Mail Order Bride

John Bruni

I0686975

PRAISE FOR JOHN BRUNI

"John Bruni is a nice kid. He's one of the next generation that I like. He's actually one of the people I like in this genre, and I don't like anybody . . . Stylistically, he's a blend of Edward Lee and Jeremy Robert Johnson."

—Brian Keene, author of *The Rising* and *Leader of the Banned*

On *Poor Bastards and Rich Fucks*:

"John Bruni is a unique visionary, granting us entrance into a world that could exist just as easily decades from now as it could a week from tomorrow. The future he crafts for us in *Poor Bastards and Rich Fucks* is both surreal and surreptitiously familiar. His is a world where, regardless of how society advances, the human condition renders characters placated by apathy and disillusionment or excess and hedonism. *Poor Bastards and Rich Fucks* is your life, tangentially explored to ease your unease . . . but only a little. After all, it wouldn't be fun if you didn't squirm a little, would it?"

—Kirk Jones, author of *Journey to Abortosphere* and *Aetherchrist*

On *Dong of Frankenstein*:

"I hope this book becomes a movie (porn or NC-17). What a beautiful and entertaining story about the glory of the penis. Bruni has a conversation with Shelley and our love of nice dongs. This is true A&E for Bizarro/Weird Erotica fans."

—Mandy De Sandra, author of *Kirk Cameron and the Crocoduck of Chaos Magick*

". . . veer[s] into almost Edward Lee bouts of hardcore violence and sex. It was an absolute blast and it had me laughing out loud on more than one occasion. Check it out if you like your comedy raunchy and ultra violent."

—Mike Lombardo, writer and director of *I'm Dreaming of a White Doomsday*

On *The Life and Times of Hieronymus Aloysis Ziege*:

"John Bruni has combined historical and hysterical into a bizarro-themed redneck autobiography for the age of the absurd. A gory, nasty, wild bout of fun we didn't know we needed, until the blood and moonshine spilled from the pages in front of us and congealed into one hell of a cocktail."

—Michael Allen Rose, author of *Jurassichrist* and *Boiled Americans*

On *And Jesus Came Back*:

"While some might see the title and think a book like this would be rife with over the top blasphemy just for the sake of it, and while they would not be completely wrong, this isn't that kind of book. Believe me, I expected it, too, and I'm really into blasphemy. This is a superbly crafted story set within the context of 'bizarro,' but the message is not hampered by silliness, nor does it get lost or murky . . . This is an excellent book from an awesome writer, and I recommend it highly!"

—John Wayne Comunale, author of *Charge Land* and *The Cadillac Man*

On "The Worm" in *Tales of Unspeakable Taste*, originally in *Vile Things:*

"[One] of the highlights for me w[as] 'The Worm' by John Bruni, which involved so much icky incest that I thought I was going to put down my book in exchange for a nice clean copy of hair-salon *Cosmopolitan.*"

—*Fangoria Magazine*

On "Bobby Yandell, Private Investigator" and "Cocksmoke" published in *Indulge for Men*:

"Thanks, John, for your fine satire! You write very well. A Pulitzer Prize is not far away!"

—Lloyd Kaufman, writer and director of *The Toxic Avenger*

TRIGGER WARNING:

Sam Pepper often thought about Tessa, the best girl he ever had working for him. She'd gone through a lot already: beatings and rape and being sold into whoring were the least of it. Who knew what she had to deal with Out West? She could run afoul of ruthless Indians or flesh merchants like the Comancheros. But white men were very capable of violence and destruction, too, and perhaps outshone the others in this regard.

He thought of the horrors she faced on a regular basis and decided that she was not new to torment and woe. She would make it just fine with Felton Reeves.

Probably.

AUTHOR'S NOTE: I know *Cyrano* did not come out until 1897, but artistic license in this case requires that it came out sooner. Apologies to pedants.

Also by John Bruni

Strip

Tales of Questionable Taste

Poor Bastards and Rich Fucks

Dong of Frankenstein

And Jesus Came Back

Blood

Tales of Unspeakable Taste

The Life and Times of Hieronymus Aloysis Ziege

Trail of Blood

Eye Cutter

Kindle only:

Pavlov's Bitches

6669: Demon Porn

John Holmes, Vampire Slayer

Dong of Frankenstein and Other Pornos You Can't Jerk It To

It Changes a Man

Mystery Sexual Theater 69000

Something to Consider

Edited by:

Strange Sex 3

To Kathy Anne Gley (née Kopoulos).
My mom, may she rest in peace.
I know this is a weird book to dedicate to my mom,
but she led a rough life. Not as bad as
Tessa's, but a pretty rough life nonetheless.
She did not have an easy time here.
I wish it could have been better.

"**P**oor bastard."

Jake Ellis looked up from the blanket he planned to buy. Brett Hartford, the shopkeeper, stood so stiff he could have been held up by a post like a scarecrow. Brett polished his spectacles with a handkerchief as his gray eyes peered through the front window.

When Jake didn't reply, Brett turned to look at him. "Felton Reeves. Poor bastard's got a new bride on the way."

The blanket fell from Jake's hands, forgotten. "How many does that make? Five?"

Brett shook his head and returned his attention to the window. "This one makes his seventh."

Jake joined the shopkeeper in his vigil. "Hell, that can't be. You think he killed the others?"

Brett recoiled. "Jesus, Jake! That's a hell of a thing to say."

"I don't know. Seems unnatural."

Both men stared through the sun-waved glass for a while in silence. Brett cleared his throat and speared his spectacles back onto his face. "Anyone else, you'd probably be right, but not that fella. He couldn't even kill the proverbial fly."

They watched Felton's stationary form dawdle outside the stage office. He was a short, skinny rail of a man, and he wore a bowler hat too small for his head. A nest of hair stuck out at all angles from beneath the brim. His child-like blue eyes twinkled in the morning sun, but anyone looking casually would have missed them. His large, goofy button of a nose distracted from them too much, to say nothing of his .45-sized Adam's apple. A slow, nervous smile twitched between these attention-grabbers, just as the rest of his body ticked and shuddered. It wouldn't have been so noticeable if his Sunday's best weren't so starched and tight.

No, Jake thought Felton couldn't have killed them. The simp didn't even carry a gun. How in hell did he live out in the middle of nowhere without a gun?

-

Joe Ridgway couldn't believe his eyes. At first he thought he'd made a mistake—that maybe he'd had a few too many after-hours shots with the customers—but Felton Reeves still stood there after Joe rubbed his eyes. Felton rested as tall as his five-seven frame allowed, and his smile twitched like a gut-shot man trying to stay conscious. A dozen flowers sprouted from his clenched fist, and Joe knew what the man had in mind.

He played it dumb, anyway. "Mornin, Fell. What's got ye into town on a weekday? Who's workin' yer fields for ye?"

"Oh, hey Joe." Felton's voice was almost high enough to be a woman's. "No, I took the day off. I'm here to pick up Tessa."

"Tessa?"

Felton's baby-face lit up like a lamp. "Yeah, Tessa! She's my new wife."

Joe nodded. "Well, damn. Glad to hear it, Fell. 'Bout time ye moved on. It gets lonely out there."

Felton pursed his lips. "Yeah, it does."

"Tell ye what. The Lucky Lou's gonna open up again in a hour. Ye want, bring the new Mrs. Reeves along, and I'll give ye a few drinks. Onna house."

"Thank you, Joe. I appreciate it, but I don't drink. Neither does Tessa."

"Aw hell. That's right. Forgot. Well, stop by anyway. Ah'd like to meet her."

"Sure."

Right, Joe thought. Tessa would be another mail order deal, but knowing Fell, he wouldn't bring her by. He'd think her too much of a lady.

He tipped his hat and went on his way. When he got a block from Felton, he looked back to see the poor bastard still standing at the stage office, waiting. Joe thought about Fell's backyard with six gravestones poking out of the ground and hoped this one didn't die on him.

-

The scarf across his mouth didn't keep much of the dust out, but it did a decent job as a safeguard. Matt coughed the grit out of his throat, and he could feel it caking the inside of the rag.

There was only one passenger in the stagecoach. Normally Matt would gripe and moan. He didn't even have any deliveries to make. But at least Tessa Reeves had great beauty, and he liked looking at her. She had a back-east figure, nothing like these western gals who tended to be built like bricks. No, you could tell this one was a lady, and a proper one at that.

Too bad she had to be wasted on Fell Reeves.

There he stood, straight as a streetlight in front of the stage office. If Matt knew him at all, the poor bastard had been standing there for at least an hour. The dust already settled on Fell's suit and bowler hat.

"Whoa!" Matt pulled at the reins, and the horses reared back to a jittering halt. A murky cloud kicked up from under the coach, and Fell coughed. He waved his free hand in front of his face.

Matt tied the straps to the brake and reached for Mrs. Reeves' luggage. He handed it down to Hank, the sweaty bald clerk. Subconsciously he kept up some small talk patter with Hank, but he only found interest in Fell. The skinny bastard cautiously approached the stagecoach as if he expected some kind of trap. Then it was like he was a match, and God had struck him aflame. Fell's face exploded into a smile, and he opened the door for his new bride.

Matt wanted to wish him luck with this one. He didn't have high hopes, though. Mrs. Reeves didn't look like she had the fortitude to survive in this forsaken land.

FROM THE JOURNAL OF TESSA REEVES:

July 17, 18—

The West is a place for savages. When I say "savages," I mean tough people with naught but violence in their hearts. As detestable as they are, I do not think I can blame them, as the heat is unbearable. The scenery would have been at home in Dante's *Inferno*. I would say that this is Death's stalking ground, but out here beyond the Mississippi, the Grim Reaper is more like a bothersome neighbor. Death is inevitable, and it is something one must put up with. This morning at a rest stop, I met a family of six. Husband, wife, and four children. They had just come back from burying their newborn baby. If I ever had a child and she died, I would have been heartbroken. I would have felt as if my soul had been rent. But they acted merely as if the family plow blade had been broken. "At least we still have four children," the wife told me. "And we can always try again."

I should never have left New York. Damn Sam Pepper's soul to hell! If he had not been so persuasive, I would still be in a civilized land.

Sam made it sound easy. Hire myself to him as a mail order bride. Let myself be sent west to some hick farmer. Then, whenever I grew tired of such a life, I would get a divorce and make my way to San Francisco, the land of milk and honey, with whatever I could get out of my rube of a husband.

I have done a lot of bad things, but I do not think I can do this.

The dust is the worst. It gets into everything. At night it spills out of my hair and grits up my bed. When I undress it comes out of my clothes, even my undergarments. It grinds against my teeth. It cakes up in my ears. When I take a bath, the water I leave behind is a grimy mess.

There are not a lot of women out here of my breeding. Most of them look tough and yet used up. I have no doubt it is because of this that men leer at me everywhere I go. I thought I was used to this kind of conduct back home, but it is much worse out here. Even the stage driver, an employee of a reputable company, stares at me whenever we take a break. I do not want to think about what would happen if he ever decided to stop in the middle of nowhere . . . but I do have Sam's derringer.

I want to go home. They say San Francisco is a wonderful place, but it cannot possibly be worth this torment.

-

July 18, 18—

I met my husband today, and I am glad to say I expected worse. He might not be much to look at, but he has all of his teeth and hair, and he is clean. He is actually a bit of a gentleman. Not very intelligent but well-mannered.

When he brought me home, I was disappointed. I am to live in a wooden shack with enough cracks in the wall to make me grateful it is summer. The outhouse is tilted, and I am afraid of what might be living down inside of it. The crops are withered and dying. The livestock is skimpy and worthless. If it were not for Felton's conduct, I would have suspected him of being an idiot.

The worst is the tiny boneyard just behind the house. There are six headstones and six mounds of dirt and six dead wives under them. Most have been conquered by the weeds, but two seem fairly fresh. Is this how badly the West uses up women?

Later—

Felton sleeps on the other side of the room, and I write this by candlelight. An hour ago we consummated our marriage, and it was not as bad as I thought it would be. Though Felton will never know this, I have shared myself with a number of men, and he is easily the best of them. I am shocked that such a small man can be so well endowed, and even moreso that he is skilled enough to use what God gave him.

But then I think about the six graves behind the house, and I know he must have had a considerable deal of practice.

Perhaps this life will not be so bad. It might take a while to hide enough money for San Francisco, as he is a terrible farmer, but I am starting to warm up to my new existence.

Goodnight.

-

July 25, 18—

I have been here for a few days now, and I cannot decide if I like it or not. For the most part, I find myself doing simple jobs, like feeding livestock, milking cows, preparing meals, washing dishes, and cleaning up around the home. Then again, there are also times when Felton needs my help to mend a fence or nail a board in the barn. Once he asked me to assist him in digging a hole. My hands are not used to this, and blisters are starting to sprout on my palms.

When things are easy, I am actually happy. I was never happy before, not even in New York. But when the work gets hard, I find myself thinking of San Francisco.

No matter how hard it gets, there is always the loving embrace of my husband and the pleasure of his bed. He never hits me, not like Sam did. I do not even think Felton has violence in him.

For this, I will stay. Maybe not forever, but I will stay. Do I love him? I do not know. But at least I *like* him.

-

September 18, 18—

It has been awhile since I have written in this journal, as I have been very busy of late. One of the things I do consists of me finding out how wrong I was about many things out here.

Back East, newspapers and dime novels would have us believe that there are gunfights and bank robberies and such on a daily, if not hourly, basis. But everyone likes each other out here. There are no range wars or drunken brawls or anything so vile.

This is a loving community. They have a nice little schoolhouse, but more importantly, there is the church. I have never been much for religion. I love God in my own way, and that's good enough for me. But I join the congregation every week. People here are so nice, and it is a wonderful joy to see them on Sunday mornings.

There is one more thing I was wrong about: Indians. Back east at school, they taught me to be tolerant of other races, but I kept hearing so much about the vicious redman, I could not help but fall under the myth's sway. On my way out here, I was very apprehensive about being scalped by "Injuns," as the dime novels call them.

I am sure you can imagine how startled and terrified I was when I walked into my home to find an Indian standing near my stove. I carried two pails of fresh milk, and I dropped them both. One hand went to my breast, as if to protect my heart, and the other went to my mouth. I tried to draw enough breath to scream, but all the fear had pushed the air out of me.

Felton, who had been retrieving a bottle of whiskey from the kitchen cabinet, rushed to reassure me that everything was all right, that the Indian was actually a friend of his.

I had never in my life heard of anything so foolish, but my Felton is so earnest, I cannot help but believe everything he says.

The Comanche's name is Iron Trail in English, and he is very courteous, almost as much as my husband. Iron Trail is tall and wiry with a mane of gorgeous dark hair. His features are stony, but his eyes are so soft and kind that I could never imagine him raiding a ranch or any of that nonsense. He wears no paint on his face, and he has no feathers. He is not the terror I expected.

Felton tells me his friend will be staying with us for a while. I tell him Iron Trail is more than welcome with us.

-

September 19, 18—

Iron Trail has taken up residence in the loft of our barn. I wish we could accommodate him better, but he says he is comfortable, that he has slept in much worse places. As I consider the dusty prairie, I do not want to think about what it must have been like for him.

Iron Trail is a model guest. He helps out with the chores, he cleans dishes and he is an excellent conversationalist. I want to know where he learned English and wit so well, but I do not want to seem condescending.

Late last night while trying to sleep, I overheard him and Felton talking by the fireplace. Both passed a pipe and a bottle back and forth. The air was crowded with bitter smoke and whiskey fumes as they discussed their adventures of the past. I did not know Felton was in the Army (and he had told me that he was not a drinker, but I have to keep reminding myself that this is the west). I cannot help but wonder if they had met in the military. Was Iron Trail a scout for my husband? I could not tell, and when they spoke of the places they had been, their references were vague and were about people with whom I was unfamiliar.

I someday hope to understand.

-

September 21, 18—

Up until today, I have never had an awkward moment with my husband. I do not mean to say anything unpleasant happened, but with Felton I find that I am always happy, whether we are making love or I am helping him with hard work. I am even starting to make my peace with the dust out here. It is just that he made me feel strange today.

Earlier, I had seen Felton and Iron Trail working in the field, so I thought I would take them some lemonade to soothe the heat. I brought it out on a tray with two glasses, but the men were no longer there.

I found them in the boneyard, and they were talking. I did not hear what they said, but their tone sounded grim. When they saw me, they stopped in mid-sentence and doffed their field hats.

What were they discussing? I do not know, but whatever it was, they did not want me to hear. Perhaps they were talking about Felton's previous wives, or maybe about some unpleasant Army battle.

But when I gave them the lemonade, any awkwardness that might have existed disappeared. Felton's smile was so bright. I hope I have brought him some happiness, as he has me.

-

September 25, 18—

Felton told me this morning that Iron Trail would be leaving us in the morning. They went to town to celebrate and left me alone with a few chores and my journal. Now, with all of my tasks completed, I relax by the stove to—

Iron Trail watched as Felton touched the heavy pouch on his belt. Though he'd seen the white man count the money twice, the Comanche wondered if maybe his business partner wanted to sift through the coins again.

Felton looked up and showed off his teeth in his usual silly grin. "I just love the heft of newly acquired money."

Iron Trail grunted. "We all do."

"Come on," Felton said. "You know it's going to be worth it."

Iron Trail nodded. They rode in silence.

When they got back to the Reeves farm Iron Trail stopped in the barn to pick up his other horse. In the dim luminescence from the moon and the stars, he saddled his second animal, mounted his first and steered them both toward the house.

When he walked in he found Felton kissing Tessa. The woman had been writing in her diary, which had been left open on the table before her.

Husband and wife broke apart.

"Hello Iron Trail," Tessa said. "I hear you're leaving us tomorrow."

Iron Trail remained silent. After having done this with Felton six times before, he knew it would be best if he didn't say a word.

"Actually," Felton said, "you'll be going with him."

Tessa paused, like all the others had, and she continued as if her husband hadn't said anything: "We're going to miss you around here."

A grin crept up the side of Felton's mouth as he took the pouch from his belt. He stuck his fingers in the top and yanked it open; from its guts came a shower of coins pouring into his palm.

"Have you ever seen this much money, Tess?"

She glanced at the pool of silver and gold in her husband's hand. "No. Where did you get it?"

"Iron Trail gave it to me." Felton funneled his hand and let the money jingle together back into the pouch.

"We couldn't take this," Tessa said to the Comanche. "It's too much. Besides, you did your share of the work around here."

It never failed to amaze Iron Trail. These women from Back East were like clockwork. None of them varied in their reactions. Still, he kept quiet.

"It's not for the hospitality," Felton said. "It's for you."

Tessa blinked. "What?"

Felton dropped the pouch on the table. It thunked like a club to the head. "I sold you, Tess. To him."

Iron Trail allowed himself a grin. So easy.

"I don't understand," Tessa said.

Felton advanced, touching her shoulders gently. "You belong to Iron Trail now."

The Comanche held out his hand. "Are you ready to go?"

Finally Tessa knew. Iron Trail could see the knowledge dawn on her face as if she were the sun spilling onto a brand new day.

But then she did something not in the script: her face grew hard, almost as hard as a typical western woman's. Iron Trail thought perhaps she wasn't the prim and proper beauty he thought her to be.

Tessa shoved her husband aside. To be expected. They all tried to fight back, but most of Felton's wives just weren't strong enough for it. This one looked too frail to last very long.

Felton backed away, holding up defensive hands. "I'm really sorry, Tess. Take a look around. I'm a terrible farmer. I have to survive somehow. Besides, this isn't the first time you've been sold. Remember, I bought you from that Pepper fella."

"Fuck you!" she screamed. "I thought you were different! You're nothing but a goofy-looking version of Sam! You bastard!"

Distantly Iron Trail wondered who Sam was, but Tessa's foul language struck him as more interesting. A woman with a dirty mouth? Nothing new out west. Some girl from Back East who looked as beautiful as this one, though? Iron Trail felt something perk up in his leggings.

Felton turned his attention to Iron Trail. "Would you please get her out of here?"

The Comanche took a step forward, but Tessa whirled away, headed for the dresser. Of course she has to be difficult, he thought, but he wouldn't have it any other way. A thing was only worth having if you had to fight for it.

The drawer scraped open, and she rummaged through her under-things. By now, Iron Trail had caught up to her. He reached out to grab her shoulder when she jerked toward Felton, and they all heard a tiny pop.

Iron Trail recoiled, and from the corner of his eyes he saw Felton do the same. Then Iron Trail saw the derringer in Tessa's hand, and she cocked the hammer for another try.

The Comanche lunged forward and hit Tessa's arm just as she pulled the trigger. The firearm popped again, and this bullet went astray like the first. Though he knew the gun to be empty, Iron Trail plucked it from Tessa's delicate hands and grabbed her in a bear hug. She struggled and screamed against his strong grip.

"Felton," Iron Trail said. "Are you okay?"

"I'm fine." Felton rubbed sweat from his forehead. "It's a good thing those guns aren't very accurate."

"Get the rag!"

"Oh! Right! Sorry."

Tessa's feet dug against Iron Trail's shins, but she simply didn't have the strength to hurt him. Soon Felton pressed his chloroform rag to her face. When she went limp, they put her on the bed and began tying her up.

-

The next day Felton tried to keep sweat out of his eyes as he dug in the ground the "grave" of his seventh wife. He decided that Tessa had died of the fever. No one ever wanted to find out for sure because no one wanted to catch anything. Besides, there was no doctor around to dispute his diagnosis, just a vet who spent most of his time and money in the Lucky Lou.

He threw in Tessa's belongings. Her clothes, her suitcase, her hats, everything. Lastly he dropped her diary into the ground. He'd been tempted to read it, just to see what kinds of things she had thought about, but in the end he decided it would be a bad idea. He considered the things Iron Trail would probably do to her, and he came to the conclusion that he didn't want to know who she really was.

As he filled in the hole he started to realize he missed her. If Tessa had been here, she would have brought him lemonade and kisses. She'd massage his aching shoulders. She'd love him.

Felton gagged and spat up a booger. Did *he* maybe love *her*? He'd never felt guilty about this before. Last night, with her side of the bed cold, he felt lonely for the first time since he'd run away from home at the age of ten.

That night, as he tried to go to sleep, he couldn't stop thinking about her. She flitted through his dreams and waking moments like a ghost.

When he woke up in a sweat he wondered if maybe he should have kept this one. It was too late, of course. He thought maybe he'd get her a good gravestone. In all likelihood Iron Trail would use her up and leave her dead in the dust of the west, but here, in a lonely farm boneyard, there would be some kind of testament to her life and love.

What else could he do for her but nothing?

-

Iron Trail thought it would be best to get as far away from Fell's place as he could, so he rode through the night, using the moon's glow to illuminate his way. Not that he needed the luminescence; he'd been down this way so many times he probably could have done it backwards and with his eyes closed.

But the pale disc above helped him keep his eye on Tessa Reeves.

After they'd knocked her unconscious Fell had taken the time to get her out of her nightgown and into something a bit more practical. Whenever Tessa woke up, she'd be grateful for those riding pants and the checkered shirt.

Iron Trail turned his attention from the dust at his feet to the horse next to him. Slung across its saddle, Tessa's unconscious form jangled, hands and feet tied tightly together. From his vantage point, her rump blocked the rest of her body. The riding pants were so taut

23

they accentuated her curves perfectly. He wanted to run a hand across her firm bottom, but he restrained himself.

This enticing image, when combined with the bounce of his horse, caused something to stir in his leggings. His erection sang to be freed and indulged, and it throbbed against the deerskin of his pants. Then the saddle bit into his balls, and it felt like his hard-on was being pinched and folded. He grunted and pushed his penis to the side so the head rested against his hipbone.

As the dirt below him turned to dust and then rock, and the moon eased up to its zenith, shrinking his shadow down to a squat oblong shape, he considered what to do with Tessa. He knew he would sell her, but could he really let her go without trying her out first? Ordinarily, he didn't like to partake of his own wares—the less used a woman was, the more her worth—but he couldn't get this one out of his head.

It wasn't just her beauty. Iron Trail had bought and sold women far more beautiful than she without so much as a second thought. No, this one seemed pretty intelligent, and while most white women he'd encountered were fickle pieces of meat, Tessa seemed to be an actual person. Not all in a good way, of course. There seemed to be something hidden in her past, and maybe this air of mystery changed her from being a product into being a person.

Iron Trail didn't know, but it turned him on. Maybe it would be better to keep her around for awhile. He remembered fondly their conversations over the past few days.

He would meet the Comancheros in a few weeks. That would be quite a bit of time to get to know someone. Perhaps Iron Trail would even take Tessa as a wife.

He shook his head and wondered why he entertained such foolish thoughts. Then he glanced at Tessa's ass, and he knew.

They were far enough away that they probably could have set up camp for the night, but Iron Trail wanted a roof over his head. There was a burnt out house about three miles away, and he thought that would be the perfect place to stop. He wanted to test out the bed in the ruins with Tessa.

He thought if he just took her, he'd get her out of his system. Still his member throbbed in his leggings, and he adjusted himself again.

A while later he found it had become too much. He got off his horse and walked around in circles, hoping it would be enough to force himself to go flaccid. Sometimes, he would feel his pants become roomier, and he would turn back to his horse. Then he would see Tessa's rear, and things once more became tight beneath his waist.

How easy would it be to just take her down from her mount and have his way with her? Who would stop him? Tessa? Her hands were bound, so she wouldn't be able to fight back. Hell, she might not even wake up during the act. Fell used pretty powerful chloroform.

No. Iron Trail wanted her awake. He wanted her to be cognizant of the situation. Some part of him wanted her to be willing.

Something flapped above Iron Trail's head, and he went for the bow and arrow on his saddle. His fingers touched the cold wood when he realized it had merely been a bat. He laughed and covered the weapon.

The sudden flush of fear had loosened up his equipment, and he felt himself hanging between his thighs again. Satisfied that he was once more an intelligent, clear-headed man, he pulled himself up into his saddle and continued riding.

A mile later Tessa started groaning, and Iron Trail brought them to a stop. He dismounted and walked around her horse so he could see her head. Gently he cupped his hand under her chin and pulled up in order to get a good look at her face. Her eyelids fluttered, and a long string of drool hung from her mouth.

"Tessa," he whispered. When she didn't respond, he lightly slapped her cheeks.

This time her eyelids slipped back, and he found himself looking into her bright green eyes. "Iron Trail?" she asked. "What . . . ?"

He watched as memory rippled across her face, smothering the initial confusion. Her mouth worked with disbelief that this could actually be happening to her, and then it all went away, replaced by cold anger.

"You son of a bitch," she said.

"You're probably very uncomfortable," Iron Trail said, "riding like that." He waved a hand at the saddle. "Your ribs must be—"

"As if you gave a damn," Tessa said.

Iron Trail lifted her up a bit so she could slide off the saddle. He didn't let go, however, as he knew that most women in such a situation would not land on their feet.

Tessa did, though. She held out her wrists, as if she expected Iron Trail to cut her bonds. "How much did Felton get for me?"

"It doesn't matter," Iron Trail said. "As long as I get more for you."

"I'm to be sold like a slave?"

The Comanche reached to the knife on his belt and pulled it out. The moon caught its surface and threw a glimmering spot of light onto Tessa's chest.

"You're not going to kill me," she said. Her voice didn't even tremble. Iron Trail forced himself not to smile, thinking this one was made from stern stuff.

He knelt and cut the rope at her feet. "So you can ride. But if you think you can run, you can't."

She looked around at the wasteland. "I know."

Iron Trail offered her a water skin. He had three more, but he wanted to see what Tessa did with this one. Most women were so angry at having been sold that they insolently open the skin and pour out all the water. A foolish thing to do out here, but Iron Trail never had a problem with women doing this.

Whenever they were finished with their rebellious act, he would tell them that they'd just surrendered their share of the water to the Great Spirit, and he would start drinking from his own water skin to irritate them.

Tessa opened the top and drank, but not deeply. When she finished, she put the top back on and held the skin out to Iron Trail.

He smiled and put the skin back on his saddle. "Do you need help getting back up on the horse?"

"Fuck you," Tessa said. She reached her bound hands up to the horn and stepped into the stirrup. She threw a leg over and sat proudly above Iron Trail. "Are we going or what?"

This time Iron Trail couldn't restrain himself. He had to laugh. "I have never met a woman like you in my life, Tessa Reeves."

"But I've met men like you," Tessa said. "Maybe they don't usually look like you, but you all have the same souls."

Iron Trail pulled himself up onto his horse. They rode on in silence. He fell back a little so he could keep an eye on her, and though her rump was not nearly as visible, the little he could see enticed him, spread apart on the saddle as it was. He figured there were a thousand poems in his heart, all dedicated to her bottom.

The moon oozed down the mountains when they reached the burnt out home. Iron Trail dismounted first, and he led their horses to the white picket fence. Still intact, it would be strong enough to hold their mounts in check. As soon as Tessa got down, he started hobbling the horses.

He nodded for her to go first while he slung his saddle over his shoulder. He followed, hoping her hips would swish a bit, but she merely shuffled forward.

She hesitated at the doorway. "It's okay," he told her. "I've been here many times before. It's safe."

"For you, I'm sure," Tessa said. But she entered, anyway.

Once inside Iron Trail dropped his saddle and pulled out his blanket. The bed was still there and in good shape. It hadn't been burned because the Comanche had brought it here well after the house had been set ablaze.

He drew his knife and cut the remaining bonds on Tessa's wrists. "Take your clothes off. All of them."

For a moment he thought he saw defiance burning in her blue cat's eyes but only for a brief second. Her jaw worked as if she were chewing cud, and she disrobed. She showed no modesty about it; she yanked her clothes off and flung them aside until she stood naked in the dim light of the moon filtering through the skeleton of the beams above.

Iron Trail stared at her, unbelieving. He'd sold beautiful women before, but never one as breathtaking as this one. Her slender body thrust the perfect globes of her breasts out at him almost defiantly, but he felt most surprised by the small strip of hair that hovered above the cleft of her vagina like an exclamation mark. Every woman he'd ever seen had more hair than a bear down there, but the slim shadow he saw was far from hirsute. It couldn't be natural. Did she cultivate it to take this shape?

His eyes wandered back to her face, and a challenge burned there. Her tiny fists bunched up, and he could see well-defined muscle slithering under the skin of her chest.

"Do you think you can take me without a fight?" she asked.

Iron Trail nodded and drew his knife. "I'd hate to cut on you, to ruin such a beautiful image. And I doubt you want me to slice off your tits. Let's just agree to disagree and do this the easy way."

Her eyes narrowed, and she bared her teeth. "I'm tougher than you might think. I grew up on a very frightening street, and I had to fight for a lot."

He believed her. It was written in the features of her face, but especially in her eyes. Not that it mattered. Slowly he put the knife back in its sheath and then put both into his saddle bag. "You're not in the east, and you're far from any street, much less a frightening one. You're out in the west. The only thing scarier than civilization is the complete lack of it."

Her hatred faltered, and he took advantage. "Besides," he continued, "you're looking at me in the wrong light. You think I'm your captor, but really I'm your protector. How far do you think you could make it without me?"

He took a step forward, and she took one back. Iron Trail smiled. He knew now that she had no fight left in her. He continued advancing as he wriggled out of his leggings.

Tessa met the wall and pressed up against it, trembling. "Felton wasn't my first man. You don't know what I might have. I've been with many."

"Good," Iron Trail said. "Then you'll know what to do with this." He reached down to grasp the base of his penis, and he wagged it at her.

She stared at it in shock. Women usually did. Iron Trail had been blessed by the Great Spirit, and he knew it. Playfully he closed his other hand around his shaft, and there was still enough room for a third.

They now stood face to face, and he tickled her lower belly with the tip of his member. Then he went further down until he arrived at her vagina.

She recoiled and tensed, as if ready to fight. "Don't," Iron Trail whispered. "I don't want to hurt you."

Her tremulous hands came to rest on his shoulders, using him to balance herself, and then she moved her thighs apart, giving him the room he needed.

He sank into her a lot easier than he'd expected. Perhaps she hadn't been lying about the number of men she'd been with, but that was fine with Iron Trail. Most men wanted virgins, innocents to corrupt, but not the Comanche. No, he wanted women of experience, and he didn't care where they'd gotten it.

He pushed her against the wall and rocked back and forth, surprised to find her already wet. Had she been feeling the same way all along?

At first Tessa went stiff, resistant, but after a while she began to respond in just the way Iron Trail wanted her to. She rolled with his movements and clutched at his back. Whenever he thrust against her, she pushed against him, and before long they were on the bed, grunting and moaning, rutting like a pair of animals. Every time he impaled her, he heard their juices slap together. She howled her ecstasy at the broken roof and the stars beyond it.

When they were done they collapsed next to each other, feeling the deerskin blanket stick to their skin as if it had been fixed on by glue. Iron Trail cradled her to his chest and closed his eyes. He drifted off to sleep listening to her steady breathing.

Not long afterward he awoke when she moved next to him. He didn't open his eyes, but he waited, wondering what would come next.

It took her awhile, but she slipped off the bed and moved toward his saddle bag. Now sure it would be safe to look, he opened his left eye just a sliver and watched as she rummaged through the contents. She quickly found his knife.

Before she could turn to face him again, he closed his eye and pretended to sleep. He listened to her feet whispering along the creaking wood of the floor until he deemed that she stood next to him. He heard a familiar scratching sound. His knife coming out of its sheath.

He waited. Though he did not hear or see her move, he felt her presence as she bent over him. She didn't even breathe as he sensed her arm move closer to his throat. The knife sang out to him, and he could feel its presence near his skin.

Now he opened his eyes. "How far do you think you could make it out here without me?" he whispered.

Tessa's dark curls hung suspended over his chest, and the blade hovered near his Adam's apple.

"Do you even know where you are?" Iron Trail asked. "You slept through most of our journey. Can you even tell direction by the sun and the moon and the stars?"

She didn't say anything.

"I can. We have water, but what if you run out? I have food, but what if you eat it all? Can you provide for yourself out in this wilderness?"

Silence.

"I can do these things. I told you, I'm your protector."

She dropped the knife to the floor, and the tip stuck into the rotting wood. "You're full of shit, but right now you're all I have."

Iron Trail smiled. "Come. Go back to sleep." He gestured for her to lie down with him.

"I'll sleep on the floor," she said.

"You'll be cold," Iron Trail said.

"I'll take my chances."

She laid out Iron Trail's saddle blanket and used his saddle as a pillow. She curled up on her side and closed her eyes.

Iron Trail followed suit, but he did not manage to get back to sleep. About an hour later he heard Tessa curse under her breath. She came back to the bed and snuggled up next to him. She felt shockingly cold against his skin, but his body warmed her up pretty quickly. He cuddled with her, and they both fell asleep in each other's arms.

-

Iron Trail woke up to a loud noise. It sounded as if someone poured out a sack of pebbles onto a slate. He sat up to see rain pouring through the hole in the roof in such a torrent that it concealed the far wall of the room. A river had grown out of the floor, but it rushed to the outside. Since the bed and his belongings were under a solid segment of ceiling, they were dry.

And because Tessa's full-figured body rested under the blanket next to him, he felt very warm.

He listened to the rain for a while before he decided to get up. He nudged Tessa. "Wake up. It's time to get ready to go."

Tessa rubbed her eyes and sat up. "We're not leaving in this storm."

"No, we're not. The rain will play out shortly. It never lasts long in this part of the world."

Tessa swung her legs out of the bed and looked down at her naked form as if seeing it for the first time. She had no regret or anger in her eyes, just a cool resignation. She wordlessly put her clothes back on.

Iron Trail rummaged through his saddlebags and withdrew a long piece of jerky beef. He snapped off a length, then broke this piece in two, and handed one to Tessa.

She glared at him, but she took his offering. Good. She knew what to do in order to survive. Very rarely did one of his women accept his food without at least complaining about it.

"I'm afraid I don't have coffee," Iron Trail said. "We'll have to do without that for a few days."

She didn't say anything. She just gnawed at her jerky.

-

By the time they were ready to head out, the rain had long since stopped. The sun now baked the moisture away, leaving nothing but dry ground. Iron Trail regretted not taking Tessa's saddle in the previous evening. Now it looked kind of shrunken, and there were cracks all over it. Tiny, gnarled strands of broken leather poked out in all directions. It would probably be very uncomfortable for her.

Tessa stepped into the stirrup and took her position without so much as a grimace. Either it really didn't bother her, or she was a hell of an actress. Iron Trail thought it might be some of both.

They rode across the hard ground, but neither said a word. Tessa kept her stoic face forward and squinted against the sun reflecting off the plain earth. Iron Trail thought to start a conversation several times, but he wanted *her* to break the silence. It was a challenge to keep his mouth shut, but he knew it would be worth it if she initiated any interaction. Even if she merely cussed him out, she would be one step further to belonging to him in her heart.

But she didn't say anything. They rested at noon, and Iron Trail gave her more water and jerky beef. She took them both without complaint. Her teeth worked at the tough meat as she stared out to the mountains ahead. The gentle breeze blew her hair back from her face, revealing red cheeks and nose. Back-East women sunburned too easily, he mused.

An hour later the quiet got to be too much for Iron Trail to handle. He didn't understand it. He was used to traveling alone, so why would he have a problem with silence? Was this woman some kind of witch?

No. Iron Trail was not a superstitious person. He barely believed in the Great Spirit, much less in people who could work magic. It was one of the reasons he'd left his tribe a decade ago.

No, Iron Trail believed in biology, and he wondered if perhaps he'd fallen in love with this white woman. This couldn't be an issue of lust or even ownership. If it had been he would have been satisfied, considering last night's festivities.

He'd loved someone, once. As a young boy he'd fallen in love with the war chief's daughter. He remembered his mind being a cluster of thoughts that couldn't connect with each other. He remembered his guts feeling like they were being wrung out by a thousand different hands. He remembered uncertainty, and it was a long time since he'd felt that.

But here it was again. It didn't feel quite so chaotic, but still it jangled his insides.

"Who's Sam?" he asked.

She stiffened next to him, but she kept quiet, as if she hadn't heard him.

Iron Trail grabbed the reins from her hands and pulled them both to a halt. "Who is Sam?"

She turned to face him. "What do you know about Sam?"

"Only that I heard you say his name back at Fell's place. He didn't sound like a very nice man from the way you said his name."

Her lips tightened into a thin cut, and she tossed her hair about her head to get a strand out of her eyes. "Sam was my pimp. Does this surprise you?"

Iron Trail shook his head.

"I guess it wouldn't surprise someone like you," Tessa said. She turned away as if dismissing him.

"And what kind of person am I?" Iron Trail asked.

"You're a savage."

Iron Trail chuckled. "I wouldn't have taken you for a bigot, Tessa darling."

"I'm not. I wasn't referring to your skin color. I meant that you're a beast. An animal. A low-down coyote. Is that a bit more clear?"

Iron Trail caressed her cheek with a finger. "I only do what I do to survive. Surely *you* can understand that."

Tessa drew back, and his finger touched nothing but air.

Iron Trail's mouth twitched. It could have been a grimace, but he thought he might have been trying to smile. That's what he told himself, anyway.

"You're a slaver and a rapist," Tessa said.

The Comanche dropped her reins. The storm had shortened them, and they only dangled down to the horse's knees. "You're free to go, if you wish."

She sneered. "Now that you've had me, you have no use for me?"

"I have a lot of uses for you," Iron Trail said.

Tessa looked behind her, across miles and miles of barren, cracked land. She then looked up to the sun, as if trying to gauge which direction she should take. Finally she gave up. "Which way do I go?"

Iron Trail smiled. "That's up to you. Freedom comes with consequences. In order to be free, you must be responsible for yourself."

"Teach me how to tell direction by the sun," Tessa said.

"Figure it out for yourself."

"Goddammit!" she yelled. Her voice echoed off the mountains to the front of them. "How would I ever do that?"

"Do you think this is innate knowledge?" Iron Trail asked. "Just think: once upon a time, someone learned how to tell directions by the sun and stars and moon. He learned it by himself. Just as someone once learned how to survive out here."

Tessa scowled and reached for the dangling reins. She shoved them into Iron Trail's fist. "Let's go."

He gave the reins back to her and nodded ahead. "That way."

The rode for awhile longer before Iron Trail spoke again. "You still haven't answered my question. Who's Sam? Besides your pimp?"

"He was my lover, too." She spoke without turning to look at him. "He's the one who convinced me to become a mail order bride."

"If he was your lover, then why did he do this?" For Iron Trail knew what he would do in his place. Hell, he *was* in Sam's place. If the pimp had possessed any brains, he would have kept Tessa, like Iron Trail thought of doing.

"I don't know," Tessa said. "Maybe lover is too strong a word for what we had. He was a scoundrel. He gambled, he beat his women, I know of at least three men he's killed."

"Why did you stay with him for so long?"

She didn't answer him, but Iron Trail thought he knew. All he had to do was think about why she remained with him, and he knew why she could never leave Sam.

"Okay, then if you loved him so much, why did you eventually leave him?"

Tessa's jaw worked, as if she were chewing on jerky. "I didn't love him at the end. Mostly I took the mail order job to get away from him. I didn't want any more men in my life."

"Then why did you go to Felton Reeves?"

"To be his wife for a while," she said. "Not for very long. Just long enough to stash away some of his money and use it to set myself up in San Francisco. I wanted to support myself. I was tired of needing men."

Iron Trail nodded.

Tessa laughed. "Have I offended you? Have I made you see me in a different light?"

"I am not offended, but I do see you in a different light. You're stronger than you think, Tessa."

"Felton's one of your friends. Aren't you pissed off at me? Don't you want to hurt me?"

"You have a strange habit of asking stupid questions," Iron Trail said. "You were a whore and an attempted thief. I've lost count of how many people I've murdered. Who am I to judge you?"

She blanched, and her face turned white, even through the red of her sunburn.

Iron Trail laughed. "Don't worry. I have no desire to murder you."

"That's not what I was thinking," Tessa said. "I remembered the way you were when Felton first introduced you to me. I recall thinking you were very decent and witty. Which is funny, because when I first saw you, I thought you were going to scalp me. And now I know that my initial reaction to you was closer to the truth."

"Scalping was started by the white man," Iron Trail said. "We took it up in an eye-for-an-eye kind of way."

"It doesn't matter," Tessa said. "Anyone who would scalp another person is a beast."

"A savage?"

Tessa glanced at him, a small smile on her face. "Yes, a savage."

-

They were nearly to the mountains when the sun started to descend. Iron Trail brought them to a halt and set up camp. A small, dead tree stood sentinel nearby, and it didn't take any effort to knock it over and break it up into firewood.

As he hovered over the pile of splintered wood, flint and steel in hand, he noticed Tessa staring at him. No, actually she stared at his *hands*.

"What?" he asked.

"Show me how to make a fire," she said.

Refusal rested on his lips, but she would probably see him do it, anyway. Besides, what did it hurt to teach her one little thing?

"Okay," he said." Come closer."

He demonstrated before putting the flint and steel in her hands. She learned quickly, for with the first few strikes a spark danced up from her fingers and landed in the kindling. Before long a fire tickled the cobalt sky above their heads. Embers drifted up to join the stars.

After they'd eaten, Iron Trail removed all of his clothes and slipped under the blanket of his make-shift bed. He left one corner of the cover turned down, as if the empty side of his sleeping gear wasn't enough of an invitation.

He didn't have to say a word. Tessa, standing in a silhouette in front of the fire, pulled off her clothes, her features hidden by the shadows. She moved across the sharp ground in her bare feet, but she didn't give any indication that it hurt her. Then she eased down to the ground next to Iron Trail and joined him under the blankets.

Iron Trail made no moves. He waited for her to make her own.

Tessa placed her head down on the Comanche's bronze chest, and her hand tickled across his lower belly until she found what she wanted. She stroked him until his member plumped up, ripe in her palm, and then she straddled him and pierced herself with his manhood. With the fire behind her, it looked like she glowed with an aura, and when they came the coyotes howled in the mountains.

The next day Tessa wasn't quite so angry, but she still felt fairly cold. She spoke only when spoken to, which suited Iron Trail. Now that they traversed the mountain pass, it would be best to keep quiet. Who knew what kind of animals—or even bandits—lived around here?

That night they took shelter in a cave. Iron Trail made sure no one—man or beast—lurked inside while Tessa gathered wood for the fire. The hole in the side of the mountain didn't go very deep, so he figured it would be safe for them. The wind got cold at night around here, and the cave would provide cover from it.

Tessa built up a bunch of kindling around a few thicker pieces of wood, as if she were a master architect. It was a beautiful structure, and Iron Trail found himself wishing he didn't need to burn it down.

She held out her hand. "Flint, please."

Iron Trail surrendered it without argument and sat back to watch her go to work. Once again it only took a few sparks before she blew gently into a smoking pile of dry wood. Again the thought of keeping her as a wife flitted through his mind.

She gave him the flint back and sat next to him, gazing into the fire as if she saw some kind of stage show playing out there. Already darkness had encroached upon them, and the flickering light reflected off her face in bright orange and red. It shone in her eyes, and for a moment Iron Trail lost himself in this image.

Then she grunted and started tearing at her clothes. It was not a sexy display, but slightly fearsome. She muttered under her breath, as if she were talking to someone, as she yanked her clothes off and threw them away. Then, completely naked, she flopped down next to Iron Trail, breathing heavily, her hair a wasps nest about her head.

"What is it?" Iron Trail asked.

"I'm sick of those clothes. They stink."

He laughed. "This is the west. Of course they stink. Baths are few and far between out here."

"I'm just not accustomed to it, that's all. I need another set of clothes."

"Do you intend to ride as naked as Godiva?" Iron Trail asked. "Because I believe such a sight would be the most beautiful thing I could ever behold."

This time *she* laughed. "No. I'll put those clothes on, even if they stink like sweat and sex."

Iron Trail slipped a hand down the front of his leggings and withdrew his cock. He took a whiff and recognized the smell of her pussy. "Is it so bad?" he asked.

She looked at his hand, but she wore an empty expression. "I'm just tired of being dirty all the time."

Iron Trail molted his clothes and tossed them in with Tessa's. "Don't worry. We'll be out of the mountains tomorrow, and there's a trading post there. They don't have baths, but they do have new clothes. We also need more food and water. We're running a bit low on both."

"If they have water, they have baths," she said.

Iron Trail laughed. "Drinking water, dear."

"It makes no difference to me. If it's wet, I'll pour it over me."

"I wouldn't do that," Iron Trail said. "Wasting drinking water like that is a crime out here, almost as bad as horse-stealing. You should

41

wait until we reach the Cibola River. It's two days from here. You can bathe when we get there."

She grimaced. "Two days?"

He nodded and stroked her breast with a rough, yet gentle hand. "Two days."

"I don't know If I can wait that long."

"You will. You'll learn to." His hand moved down her belly until it found the cleft it sought. She was dry, so he stuck his index and middle fingers in his mouth, wetting them until they glistened in the firelight. He grinned when they found what they were looking for again, and she arched her back and pushed against his hand.

-

The next morning Iron Trail opened his eyes to find Tessa sitting near the fire, wrapped in a blanket. Her jaw pulsed as she gnawed at a piece of jerky. Though her hair was stringy with sweat, and her face had dust and filth caking it, she was easily the most beautiful woman he'd ever seen.

When he sat up he felt his muscles groan and his back stretch. He felt young again, as if he were freshly unvirgined, discovering aches in muscles he'd never known he had. The scratches on his back had to be deep, considering how the scabs pulled at the rest of the skin. His shoulders and biceps bore the marks of her fingernails, and they sang wonderfully.

She must have heard him move. She offered him a piece of jerky without turning. He took it and jabbed it into his mouth. His tongue ached from the night before, but the burning sensation felt wonderful.

"You are wearing me out," he said. He took a seat next to her and put his arm around her shoulders.

She didn't say anything. The fire withered down to embers, and a thin wisp of white smoke lifted from the ashes. The warmth staved off the slight morning chill.

Iron Trail wondered what would happen if he turned her head and planted a kiss on her lips. Though they'd been in many positions the previous evening, and they had performed many acts upon each other, they had still yet to kiss, and he very much wanted to do this.

But the blank look in her eyes convinced him not to try.

-

Three hours later they cleared the mountains, and an hour after that they reached the trading post. It didn't look like much, and it seemed from a distance to be short enough to only house Swift's Lilliputians. Upon closer examination, however, one could see a set of stairs leading down into a much more expansive building. A stone chimney sat in the middle of the structure, but no fire burned, for now the day had grown a bit hotter. There were a few horses tied to a hitching rail, and some livestock roamed around behind the trading post in a corral.

Iron Trail dismounted and tied his horse up with the others. He watched as Tessa followed suit, but as they approached the stairs leading into the building, the raucous sound of men came pouring out. Tessa paused.

Iron Trail came to a halt and turned to face her. He didn't need to say anything.

"Do you want me to stay out here?" Tessa asked.

"No," Iron Trail said. "You'll be safer by my side."

She nodded, and they stepped down into a dimness lit only by lanterns. The post was divided into two parts: the store and the bar. They found themselves standing in the latter.

The counter consisted of a board hammered onto two other boards, and the mirror behind it was so dingy only the outlines of reflections could be seen. Whiskey bottles gleamed on a bookshelf behind the bar, along with glasses turned upside down. None of the glasses looked clean, at least not on the outside.

There were five stools, and two of them were occupied. The first man had hair all over him except for the bare pate of his head. The fringe of hair around the sides had grown out all the way down to his waist, and a bushy beard concealed most of his chest. His eyes were uneven, and blood-splatters decorated his clothes. It had dried there a while ago, and considering the size of his rifle and the enormous knife on his belt, Iron Trail took him for a buffalo hunter and disliked him immediately.

The second man, almost as contemptible, was skinny enough to be a skeleton. He had a full head of short blond hair with none on his face. Though he looked to be about forty, Iron Trail had doubts that this man could even grow anything on his chin. His pink skin looked as if he'd just scrubbed himself as hard as he could, but his hands were large and chapped. This one wore two guns on his hip, both about the size of babies.

Both men looked over when Iron Trail and Tessa had entered, and when they saw the Comanche, they grimaced. But when they saw the woman, their eyes brightened a bit.

"Howdy," the hunter said.

"Ma'am," the gunfighter said. He reached up to his forehead, as if to doff a hat, but when he touched his hair, he let his hand drop again.

Tessa drew closer to Iron Trail, and he could feel her fingers tighten around his arm. He nodded to both men and moved toward the store segment.

A grizzled old man sat slumped behind his desk, his spectacles up on his thinning head and the neck of a whiskey bottle plugged into his small mouth. His mustache glistened with previous drinks.

"Bud," Iron Trail said.

The old man put the bottle down and lifted his eyebrows. As a result his glasses plopped down on his nose and slid to the end. "Iron Trail? That you?"

"It's been awhile," the Comanche said. He stepped forward, offering his hand.

Bud wiped off his own and took it. "Well, damn! It sure has! And who is this?"

"A friend," Iron Trail said. He reached behind him and folded her hand in his.

The old man cackled. "I'll bet! Well, what can I do for you?"

Iron Trail gave him a verbal list, and Bud scratched it all down on a pad of paper. As they did this the Comanche felt Tessa draw away from him. He turned and watched her stepping toward the wall. It looked like she had taken an interest in something, but she stood in the way, so he couldn't see what it was.

And then she turned, holding a notebook in her hand. A journal. A diary. Men kept journals. Women kept *diaries*.

"I wish you hadn't left my old one with Fell," she said.

"I hadn't thought," Iron Trail said. "I'm sorry."

"Can we get this?" she asked.

He turned to Bud. "Add it to my bill. And pencils, too."

"Hell, I'll throw it in, free of charge," Bud said. "Nobody buys that shit around here anyway. Ain't a literate soul this side of the mountains."

Tessa smiled and hugged the journal tightly to her breast. Iron Trail thought back to when he'd bought her from Fell, surprised to find that he really did feel sorry for not bringing any of her belongings. A lot of things surprised him about this woman. He wondered what she'd said about him in her previous diary.

"That all?" Bud asked.

Iron Trail snapped back to the real world. "Pardon?"

Bud looked from him to the woman, and the Comanche could see the gears turning in the old man's head. Maybe Bud didn't think the two of them were in love, but he sure understood lust well enough.

"You need anything else?" the trader asked.

"No, thank you."

"Okay. It'll take a bit for me to get all these things together. You got a wagon?"

"No, just two horses."

"Need a new saddlebag?"

Iron Trail looked to Tessa, who ran her fingers over fresh, blank pages, probably wondering what she would cover them with. All she had was a saddle, so she should probably get some bags.

"Now that you mention it, give me a new set," he said.

"You got it. Why don't you go to the bar and have a few drinks while I'm getting everything."

Iron Trail almost said no, that he didn't like the looks of the other two patrons, but the old man called into the bar. "Sally! Get out here and serve our customers!"

A hefty woman with a bun of hair pulled severely back from her forehead staggered out from the back room. Strands had come loose from the structure on top of her head and ran across her smudged, plump face. The rags around her waist swayed with her movement, and she stank of whiskey.

"My wife," Bud said. "Don't look like much, but her pussy practically sucks the balls through my dick hole." He cackled, and Iron Trail smiled. "Sally, pour them what they want. First drink's on me."

Tessa looked at Iron Trail, and though he knew her to be a strong woman, he saw something in her eyes. She clearly didn't want to go into the bar, and he knew the reason why. He returned her fear with a confident gaze, and when her features softened, he nodded toward the bar.

She took a seat at the end, and Iron Trail positioned himself between her and the other two customers. Sally went behind the bar and took down a bottle of whiskey with two glasses. Iron Trail thought to ask her, "What if I don't want whiskey?" Then he looked around and saw nothing else to drink.

"Did you want a whiskey?" he asked Tessa.

She looked at the empty glass in front of her and frowned. "I don't drink."

"I'll take it, then," the gunfighter said. "It being free and all."

Sally glanced at him and poured into his glass instead of Tessa's. She then put the empty glass back on the shelf and poured one for Iron Trail. The Comanche sipped on his whiskey.

The buffalo hunter mumbled something, and the gunslinger laughed. Something tickled Iron Trail's brainstem, but he ignored it. He wanted supplies, not trouble.

Iron Trail took another drink, and he felt Tessa's slender hands wrap around his bicep. She squeezed, and he turned to look at her. She stared around him, and he turned to see what had her attention.

The buffalo hunter. His crooked eyes had settled on her, and his tongue worked at his lips as if he were licking a bit of stray grease away from himself after a messy meal. A glass of whiskey sat in front of him, forgotten.

Iron Trail put his arm around Tessa and held her, his hand gently pumping her shoulder. He continued drinking.

"You look familiar, friend," the gunfighter said. His clear blue eyes flashed, and he showed his tiny, jagged teeth. "Have we met before?"

"No," Iron Trail said. He drank and asked Sally for another.

"He's Iron Trail," the buffalo hunter said. "Comanche scum. Trades with the Messicans."

"Well now," the gunfighter said, "that name does sound familiar. I think I read it in the papers once. I can read, you know."

Iron Trail ignored them both and continued to drink.

"Maybe you heered of me," the gunfighter continued. "Nick Ford. I killed two dozen men. All legal, of course."

The name did not ring a bell. Iron Trail stared at the dirty mirror and tried to see himself through the grime.

"They call me Nick the Quick," the gunfighter said. "It's on account of how fast I am on the draw."

Iron Trail ground his teeth and wished this dime novel phony would go away.

Ford hooked a thumb to the buffalo hunter. "This here's Paw Skrowl. He's my partner. Most times, anyway."

Skrowl grunted and downed his glass. He reached behind the bar for the bottle, and Sally didn't stop him, not even when he forsook the glass for the source.

"You trading anything?" Ford asked. "We got a few things, if you got a few things." He glanced at Tessa when he said this.

Skrowl slapped him on the shoulder.

"Calm down, Paw. I gotcha." Ford turned back to Iron Trail. "A Comanch like you can't be with no white woman, not out here. You'd be skinned alive by the first white man who saw you. No, she's your property, ain't she? How much?"

Iron Trail put the glass down. "Not for sale."

Skrowl grimaced, showing off what remained of his black teeth.

Ford ignored him. "What? You're gonna' sell her to Messicans? What good'll that do anyone? She is top notch pussy, and we'll pay top dollar for it. What'll you get out of Messicans?"

Iron Trail glared at them. "Not for sale."

Ford chuckled. "Okay, I get it. You heered Paw's comment about you, and that turned you off us. I apologize for Paw. He comes from a different time, when Indians and whitefolk didn't drink with each other. Let me assure you, friend, green is the only color I give a shit about."

"We are not friends," Iron Trail said, "and she is not for sale."

Ford frowned. "Don't be like that. I think ol' Bud over there would appreciate it if we didn't have to kill you. You seemed like friends, and I don't want to piss Bud off."

49

"Then let's just stick to the drinks," Iron Trail said. "We'll be out of here in a few minutes."

Skrowl shoved at his partner's shoulder, this time a bit harder, and the gunfighter nearly fell over. "Damn, Paw! We're just in negotiations. 'No' don't mean a fucken thing yet."

"This red nigger's a hard-ass," the buffalo hunter said. "Only way we're getting her is by cutting his throat."

Iron Trail kept his eyes on these two while he finished off his drink. He felt Tessa lean toward him, but he resisted the urge to look over at her. "Let's just go," she whispered.

He ignored her and waited for Ford to open his rotten mouth again.

He didn't have to wait for long. "Listen, Iron Trail. We're menna the world. You don't have to fuck around with us. We know how things go out here. I see yer a drinking man. How about five bottles of whiskey for her? I'll throw in a pouch of 'baccy, since we're such close friends."

Sally reached down and pulled up a shotgun. She didn't point it at anyone, but she made sure everyone saw she had it.

Iron Trail looked Ford in the eyes, and the gunfighter didn't flinch. Usually the idiots who have read too many dime novels and wanted to try their hand at Colt's game had no steel in their spines. Maybe Ford wasn't just bragging after all.

But that didn't change anything. Iron Trail knew himself to be ten times the man Ford was, and the gunfighter would lose his nerve and drop his clear blue eyes.

Ford swallowed, and his Adam's apple bounced. A bead of sweat ran down from his hairline, but his gaze did not falter. His eyes were so light that Iron Trail thought he could see the wrinkles in the gunfighter's brain through them.

Ford's easy smile twitched. "Okay, fella. Maybe I was lowballen you. You should see some of the skins Paw's got. He's got a giant buffalo pelt that's guaranteed to keep you warm throughout all the winters you got left in you. Plus I'll throw in the whiskey and 'baccy. And we'll even buy all your supplies today. You really can't get a better deal than that."

Iron Trail continued to stare at him, as if his dark brown eyes were daggers pushing through the gunfighter's soul.

Ford was not impressed. "What are you going to get from the Messicans? A couple of bottles of mescal? Maybe a saddle with silver studs? You *do* wanna make a profit, right?"

Iron Trail shook his head. "Not. For. Sale."

Skrowl pushed his partner aside and yanked his skinning knife from its scabbard. "How about you just give her to me, fuckbag?"

Light reflected off the blade and into Iron Trail's eyes, but he did not flinch. "I don't know how many times I can say it. I'm not selling her to you."

A dry cough came from the other side of the room, and Skrowl turned to see Bud standing in the doorway. "Iron Trail, I got your stuff all set up."

The Comanche didn't look away from the buffalo hunter. "Thank you, Bud. I'll be leaving now. How much?"

Bud opened his mouth to quote a price, but Skrowl wasn't interested. "You're staying right there, red nigger. You ain't leaving till we've settled on a price."

51

Ford laughed as he lounged against the wall, balancing his hands on the butts of his guns. "You should have taken my deal, Iron Trail. Now you ain't got a chance."

Iron Trail drew his lips back from his teeth, showing off canines almost long enough to be a wolf's. "Get that thing out of my face, or I will kill you."

Skrowl gurgled. He had probably meant it to be a laugh, but he was so drunk it could have been anything at this point. It could have been indigestion. "You're not armed. How you gonna' stop me?"

A good point. Iron Trail wished he hadn't left his knife in his saddlebag. This would have been a lot easier if he'd had it. He supposed he would have to improvise instead.

"I'll think of something while I'm fucking your mother," Iron Trail said.

Skrowl's face drooped, but his eyes brightened as if someone had flicked a switch behind them. "My momma just died last year. Why you gotta say something like that about her?"

"It doesn't matter to me," Iron Trail said. "Living or dead, pussy's pussy."

Skrowl roared and lunged forward with the skinning knife, just as Iron Trail had hoped he would. The Comanche grabbed Ford by the shirt and yanked him forward, directly into the path of the blade. Something flashed, and the knife bit into Ford's back, halfway to the hilt.

Ford gasped, and blood oozed from the corner of his mouth. Iron Trail didn't have the time to care. His empty hand went to the gunfighter's belt and pulled out a Colt .45. Using Ford as a shield, in case the buffalo hunter could yank the knife free and attack again, Iron

Trail cocked the hammer and started firing into Skrowl's formidable bulk. Three shots went directly into his guts, the fourth into his chest, and the fifth into his gigantic head. The sixth passed through the hole that was already there. For a moment Skrowl remained standing, holding the knife like it was a lever he wanted to pull, and then he collapsed, a pool of blood forming around his body.

Ford's mouth worked, but no sound came out. The knife still stuck into his flesh, and judging from its location, Iron Trail figured it had punctured some important organ or other. Perhaps more than one, considering the size of the blade. He thought it might be humane to push the damned thing further in, but maybe it would be quicker to just put a bullet in the gunfighter's head.

Iron Trail chose the latter course of action. He gently removed Ford's other gun and placed the barrel directly between the gunfighter's eyes. He didn't think Ford knew what was happening, but if he did he probably experienced something along the lines of relief.

Iron Trail fired, and Ford's brains jumped onto the grimy mirror behind the bar. His skinny frame fell in a tangle at the Comanche's feet, where it twitched for awhile before the nerves had a chance to die.

"Jesus." Bud still stood as far away from the action as possible. His pate shone with sweat, and the bill for Iron Trail's goods sat wrinkled and forgotten in his hand. "That was a cold piece of work."

Iron Trail looked at the gun. "This is actually a pretty good piece. I don't really care much for firearms, but this is very nice."

Sally grunted and stowed the shotgun under the bar. "They say he treated his guns like women. Polished 'em every day. Even slept with them next to him on the pilla."

Iron Trail was surprised to find there were no notches on the butt. He checked the other gun and found the wooden grip to be immaculate. No disfigurement. Then again, if Sally had heard right, Ford would never have wanted to carve into his babies. Perhaps he kept a list of people he'd killed somewhere else.

"If no one objects, I'm going to keep these guns," he said. He paused, waiting for someone to speak up, and then he removed the gunfighter's belt, put the guns back in place, and rolled it up like a package.

Bud approached, looking down at the bodies. It wasn't hot enough for the flies to have arrived, but the stink of blood cut sharply through the odor of gunsmoke. "Jesus, would you look at that mess?"

Iron Trail wanted to apologize to his old friend, but he hadn't started the scuffle. Instead he made a promise. "I'll help you bury them."

Bud looked around him to Sally. "Would you get the lye soap? Something tells me this is gonna' be a hell of a blood stain."

Iron Trail put the gunbelt on the bar and reached down toward the gunfighter. He grabbed Ford by the shirt and hauled his skinny ass up, flinging him onto his shoulder. The blood was prodigious on the other side, where the knife still stuck out, so instead of holding the corpse by the back, he twisted a dead arm around his neck and held him in place like that.

When he turned he saw Tessa staring at him. At first he thought she might have been horrified by the sudden display of violence. It occurred to him that he might want to apologize to her, too, but when he saw the corners of her mouth, he knew such a thing would not be necessary.

If he wasn't mistaken he thought Tessa might actually approve of these killings.

-

An hour later both men were buried. Bud wasn't much good at digging, considering his age and his bad back, so it fell to Iron Trail to do most of the work. Sally helped, but Tessa stood off to the side writing in her new diary.

With the deed done Bud invited everyone back inside for a drink. Iron Trail looked up at the sun and decided they had enough time for at least one. Tessa stayed outside with the horses while the Comanche went in with Bud and Sally. They took seats at the bar and tried to ignore the smell. Though they had vigorously scrubbed at the bloodstains, and no visible mark remained, the reek of death still burned strong inside the trading post.

Bud poured them each a drink. "Here's to the right people dying."

Iron Trail nodded. "Amen."

F ROM THE JOURNAL OF TESSA REEVES:

September 27?28?, 18—

I have lost track of the days, so I am unable to tell for certain when this is. I suppose time is not so important right now, anyway.

I wish I still had my other diary. Has Felton thrown it away? Or does it rest in my "grave"?The latter strikes a more veracious tone in my head. Felton would probably not keep something so incriminating in his home.

Back when I first arrived here in the West, I had thought life to be cheap and unimportant to its denizens. And then I met my husband and his friend, Iron Trail, and they seemed like such nice people that I changed my mind.

Now I have changed it again. As I sit here, scribbling away in my new diary, my captor is digging a pair of graves.

In my previous diary, I discussed Iron Trail to some degree. He is a very erudite and articulate person, so much so that one would never believe him to be capable of such incredible and swift violence. Nor, I suppose, would one even suspect that he is a flesh merchant, but he clearly is. I am his merchandise, after all.

Here we are, at a trading post in a part of the country with which I am unfamiliar. Iron Trail has just killed two very rude men. It was in self-defense, but nevertheless quite brutal, perhaps unnecessarily so. These two bi-pedal creatures wanted to purchase me, and he would not sell. I do not know why he refused. Perhaps he has another buyer in mind for me. Regardless, they moved to kill him, and he promptly returned the favor.

I am watching the Comanche dig their graves. Actually, it is a single grave which the two men will share. Back East, such a thing would be unheard-of, but here, things are different. Wasteful actions tend to be dangerous. Besides, I do not believe these two curs deserve the respect a proper burial would afford them.

Iron Trail's powerful muscles bulge, and the sweat that runs across them shines in the sunlight, accentuating his handsome qualities. Under other circumstances, I might be able to love him.

But he is just as much of a beast as the men he is burying.

It has not stopped me from letting him fuck me. As shaming as it is to admit this, he is the only thing that stands between me and death in this godforsaken hellhole. Though he is my captor and undoubtedly intends to sell me like livestock, he is also my protector.

But perhaps not forever. At first, I was reluctant to share my sex with him, but when I realized the power I had over him, I found myself growing accustomed. It helps that he is attractive. Far more attractive than anyone I have ever been with, even that bastard, Sam Pepper, and he was the prettiest man I've ever known until now.

Since my reluctance has fallen away, Iron Trail trusts me more. He is teaching me many things, perhaps inadvertently, about how to survive out here. Should the day ever come when I feel I can fend for myself, I shall do so.

On the first night, when I attempted to slit his throat, he only caught me because he was wary of me. Soon, his paranoia will slip away, and then he will be mine to do with as I please.

The graves are filled in, and he is going in with Bud and his wife. I do not want to be inside that filthy hovel again, so I told them I would remain out here, writing in my diary. Iron Trail smiled condescendingly at me, as if he were indulging a precocious child.

I can hear them drinking a toast to the dead. No, that is not quite right. The old man said, "Here is to the right people dying." A good toast for the living, but I find it insulting to the dead.

Yet I think I will make an exception in this case. The gunfighter and his fat friend were not very nice people.

I have just reread what I have written. Am I becoming a Westerner? I believe I am turning more callous with each passing day. The New York City Tessa would probably not recognize me, but this is most likely for the best. If I am to survive out here, I will need to be tough. I will need to be callous. I will need to be a Westerner.

They have just finished their drinks, and I can hear Iron Trail paying for our goods. He is apologizing for the killings. And now, he is walking up the steps and out into the sun.

He smiles at me and asks if I'm ready to go. How can such a vicious killer of men be so . . . amiable? Charismatic?

I wonder if there is a part of me that actually likes him. I hope not, because I intend to kill him someday.

Later—

When we stopped for the evening, we found ourselves in a tiny grove of dead trees. The gnarled wisps of bark twisted into the cobalt sky, jutting branches that could not possibly have grown leaves at any point in the memory of man. The ground became a bit more solid, less dusty, than that with which we were accustomed. I started to wonder if perhaps we were leaving the unforgiving desert behind.

I mentioned this to Iron Trail, and he gave me his usual condescending smile. "No," he said, "this is a mere oasis. Tomorrow, we will be back to the sand, as unpleasant as I'm sure you find that."

"Will we ever come to a town?" I asked.

"Yes. Not today or the next day, and probably not the next, but within the week. Still hoping for a bath, I take it?"

"What happened to two days?

"Sorry, I lied. I didn't want you to lose all hope."

I wrinkled my nose and smelled the sour sweat on my own skin. My arms stuck to my blouse, and I could feel the stubble on my legs catching on my riding pants every time I moved. I wanted nothing more than to feel smooth and fresh again. I was grateful that my womanly time was still three weeks away. If I started to flow, I don't know what I would have staunched it with.

Iron Trail moved about camp, gathering some dry wood for a fire. The sun dipped behind the mountain, and from what I had learned, that meant we were headed east. A slight chill insinuated itself in the air, and I fished the flint from Iron Trail's saddlebag.

When he had prepared the wood, he asked me to do the honors. Before long, we had a healthy fire burning in the middle of a circle of stones. We had purchased beans and bread while we were at the trading post, so we opened a can of the former and broke up a loaf of the latter. After having nothing but jerky for so many days, the smell of cooking beans filled my mouth with stinging wetness. I stuck a hunk of bread between my lips, and the saliva dissolved it before it touched my tongue.

As we ate, the stars appeared in the sky, almost one at a time, each declaring their presence with a twinkle. The moon shone as a sickle floating in the sparkling brew of night.

"How can you tell direction by stars?" I asked.

"You mean, you don't know?"

I grimaced. "I come from a place where you don't need stars to tell you where you're going. Street signs will do that for you."

He chuckled. "I was just teasing you. Do you see that dipper shape up there?"

I squinted at where he pointed, but I could not make sense of the celestial mess twirling about our heads. "It all looks like a bunch of tiny lights to me."

It was Iron Trail's turn to grimace, but only as a momentary flash across his stony face. "Do you at least see that very bright star? And the line of other stars leading to it?"

I tried to see what he was talking about, but again, I only saw a chaotic jumble, as if God had accidentally spilled the stars across the galaxy like a child would spill a glass of milk.

"Have you no imagination?" he asked. When I remained silent, he put his plate aside and scooted over to sit next to me. With one arm around my shoulders, he gestured at a thousand constellations, trying to point out their shapes to me and where they were supposed to be in the night sky at this time of year. Sometimes, I could see the patterns, but most times I found myself nodding just to agree.

It was too much to take in. After a while of trying, Iron Trail gave up. He told me that at least I had learned something. Later, we would try again.

We finished up dinner and . . . I hesitate to call it love-making. It is something more animalistic than that. Yes, it is definitely fucking. But there is something stirring within me for this Comanche. I had heard tales of women who have been taken prisoner suddenly falling in love with their captors. Is this happening to me?

Iron Trail sleeps across the fire from me. When I left our blankets to write in this diary, he did not even stir. If I wanted to, I probably could have killed him this time.

But not yet. I wouldn't last a day out here alone. He has a lot more to teach me.

-

September 29, 18—

Yes. This sounds like a good date, and I think it will suit my purposes. If I find out later that I am wrong, I will change it, but for now, I believe it is the 29th.

When I woke up this morning, I reread what I had written last night as Iron Trail slumbered nearby. I thought perhaps I should not write about such things. Iron Trail is no fool. He is a studied, well-educated man, which means he can read. If he ever took it into his head to read my diary, he would know what I intend to do to him eventually.

I was tempted to tear the pages out and throw them into the glowing remains of our campfire. At the time, the only thing that stopped me was the fact that he was awake and was cooking our breakfast over that exact fire.

But now that I have had time to think about it, I have come to the conclusion that Iron Trail would never read this diary. Is he a villain? Indeed. Is he violent? Absolutely. But he is also a gentleman, a trait I suspect was bred into him wherever he had been educated by white men. He respects my privacy, even when I get dressed in the morning. Despite his carnal knowledge of my body, he turns away so that I might cover myself up.

He bought me new clothes at the trading post. They did not resemble anything I would have worn Back East, but they are quite suitable to making my way through this barbarous desert.

We had eggs and bacon for breakfast. Even though it had not been long since Iron Trail had taken me from my home, it still felt like it had been longer, a lifetime, since I had had such decent food in the morning.

Shortly afterward, we packed up our things and started off into the wilderness.

Iron Trail had not lied when he said we were going to be traveling across sand again, but I thanked whatever god might care to watch after me that it wasn't the loose, shifting stuff we had been on before. No, the ground was more solid, and it was merely gritty rather than grainy.

The land around us was no longer flat and barren; it had become more hilly. We went down a few steep slopes that I thought our horses would never be able to traverse. Still, our equine companions were more fleet of foot than I would have expected, and we arrived at the bottom safely.

We broke for luncheon when Iron Trail said the sun was high enough in the sky. When I questioned him about this, he gave me a quick lesson in what the position of the sun meant. I grasped this a lot quicker than I did the constellations. By the end of the day, I became very adept at this.

"Then, we're headed east?" I asked. "Maybe closer to northeast?"

He smiled. "Yes. You are learning."

I blushed and gave him my best aw-shucks, and he seemed pleased.

We continued on our way, and about an hour later, we came upon a town. I asked him why he had said we would not see such a place for a few days, and he told me that Pilgrim City did not count.

"It's a ghost town," he said.

I had heard of such things from newspaper and magazine accounts, but I doubted their existence. "How could a town just become abandoned?"

"When it's no longer profitable," Iron Trail said. He pointed off to hills in the distance. "There used to be gold out there. When the vein ran out, so did the people."

"People just left their homes?" I asked. "Without selling them?"

"What would their homes have been worth?" he said. "What fool would buy them?"

"That's hardly the point," I said. "A home is more than just a piece of property that may have some monetary value. Memories are held between a home's walls. A sense of family."

"If there are any memories left behind here," he said, "they are dismal ones, and they are worth forgetting."

I watched as he rode into the center of the town, where a water pump and a trough was the main attraction. He dismounted and strode to the pump, where he grabbed the handle and began pushing it up and down. I heard a metallic squeal, and even from a distance, I could see a cloud kick up from the joints. He continued to do this for a minute before he gave up.

I urged my horse forward just as he led his away toward a hitching post. "Why did you do that?" I asked.

"I had to try."

"We have plenty of water."

"Maybe. We also have two empty water skins. Who knows how long we will be out here at nature's mercy?"

I didn't push him on it. He was right. It was one of the most important lessons I had learned from him so far. I kept thinking about the single grave he'd dug for two men.

"Help me look around town," he said. "I'm sure they took everything of value when they left, but it is possible that they couldn't carry everything."

I shook my head. "This is pointless. If they left anything good behind, it would be useless by now."

"Canned goods never go bad," Iron Trail said. "Check restaurants and bars mostly. Liquor doesn't go bad, either. Perhaps we can find something to trade later."

I tied my horse to the hitching rail as he moved on, entering a general store. This town didn't offer much, but I decided that Iron Trail would look at his side of the street while I would check the other.

I hopped up on the dusty boardwalk and passed a dentist's office, a lawyer's office and a bank before I found a saloon. There were boards across the doors, but they came away easily. The nails did not scream when I pulled the wood back; they simply broke with a cloud of filth.

Behind the outer doors, I saw a pair of batwings, which I pushed through. One protested with a wail, and the other snapped off its hinges. The slate clattered on the hardwood floor, and I thought I heard something scurrying in the darkness. Rats?

Most women would probably jump up on a table, but not I. They were practically raised with me as siblings in New York.

A lot of dusty bottles remained on the wall behind the bar. The mirror was obfuscated by cobwebs and grit, but not so badly that I could not see my own reflection. I found nearly ten bottles full of amber spirits. Seven were whisky, and three were rye. I lined them up on the bar and made a note to myself to pick them up before we left town.

Under the bar, where the tarnished beer spigots cast their death-gaze up at me, I found something much more interesting than alcohol: a shotgun.

It was old, but the lack of rust indicated a serviceable weapon. Maybe it needed to be oiled, but it looked deadly without it.

I ran my fingers along the stock, and while the wood felt rough, it was sturdy. Rot had not touched this device. But would the ammunition be intact?

I could tell directions from the sun, and I knew a few constellations. I knew how to build fires. There was plenty of food in our saddlebags. Perhaps now would be the perfect time to have my vengeance. I could make it back to civilization on my own.

I cracked the shotgun open, and I pulled out the shells. Both seemed to be in perfect working order. Granted, I didn't know much about such things, but I felt certain they could send buckshot into Iron Trail's vicious heart.

I found a box of spare cartridges near the broken cash register, but when I opened it, I found the contents were slightly on the soggy side. The two in the gun were probably my only chance.

I took the shotgun with me to the front door and hid behind the remaining batwing. Across the street, I could see Iron Trail stepping into a restaurant. He carried with him a sack of canned goods. It would be all too easy to blow him out of his leggings when he came back out. From this distance, it would be no problem to hit him. The cloud of buckshot would pepper him so badly that he would not be able to resist long enough for me to get close to him for the finishing shot.

I have done many horrible things in this life, but I have never killed anyone before. It was this knowledge that stayed my hand. I do not know if I believe in Hell or not, but I am fairly certain that there would be too high a spiritual price to pay for this.

Maybe I had another reason, but I do not think I will entertain it here. Suffice it to say, I lowered the weapon long before he stepped outside again.

But my mischievous nature did not leave me. I cracked open the shotgun and removed both shells before snapping it shut. When I saw Iron Trail emerge from the restaurant, carrying only the bag of canned goods he'd had before, I strode out of the bar, holding the gun loosely in my hands. I was not aiming it anywhere, but I knew its presence would disturb him.

I made it halfway across the street before he noticed me, and for a moment, I saw every muscle in his body tense. He paused in mid-step, and I could see he was ready for me. There was no firearm on his body, but he did have a knife on his belt, and I knew he could easily hurl it into my throat, if he had to.

But he saw that I did not aim the gun at him, and his body loosened up. Not enough to come completely uncoiled, but enough to show that he no longer feared me.

"Look what I found," I said. I presented the weapon to him carefully, so he knew I meant no harm.

He took the shotgun from me and gave it a cursory glance. "This will not fire."

My brow furrowed. "How do you know?"

"See this rust?" He pointed to the barrel.

"No, I . . ." I trailed off, for very shortly, I noticed how the end of the barrel had eroded over the years. There were tiny pock marks at the end, and the sight was crooked. I had not noticed these deficiencies in the darkness of the saloon.

"Anyone who would fire this weapon would only have it explode in their hands," he said. "You are very lucky you did not test it out."

Test it out. I believe he meant to say, "It's a good thing you didn't try to shoot me." Even though I had shown no intention to kill him, I knew that he had seen through my little game.

I played dumb. "It crossed my mind, but I have no experience with such things. I wanted to give it to you."

He grunted. "Even if it was in perfect working order, I would have passed. Firearms are inferior weapons. I'm not much of a traditionalist, but I do favor the bow and arrow over the white man's faulty craftsmanship. The Cherokee believed in such death machines, and look what it got them."

Iron Trail spat and dropped the shotgun into the dust. "Did you find anything else in the bar?"

"There was some whisky," I said.

He smiled. "Good. Show me."

I stepped into the saloon first, displaying my back to him. By this time, I knew he would not hurt me, so I felt safe in having him in my blind spot. Once inside, I pointed out the line of bottles, and he approached the first. The label had rotted away long ago, so he didn't bother trying to read its name. Instead, he popped the cork and smelled the contents. Both eyebrows raised, and he took a tiny sip from the bottle. He sighed. "Kentucky Bourbon. Lawrenceburg, I believe. Do you know how hard it is to come by such things this far west?"

I did not, so I remained quiet.

"We can't take them all," Iron Trail said. "Maybe three bottles of whisky and one of rye. Pack them up and put them on your horse. I'll search the rest of the town."

I followed orders. When I finished, Iron Trail came back with a few paltry goods. Canned foods, mostly. He came away with some medical supplies from the doctor's office, but it wasn't much. Just aspirin and some bandages.

It did not take us long to pack everything away, and soon we were back on the trail. The rest of the day was uneventful, and as per usual, we made camp at sunset, where we ate a magnificent dinner and made love under all the stars in creation.

-

September 30, 18—

I heard the river long before we saw it. The land had evened out, and across the long grass and skimpy trees of the prairie, I listened to a rushing sound that reminded me of Niagara Falls Back-East.

"What is that sound?" I asked.

"The Brown River," Iron Trail said. "Folks around here call it Shit Creek. It's not a very aesthetically pleasing body of water."

"It sounds like we're very close," I said.

"We still have five miles to go."

I shook my head. "Impossible."

"I know this land," Iron Trail said. "I know there are exactly five miles between us and the river. Sound travels very well over the prairie."

I chose to believe him, although his theory did not sound very plausible. However, after riding for another three miles, I still did not see the river.

On the fourth mile, I could smell it. There is something about being in the wilderness for so long, being baked under an unrelenting sun, that makes one constantly thirsty. Every time I took a drink from my water-skin, I felt tempted to take a long draught. It took every ounce of willpower to place the cap back on. Now that I could take in the scent of the river, I licked my lips.

"It smells delicious," I said.

Iron Trail grunted. "Wait until you see it. I warrant you won't want a drop of it to get on you."

We briefly broke camp and had a quick luncheon, and within the hour, we were close enough to see the rushing waters of the Brown River.

I will grant that I have not seen many rivers Out West, but the few I have seen were usually frothing with white foam as they blasted by. This one looked like something that would have been at home in New York City. It was such a deep brown color that I thought it had to be a rushing glut of diarrhea. I do not know why it did not smell of sewage, like a city river would, and Iron Trail does not know the answer, either.

"That's strange," he said.

"Huh?"

"There's supposed to be a ferry here."

"There was a heavy storm a few nights ago," I said. "Maybe it washed the ferry away."

Iron Trail shook his head. "The waters are strong and high, but not enough to break up a ferry. Look." He pointed.

I shielded my eyes from the sun with my hand and squinted. "What I am looking for?"

"Those wooden posts," he said. "Those mark the ferry landing. You can't see it through the grass, but there is a platform beneath them. The ferry should be there, along with a rope crossing the river to the landing on the other side."

I noticed a shack about several yards away from the landing. "Perhaps we can ask the ferryman." I pointed.

Iron Trail glanced at the shack. It did not look lived-in, but then again, this was the West. People were known to live in homes that looked weak enough to collapse under a slight breeze.

"Keep quiet," he said.

"Why?"

"Just do it."

I watched as he dismounted and removed what looked like a stick from the side of his saddle. He then pulled a string out from his bag and began to bend the stick over his knee. It took me a moment to realize he was stringing a bow.

From the side of his saddle, where most men carried their rifles, Iron Trail pulled a quiver full of arrows, which he slung over his shoulder. He nocked an arrow and approached the shack at a crouch. Even though I was watching him, he seemingly disappeared into the tall grass as if he were a ghost.

The next time I saw him, he appeared in front of the shack. He shuffled up to the door from the side, and he used his foot to nudge it open. He went in for a brief moment, and when he came out, his arrow still on its string, he cast his glance around the area.

Iron Trail's eyes fixed on something, and he lowered his weapon. The arrow remained in place as he slowly advanced through the grass.

Without slowing his pace, he ducked down and grabbed a rock, which he hurled at something I couldn't see. There was a loud squawk, and several birds took to the air.

Carrion birds.

I grabbed a rock of my own and started leading the horses down. By the time I'd arrived, I could see what had attracted Iron Trail's attention: a badly rended corpse. It had been an old man in life, but now it was a hunk of decaying meat. His face was gone, having been eaten by buzzards. Still, the cause of death was obvious. There were large holes above his empty eye sockets. I judged them to be .45-caliber.

I was getting good at this.

Iron Trail pulled a rope from the river, but he had still taken the time to notice me. "This doesn't make you ill?" he asked.

"It's unsettling," I said. "But I've seen death before. Most recently, thanks to you."

"For one to know death is to preserve one's own life."

"You sure know a lot of catchy one-liners," I said. "You should write a book."

"I have," he said. "Several, in fact. But not books as you would know them. Scholars have a phrase for it: oral tradition. I've passed on epic stories to my children and wives and anyone else who cared to listen. I will be remembered long after I'm dead."

It sounded like a fallible way to pass on stories. I liked the idea of writing something down (as if you couldn't tell). But who knows? Perhaps paper will someday be fallible, too.

"What happened here?" I asked.

He held up the end of the rope. It was not frayed, but it looked very even. "Someone cut this from the other side and sent the ferry adrift. There are some busted up boards down there." He pointed. "I think that might be the remains of the ferry."

"Why would someone do that?"

He glanced at me. "You're smarter than that, Tessa. You tell me."

"Well, I guess someone didn't want to be followed. A very bad person, considering how he shot this poor old man in the face."

"It wasn't just one person," Iron Trail said. He pointed to a multitude of tracks, both boot prints and horse hooves. "I'd say there are five people here. It's hard to tell for sure. One of them might be wounded badly."

"How can you tell?"

"There are several drops of blood mixed in here." He pointed. "It might be from the ferryman, but there is quite a distance between him and these dots."

I laughed. "You're a regular Sherlock Holmes!"

"Who?"

I quickly explained about *The Strand* magazine, to which I have subscribed for several years. I had to cancel it, due to my marriage to Felton.

From the stoic way he listened to me, I thought perhaps I'd bored him with my summary of Mr. Holmes's character, but he surprised me. "It sounds very interesting. I should like to read such tales someday. But we have other, more pressing, issues to consider right now."

"The scoundrels?" I asked.

He nodded. "They're going the same way we are. We might run into them, and judging from their ruthlessness, I'm not sure I can take them. We also have another problem."

"What?"

"How are we going to cross Shit Creek? The waters are too high and fast for our horses."

"You know this territory better than I. What do you suggest?"

Iron Trail sighed, brushing his hair back from his face with his fingers. "The river thins out a bit south of here. And by 'a bit,' I mean fifteen miles."

At first, the thought did not appeal to me, but then I remembered my situation. This was no gentle ride through the countryside. I was a captive, and I would probably be sold soon. Why would I protest such a delay?

"I find no objection to this," I told him.

"I do. I have an appointment to make in a few days. It would not be very professional for me to miss it."

I did not need to ask what he meant by this. "Are there any alternatives?"

He shielded his eyes from the sun with his hand and squinted across the river. It was as if he wanted to attempt the crossing, regardless. I stared at the roiling, brown water, and I knew we would not make it.

Even if our horses were strong enough, I dreaded the very idea of this fetid water touching me.

Iron Trail ambled toward the ferry landing and stooped down to pick up the rope. He went over it inch by inch, not seeming to care that his hands were now soaked with Shit Creek. When he had a good length of it before him on the dock, he peered to the other side of the river, as if gauging the distance.

"Can you swim?" he asked.

"You surely don't mean—"

He whipped his head around to face me. "Can you swim?"

"I . . . yes."

"Good. I'm sure it won't come up, but I had to make sure you could fend for yourself if anything happened."

My heart turned into a wild beast in my chest. "What do you mean?"

"The rope isn't long enough to reach the other side," he said, "but I'm pretty sure it will reach that rock in the river." He pointed to a stone outcropping almost to the other embankment. Water rushed past it on our side, but on the opposite, it seemed considerably slower.

"I'm going to try swimming to the rock," he said. "I'll take the cut end of the rope with me. I'll loop it around the outcropping and hold it taut. I then want you to hold the rope and use it as a guide to bring you and the horses across to the rock. From there, our horses will be able to swim it on their own to the other side."

I wanted to object. My mouth opened to do so. I wanted to mention the crossing fifteen miles away. But I could see it in his eyes: he was dead set on giving this a try.

My own face had to be just as easy to read. "The worst that happens," he said, "if I don't make it, I will be washed down the creek a bit, but I will still have the rope. It will eventually bring me back to this side."

And then, another thought occurred to me. There was a knife on the dead man's belt. As soon as Iron Trail made it halfway across, I could very easily cut through the rope and make my escape. How would he be able to stop me? Besides, now I knew enough to vaguely know where to go. I had a good supply of food and water on the horses. It wouldn't be very difficult to manage this.

I looked down at the old man's corpse. Its empty eye sockets stared back at me. My heart begged me to ask Iron Trail to bury the man first, but then I wouldn't be able to get the knife. It was a war in my breast between the Christian thing to do, and the smart thing to do.

I chose the latter. "Good luck," I said to him.

Iron Trail stripped out of his shirt and put it in his saddle bag. Next came the rest of his clothes until he was stark naked. His chest and back rippled with muscle, and when he knelt down to pick up the rope, I could see his buttocks tense into a very grab-able shape.

He looped the rope at the end, and he put it around his waist. His hands wrapped around the rough hemp and pulled. More of Shit Creek spat out from its fibers, but the rope held.

Iron Trail walked along the creek for a while, and I wondered what he was doing. He kept staring at the rock as he went, but he stepped in the opposite direction. I was about to ask him about this when he jumped into the putrid waters.

It was shocking, how well he swam. Though I thought the current would sweep him away, he moved like a knife through the creek. He reminded me of a seal I had seen back at the zoo in New York.

I knew then I couldn't possibly cut that rope. I did not even glance at the blade on the old man's belt. If I had severed his lifeline, he would drift for a while, but not far enough for me to get away. I did not think he would kill me, or even get rough with me (I am, after all, merchandise), but there are other ways to torment a person. Iron Trail struck me as one who knew all about cruelty.

Even if I tried, he had almost made it out to the rock now. If I went for the knife, he would be safe by the time I had the chance to use it.

I now knew why he'd walked up the creek a little bit; the current bore him directly towards the outcropping. It was almost a geographical magic trick, the way he'd managed this.

I blinked, and he climbed up on the rock, panting. I had expected him to emerge from the river covered in brown slime, but his muscles gleamed in the sunlight, seemingly fresh.

"Grab the horses!" he shouted.

I turned and retrieved our horses, leading them both by the bridle to the creek. "How do I do this?" I called back.

"Get on my horse! She's stronger!"

I followed orders. My feet did not quite reach the stirrups from where I sat in the saddle, but I felt stable enough.

He removed the rope from his waist and looped it around the rock. Then, he jumped into the water and pulled, yanking the rope taut like a clothesline. "Wrap the reins of your horse around the saddle horn of mine!"

Again, I obeyed. "Now what?"

"Inch into the water, but very carefully! Grab the rope and hold tight! The horses will do the rest!"

I peered down over the edge. There had to be a slight downgrade in the bed, but because the water was so thick and filthy, I couldn't see it. Still, Iron Trail knew the territory. I had to trust him.

But first, I reached back behind me, to my saddlebag. I retrieved this journal, only because I was afraid it might get wet. It was thin enough to hold between my clenched teeth, so this is what I did.

I then nudged the horse forward, and she started moving slowly. First one hoof vanished into the brown murk, and then the other. Before I knew it, my legs were in the water, all the way up to my thighs, and it felt every bit as slimy as I expected it would. I thought about the ubiquitous dust of the West, and I decided I would prefer it to the creeping, crawly feeling I got when the water eased up over my hips.

It was such an horrendous feeling, that I almost forgot to grab the rope. I did so at the last moment, holding it with my right hand while I held the reins in my left. Both of my hands clenched tightly shut. I could see the veins and muscles in each standing out against my tanned, almost sunburned skin.

Something tugged at my rope hand, and I realized that I couldn't hold it as tightly as I wanted to. I had to use it as one would use a handrail. The rough material, muted somewhat by the tepid water, scratched against my palms almost badly enough to burn. I then decided it would be easier to hold the reins with both hands and put the rope between my arm and my side.

It took only a moment to accomplish this, and when I did, the going became suddenly smoother. I did not even panic when I felt the horse's hooves leave the firma and begin to pump against the water.

Until that moment, I did not know horses could swim, much less swim well.

The current pushed against us, but the rope held us in place. The other horse struggled a bit more to stay on this side of the rope, but Iron Trail's strength was so powerful it need not have worried.

Something snapped under my hands, and at first I was afraid it was the reins. For a terrifying moment, I thought I was going to fly off the horse and get dragged through all creation by the demon-pace of the river's current. When I remained in place, I checked the reins and was happy to note they were in one piece.

"Tessa!" Iron Trail yelled. "Grab the reins!"

"I have them!" I yelled back. My words were slurred around the journal in my mouth.

"The other reins!"

The horse behind me shrieked as the current beat her so badly she was swept under the rope. I went to grab her reins from my saddle horn, but I was shocked to find that they had snapped.

The horse slipped out of reach. She tried to swim, but her form was too unwieldy. She shot down the creek to the mess of what had once been the ferry. Her body was battered and broken on the pile of jagged wood, and the next time I saw her, she floated motionlessly.

There was no time to think about the horse. I still had to make it to the destination myself. I urged the remaining horse forward, and she continued swimming until we reached the rock. By that point, the waters were more or less placid, and the horse was able to easily swim to the bank.

Iron Trail came up behind me. "What did you have on your horse?" he asked.

I dismounted, feeling as if I had been swimming in sewage. My jaws creaked from holding my diary between them for so long, so I pulled it out and stuck it in my belt. "Just some food. My water skins. And the whisky from the ghost town."

He cursed and began to check his own supplies.

"Are we going to be okay?" I asked.

"I don't know," he said. "At least all of my stuff is still there. We can survive off of this for a while."

"How close is the next town?"

He grimaced. "Too far to think about. But we have a chance if . . ." He trailed off, and he did not seem ready to continue.

"If what?" I asked.

"Well, let's not consider that just yet. I'll let you know when and if it comes up."

I started to object when he said, "Get undressed. You need to let your clothes dry."

I smirked. "You just want to see me naked again."

"Who wouldn't want that?" he asked. He leaned forward and kissed me gently. "But we do need to rest. It's late enough, so we can break camp here."

So, we did. I stripped down and hung my clothes up on a tree branch. As I did this, I thought about my horse and the clothes she had carried in her saddlebags. I found myself wishing for a fresh set of garments. The sun pleasantly warmed my skin, but I knew by night I would be shivering. I would be wrapped up in a buffalo skin with Iron Trail's body heat to keep me company, but sometimes the cold of the prairie at night seemed to cut through all barriers. I dreaded seeing the sun go down.

We ate from Iron Trail's saddlebag, but as the world grew darker around us, he turned away from me. He kept peering into the night, as if he'd heard something.

"What is it?" I asked.

"You don't see it?"

I squinted, but I saw only darkness. I told him so.

"You'll see soon," he said. "It's just not dark enough yet."

I moved to put more kindling on the fire, but he grabbed my wrist and said, "No."

"Why? It's going to be cold soon, and my clothes aren't dry yet."

"Let the fire die. I'll keep you warm."

"I think I'll need a something more—" I started. He silenced me with a finger to his lips.

"Not so loud. They might hear. Sound travels well across the prairie."

"Who?" I whispered.

He pointed, and I squinted again. This time, I *did* see something: a campfire in the distance, perhaps a mile or more away. I started to ask who it could be when I remembered the old man.

"You don't think. . . ?" I asked.

He nodded. "I'm not sure, but why not be careful?"

All of a sudden, I wanted our fire to be put out. Fear overrode my sense of comfort, but Iron Trail had shown no indication of wanting the same thing. I had to trust his instinct. This was his world.

A short while later, I heard someone laughing from the other camp. There was a gunshot, and then more laughter. "You're a motherfucker, you know?" someone shouted, and more laughter and unintelligible speech followed. The hilarity baked in the air almost tangibly.

"Go to sleep, Tessa," Iron Trail said. "We'll find out who those people are tomorrow morning, just before dawn."

"Why do we want to find out who they are?" I asked.

"Because they might have supplies," he said. "We need supplies, and if they're the ones who killed the ferryman, I'm going to kill them and take whatever they have."

I was surprised by the animosity in his voice, so I mentioned it to him.

"I knew the old man," he said. "I wouldn't say we were friends, but we've shared each others whisky more times than I can recall. If I can get vengeance for him, I will do so. That they have supplies we'll probably need only sweetens the pot for me. Besides . . ." He trailed off, looking to their campfire. "Besides, it sounds like they have whisky, and I could sure use a slug or two."

Shortly after, he fell asleep, or at least I think he did. It is very difficult to tell with him. Perhaps he merely dozed, but his paranoia kept his sleep shallow. In the meantime, I am wide awake with the thought of a band of cutthroats so close tome. I opted to stay awake and write in this journal, but now I am finally feeling tired. The moon tells me that it is about midnight, and now would be a good time for sleep.

-

October 1, 18—

The sun had not yet risen when Iron Trail shook me awake. He put a finger to his lips, then pointed to my clothes. They were dry but cold.

I almost dreaded putting them on, but I remembered the villains camped nearby, and I hastened to cover myself.

The fire went out, and from the way it did not smolder, nor did it faintly glow, I determined it had been put out long ago. The moon offered very little light from above, and the iridescence in the east was far too diaphanous to be of any substance, at least not for another hour.

Iron Trail drew close to me and held up both hands. In one he held his knife, honed to an uncanny sharpness; in the other rested a small lady's pistol. He lifted his eyebrows, and I understood his question. I knew I would never be able to use something as savage as a blade on another human being, but I equally knew that I could send a piece of lead hurtling through a person's body from a distance.

He gave me the lady's gun, and I placed it in my pocket. As I put my boots on, I noticed that he had strung his bow again, the quiver strapped to his back.

I wanted to say something, but he beckoned for me to follow him. We headed for the other campfire, which still distinctly showed in the early hours of the morning.

Ahead of me, Iron Trail moved silently through the sparse, brown grass. It was brittle stuff, and it crumpled against my boots. Iron Trail's step, however, was far lighter than mine, and he did not leave a single broken blade in his wake.

We reached a small grove of dead, wind-twisted trees, and at the center guttered a campfire, almost down to the embers. Four men, concealed in their sleeping accoutrements, rested in a circle around the dying flames. Their sleep was deep and whisky-wrought, but the fifth member of their party did not rest easily. His face beaded with sweat, and his breath came harsh and ragged. He twisted and turned, as if plagued by a hideous nightmare, but even a fool could see the only thing he suffered was fever.

Iron Trail nocked an arrow and drew back, aiming for one of the sleeping forms. He gave every indication that he was going to shoot, so I intervened. I placed my hand on his shoulder.

"How do we know they killed the old man?" I whispered.

He loosened the bowstring and turned to me. Holding both bow and arrow in one hand, with his other he traced the bottom of his foot, then pointed back at the four men. It took me a moment to realize he meant for me to look at their boots.

Even with the dim light in the sky, I could see the shiny dark spots on the bottoms of their footwear. Unmistakably blood. I then remembered that Iron Trail thought there were five of them, and that one was injured.

I needed no further explanation.

He nocked the arrow again and took aim. He seemed to deliberate for a moment, as if trying to decide which man to shoot, when he settled on one and let the string go.

I was surprised by how quickly the arrow sliced through the air. I could barely follow its path with my eyes. One moment it rested safely in the bow, and the next it landed in the chest of a sleeping man. It went directly into his heart. He was probably in hell before he knew what had happened.

The impact sounded hollow, like when one knocks on a clothing chest. Loud enough to cause the others to stir, they rose, logy, but were undoubtedly blinded by their hangovers. No one seemed to notice what had happened.

Iron Trail let loose with another arrow and struck a second man in the heart, killing him instantly. By now, the remaining three men knew they were being attacked, and they scrambled for their weapons and a hiding place.

I remembered the lady's gun, and I stuffed my hand into my pocket to retrieve it. By this point, I knew I would not have to use it, but I wanted to feel safe, regardless. Its metallic weight comforted me.

Iron Trail managed to shoot a third man, again, in the heart, but the fourth took refuge behind a tree.

"Who the fuck's out there?!" the man screamed.

"Don't leave me!" the remaining wounded man shouted. "Please, Gorton! Don't leave me! I don't want to die!"

"Shut up! Just shut the hell up!"

The wounded man mewled in the dirt, twisting and turning, trying to reach a dead man's gun, but the bandages around his guts held him back. A string of indecipherable words dropped from his mouth, but I did manage to catch one: "Savages!"

Iron Trail smiled at this.

"Who goes?" Gorton shouted. "I'm . . . I'm unarmed! Show yourselves!"

Iron Trail held his finger to his lips and pointed to the ground. I understood his command as he slipped into the tall grass and vanished from my sight.

"They're gone!" the wounded man cried. "They gots to be!"

"Shut up, you fool! Since when did those savages ever leave survivors? Be quiet, or you'll draw their fire!"

The wounded man whimpered, and I could hear even from this far his ragged breath, as if he were out of air but didn't want to start panting too loudly.

Something flashed near Gorton's tree, and a figure staggered out of the shadows, holding his throat. Gorton fell to his knees, and he tried to hold his gaping throat closed. Blood spilled out from between his fingers and from out his mouth.

Iron Trail stepped from behind the tree, and he wiped something off of his knife, which he then sheathed. He leaned against the tree with his arms crossed while he watched Gorton drown in his own blood. The look in his eyes was cold, as if he were studying a math problem that didn't particularly interest him.

I wanted to ask him to end this poor man's suffering, or to perhaps even do it myself with the lady's gun, but paralyzed, my mouth remained shut. If I could move my feet, I would have probably tripped over them.

The wounded man went beyond fright. His mortification froze him as much as I. His frame shook, and slobber oozed down his chin. His eyes were saucers, transfixed on his partner's slow, unending death.

Except, it finally did end. Judging from the gentle lift in the sun, peeking over the horizon from the east, I supposed it had taken fifteen to twenty minutes before Gorton's body stopped moving.

And Iron Trail turned his eyes on the wounded man. "I know you."

The wounded man gagged and started coughing. When he was able to speak, he said, "Is that what this is about? The bounty?"

Iron Trail ambled over to a dead man and pulled his arrow out. I would not think it would be very difficult, but it took him a moment of twisting and wrenching before the point came out. Even then, it had a curlicue of glistening flesh around the tip.

"We got more money than you'll ever get off our hides," the wounded man continued. "Just let me go, huh?"

Iron Trail went to the next dead man and did it all over again, but this time, when he examined the shaft, he must have determined it to be faulty. Rather than clean it off and stick it back in his quiver, he threw it into the dying flames. It smoldered for a moment, and then it caught fire.

"Talk to me, you fucking savage!" the wounded man screamed. His voice cracked near the end of his exclamation, and he spent the next minute in a spasm of coughing.

Iron Trail retrieved the final arrow and found it to his liking. "You're Brent Benjamin, otherwise known as Bullet Brent. Known for robbing thirty banks and ten trains, and never getting shot in all of that time. Luck run out?"

Brent glared up at him. "Who cares? You just want the money, right? You can have it, just let me go."

"Even if I let you go, you'd die," Iron Trail said. "It looks like you caught a slug in your guts, and from the look of things, it happened two days ago. I'm surprised you're still alive."

"You sure are mouthy for a bounty hunter," Brent said. "And I didn't know your kind came in that shade of red."

"I'm not a bounty hunter," Iron Trail said. "I don't care about any money you may have stolen. Although I have no aversion to taking it after I kill you."

Brent gagged, or perhaps he laughed. He had a slight twinkle in his eyes, and I thought it was more than just the rising sun. "Then what the hell're you doing here? Why're you killing me?"

"I saw your sign back at the ferry crossing," Iron Trail said. "I wasn't entirely sure it was you, but that was probably because you were limping. Do you remember the old man you killed?"

"The ferryman? I didn't do that. It was Decker, the guy you throat-cut."

Iron Trail smiled. "I don't care which of you did it. The old man was harmless, and he liked to share his whiskey." He turned toward me and called my name.

"I don't get it," Brent said. "You're killing me because of some nobody?"

Iron Trail didn't answer him. "Tessa! Come on out! It's safe!"

I hesitated a moment longer. I knew he told the truth, but there was so much death down there it made me think twice. But this, the bloodthirsty West, had adopted me and I could not turn away. I descended, the lady's gun at my side.

"This ain't fair!" Brent continued. "I'm supposed to die in some blaze of glory, or something! Not like this! I don't even know you! Are you even famous?" He screamed so loudly that something must have ruptured inside of him; blood seeped from the corner of his mouth and bubbled in his nostrils.

When I reached him, Iron Trail said, "Tessa, I want you to shoot this man in the head."

At first, I laughed. It sounded like some kind of joke. How could I possibly send a bullet into another person's head? But then I saw his stoic face, and I knew that he was not joking.

"No!" Brent screamed. Red sprayed from his lips and dribbled down the front of his shirt. Dirty bandages were soaked through with fresh crimson. "I won't be killed by some girl! Fuck you!"

I looked at Iron Trail. "I don't . . . I mean, I don't think I can do this."

Iron Trail nodded. "You can. You have to. You've come a long way in very few days. You need to come a little way further, and this will help."

"Help what? Toughen me up?"

"If you see it like that, then yes. This is tough country, and you need to be able to survive it. I'm not always going to be by your side."

"You mean, after you sell me."

Iron Trail shrugged.

I felt a slight urge, just a tickle, really, to use the lady's gun on Iron Trail. This close to him, it would certainly put him in the ground. Once more, it occurred to me that I could probably survive without him now.

Except our supplies were low. I could not hunt and kill my own food. Even if I could, I would not know how to prepare it. No, I could not kill Iron Trail.

I turned my gaze to Brent. His bandages were now sopping wet, and blood gushed from his mouth. Clearly, he was almost gone from this world. Did it really count as murder if the person is already dying?

"Why can't we just wait for him to die?"

"It's inhumane," Iron Trail said. "Bullet Brent is a rabid dog, and he must be put down as such."

"But . . ."

"I have been many things in my time, but I'd like to think that I'm not deliberately cruel."

I thought these were strange words for a slave trader, but they locked in my throat. I remembered a time when I was very young, when I still had a family, when we had a dog. It was my brother's dog, and it had been missing for several days. When it came back to us, my father saw its foaming mouth and declared that it had rabies. He did not hesitate in taking down his rifle and shooting the mangy thing.

My father was very much a cruel man, but when he saw my brother's tears over the event, he imparted this lesson upon the both of us: a creature must never suffer needlessly. When the inevitable is obvious, something must be done.

I aimed the lady's gun at Brent's face, and he muttered something. I could not tell what, because there was too much blood in his mouth, but I think he called me a cunt. His hands feebly reached for the gun, probably to knock it away, but they could not extend far enough.

I pulled the trigger, and one of his eyes winked away. The empty hole began to cry blood, and the villain slumped down, lifeless.

I expected to feel differently. This was, after all, the first (and hopefully only) time I have ever killed a person. I thought I might experience a streak of shame, or perhaps I would weep. My innocence has had a long and tarnished past, but it has never been dirtied with such a death.

But I felt nothing. It was incredibly easy to do, and for the first time, I found myself understanding these Westerners and their readiness to deal death.

Iron Trail gently removed the gun from my hand. "You did very well, Tessa."

I cocked my head and watched the last of Bullet Brent's life flow out of him and into the dirt. "It's a shame," I said.

"What is?"

"That killing is so effortless."

"Maybe," Iron Trail said.

"Should we bury them?" I asked.

Iron Trail looked up at the sun. "No. It would take too much time, and besides, nature is good at taking care of corpses. Bird or worm, it makes no difference to me."

We spent the next half-hour or so picking through their belongings. We found some money but not a lot. Either they had hidden the rest elsewhere, or the bank they had robbed was not very well stocked.

There were plenty of supplies. Food, water and whisky, they had it all. Iron Trail stopped his search long enough to take a couple of slugs of booze.

He removed the ammunition from their guns and packed them up as well. "Comancheros can always use more weapons," he said.

By the time we left their bodies behind, their fire had finally died. When we got back to our camp, we started a new flame and prepared a meal.

"It's funny," I said. "We killed a bunch of men, stole their money and stocked up on supplies, all before breakfast."

"Welcome to the wild West," Iron Trail said.

It was a witty thing to say, and yet too close to the truth to amuse. Neither of us laughed as we finished our food and packed up our things. We now had a group of horses in tow, so we didn't have to worry about overburdening Iron Trail's any longer.

The sun was all the way up when we continued on our journey.

October 4, 18—

Nothing worthy of mentioning happened since last I wrote in this diary. We traveled and did not do much else. Iron Trail taught me a few things, the most important of which was how to prepare rabbits for dinner. He managed to shoot a couple with his arrows, and he showed me how to skin them, disembowel them, and cook them over a campfire. I did not much care for pulling their guts out, but the rest of it came fairly simple. I thought skinning them would be more difficult, but once the initial cuts were made, the skin came away easily.

I asked him if he would teach me how to hunt, but he declined. "I don't think you're ready for something like that just yet," he told me. However, I believe he merely did not want to teach me how to shoot a bow and arrow. Maybe he thought that would make me too dangerous.

As we set up camp tonight, he cast his gaze to the east. It was too dark for me to catch anything, but I have learned over the past few days how sharp his eyes are. His ability sometimes seems supernatural.

"What do you see?" I asked.

"There are lights in the distance," he said. "Streetlights. Tomorrow, we'll be in the town of Tramonto. It's quite a civilized place, much more so than anyplace I've taken you so far."

"I would kill for a bath," I said. The grime that constantly clung to my skin grated at me, and I hated the way my greasy hair hung about my face in ugly strands.

"We have enough money for a night on the town," he said, "thanks to Bullet Brent and his stooges."

"Could we buy some new clothes for me?" I asked. "This is all I have, and already they're getting a bit ragged."

He turned from the coming night and looked at me. "There will be plenty of opportunities for you to escape or tell tales. But you wouldn't do that, would you?"

Honestly, the thought had not occurred to me. The extent of my in-town fantasies were new clothes, a bath, restaurant food, and a roof over my head, a bed under my body. Escape? Where would I escape to? If I managed to get away from Iron Trail, where would I go? I would have nothing, and I knew no one around here. I suppose I could have indulged my desire to travel to San Francisco, but how would I get there?

I told him these things, and he smiled. "Good. I would hate to lose you now."

He said it so tenderly I felt myself melt a bit. We approached each other and kissed around the campfire. I felt his tongue probe deeply into my mouth, and I returned the favor. I do not know how long we stood there like that, but as the bigger logs towering in the midst of the kindling caught, we disengaged.

"We should eat first," he said. He produced a couple of rabbits he had shot earlier, and he handed me his knife. I went to work slaughtering their little bodies. After our meal, we made love, and now I am tired. I shall set aside my pen and dream about the wonderful things I will undoubtedly encounter in town tomorrow.

-

October 5-6, 18—

My goodness! I have so many wonderful things to relate in this journal! I have spent the greatest day of my life in the town of Tramonto! I am told the name is Italian for "sunset," but I do not think the sun will ever set in this place, at least not in a metaphorical sense.

It is three o'clock in the morning—and I know because I can see the clock on the wall!—so I suppose this is really the sixth of October. My estimations, by the way, were correct. I sought out a calendar and was pleased to discover that my notations on the passing of time has been perfect.

But mechanics aside, I must describe what has happened today, so I can remember it for always! Though I dislike Jane Austen, I feel like one of her heroines!

It began when I awoke this morning and donned those filthy clothes for what I hope will be the last time. We ate a swift breakfast and started on our way to town.

Though we passed several homesteads on our way, we did not arrive into the town proper until noon. Our first stop was to the livery stable, as we had six horses and we didn't want to drag them with us all over town.

The liveryman looked askance upon us, in particular Iron Trail, perhaps because it was unusual to see a Comanche with so many horses. I am certain he overcharged us, but Iron Trail did not seem to care. He peeled off a few bills we had gotten from Bullet Brent and his companions, and we went on our way.

"What do you want to do first?" he asked me.

There was no contest: "I want a bath."

"Very well," he said. "I think we could both use a bath, but it would hardly be worth the effort if we didn't have clean clothes to wear when we're finished. Shall we get you something new to wear first?"

I did not argue.

We went to the nearest clothing shop, and before we went in, Iron Trail whispered to me, "Money is no object. If you see something you want, it's yours."

The next thing I knew, ladies surrounded me, all taking my measurements as I tried on a grand dress that would have been the talk of the town back in New York City. I don't think Tramonto had a more expensive dress.

In the other room, I could hear Iron Trail being fitted for a suit of his own. I could not see anything, of course, but I could hear his pleasure with what he saw. It felt as if we were being prepared to go to a ball!

There were a few adjustments that were needed on my dress, so the tailor said that it would take an hour before it would be ready. Iron Trail had the same problem with his clothes, so he told the owner that the adjusted garments should be sent to the bath house, where we were going next.

Ah! I cannot tell you how much I enjoyed a bath after so long in the wilderness! To feel the suds soaking into my skin, pulling the wretched dirt out from my pores, it was akin to heaven! I scrubbed deeply, wanting to eliminate all the filth. I had the feeling that I wouldn't be able to have another bath for a while, so I luxuriated in this one. Even when I was utterly clean, I leaned back and closed my eyes, smiling at the warmth of the water around me. I couldn't remember the last time I was so happy! Perhaps it had been when I lived with my Felton, but in the end, that had been a false happiness, had it not? I do not think I was ever really happy in New York City. Maybe I was when I was a child, but I do not think it very likely.

I never truly understood what the philosophers meant when they said we needed misery to truly experience happiness, not until that moment in the tub. It felt like I had been through a thousand hells; would I have been so satisfied with this bath if I had not?

The maid soon entered with a delivery from the tailor. She gave me not just my clothes, but Iron Trail's as well. "He finished his bath earlier," she said. "He told me to tell you that he's at the barber, getting his hair trimmed, and that you should bring his clothes there."

I agreed, and when she left, I dried off and dressed in my new clothes. The old ones had been sent to a launderer, but honestly, I hoped to never see them again. They were filthy things, and from now on I would wear nothing but the best, for as long as I could!

I followed the maid's instructions to the barber shop, where I stepped in, carrying Iron Trail's package. I found him sitting in the chair while a barber clipped at his hair. It would never be cut short. As I understand it, a Comanche male's hair should never be short. It is a matter of masculinity. But it had been ragged of late, and the barber seemed to be trimming up everything so it looked even.

The barber stopped snipping when he saw me, and Iron Trail gasped. The other barber, busy pulling a customer's tooth, paused to take me in. The customer screamed in pain, but even so, he took the time to cast an eye in my direction.

"Tessa," Iron Trail said. "You look more beautiful than I could have ever imagined."

"She's your wife?" the barber asked.

The Comanche gentleman paused a moment, as if at a loss for words. Then, he said, "Yes. She is."

His words might have been flattering to anyone else, but I did not find them so. I never wanted to be another man's wife, not after what Felton Reeves did to me. For a moment, I was furious with Iron Trail, and I wished I had had the nerve to kill him when I had the chance back at Shit Creek.

But the feeling passed.

He stood, pushing his bib away. As he approached, it looked like he wanted to embrace me, but remembering that he still wore his filthy clothes, he paused. Instead, he reached across the space between us with just his face and planted a gentle kiss on my lips.

"I am very blessed," he whispered.

"That'll be two bits, mister," the barber said.

Iron Trail grimaced and turned away from me. "That's your price for a shave and a haircut. I only received a haircut."

"That's the standard fee. It's not my fault you savages can't grow facial hair."

It was so odd that I had never noticed that before, but when I cast my memory back on my time with Iron Trail, I could not help but acknowledge the barber's wherewithal. Not once had I seen Iron Trail shave, and his body had no hair except for a thin layer around his member.

I saw Iron Trail's muscles tighten, and from experience, I knew he meant to strike out at the barber. Before he could take action, I touched his arm. "Please don't. We're affluent enough to pay this man's price, and we've been having an awfully good time. Please don't ruin it."

Iron Trail paused, but I knew even before his muscles relaxed that he would heed my request. He slapped two bits onto the barber's desk. "Do not expect a tip."

"Your kind never tips," the barber said.

The customer's screams renewed and the other barber nearly fell back with the force of his pull. He balanced himself, holding aloft his customer's tooth between a pair of pliers. The gruesome display shook me, and I hoped I would never have to suffer the act of having a tooth pulled.

I made a mental note to brush my teeth as soon as I had the facility to do so.

Iron Trail ignored the barber's final insult, and we walked down the road to seek out our lodging for the night. We did not have to go far before discovering the Tramonto Inn. I have stayed in nicer looking houses, but not many.

The clerk was a gentleman, and he did not seem to have a problem with my partner's race. We were swiftly served, and before long we rested in our quarters. We had a dressing screen, but Iron Trail did not make use of it. We had seen each other naked so many times that it did not matter.

As he dressed in his new clothes, he said, "There is an art exhibit in town. After we have luncheon, would you care to peruse the display?"

"I would love to," I said.

"Good. There is also a photographer's shop down the block. I think we should get a portrait taken of us."

"That sounds marvelous."

"The barber told me that there is going to be a shooting exhibition, as well. It's a low form of entertainment, but since we're living the high life, maybe we should be in attendance."

"I wouldn't have it any other way," I said.

He struggled with his bowtie. "The tailor told me that there are actors in town. They are going to do some scenes from Shakespeare and Moliere. If they take requests, I'm going to ask for the first act duel in Cyrano. What do you think?"

"I've never been to see a play before. I'm afraid I don't know what Cyrano is."

"Cyrano de Bergerac, the great cynic. It's the tale of a very witty, very insecure man with a very large nose. It's humorous and sad at the same time."

"If it interests you, I would very much like to see it."

"Good! After the play, I thought perhaps we would have dinner at the local Delmonico's, and afterward we might enjoy a few drinks."

"It sounds like you've put a lot of effort into tonight's festivities."

He finished with his tie and beamed at me. "I have. Who knows when next we'll get the chance to be so free with our money? How do I look?"

I never expected a red man to look so handsome in a white man's fineries. I know that sounds like an uncivilized and ignorant thing to say, but keep in mind that I have been raised on news stories of the west from the far distant land of New York City. All I have to go on are newspapers and dime novels. I would have never expected to see such an image, nor would anyone else I knew from Back-East, I suspect.

"You look amazing," I said.

He smiled. "I'm glad. Considering how gorgeous you are, I had to make sure that I could keep up. It wouldn't look good to have you look so incredible while I went around like a slob."

I giggled. "Hush."

He embraced me, and I could feel his heart beating through his chest into mine. "I have never met anyone like you, Tessa."

"Nor I, you." Even if I were still angry with him, it would be the truth.

"It's taking every ounce of restraint for me to not tear these clothes from you," he said.

"There will be plenty of time for that later," I said. I meant it. I have been trying to deny it in these journals for far too long, but I think I am in love with him! As I read over everything I have written before, it seems very obvious to me. I cannot see how it has happened, but I love Iron Trail, and I suspect the feeling is mutual. I have read stories, back when I was in New York City, about women who have been kidnapped and then they fell in love with their captors, but I do not think that is the case with me. Had anyone else taken me as prisoner, I do not think I would have so readily fallen in love with them. No, it is Iron Trail and he alone whom I love.

We went down to the art exhibit, but it was not yet open. To pass the time, we went to the photographer's shop and paid for a portrait. At first, the owner seemed reluctant to do this, but as soon as Iron Trail produced the money, he became Johnny-fetch-it.

I remember seeing daguerreotypes from Back-East, and I always remarked on how unhappy the people depicted tended to be. Now I know why this is the case; it seems to take forever to get a picture taken. The photographer asked us to remain absolutely still. At first, I smiled as heartily as I could, but so much time passed that I could not keep it up. I do not know how long it took, but after what seemed like an eternity, the photographer finally replaced the lens cap and told us it would be some time before the picture was ready. Iron Trail paid the man and said to deliver the picture to our room at the Tramonto Inn.

Since the gun show was not scheduled until later, we stopped in at a restaurant for luncheon. We merely had a few sandwiches and some drink. I had milk, and Iron Trail had sarsaparilla. I cannot tell you how relieved I was to have a meal under a roof, using utensils like spoons and forks. It made my time in the wilderness seem like a nightmare.

After luncheon, the gun show went on as planned. There were two sharpshooters involved, and they both shot the centers out of coins, blew airborne bottles to pieces and the like. One of them was an expert with slight of hand. He asked me to pick a card and then place it back in the deck. He then threw all fifty-two into the air and shot at it. The only one that he nailed came fluttering down into his hand. It was my card, and it had a hole in the center. It was a sheer marvel to watch them work!

Iron Trail said it was an old trick, and he even described how to do it, but I paid him no heed. I wanted my illusions to remain intact. It was not fun otherwise.

By then, the exhibition opened, and I quickly saddened to discover it to be mostly a collection of pictures of dead outlaws. They were all stretched out on boards, showing the gunshots that had ended their lives. A morbid display I could have done without.

But aside from these grim pictures, there were a few others that had grabbed my attention, photographs of railroads stretching off into nothingness, two rails stretching off until they converged in the distance. Artful pictures of lonely, gnarled trees. Daguerreotypes of dirty children from the wrong side of the tracks. Cowboys in saloons with pints of beer and drooping mustaches.

Much to my surprise, Iron Trail bought a photograph. I did not see it until much later, when we had retired to our room. At the time, he had asked the artist to wrap it up and send it to the Tramonto Inn. He would not show it to me at the time, but when I finally saw it, I marveled at its simplicity. It was a picture of a long forgotten graveyard from Back-East. I could tell it was not from here, or the stones would have been made of wood. No, the markers in the picture were stone, and they bore dates back to the 18th Century. Normally, I would not care for something like this, but accomplished with such artistry, I could not deny Iron Trail's eye for beauty.

We then headed over to the opera house, where the actors prepared for the evening play. We arrived early, so we could get good seats. As we waited, Iron Trail fetched us some drinks. He got whiskey for himself, and since he noticed my curiosity, he got the same for me. I have to say, the taste was bitter, but the effect very much satisfied me.

When the actors took to the stage, they delivered memorable scenes from several Shakespeare plays, but my favorite was Aaron's speech from *Titus Andronicus*. It is a horrid display, but it is so well-worded that I was willing to overlook the implications of said speech.

They also performed scenes from something called *Dr. Faustus* and *The Shoemaker's Holiday*. The former was decent, but the latter lacked. They started to lose me, but then they delivered from *Tartuffe*. I am unfamiliar with the play but found it most engaging.

Much to Iron Trail's pleasure, they did indeed take requests. Judging from their offhand way of stating this, I do not think they expected anything from us. Perhaps they have been traveling the West for too long. I think they were pleasantly surprised when Iron Trail asked for the duel from Cyrano. I do not think I have ever seen a troupe of actors so pleased.

There was another scholar in our audience, and he requested a scene from John Ford's *'Tis a Pity She's a Whore*. It seemed to be a tasteful rendition, but the owner of the theater asked the actors to stop. As a finale, they did something from Oscar Wilde, but I have never heard of him.

Iron Trail approached the other scholar and determined he taught philosophy by the name of Smalls. Dr. Smalls eagerly accepted an invitation to have drinks with us, since it was still early.

I wish I could give a good report as to what was said at this meeting, but I am afraid I could not follow what Iron Trail and Dr. Smalls said to one another. They were both very clearly versed in the history of literature and drama, but they kept mentioning names with which I was unfamiliar. My education surpassed most who went to school with me, but I still could not keep up with these two gentlemen. At one point, they traded quotes from someone named Dr. Johnson back and forth. I am vaguely familiar with a British scholar by the name of Samuel Johnson, but I am not sure if this was the person they meant. Maybe they meant Ben Jonson, but I am not sure.

After a while, Dr. Smalls's wife called him away, and Iron Trail and I retired to Delmonico's for dinner. I did not expect much from this quaint restaurant, but I have to admit they delivered the finest meal I had had since those I had prepared for Felton. There were a few places

Back-East that could have matched Delmonico's, but not many. The steak I indulged in was very delicious. As I consumed the last of it, I shivered to think of the substandard meals I would be subjected to once we left this town.

We paid for our dinner, and Iron Trail asked the waiter as to where a gentleman could go for a drink. He did not want to go to any of the saloons, as they tended to be wild places unfit for a lady's presence. There were a few high-class places to which we could go in order to unwind for the evening.

We settled on a place called the High Ball. They specialized in fine whiskies and Scotches. I had never tasted the Glenlivet before, but as soon as it touched my tongue, I knew I had found the proper alcoholic beverage for me.

I ordered several more of Scotland's finest, and I was readily indulged. At first we cast ourselves about the club as Iron Trail tried to gauge the environment. He eventually found a few wives I could converse with while he gambled with the remainder of Bullet Brent's money. I watched from afar, impressed with the ability of everyone at the poker table. In fact, they were all professionals. None of the ruffian "tinhorns" you would read about in dime novels were present. No, these were all gentlemen, and if they lost a hand, it was without complaint. I do not think any of them were carrying weapons.

I tried to keep up my end of the conversation with the gamblers' wives, but I am afraid we did not have much in common. As far as I could tell, they were actual ladies with excellent pedigrees. I think they would have ejected me if they learned that I was merely a mail order bride from Back-East. They seemed enchanted with my accent, which I could not understand. It was they who had accents, not I.

Regardless, I must have seemed exotic to them, so I played it as best I could. I had not lost my ability at embellishment; they were practically convinced that I was royalty. If any had cause to doubt, all they had to do was look at my expensive dress, and their worries quickly dissolved.

At eleven of the clock, the crowd started to disperse. Iron Trail took it to mean that the appropriate hour of retirement was upon us. I found that he had, in the parlance, broken even. In other words, he had not won or lost, but he came out of the game with the money with which he had started. Actually, he came out a little ahead. As a token of his appreciation, he bought a round for everyone. I received my glass of the Glenlivet with a smile.

I hoped we would come upon another such town in the future. I hated to think this might be my last taste of the finest alcoholic beverage I have ever known.

We paid our bill, and Iron Trail escorted us back to our hotel room, where we made exquisite love by candlelight. I have been with many men, but none were ever quite as satisfying as Iron Trail, not even Felton Reeves. Not even Sam, and as much of a bastard as he could be, he was more than adequate in bed.

No, Iron Trail was in a class of his own, and not just because of his size; he knew how to use what God had given him. I do not know if we have words in the English language—or any other, for that matter—to describe the passionate night he and I have just shared, pleasure so intense it was almost unbearable. I have never felt my insides explode in such orgasm. Was it just a matter of environment? Iron Trail was certainly exceptional in the wilds of the West, but now that we were in a bed under a roof? Was this all that made the difference? I do not think so.

I remembered him hovering over me with all the stars of the universe behind his thick, wreathed hair, and while it is a romantic enough image, it did not match up to the sensation I experienced in the Tramonto Inn this night.

Finally, when both of us were spent and sore from such an epic bout of lovemaking, he fell by my side and rolled a couple of cigarets for us. He had also procured a bottle of the Glenlivet from the High Ball, and he poured us both drinks. We lay in the darkness, smoking and drinking and luxuriating in each others presence, when he said, "My father was always displeased with me."

This was a confession I had not expected, but I did not want to ruin the moment. He clearly needed to get something off his chest, and I did not want to shame him into keeping reticent on the matter.

"All I ever wanted was to make him happy," he continued. "I tried so hard, but the only one I ever pleased was my mother. She was my father's third wife, which perhaps explained his general callous feeling toward me. He was a great warrior, you know."

I did not know, but I remained silent.

"My mother was the philosopher. Without her, I would be another ignorant savage, as the local whites call my brethren. Then again, it was her teachings that also exiled me from my family and friends. I believe I've told you before that I am no believer in the Great Spirit."

I nodded.

"My father was a war chief. Had he lived to old age, he would have become an elder. He would have had a place at the Lodge. He was a great believer and a great storyteller. His tales were usually about the warriors of our past and of his own exploits. I wanted to live up to these characters, but I found more solace in my mother's tales of wisdom."

"You wouldn't be the first son to ever disappoint his father," I said.

"I killed him," he said. "I don't think I'm the first son to ever do that, either."

I wanted to know why someone who desired to please his father so much had resorted to killing him, but again, I remained silent.

"He tried to kill my mother, not because of some infidelity or betrayal, but because of her ideas. He thought she was poisoning my mind, and perhaps he was right. But I had to choose between ideals on that day, and I chose education over violence." He grunted. "I know, that sounds absurd. How can a murderer advocate the value of education over violence? I was young. I did not appreciate the discrepancy."

I felt his hand go through my hair, fingers separating strands. "Am I a violent man, Tessa?"

I could have lied, but that would have been foolish. "Yes, Iron Trail. You are. But I do not think you are cruel. That makes a difference."

"Does it?"

I nodded.

"I bought you." It seemed like a feeble argument, but I understood what he meant.

"Yes, you did. But I do not think you intend to sell me."

He shook his head, and I kissed him. We made love yet again, and afterward, he went to sleep.

I tried to join him in slumber, but the excitement of the day was so fresh in my mind that it kept me awake. After a while, I knew I would not be able to sleep until I made note of everything that happened today. So, here I am, sitting by the flickering candle, writing about the greatest day of my life.

Iron Trail is not going to sell me, and I think this is a definite sign of how well my fortune has turned. I do not think we will ever live in luxury, but I know we will live in bliss. We love each other, and nothing short of death can ever separate us.

My eyes are finally as weary as my writing hand. In a moment, I will set the pencil aside and retire to bed with my lover. For these final moments, I want to gaze at Iron Trail's sleeping, naked form. He is a beautiful man, but his attractiveness is more than just the features of his body. There is something inside of him that acts as a magnet to my heart.

Goodnight, diary. Until tomorrow night . . . .

The town clock struck six in the morning, and Iron Trail opened his eyes. Beside him, the naked form of his lover stirred, but she did not awaken. He cast his eyes across her supple flesh, now clean from the bath of yesterday. The sharp tang of the soap she had used tickled his nostrils, for which he was grateful. He would have Tessa anyway she cared to offer herself, but the cleanliness greatly helped.

He remembered when he was a youth, barely on the cusp of manhood. His companions would trade stories about how they had stolen the maidenhood of squaws around them. More than half of them were straight-faced liars, but Iron Trail had been attentive enough to notice at least one thing: these other boys loved the scent of the trail. They loved the sweat and the grime and the dust and the dirtiness that came with laying a woman in the middle of the wilderness.

Not Iron Trail. He could withstand such things, but he had refined tastes. He preferred a fresh, clean woman, and Tessa was such a person right now. He breathed in her hair and her skin. If he could smell himself, he would be able to detect his sweat—among other bodily fluids—all over her body.

He remembered their conversation from the previous evening, the one about selling her. All this time he had fooled himself into believing that he would give her up to the highest bidder, but he knew he could never relinquish the finest lover he had ever known. Others would have turned her away, or perhaps would have killed her as damaged goods, but not Iron Trail. He knew horrible things must have happened to Tessa to make her such a marvel in bed. Never before had he been brought to such screaming, nearly-unbearable orgasms. To sell her would be foolish.

But at the same time, he knew himself. In two days he would meet with the Comancheros, to whom he'd intended to sell Tessa, along with a number of other goods. No matter how well-educated and experienced he was, he was still a pimp and a scavenger. And a killer.

He hoped there really was no such thing as the Great Spirit. If there was, he'd be doomed to an eternity of punishment.

He had the finest of his father and mother in him. He could quote the poets of old in one breath and condemn a man to death with the next. How did such people manage to exist?

He didn't consider this for very long. He knew he would not sell Tessa Reeves to the Comancheros. He had many other goods they would be satisfied with, and if they wanted more, he was skilled at the fine art of dispatching souls to their maker.

Iron Trail let Tessa sleep another hour. In the meantime he stared at the ceiling, wondering what it would have been like if he'd found this wonderful woman before Felton had. Would things be different? Or would he have sold her long before learning what a singular woman she was?

He hated to think about what he might have missed out on. Was it even possible that he would retire from this business? Could he settle down with Tessa for the rest of his life with whatever he managed to make off the Comancheros? He didn't think he could continue like this for that long. Eventually he would have to grow old, and then what?

He probably wouldn't be able to retire on this deal, but now would be the best time to start saving up. He'd deposited a considerable sum in various Wells Fargo banks across the West, and if he managed to get them all together he might have enough to retire with, but he doubted it. Perhaps a few more deals would do the trick.

Tessa stirred slightly, and he wondered if she could sense his thoughts. The rational side of him knew she couldn't, but there was a tiny part of him that thought it might be possible. Considering how many times they had joined, wasn't it likely, even, that they might be able to read each others minds?

No. He had told her he had no intention of selling her, and he thought it would be best to live up to his word. The Comancheros might not like that, but he did not care about what they fancied. Besides, he thought he might have Tessa hang back while he went in to make the deal. They might be pissed that he didn't have a white woman to offer, as he usually did, but so what? No one's perfect.

He thought maybe he shouldn't even meet with them, but as soon as the idea had formed, he dismissed it. Why should he care? And did he actually fear these people? No. Not only did he want to continue to maintain his reputation as a hard man, he also wanted to sell these goods in his saddlebags.

The clock struck seven, and he nudged Tessa awake.

She murmured in her sleep.

"It's time to get up. Are you hungry?"

"Hm," she said.

"That's fine. Get dressed, and we'll head down to the restaurant for food."

"Hm," she said.

Iron Trail pulled himself out of bed and started washing up in the basin on the night table. He made sure to leave enough water for Tessa, should she feel energized enough to get out of bed.

While he wasn't exactly in the throes of a hangover, he did feel slightly off balance, so he thought a little hair of the dog would suit his purposes. He felt grateful for his drunken foresight. The desk in the corner still had a bottle of Scotch on it. He poured a finger's worth of the Glenlivet, and just as he downed the drink, he noticed Tessa's diary, along with the quill pen and inkwell. He did not remember her getting up in the middle of the night, and that was the only time she could have written anything. His vigilance had failed him. Was he getting too old for this line of work?

No. The only reason he'd let his guard drop was because he trusted her. Hell, he loved her, and she probably loved him back.

He fingered the cover of the diary, and he wondered if he should indulge himself in a few passages. Granted, he did not know a lot about his lover, but he knew she was educated if not well-educated. She had mentioned a British fiction magazine a few days ago, hadn't she? She might have been a prostitute Back-East, but she definitely had a brain inside her head, and it wasn't just the kind of smarts that were earned on streets. A lot of it came from book learning, and he knew that wasn't common.

What exactly did she write in this diary? He thumbed the cover back, and with his index finger, he flipped through the pages. Most were blank, but the first few pages were cramped with Tessa's petite, even letters. They did not have a lot of flourish, which Iron Trail thought was an interesting detail. Her handwriting was very practical.

The temptation to actually read the words nearly overpowered him, but he decided to let the cover fall back into place instead. They were lovers, but she deserved some modicum of privacy at the least.

He finished off his drink and began to get dressed. By the time he had put on his pants, Tessa got out of bed and started washing up.

"When are we leaving town?" she asked.

Iron Trail watched her scrub her face and knew she didn't want to hit the trail just yet. "I'm afraid we must leave by noon."

She picked up the towel and patted herself dry. "Must we? It's just that I've been enjoying myself so much. It would be a shame to leave it all behind now."

"I know, Tessa. But we have an appointment in three days, and we'll be late if we don't leave by noon."

She looked at him, the towel impotent in her hands. "Meeting? With whom?"

"The Comancheros," he said.

"But you said last night that you wouldn't—"

"And I won't," he said. "But I still have business with them, and it will not be good for us to be late. They might not wait."

The towel dropped from her hands. "I see."

"We still have a few hours," Iron Trail said. "I know an excellent place for breakfast. Get dressed, and you'll have the finest steak and eggs you've ever had."

He turned away so he could put on his moccasins, but not before he noticed the look in her eyes. She still feared he would sell her. A part of him wanted to allay these worries, but what good would that do? She would only think he was lying.

Iron Trail did not like clichés, but "actions speak louder than words" seemed straightforward and adequate for this situation. He would have to let his behavior prove himself to her.

-

When they got back from a belly-filling breakfast, their laundry had been returned to their rooms. At this point Iron Trail suggested that they get into their riding gear. It might have felt fresher to head out into the wilderness in fine clothing but not very practical. Tessa reluctantly saw the wisdom in this, and she got back into her old clothes.

They finished packing and checked out of the hotel. After a short walk they were back at the livery stable, where Iron Trail paid off the owner, and they were back on their way east to their meeting with the Comancheros.

That night, as they relaxed near the campfire, Tessa thought she should write in her journal, but she wasn't in the mood. She missed Tramonto, so instead of making a new entry, she read the old one, wishing she were still back at the inn, or eating at Delmonico's, or drinking at the High Ball.

They still had some Scotch, so she indulged herself a little. If she closed her eyes she could pretend. Maybe not accurately—the smell and sounds of the wilderness around her were too acute for something like that—but it satisfied her.

-

The next day went uneventfully, much like their other days in the wilderness. Halfway through day Iron Trail stopped to rest the horses, and he snapped off a length of jerky for himself and Tessa.

"We're ahead of schedule," he said.

113

Tessa smiled, squinting into the sun so she could look at her lover. "Is there enough time for you to teach me something?"

Iron Trail gnawed at a hunk of jerky, thinking. He had already taught her a lot about surviving in the wide open spaces, and while there were many other lessons he thought he could impart upon her, he thought of only one that might be relevant at any moment.

"Would you like to learn how to shoot?" he asked.

"Guns?"

He grunted. "White men are good at making machines that break down. No, I mean with a bow and arrow."

She grimaced, looking down. "I was kind of hoping that, well, you know . . ."

"Forget it," he said. "You don't need guns. They jam. A bow never jams."

Iron Trail strode toward his grazing horse, and he took the bow from the rifle roll. "The first thing you need to know is how to string a bow. Are you familiar with the story of Odysseus?"

"I've been taught *The Odyssey*," she said.

He smiled. "But did you *read* it?"

She blushed. "Maybe not."

"I thought as much. Regardless, do you remember how it ends?"

"Odysseus comes home from his long journey and kills all the suitors who have been trying to win Penelope's hand."

"True," Iron Trail said. He put a bowstring in her hands and laid the bow at her feet. "But that's not the part I meant. Odysseus comes home in disguise, and the way he reveals himself is by stringing a bow only he is strong enough to string, and he then uses this weapon to dispatch the scoundrels trying to eat him out of house and home."

Tessa looked at the string. "You want me to string this bow?"

Iron Trail nodded. "I think you'll find it quite difficult. Not impossible, but it will still be a hard task."

Tessa took up the bow and slipped the string in the niche. Then she tried to bend both ends so that she could fit the other knot into the corresponding niche. It gave a little bit, but it wouldn't go much farther than an inch.

Iron Trail didn't move an inch, either.

Tessa thought back to the last time she'd seen him string the bow, and she remembered he had bent it across his knee. She grunted as she tried this, but again to no avail.

Iron Trail took the bow back. "I've got it worked out pretty well, so that I can have it strung quickly if need be. Since you are a novice, I would do this." He put the bow on the ground and knelt on it so he could bend it to his liking. Within seconds, it was complete.

"Do you know why this is the preferred weapon?" he asked. When she didn't answer he continued. "Have you heard of the battle of Crecy?"

"I remember it vaguely from some childhood lesson," she said.

"It was a decisive battle. When all else failed the British Empire, the bow and arrow saved them. They had the finest archers in the world, and without them, the French would have treated them like dogs for the rest of eternity. It was so damaging to the French that whenever they caught British archers, they cut off their index and middle fingers, so they would never be able to fire an arrow ever again."

"That's horrible!"

Iron Trail put on his quiver. "But they let them live. Which is humane treatment for prisoners, I suppose. Regardless, to this day, whenever an Englishman is upset with you, he will hold up his index and middle fingers in a taunting way. This is because of Crecy. Whenever the French were defeated, the British made fun of them by waving their two fingers, showing that they still had them and would put them to good use in a future battle."

Iron Trail whipped an arrow from his quiver and nocked it. Before Tessa even knew what he was doing, he'd drawn the string, and the arrow had sailed across space into the heart of a tree.

"Firearms can be accurate," he said, "but I wouldn't trust my life with anything less than this fine weapon."

He handed the bow to Tessa, and he surrendered an arrow. "Try to hit the tree I just shot. And be careful with the string. If you don't hold your forearm out a bit, then you will be stung."

She didn't listen to this advice. The moment she fired her first arrow, the string snapped up on her arm, and she yelped, dropping the weapon to the dusty ground. The arrow hadn't gone more than ten feet.

Iron Trail suppressed a smile. "I warned you."

"I didn't think it would hurt that fucking much," she muttered. No cut could be seen, but her arm had turned red from elbow to wrist.

Iron Trail picked up the bow and demonstrated. "Try holding it like this when you fire."

It took her a moment to gain the courage to try again. Memory of the pain still lived in her, she held her arm out so far that it would be impossible to draw the string back properly.

"Don't be afraid of it," he said. "You can get a little closer."

She gritted her teeth and reluctantly followed orders. This time when she fired, the arrow cut through the air in a straight line, but it missed the intended target.

"Much better," Iron Trail said. "You just need to learn how to aim."

He took up a position behind her, placing a hand upon hers, the one holding the bow. He then took another arrow from his quiver and helped her nock it. "Watch right here." He indicated by lifting a finger on the first hand. "Line it up with the tree, like so."

"Okay."

He lowered his head, so he could see on par with her vision. "Then, pull back and just release. It helps if you breathe out when you do so. Ready?"

"I think so."

Iron Trail slipped away from her. "Then let go."

She did, and when the arrow reached its destination, it split the original in two.

"Wow!" she yelled. "It's like something out of Robin Hood! I can't believe I just did that!"

Iron Trail produced another arrow. "Try it again, this time without my help."

When she fired again, it missed the arrow, but she still managed to hit the tree. With Iron Trail's aid, she continued her target practice, and she seemed to always hit the tree, but never came close to her first arrow.

After the arrows were all spent, Iron Trail went to retrieve them. Some were bent beyond repair, but most were still in good working order, even if he had to dig them out of the tree with his knife.

"Do we have time for more?" Tessa asked.

Iron Trail looked up to the sun. "I'm afraid not. We should resume our journey. Get the horses together."

That night Tessa felt tempted to write in her diary again, but she just didn't want to. She hoped it wasn't a sign that she'd grown lazy. The journal was supposed to tell the story of what happened to her as it was happening, and if she couldn't write, then what was the point?

Instead she relaxed in Iron Trail's arms and made love to him once again. This act seemed infinitely more important than writing in some diary.

-

When Tessa woke up the next day she felt the immediate urge to kill something with the bow and arrow. She'd dreamt about chasing a buffalo, and then firing a small arrow into the giant beast's throat, putting it down with a snap of her fingers, but now that she sat by the campfire with Iron Trail she felt like she was less of a person for not having killed a buffalo in such a fashion.

Instead she found Iron Trail's jerky beef, and she snapped a bite off. Though there wasn't as much dew as she was used to Back-East, it was enough to make her believe she lived at home again. The tang sharp in her nostrils was the only thing that prevented her from tricking herself. The dryness and the desert around her would never have allowed the illusion to take hold.

The jerky filled her mouth with juice, so long as she didn't swallow. She continued to chew and suck, filling her mouth with the stinging flavor of smoked meat. She knew it wouldn't be enough sustenance for her lover, but for now, at least an hour before Iron Trail would awaken, this was good enough.

When she finished she looked through the saddle bags for bacon and eggs, but there were only three of the latter and nothing of the former. Had they not just been in town? Were they out of supplies already?

No, she supposed not. Why would Iron Trail buy such supplies in town when he knew he could get them cheaper from the Comancheros? And how far ahead were they at this point? If memory served correctly, they would be upon them by the time the sun set on them today. A scary thought, but when she considered it, she knew Iron Trail would not sell her.

An hour later they had packed up and were on their way to the meeting with the Comancheros. The trail was long for the day but uneventful.

As the sun dipped toward the western horizon, they came upon a grove of sparse trees, and Iron Trail brought them to a halt. "We'll make camp here," he said.

Tessa dismounted. "I thought we'd see your business partners today."

Iron Trail grunted. "This is our meeting place. They'll probably be here by dawn tomorrow. I just wanted to be here early. It always pays to be the early bird in such dealings."

Tessa raised an eyebrow. "How do you mean?"

"You get the lay of the land, and if any surprises need to be set, you get to set them."

Tessa went about making a fire for the evening while her lover took to the wilderness with his bow and quiver. By the time he came back with two rabbits, she had a blazing flame in the center of their camp. She had also taken the time to set up a spit for their dinner.

Iron Trail gave her the rabbits. "Prepare them, please. Both, just in case we have visitors."

"I thought you expected them in the morning," she said.

"They might get the same idea, in regards to surprises," he said. "They might be suspicious of our . . . punctuality, and a cooked rabbit usually helps smooth out such ideas."

She nodded and took the knife from his belt. Before she finished skinning the first rabbit, Iron Trail perked up. "Do you hear that?" he asked.

Tessa paused, listening. "No."

"You will. Keep working."

She cooked the first rabbit and started preparing the second when she heard the riders. She didn't quite trust her ears yet, but she thought there might be seven of them, all on horseback except for one on a covered wagon. Regardless, they were loud, and she was surprised she hadn't noticed them before.

The two of them were getting ready to eat when the Comancheros breasted a nearby hill and rode toward the circle of trees. As it turned out there were ten of them, but one of them, indeed, rode a covered wagon. It looked to be empty, judging from the way it swayed back and forth like a drunk.

Iron Trail did not give Tessa so much as a glance. Instead he stood and belted on his knife. He did not take the bow with him, and aside from his pants, the blade was the only thing that accompanied him when he walked out to meet with the Comancheros.

Tessa began to stand, but Iron Trail motioned with one hand for her to remain in place. She hunched back down over the fire. The first rabbit was done, so she removed it from the spit and laid it to rest on a deerskin blanket. She placed the second rabbit on the former's spit, where she started turning it over the fire. She pretended to be engrossed in the woman-work, just as any man out here would expect her to be, but she kept her ears open, and she watched Iron Trail in case he needed help.

The Comanche strode out to the ten Comancheros, exhibiting no fear, keeping his stoic face in order. Tessa knew that if it had been her out there, she would have lost it. She'd be able to maintain her position—she would force herself to do so—but she also knew she might quiver or blubber or something that would give away her fear.

Iron Trail addressed the Comancheros in another language. She didn't know if it was his own or Spanish, as she had no experience with either one, but it had a gruff sound. It ran across her eardrums like sandpaper, and she wondered if perhaps the words would have sounded different coming from another set of vocal cords.

Regardless, she couldn't keep up with it, so she paid more attention to behavior. Her father, while he wasn't much of a person, had at least left her with this advice: "Never mind a person's words. They're not important. It's how they act that defines their character."

-

It had been at least a year since Iron Trail had spoken the Comanche/Spanish mix that the Comancheros used, but he grinned upon finding his fluency had not faltered. "Good evening, Ortega. I hope I have found you in good health."

The squat Comanchero glared down at him from his perch on the silver saddle. Gold teeth glinted in the dying sun from between his meat-slab lips. A wispy mustache clung to the underside of his nose

121

despite the sneer. "Iron Trail. It has been a long time. I wasn't sure if you would meet with us again."

Iron Trail smiled, but was careful not to show his teeth. He had heard that ape-men in Africa were in the habit of assaulting people who smiled while showing their teeth. He didn't know if these ape-men existed or not, but he knew Hector Ortega existed, and that was enough for him to take caution. "I have never missed a meeting with you, Ortega. Why would I start now?"

"Your kind are dying out," Ortega said. "In fact I heard you were a conquered people. What are you still doing kicking about? Only the outlaws remain, and I have never seen your name mentioned in a newspaper."

"Is that a bad thing?" Iron Trail asked. "You know I like to keep away from the attention of the public. Don't you think it would be bad for business if everyone knew about me?"

Ortega laughed, showing off every golden tooth in his head. They twinkled like stars in the twilight as he jumped from his mount and grabbed Iron Trail's right wrist in a hearty shake. "It's good to see you haven't changed, friend. Too much around us changes every day."

"And it won't stop changing," Iron Trail said. "Take a look around you. Very soon, there will be a town where we stand. Perhaps it will make it, and perhaps it won't, but ten years from now there will be buildings where this grove of trees once existed. We are fighting a losing battle. I believe we will both be dead by the time this comes to pass. Well, you will most likely be gone. I can pretend enough to make it in the white man's world. It's all a matter of whether or not they buy it."

"They will suffer," Ortega said, "before they put me in the ground. There is no doubt about that."

Iron Trail smiled. "No, friend. Would you care for some rabbit?"

Ortega nodded, and Iron Trail motioned for Tessa to give the Comanchero the first rabbit. At first she seemed confused, but before long she got the idea. She gave the entire thing to Ortega, who took a giant bite from its flank before passing it on to his men. As he chewed, the rabbit's grease gleaming on his hairy chin, he stared at her, his head tilted like a drunk's. His eyes moved up and down her body as if he were appraising her.

Iron Trail stepped between them. "I have a few interesting things for you. I hope you have a few for me."

Ortega's muddy eyes shifted up to Iron Trail's. Had he been drinking already? Iron Trail inhaled, and he could smell the bitter fumes on the Comanchero's breath.

"I have jerky," Ortega said. "Some food, as always. I have a daguerreotype of a naked lady."

Iron Trail shook his head. "I think I would much rather have money."

"That, we have plenty of," Ortega said. "What are your offerings?"

"Come." Iron Trail motioned with a hand toward his horse, and the Comanchero followed.

Over the next half-hour Iron Trail and Ortega poured over the Comanche's offerings. The Comanchero had a few things to trade, aside from the money. He really tried to push the daguerreotype, but Iron Trail showed no interest. He managed to get more bacon and eggs out of Ortega, though. A good thing, considering how they were out.

He also got a good price for the bottles of whiskey they'd found in the ghost town. Ortega was also interested in the remnants of the bottle of Scotch from Tramonto, but Iron Trail told him no. "Not for sale."

"It looks so fine," Ortega said. "Ten dollars."

"You'd only swill it like it was any other kind of booze," Iron Trail said. "It's not for sale."

"I'm a conn-ee-sewer, old friend. Fifteen."

"I will not barter with you on this. It is not for sale."

They moved on to a few other goods Iron Trail had managed to collect over time, and before long the negotiations came to an end. The Comancheros celebrated by passing around a newly-acquired bottle of whiskey. Ortega drank deeply as his underlings loaded their new possessions into the wagon.

Tessa pulled the remaining rabbit off the spit and started preparing it for her lover, completely unaware of the way Ortega stared at her. When she looked up the Comanchero fingered his scant facial hair, his dull eyes never moving from her bottom.

"Iron Trail." His lips barely parted with speech. "How much for the girl?"

Iron Trail looked up from putting money in his saddlebags. "Not for sale."

The Comanchero broke his gaze and laughed. "What? She's your wife or something?"

"That's none of your business," Iron Trail said.

Ortega reevaluated Tessa. "This isn't a proper lady, even by your savage standards. She's not even concubine material. She looks like a whore from New York. I'll give you a couple hundred for her."

Since they weren't speaking English, Tessa couldn't understand what they were saying. She had a pretty good idea, though, and she looked to her lover, eyebrows raised.

"I told you," Iron Trail said, "she's not for sale."

"Three hundred?"

"No."

Ortega grunted. "She's a mighty fine piece. She good in bed? She got a sucking pussy? I'll bet she does."

Iron Trail let the straps on his saddlebags go, and he stood. A hand dangled closely to his knife. "You will never find out, Ortega. She's not for sale."

Ortega smiled, showing off his twinkling teeth. The gleam went out as the last of the sun disappeared behind Iron Trail. "Five hundred."

"Maybe we can rent her," one of Ortega's underlings said. Both men ignored him.

Iron Trail shook his head, and the message was clear.

"What's going on?" Tessa asked. Although she knew.

"He's trying to buy you," Iron Trail said. His placid dark gaze never left Ortega's eyes. "He doesn't want to take no for an answer."

Then, in perfect English, Ortega spoke again. "We're offering far more than you're worth, whore. Keep your mouth shut and let the men do the bargaining."

Iron Trail's knife snicked from its scabbard before anyone could figure out what happened. He threw the blade at Ortega, nailing him directly in the chest. The Comanchero's eyes nearly popped out of his head as he grabbed at the hilt protruding from his breastbone.

Iron Trail wasted no time. He went for his bow, still strung, and his quiver. There were only seven arrows, and there were nine men left standing. He thought he might need a gun for this, and he made plans to take one off a dead man in the next few seconds.

The Comancheros quickly drew their weapons, but by the time they had anything to aim at, Iron Trail had sent two arrows sailing into the skulls of their comrades. He nocked a third when the volley of gunshots went off, echoing across the plains.

Most of the bullets missed him, but two found their mark, one in the shoulder and the other in his side. The pain nearly overwhelmed him, but as a young man he'd been trained by his father to muscle through such things. Though it was a fire throughout his body, he turned his reaction to it off as he took aim again.

A third Comanchero fell dead, and a fourth caught an arrow in his leg, but the rest fired once again.

This time three bullets found him. His kneecap exploded into shards of bone just as two bullets passed through his stomach. Iron Trail gritted his teeth, swallowing the pain back down his throat. Sweat dripped down from his forehead as blood oozed down the rest of him. It seemed to be spilling from his guts like a bucket that had been knocked over.

He had the strength to nock one more arrow, but it never left the bow. Iron Trail collapsed, breathing heavily into the ground. Plumes of dust took to the air around him.

Tessa watched as the Comancheros gunned down her lover, and she wanted to scream. She *tried* to scream. But nothing came out. She didn't have the air for it, and it felt like her heart was clogging her throat.

Ortega let out a string of curses as he pulled at the knife in his chest. Had it been an inch lower, it would have pierced his heart, and he would have joined his fallen compatriots.

The remaining five Comancheros split up. One went to help his leg-shot friend, another went to his leader to help him with the blade. The remaining ones circled around Iron Trail's bullet-riddled body, watching as blood ran out of him as if he were a faucet in a water pump. He still breathed, and his body twitched as he tried to roll over, to try to get to his feet, to do anything.

One of them pressed his gun to the Comanche's head and cocked the hammer.

"No!" Ortega shouted. "Don't you dare! I want the piece of shit for myself!"

The Comanchero grimaced, but he backed away as their leader hobbled over to the fallen Comanche. "Fuck your mother, you fucking savage piece of dick!" He grabbed Iron Trail by his long hair and pulled back so he could kick the Comanche in the face.

Finally Tessa's scream came out, a garbled inarticulate thing of no words, but the despair was so heartbreaking that everyone who heard it couldn't help but stop in their tracks, even Ortega.

But it didn't distract him for long. Ortega went around Iron Trail's body to where the bullet had destroyed his kneecap. The Comanchero stepped on the exit wound and twisted his heel.

Finally Iron Trail mustered the strength to scream.

"Stop it!" Tessa wailed. "Please! You're hurting him!"

Ortega grinned, and even in the darkness of dusk, she could see his slimy teeth gleaming. "I know," he said in English. He flipped Iron

Trail over and stuck his fingers in the bullet holes, one by one, cherishing the howl Iron Trail gave with each probing.

Tessa shrieked as she rushed toward the Comanchero, drawing her lady's pistol. There were only two shots, and she intended to use them both on Ortega. She didn't care what the others would do to her, so long as Ortega left this world.

One of the other Comancheros didn't see the gun, and he laughed as he stood in her way, thinking he would catch her in his arms and subdue her. He got the surprise of his life when two Derringer bullets went through his chest and lodged in his heart.

She still charged at Ortega over the dead man's body, tears running down her reddened cheeks, a harpy's war cry coming from her mouth. Her finger twitched, still pulling the trigger and coming up with nothing.

Tessa drew the gun back to try and club the Comanchero with it, but to no avail. Ortega grabbed her throat and pushed her away. She stumbled back, the gun flying from her hands, but she didn't fall yet.

This time when she came for him, Ortega threw a fist into her belly. He never hit women in the face. He wanted something good to look at when he used them.

"Tie that bitch up," Ortega said. "I want her to watch while I murder her lover. And then I'm going to fuck the shit out of her."

-

Murder is too easy a word for what Ortega planned on doing to Iron Trail. The connotations of murder are brutal but didn't usually entail the hours and hours and hours of torture that Ortega devised for his former Comanche friend.

And Tessa had to watch it all. "If you close your eyes, I'll carve off your pretty little eyelids," Ortega told her. He brandished the knife that had once belonged to Iron Trail. She knew he wouldn't do it, since he planned to sell her later, but she didn't want to test him.

Ortega took his time jamming the blade under Iron Trail's fingernails and prying them off one by one. The customarily stoic Comanche managed to keep quiet for the first two, but he screamed and squirmed for the rest.

The Comanchero then had some fun cutting the bullets out of Iron Trail's body. It took some considerable digging, and the night rang with Iron Trail's suffering.

"I like your hair," Ortega said. He used the tip of the knife to pick between his teeth. "I think it would be best if I took it. To remember you, of course."

Tessa screamed against her gag as the Comanchero dragged the knife across the top of Iron Trail's forehead from temple to temple. He then pried his fingers into the slit and pulled back, exposing the top of Iron Trail's skull to the sky.

Iron Trail remained surprisingly silent, and Tessa thought he might have died. Blood dribbled into his eyes, and while he didn't blink, his breathing took on a quicker pace.

Ortega ripped the scalp away, leaving only a fringe of hair around Iron Trail's ears and neck, as if he were just an old bald man rather than a scalped Comanche.

Ortega laughed, examining his prize in the moonlight. "I hear you savages never cut your hair. This must have taken you all your life to grow, huh?" When Iron Trail didn't respond, he kicked him in the chest. "Answer me!"

Iron Trail opened his mouth, but only a thin stream of blood came out. He managed to emit a strangled grunt, nothing more.

Ortega put the scalp over his own head and did a pirouette. "What do you think, boys?"

The other Comancheros laughed, and Tessa gagged, hoping she wouldn't vomit, not with this cloth stuck in her mouth.

Iron Trail tried to stand against his bonds. Ortega noticed this and snarled. "You think you still have a chance of getting out of this?!"

And he quickly severed both of Iron Trail's Achilles tendons.

He spent some more time carving curse words into Iron Trail's chest and giggling with his comrades. When the Comanche wouldn't give Ortega the satisfaction of screaming, he lashed out with the blade and cut one of Iron Trail's eyes out. Once again the placid, stoic look on Iron Trail's face disappeared, and he howled like a coyote at the moon.

An hour later Ortega squatted down in front of Iron Trail. "I hear you're an edge-u-cated savage. Recite some pomes for me."

Iron Trail's remaining eye squinted. He garbled, "Do . . . y-y-you have . . . any re-requests?"

Ortega sighed. "You try to be nice to a bastard, and all he does is spit in your face." He then grabbed Iron Trail's lower lip and sawed it away, leaving his wet jawbone to gleam in the firelight.

Finally Tessa looked away, hoping no one would notice. Ortega saw this right away and brandished the gore-streaked blade at her.

"Don't make me do it, cunt," Ortega said.

Tessa looked at the ruin of her lover, and she couldn't find her breath. She gagged on her tears and begged whatever god there might be to end Iron Trail's misery.

As usual no one listened to her prayers. Ortega went back to cutting Iron Trail, but never in a place that would lead to a swift death. Sometimes the pain grew so much that Iron Trail would stop screaming. On these occasions Ortega felt it important to cut something bigger off. First an ear, and then his nose. Then his fingers. He pried out a bunch of teeth.

But soon this stopped working, too.

Ortega turned to one of his men. "Moreno. Grab his dick."

"What?"

"You heard me. *I'm* not going to touch it."

Moreno, who never thought joining a group of Comancheros would ever lead to him one day grabbing a Comanche's cock, thought about taking a stand. This was humiliating, and the others would in all likelihood call him a faggot for the rest of his life.

But he also knew the kind of man Ortega was, and he knew his boss would never take no for an answer. He knelt down and extracted Iron Trail's penis from his leggings.

"Stretch it out," Ortega said.

Iron Trail's remaining eye widened, and he muttered something unintelligible. He tried to pull his hands apart, but the rope wouldn't give, and he no longer had strength.

Ortega moved in and drew the blade across the taut skin once, twice, and with a third time it came away from the rest of Iron Trail's body.

The initial scream turned into a whimper, and Ortega knew that Iron Trail had finally broken. There would be precious little fun left in him.

Moreno gagged, holding the chunk of flesh. He was about to drop it when Ortega shook his head. "Give it to the girl." He called over to her: "Cunt-whore! We have a present for you!"

131

Moreno threw it at her, and it thumped against her chest before it rolled down her body and came to rest on her legs.

Ortega laughed. "Good aim, Moreno!"

Moreno sheepishly grinned. He liked the praise, but he wished he hadn't had to do that.

Tessa wanted to scream, but she had nothing left in her. She stared at the dismembered piece of Iron Trail. Already it looked withered, less than what it had been.

She barely noticed it when Ortega stood over her, tapping the knife against his front teeth. A spot of blood shone on one of them. Then, silently, he brushed the hunk of meat away with the blade and removed the gag from her mouth.

She tried to say something, but her mouth was so dry she could only croak.

Ortega turned her around so he could cut away the rope around her hands. He left the bonds around her legs and dragged her to her feet. She thought he might set her entirely free, but he only dragged her over to Iron Trail, whose breath whistled through the hole where his nose had been.

"Think he's had enough, cunt-whore?" Ortega asked.

"Please," Tessa gasped. "Please stop."

Ortega presented the handle of the knife to her. "I think you should do the honors, don't you?"

She stared at the hilt and considered sticking the knife into Ortega's guts. He wouldn't be the first person she'd killed. But one look into his eyes proved that he waited for such a move, and perhaps he even welcomed it.

Tessa looked at her lover and thought—hoped—this was a nightmare brought on by too much Scotch and not enough food. How could this pile of flesh be Iron Trail? The top of his skull open to the world, his face a ruin, more bone and blood than skin and hair. She didn't understand the words carved into his skin, but she didn't need to. The hole in his crotch spoke all, his manhood gone.

Iron Trail moaned, and it sounded like there were words in the noise.

"Take the knife and do it," Ortega said. "Or I'll start cutting his asshole out."

Iron Trail made more effort this time. "I . . . luh you, T-t-t-tessa."

She took the knife and put it to her lover's throat. She waited, wondering how to do this. He'd suffered enough; why make him suffer more?

As if he'd heard this thought, Iron Trail nodded. He said something else, but she didn't know what it was.

She thought it might have been, "Do it."

So she did.

-

From that point it took ten minutes for Iron Trail to bleed out and die. He choked for quite some time, but from the way crimson barely crawled out of him, Ortega thought the blood loss had killed him before the asphyxiation had a chance. By then his men had the chance to look at his knife wound. It looked worse than it was, and they'd stitched and bandaged him up while he watched Iron Trail and Tessa.

Tessa waited with her lover, holding his hand for every second of life Iron Trail had left in this world. When he finally passed on she

133

held the knife in her limp hand, staring into the empty eye of the Comanche.

Ortega gently took the blade from her. "Do you know what my favorite thing about killing Comanche is? They're trained from a very young age to take pain. This means they take so much longer to die, and this gives me much pleasure."

She did not respond.

He examined the knife. "This is the finest blade I've ever seen. I'm glad it's mine now."

Tessa remained silent.

Ortega sheathed it and stood. "Say your goodbyes to his corpse, cunt-whore. Tonight I will have you."

The beast walked away from her, leaving her with Iron Trail's empty husk. Very little remained to remind her of the man he'd been. To think, after all this time of wishing him dead, now that he finally was, she no longer wanted it. Death came ugly to those with whom it was well-acquainted. The bits and pieces Ortega had cut off were still on the ground, and Tessa felt moved to put them back where they belonged. She couldn't believe this mutilated flesh used to be a human being.

Iron Trail, perhaps not the best of people, was still an intelligent soulful man, and how could someone as unsophisticated and brutal as Ortega kill him? Would this have happened if she had stayed in New York with Sam Pepper? She didn't think so, but at the same time she knew not to dwell on such thoughts.

Ortega deemed that she'd had enough time. He grabbed her by the hair and dragged her away from the corpse. She screamed, more out of fear than the pain that assailed the roots of her hair. Out of instinct she reached up and grabbed Ortega's wrist, so he pulled her along by her arms instead.

Two other Comancheros held her wrists while Ortega ripped her shirt open and pawed at her bare breasts.

"Ripe for the picking," Ortega muttered. The corners of his wormy mouth were wet. He reached down to her legs and cut the bonds at her ankles before pulling her pants down and sticking his fingers inside her.

"Stop!" But no one heeded her.

Ortega opened his own pants and showed her his erect penis. As long as a pencil and just as thin. Big enough, though, and he proved it by thrusting inside of her.

She wanted to beg for mercy, but she knew it would be futile. All she could do was look up at the moon and try to pretend this wasn't happening.

Before long she started sinking into herself as Ortega filled her with his seed. She found other worlds to explore as the rest took their turns. Some of them hit her, but she didn't notice. She was too far gone to think about what happened to her physical body.

-

The next day she awoke before the others. Not that it did her any good, considering how they'd left her naked and bound so they could rest easily. Their stinking drunken shapes littered the campground. The fire had guttered and now smoked in the dawn sun.

Iron Trail's body. There were a few purple splotches of decay on his corpse, not that it much mattered. The vultures had already descended and were pecking away at the rotten meat.

At least Iron Trail wasn't alone. The scavengers also feasted upon the bodies of the dead Comancheros.

Tessa shrugged out of the shreds of her shirt and used the cloth to dry the dampness between her legs. How many had taken her? Did it matter? Who knew what diseases these beasts carried, but at least she knew one thing: she was barren. Sam Pepper had once gotten her pregnant, and the abortionist had not been very skilled. Never before had she considered this result fortunate, but now she smiled, knowing that none of the scum who had raped her could get her pregnant.

Nearby she saw the shattered remains of the bottle of Scotch. The memory seemed dim—it had happened shortly after the first rape of the evening—but she recalled Ortega pulling the bottle from Iron Trail's saddlebag and guzzling it like it was cheap whiskey. It had dribbled from the corners of his mouth and down his chin, as if it hadn't meant a thing in the world. And then the Comanchero had thrown the bottle aside, breaking it to pieces before he went to retrieve another bottle.

Now Ortega sat with his back to a tree, a limp cigarette dangling from his lips, leafing through her journal. Whenever he finished a page he tore it out, balled it up and threw it behind him.

Her bound wrists went to her breasts, and her hands twisted together, covering her mouth. She gagged at the sight of the Comanchero, but even worse was the violation of her diary.

When she moved, Ortega glanced over the top of the book. He laughed, puffing out smoke as he did so. With a lazy hand he removed the cigarette from his mouth. "You know, it's not that uncommon."

Tessa turned away from him, not wanting to see him. The smell reeked badly enough.

Ortega stood and dropped the diary, and he walked up to her, sitting where she couldn't look away from him. "I have captured many people in my lifetime." He spoke as casually as if he were ordering a drink in a saloon. "Women and kids, mostly, but occasionally I have held a man captive. More often than you would think, one who is captured sometimes falls in love with one's captor."

Tessa gritted her teeth and hid her face in her arms. Ortega pulled her hands away. "Perhaps it will happen with you and me, no?"

She spat in his face. Her saliva dotted his cheek and ran down his jaw line. He laughed, wiping it up with his fingers and sticking his findings between his lips.

"You're an animal," she said. "Iron Trail was ten times the man you are."

Ortega's smile faded, and he wiped his fingers off on his shirt. "Maybe. Honestly I don't think I would have killed him if I wasn't so drunk last night."

He stood and wandered back over to where he'd left the journal. He picked it up and flipped through the pages that remained. "He was probably one of the smartest people I've ever known. A hell of a trader, too. I cannot tell you how many blonde-haired, blue-eyed white women he brought to me, and for a good price, too. A hundred dollars for prime pussy? Not bad at all. I would have given hundreds for you, though. No wonder he wanted to keep you for himself."

Tessa felt anger, but she didn't know why. Surely she'd known what Iron Trail was capable of, that he'd traded in flesh for many years. Ortega hadn't told her anything she didn't already know. But why did it hurt like this?

"Hell, I was thinking of maybe keeping you for me, too," Ortega said. "But now that my men have had their turns, I think I'll pass. Don't get me wrong, I'll still fuck you till you bleed, but when I'm through with you, I'll sell you."

He dropped the journal into the smoking remnants of the fire. The pages caught on an ember and blazed up quicker than expected. "I don't know how much I could get for you, used. Maybe fifty bucks. Get you down to Mexico and sell you to a bartender who'll make up his expenditure by whoring you out, getting you to clean tables. What do you think?"

Tessa refused to dignify the Comanchero with an answer, belligerent or otherwise.

Ortega strolled over to Iron Trail's body. The vultures looked up at him, but when he made no sudden movements, they decided he was harmless and continued consuming their meal.

"Smartest savage I've ever known," he muttered. "My own mother told me once that I'd never amount to anything. Yet here I am, probably the dumbest fuck in the world, and there Iron Trail is. What's all this effort supposed to be for, this so called intelligence, if we all just end up as empty husks, anyway?"

He kicked Iron Trail's empty head, and the scavengers flew away, leaving feathers and bird shit in their wake. They would be back, though, not that Ortega cared.

"Sure was fun to kill him, though. Comanches breed their sons to be tough. Makes 'em last longer. More fun for me."

He then turned and walked up to one of his sleeping men and kicked him. He spoke in Spanish to the man, who Tessa thought was named

Hernandez, and the man got up, stumbled about, and started preparing breakfast.

-

An hour later, after they'd eaten, they thought it might be best if they fed their captive, too. They prepared a couple of eggs and some bacon for her and handed her the plate. At first, Ortega thought she would express her hatred for them by not eating their food, but she made quick work of what they'd given her. Had she learned survival from Iron Trail? Or did she already know this?

Shortly thereafter they started packing their things. Tessa said, "I have to answer nature's call."

"You mean, you have to take a shit?" Ortega asked. "Just go."

"In front of you all?"

"We don't care. Hell, I think Hernandez might actually like that kind of thing."

Only half of the men understood English, and they started laughing. Hernandez leered at her, showing that most of his teeth were missing. Judging from the lack of rot, he'd probably had them knocked out in a fight.

"You can use your shirt to wipe with," Ortega said. "Remember, if it sticks to the sides of your ass, don't be afraid to get in there and get it clean. Nothing upsets me more than fucking a dirty asshole."

She gritted her teeth and wondered at how she'd once hated the West because of the dust. Had she really been that angry with such a small detail? With resignation, she took her shirt and started heading for a tree.

Ortega grabbed the rope that bound her hands and pulled her back. "Not out there. Over here."

She wanted to retort, but considering everything she had gone through, what dignity did she have left? She squatted down and looked into Ortega's eyes as she did her business. She stared holes into him, and as the first of her spoor slapped the ground, Ortega turned away, a grimace on his face. A small victory, but a victory nonetheless.

She finished. "Do I get to wear any clothes?"

Ortega still couldn't look at her. "Moreno, fetch her some pants and a shirt from the wagon."

Tessa found her boots near the campfire, where they had been thrown after she tried to kick one of her rapists in the balls.

Her bonds were cut long enough for her to get dressed and put the boots on. Then they were wrapped around her wrists again, and she got up into the wagon, along with the other possessions of the Comancheros.

There were a few blankets and bedrolls back there, so Tessa made herself comfortable. The rocking and bucking of the wagon would not do wonders for her, but she figured the padding would at least help. And if she got hungry, she had some jerky beef, too. Hell, if things got hairy there were a few bottles of whiskey.

She saw Ortega pass by the opening of the wagon, and she called out to him. "Where are we going?"

"Why? Are we keeping you from something?"

Tessa held up her bound hands. "What difference does it make?"

He smiled, and he almost looked pleasant. "Good point. Well, we're going to meet up with the rest of my group."

Tessa swallowed, and the movement was so labored that Ortega noticed it.

"Don't worry," he continued. "They probably won't all use you. Most of them like hairless boys. Besides, I think your pussy's been used enough. We don't want to break it or anything."

"How . . . how many?" She didn't know how much more she could take. Miraculously, they hadn't torn her last night. Then again, most of them had tiny dicks. Ortega was long but skinny. Moreno, however, was almost as big as Iron Trail had been. She thought she could survive, just so long as there were none others like Moreno.

Ortega took one of her hands in his, stroking up and down. "I don't like it when people ask me questions. It ignites something in me, and it burns me up. I recommend you keep your cunt-whore mouth shut." He said it with no animosity as if he'd earnestly meant it as a warning.

Before she knew what had happened, Ortega had twisted her pinkie finger back so hard it snapped, the nail touching the back of her wrist. She screamed more at the way it looked, rather than the pain, although the latter certainly let her know its presence. Tears ran down her cheeks as she tried to hold her wound with her good hand. The bonds, however, prevented this.

"Quit it," Ortega said. "See this lump here? That means it's just dislocated. It's an easy fix."

"Fix it!" she cried. "Please, God, fix it!"

Ortega smiled, and this time it was in much the same fashion as he had when he was torturing Iron Trail. "As you wish, ma'am." He squeezed her hand, and the finger popped back into place with a loud click.

This time, the pain knocked her out. Tessa fainted backwards into a pile of blankets, and Ortega laughed. "Let's get this show on the road!" he called out to the wagon driver.

When she came to she found herself surrounded by a new group of Comancheros. Like the previous assemblage, most were of Mexican descent, but there were a handful of Indians—she wasn't sure which tribes, but one wore the same fashion as Iron Trail, so she assumed he was Comanche—and white men. She immediately thought to appeal to the white folks to save her from these savages, but the idea quickly died as the two whites pawed at her breasts, squeezing and massaging.

One of the young white men had a cleft palate, and when he leaned down to grab between her legs, drool slopped out of his mouth and left a trail on her clothes. "Panth're too thick," he lisped. "Can't feel nuthin'."

One of the Mexicans spoke but not in Spanish. It was the weird Comanche and Mexican mix she'd heard the previous evening. From the way he talked, she guessed that he wanted to be the first to try the merchandise.

"Nuh-uh," the other white man said. "She's one of us, we gets to try 'er first, ain't that right, Norbert?"

Norbert wiped spittle from his deformed mouth. "That'th right, Brother Dethmond."

Desmond drew his Bowie knife, but he didn't brandish it at anyone. "I don't think there's any question, right boys?"

Ortega slapped the blade from Desmond's hand. It flew through the air and stuck itself into the ground. "No one's using this one," Ortega said. "We need to keep that pussy tight. Only guys with little baby dicks get to do her."

Most of the men looked away at this, not wanting to admit such a thing, even if it was for the cause of pussy. Norbert didn't much care, though. "I don't got muth, botthh. Can I have a go?"

Ortega raised an eyebrow, as if he hadn't expected anyone would take him up on the offer. "Hell boy, ain't you got shame? Des, what kind of idiot brother you got tagging along with you?"

Desmond shrugged.

"Fuck it. Okay, Norbert. You got it. Take her into the wagon, but don't hurt her. Remember that. Do. Not. Hurt. Her. Do you understand?"

Norbert nodded, his lazy eyes locked on Tessa's breasts.

"If she winds up like that last one," Ortega said, "I'll cut your dick off and make you eat it. Are you hearing me?" But when he said all of this, he looked at Tessa with a gleam in his eye. Had he made this up about the "last one" to scare her?

Norbert nodded, so maybe he hadn't.

"Desmond, go with your idiot brother and make sure nothing happens. If things go well, you can break a piece off for yourself, too. But no one else touches this woman, understand?"

No one disagreed with him.

"And don't you fucking rip her clothes. I already gave her some from our supply, and I don't feel like giving her more."

Norbert didn't pay attention. He was too busy staring at Tessa's breasts and drooling.

Desmond nodded. "You got it, boss."

The other Comancheros glared at the white men, and Norbert didn't notice. Desmond did, and he shrugged. "Sorry, fellas. White's a

143

privilege, you know. Maybe some of yez with lighter skin might get a go after we're done. Sanchez, I guess you're shit out of luck."

Sanchez had skin so dark he could have been mistaken for an African. He snarled, showing bone white teeth, all so crooked he could bite someone without opening his jaw.

Desmond stooped down to grab the length of rope that trailed from around her wrists. With a deft movement, he looped it and stuck it around her neck. By the time she realized what he planned to do, it was too late. He yanked, and she jumped off the ground, grasping at the rough material around her throat.

"Don't slip, darlin'," Desmond said. "Don't want to choke, do ya'?"

She stumbled, but when she got her bearings, she managed to find Desmond's pace and keep to it as he led her to the wagon. She couldn't see it, but Norbert was trailing behind them, staring at her ass and sucking at his lower lip. A slurping sound came from the cleft in his palate.

"Up and at 'em," Desmond said. He grabbed Tessa around the waist and boosted her up into the back of the wagon. He had practically thrown her, and she rattled around a bit on the floor inside as he mounted the wagon and ducked in.

Norbert followed, and he slumped on top of her immediately, pressing his disfigured face against her own, his ruined lips rubbing all over her chin, as if he'd misjudged the distance.

His tongue found her mouth and darted in, slithering over her teeth and then probing deeper. The slobber from his cleft palate—hairy because he didn't bother shaving within the crease—adorned her lips, and when he drew back to look at her, strings of slime connected the two of them.

Tessa gagged, and her breakfast came up, splattering all over Norbert's face.

Desmond nearly retched. "Ah, Jesus!"

Norbert didn't seem to notice what had happened, or perhaps this was a common occurrence for him. One way or the other he went for another of his sloppy kisses, and Tessa dry heaved.

Desmond couldn't help it. He handed over a bandana." Brother Norbert, I'd greatly 'preciate it if you'd clean yer face."

Norbert reluctantly took the hint and followed his brother's suggestion. Then he took the care to unbutton the thick scratchy shirt Moreno had given her. She wore nothing underneath it, and Norbert didn't waste time in pawing and squeezing her flesh.

"Enough with the games, brother," Desmond said. "Get yer dick wet so's I can get mine wet."

Tessa forced herself to calm down. One of the things that had gotten her through last night was pretending to be dead. With no resistance the men were less likely to hurt her. Another thing: fixing her gaze on something. The moon had been a bright and easy target, but now all she had was the canvas of the wagon.

She found a hole in the top where sunshine managed to crawl through. As Norbert wiggled her pants down her thighs, she stared at the hole and at the motes of dust floating in the sun's wake. She imagined that she looked at the universe, and the dust particles were planets and stars.

And then something brought her out of this escape mediation. Norbert struggled to get inside of her. It felt like there were two dicks down there. Had Desmond decided to join in? No, she saw the handsomer of the two looking down at her with a thoughtful look.

When she looked at Norbert she saw that his palate wasn't the only thing that had a cleft on his body; his penis was forked like a serpent's tongue, and the ends looked like two smaller penises. Both were hard as rock.

She screamed, and Desmond laughed. "Yeah, everyone gets a kick outta' that the first time they sees it. Some cunt got tired of him fuckin' her all the time. So she put a razor in her pussy and let him fuck her. The sheriff still hasn't found all of her. You believe that?" He laughed again.

"Is that what happened to his mouth?" The words were out of Tessa before she'd even realized it, and Norbert didn't hesitate to shove them back in with a sharp backhand.

"Calm down, Nor," Desmond said. "Remember what Ortega said. 'Sides, who cares what a fuckin' hooer has to say?"

Norbert grunted, which seemed to be an indicator that he'd finished beating her. Instead he focused his concentration on pushing the forks of his dick together with one hand and holding her open with the other.

Tessa didn't want to see this. She refocused her attention on that hole and tried to ignore the sensation. It felt like someone ham-fisting a couple of worms inside of her.

And then she found her mental escape in the floating motes of the universe.

She was dimly aware of Norbert's quickness. Two minutes might have passed in that time, but certainly not three. She heard movement as Norbert pulled his pants back up and stepped out of the wagon, leaving her alone with Desmond.

"Baby, you have beautiful hair." His voice seemed to come from next door, and the hand that brushed at the sweaty strands across her forehead belonged to a ghost. A buckle struck the wooden floor, and hands moved up and down over her body. The ghost murmured so distantly she couldn't make out any words.

Something brushed at the insides of her thighs. At first she thought it might be Desmond getting ready to take his piece of her. Then she realized there was a rough cloth down there, probably cleaning up what Norbert had left.

Now she knew it would come, and she hoped she was far enough away not to feel it. But too much time passed, and she looked down at Desmond. One of his hands rested on her breast, pumping away, while his other encircled his flaccid, flopping penis. His teeth were gritted as he worked his crank, but nothing seemed to be happening down there.

Tessa uttered a chuckle, a dry, flat sound, but it seemed to be full of mirth. "Your brother's dick is ruined, but he can still get it up," she whispered. She let the implication settle.

"Fuck you, hooer!" Desmond raised his fist, and Tessa was certain he'd use it on her. Then he remembered Ortega's orders. Instead of punching her, he grabbed one of her nipples between his index finger and thumb. He squeezed, digging his nail in as hard as he could.

She screamed, her escape mediation forgotten. She definitely returned to here and now as the sharp pain raced through her chest. It felt like her nipple had been cut away.

Satisfied, he released her. As he pulled his pants up he muttered nonsense. Then: "Cunt."

Outside he saw Moreno running up to the wagon. "What just happened?" he asked in Comanchero.

Desmond offered his best smile. "I fucked her so hard she couldn't take it. What can I say, Juanito? My dick's like a cannon."

The men all laughed while Tessa laid back in the wagon, crying into her palms. She found no damage to her nipple, but it would be tender for days to come.

She thought she should pull her pants up and close her shirt, but she didn't have the energy. Besides one of the other men would want to take her, too, and they would only bare her flesh again.

Shortly after Desmond had left, a shadow entered Tessa's periphery. She looked up to see another Comanchero at the wagon flap. The sun was to his back, making him nothing but a silhouette, but she knew he was staring at her.

Restraining a sob, she laid down on her back and spread her legs. It took her a moment to find the hole in the canvas, but when she did, she stared and waited, hoping this wouldn't take so long. She tried to think of it as a doctor's visit, uncomfortable but necessary.

The Comanchero placed something in the wagon. It thumped on the floor, sending a thick vibration through her body. She heard a rattling sound as he climbed into the wagon with her. But when he knelt in front of her, he did not open his pants. Instead he gently touched both of her knees, moving them together.

Tessa abandoned the sunlight hole and turned her gaze to the Comanchero, a young and almost wispy man, no older than twenty. He kept his thick dark hair swept back, and it shone in the single beam of sunshine. A scant mustache rested on his upper lip in patches.

He closed the flaps of her shirt and turned away to pull the bucket of water he'd brought with him closer. "There's a rag in there," he said. "I found some soap, too. Have a few sips before you bathe. You look dehydrated."

"What's your name?" she asked. Her voice was nothing more than a whisper.

He didn't look at her. "Eduardo Molina. I'll see if I can get some food for you."

"I'm Tessa Reeves."

"You'll probably have an hour to yourself," Molina said. "After that Ortega will want to use you again. I think he'll want you to himself, though. After that you'll be housed with the other prisoners. Is there anything I can get you?"

Tessa wanted to ask for whiskey to help with her nerves, to even dull whatever pain Ortega might deal out to her tonight. But that was no answer. Was she really just going to give in to these scum? Was she really going to surrender her life to them? No. Iron Trail would have looked for a way out. Perhaps he had taught her enough to survive.

"Do you think you can get me a pencil and paper? A notebook, perhaps?"

Molina's eyebrows arched, but he said nothing. On his way out he closed the flap entirely so no one could see her.

She thought she'd seen about twenty Comancheros. Was it possible that one among them could be called a good person? Probably not. Molina was one of them. He had to be savage and twisted in some way. Still he was the only one who had been decent to her, the only one who so far expressed no interest in having her.

Or perhaps he liked little boys, like Ortega had said. Yeah, he had to be like that.

She reached both of her hands into the bucket and cupped some water to her mouth. After she'd had enough to make her feel bloated, she put the rag in with the soap and started washing Norbert and Desmond away.

-

She'd started putting her clothes back on when Molina returned. "You decent?"

"Wait." Tessa finished buttoning her shirt. "Okay. Come on in."

Molina hopped up into the wagon and handed her three pencils and a handful of blank pages. They all seemed to have come from the same notebook, a ledger. The pencils were as sharp as they could be out here in the wilderness.

"When they get stubby, let me know," Molina said. "I'll sharpen them for you."

She wanted to say that she'd hoped for a notebook rather than a bunch of loose sheets, but considering how she was probably lucky to have this, she kept her mouth shut. "Thank you."

He nodded. "Don't let Ortega catch you with that."

"If he does, he'll never find out where I got them."

"He'll know it was me. I'm the only one who ever writes things down around here."

What kind of things? Could it be possible that young Molina was a poet? Or did he write letters home to his mother? It wasn't any of her business, so once more she kept quiet.

Soon Molina left, and Tessa found herself writing feverishly of all the things that had happened to her. Had it only been yesterday that she and Iron Trail had set up camp and waited for the Comancheros?

It seemed like it had been months ago. She had so much to tell, and her hand didn't move fast enough to keep up with her mind.

After the first three pages her hand cramped up, and she forced herself to stop and flex her fingers for a minute. Then she started again, her usual lady-like cursive giving away to hastily scrawled chicken-scratch.

When she finished she put the pencil down and cracked her knuckles. It sounded like a bundle of sticks being broken. She cast her gaze around for a place to hide her work. She certainly couldn't keep it on her body, or someone would find it when they raped her. No, it had to be somewhere in the wagon. In the heap of bedrolls? No, they'd find it at night.

Then she noticed a rip in the hem of the wagon's canvas. Tight, but she thought if she rolled up the pages small enough, they might fit in.

She evened out her new journal and started to roll it up, but it didn't take long for her to figure out that the bundle would be slightly too big for the rip. No, it had to be somewhere else.

Tessa moved things around in the wagon, looking for hiding places. She started to give up when she found, under a rag pile, a stack of books. What had Molina said? That he was the only one who wrote anything down around here. Perhaps he was the only one who knew how to read.

Then why did they have books? Perhaps they were rare and the Comancheros were going to sell them to collectors. Unlikely, but at the time they seemed to be the best hiding place. She found a large volume and hid the pages between the front cover and the first page.

No sooner had she covered the books up with rags again than Ortega threw open the flap at the back of the wagon. "Come on, princess. It's time for us to get more acquainted."

She forced herself not to cringe. Just like going to the doctor, she thought, and she let the Comanchero help her to the ground outside.

FROM THE JOURNAL OF TESSA REEVES:

I no longer know what date it is, so I am going to refer to this as the first day of captivity. Considering what I have written in previous diaries, this may seem a bit strange (if you will remember, haha, my first captor was Iron Trail, so I have been a prisoner for quite a while), but I can never think of my previous incarceration as such. Iron Trail became my lover. Hector Ortega is nothing but scum.

When he took me out of the wagon today, I saw that the sun approached the horizon, and twilight encroached upon us. The day felt cooler already, and a slight breeze picked up, just enough to rustle through my hair.

Ortega led me to a campfire which had just been started. The light from within the logs barely flickered, and the smoke cast its wispy shadow on the dead ground.

On the way, I saw Juan Moreno speaking with a couple of Indians. They were not Comancheros, and I could not tell what tribe they were from, but they seemed to be bartering for a little white girl. The girl stared ahead with a dull look in her eyes, and I doubted that she understood her predicament. Perhaps she no longer knew who she was. My first day of captivity, and already I doubted my own existence.

The Comancheros settled on seven horses from the Indians. Nearby, I heard someone laugh. He said to Desmond Hertell, in English (presumably so the Indians wouldn't understand), "These dipshitth must really want that little girl."

Desmond smiled back. "Yep. I'd've given just three horses. Maybe four."

Norbert shook his head. "She'll be worth it when she grows up and getth a good thet on her."

Desmond giggled, almost like a girl himself, and I felt the urge to cut him so he would look just like his repulsive brother.

I watched Moreno take the tether of seven horses as the Indians took possession of their purchase. For one brief moment, the little girl's eyes locked with mine, and I saw nothing in them. Whatever they had done to her, she had died, yet still she walked. I wanted to reach out to her, to comfort her, but what good could I do?

Ortega yanked on my arm, and I fell by the side of the campfire. "Cook this." He dropped a skillet onto the ground, and then he tossed a slab of meat into it. The steak slapped the hard metal, and I thought about when Norbert had backhanded me. I winced, but this did not prevent me from picking up the skillet and putting it over the fire.

I did not cook much Back-East, but Iron Trail had taught me how to make do with what I had out in the West. I took up a stick and used that to push around the meat.

Ortega waited long enough to be satisfied that I knew what I was doing, and he then walked away to admire his new horses. I looked about, hoping to see Eduardo Molina. It took me a moment, but I spied him sitting with his back to a tree, reading a book. He sat so the last of the sun would illuminate the pages. I could not see the title from where I knelt by the fire, but the book seemed very old. The pages crumbled as he turned them.

I considered waving to him, but I knew that would not be smart. He had already gone out on a limb to help me, and if the others knew that, he might not be safe, which meant that I would not be safe.

Molina must have sensed me staring at him, for he looked over the top of his book and gave me as light nod before returning to his reading material.

I assumed that a beast like Ortega would want his meat rare, so I did not cook it for very long. On one hand, I wanted to please him so he would not be so rough with me. On the other, I hoped the undercooked meat would make him ill, would maybe even kill him.

I presented it to him, and he nearly pressed his nose into the skillet to smell it. "Very good," he said. "Great pussy, and you can cook. Yeah, I would have had to have killed Iron Trail to get you. He was a walking dead man this time yesterday."

He carved off a portion for me, but he did not give me utensils with which to eat it. I placed it on my thigh, and I waited for it to cool off before I could pick it up. The heat baked through my pants leg, but the sensation didn't feel so bad.

As soon as I started eating, Moreno came by and poured water for everyone. He stopped by me last only to give me the dregs from the bucket.

I found it to be better than nothing.

After dinner, when the sun dropped completely from the sky, Ortega ordered Moreno to get a couple of bottles of whisky. They started passing them around, and before long, I saw that the men stared at me with glassy eyes. Their mouths hung open. In Norbert's case, drool spilled down his chin.

155

But then Ortega sat next to me and put his arm around my shoulders. "Don't worry, princess." His breath stank of whisky. "They know you belong to me."

Ortega had a bottle that he started to pass on to Hernandez. Before the Comanchero could take it, I grabbed it from my owner and took a deep swig. When I handed it to Hernandez, he glared at me, but it disappeared into a fake smile when Ortega laughed.

"That's the spirit, princess!" And he hugged me so tightly I could feel my pulse rocking through my body.

I do not have the stomach to describe what happened next, although you probably have a very good idea. When Ortega was done with me, and when I had memorized every crater of the moon, he gave me to Moreno.

"Put her back in the wagon," he said. "Then get the other cunt-whore. They're going to be roommates."

"Can I have a turn at this one?" Moreno nodded to me.

"No. You can fuck the other one's brains out for all I care, but this one's mine, at least until my dick gets tired of her."

Ortega dismissed the both of us, and Moreno escorted me back to the wagon. When we were sheltered from the others behind the vehicle, Moreno stopped us. "I don't care what the boss says. My first taste of you was so good, I have to go back for seconds. And if you scream, or if you tell on me, I will cut your fucking tits off and make you eat them. Understand?"

I understood. Without being prompted, I lowered my pants and prepared to let him do what he wanted to me.

I heard soft, raspy sounds as he untied his pants, but when he pushed his hardening member against me, he did so against the wrong part. It

156

took me a moment to realize that he wanted the other hole, the one that Sam Pepper liked so much.

I found no moon to look at. Nothing on which to focus my attention. I had only the canvas of the covered wagon, and I did not think I could lose myself in it.

"Come on," Moreno whispered. "Loosen up back here." I could hear him spitting into his palm behind me.

And then, Eduardo Molina came around the corner. He paused, but it was very evident to me that he had expected to see the display before him.

I felt Moreno shrink instantly, and he hurriedly placed himself back in his pants. He spouted off in his own language, and though I had only spent a day with them, I picked up a few words. Whatever he said, it involved some very naughty language.

Molina said a few things in Spanish, and Moreno reacted angrily. They had a brief, but sharp, discussion, and it ended with Moreno stalking off, leaving me with Molina.

"Thank you," I said.

"*De nada*," he said. I think this means "you're welcome." "Let's get you into the wagon. Moreno's coming back with Gracie, your roommate. He might be a while. Since he didn't get anything from you, he'll probably take it out on her."

"That's horrible!" I thought about what had been meant for me, and it made me sick that someone else would get it because of my conduct.

"She won't feel a thing," Molina said. "She's far too gone for that."

"What do you mean?"

"You'll see when you meet her."

He escorted me to the inside of the wagon, where I started to write this account. I had to take a break when Moreno brought Gracie to me. It was easy to keep watch for him, since he was drunk and angry. Judging from his smell, he had used Gracie at least once before bringing her to the wagon.

How can I describe my companion? My fellow victim? I think she was once pretty, perhaps even beautiful. Her long blonde hair was tied back into what must have been a painfully tight ponytail. Her blue eyes were faded and glassy, and I am fairly certain that she never blinked. I could not watch her all the time, but whenever I did see her, her demeanor remained the same. Wide eyes and wide smile, almost like a mannequin in a department store back in New York City, except she clearly lived. Despite the sun to which she must have been exposed, her skin was very pale.

There were no bruises on her face, but I saw plenty on her arms and legs. When Moreno delivered her to me, her clothes were open, so I could see the rest of the bruises on her. I could see the blood on her thighs. It wasn't fresh, so it probably wasn't Moreno's doing, but to have left dried blood on a person for so long seemed inhumane.

When Moreno dumped her into the wagon (and this is no exaggeration; he had grabbed her by the legs and had thrust her up and into my domicile), after this cursory examination, I felt compelled to bathe her. From her appearance, it had been quite some time since someone had done that for her.

Molina's bucket was still in the wagon, so I put some more soap in and began to wash her with the rag. At first she didn't resist, but when I cleaned beneath her neck, I could feel her heart beat quicker, and her muscles tensed, as if ready to attack.

I spoke softly to her, trying to reassure that I would not cause her any pain. This seemed to work until I started cleaning Moreno's leavings out of her. She screamed and lashed out with her sharp nails, but I was ready. I held her hands together and whispered soothingly to her. It unsettled me, looking into her marbled eyes, and I wondered what Ortega and his men had done to her to cause her to look like this.

She turned her face away from mine, and as I watched her, it seemed like she focused her attention on the very same hole in the top of the wagon that I had earlier. I thought I had been clever in doing this; it educated me to witness another doing the same thing without prior knowledge of my existence. Perhaps human beings are not as different from each other as we tend to believe.

I carefully washed Moreno's spunk away. It took some time because it was deep inside her, but I did so gingerly. If she experienced any pain, she did not alert me to it. While I was down there, I discovered several tears where the blood had originated. They had scabbed over, and I made sure that I did not rip any of them away.

As I cleaned her hands, I noticed that she didn't have all of her fingers. The first joints of the index and middle on her right hand, and her thumb on her left. The cuts were even-edged, so I assumed it had been done to her purposely. They'd scabbed over pretty well, just like the tears inside of her.

When I finished, I closed her pants and shirt and said, "All done."

She did not respond. In fact, she did not reply to anything I said. She continued to look up at the hole in the canvas, as if it were her entire world.

I would not have disagreed with her on that.

I tried talking to her, introducing myself, but nothing shone behind her glassy eyes. Every once in a while, she would emit a sound that resembled a giggle, but this possibility was too ghastly to even consider.

Now, as I write this, she stares at me with her empty eyes, and she does not say a word. Her eerie smile is so open I can see each and every one of her teeth. Considering how long she must have been out in the wilderness with the Comancheros, her grin is surprisingly white and even.

I wish she could talk with me. Not just for her sake, but for mine. Here I am with someone who is on the very same level as I am, and she cannot talk. Did that sound selfish? Probably, and I apologize for it. She is obviously tougher than I am. How else has she survived this long?

For now, I must hide you away. Tomorrow, I will write more.

Later—

I just woke up a minute ago, and I felt the need to write this down, though I can barely see by the light of the moon coming through the hole in the canvas. I peeked outside and saw that the festivities were over, that my captors were passed out from the whisky around a guttering campfire. There is very little warmth for those of us in the wagon.

I do not know what brought me back to the waking world, but when I looked over to my side, where I had helped Gracie bed down, I saw that my companion was wide awake and staring upwards. The blank look of frozen glee on her face startled me, and I felt a chill run through my blood.

It took me a moment to realize that she actually was asleep, that this was how she slept. Her breathing registered too evenly and relaxed for her to be awake.

How could someone sleep in such a fashion? And what did such a person see in her dreams? This thought is too morbid for me to consider.

I should get more sleep.

-

DAY TWO OF CAPTIVITY

Although I had only two days by which to consider, I am beginning to think that the Comancheros are late risers. Despite the horrors I have been through, I still woke up with the sun, just as I had with Iron Trail.

I exited the wagon with the idea of getting food and water for breakfast, but when I cast my gaze about the sleeping masses of Comancheros, I wondered if perhaps I could escape. Would anyone notice for several hours? I did not believe so.

I could not leave Gracie, though. And I had no idea where the nearest town was. For all I knew, there could be miles and miles of wilderness around me. These were hard men well versed in the art of survival. I did not think I would be able to evade them.

No, for now I was stuck.

I headed for the fire with the intention of stoking it. There were some eggs I planned on cooking. However, when I knelt down I saw the silhouette of two men a slight distance from camp. They were Comancheros, and they stood guard. Perhaps escape would be more difficult than I thought.

Since no one stopped me, I began preparing my food. While the eggs cooked, I splashed some water about my face and arms. It did not do much to refresh me, but it was something. Out in the West, you have to take what you can get, when you can get it.

The aroma of cooking food caused some of the men to stir, but no one woke up. I quickly ate what I had prepared, and I then made another batch and brought it back to Gracie.

Unlike those around us, she had awakened and had pulled herself up into a sitting position. She was still a blank slate, staring into nothingness, but her hands twitched and fiddled with the folds of her blanket.

"Can you eat?" I asked.

I did not expect an answer, and she did not give one.

I sat down next to her and fed her. She responded as a child would, and over the course of the next half-hour, I put some eggs and sausage into her. Chewing did not trouble her, but she got a bit sloppy around her mouth. I had to constantly wipe at her lips and chin so as not to make too much of a mess.

When she finished, I took the dishes outside and cleaned them. I then made it my business to start tidying up the campsite. Iron Trail never left a mess, had thought it uncivilized. These Comancheros were the biggest slobs I had ever met. Bottles and scraps littered the ground everywhere.

It took me about an hour to pick it all up, and I had no idea what to do with the trash. I left it in a pile for the time being.

By then, some of my captors had woken up. Most were groaning, rubbing at their temples. Others rubbed at their backs while they had their morning pisses.

Ortega yawned as he stumbled toward me. "What's this?" He pointed to the pile of garbage.

I remained silent because I did not know how to answer such an obvious question without sounding rude.

"Did you do this?" he asked.

I nodded.

He kicked the pile and sent the garbage flying. It scattered about the camp, all my work for naught.

"Do something useful, cunt-whore," he said. "Make me breakfast."

I looked at the trash twinkling under the morning sun, and I could feel my mouth tighten. The urge to clean it up again beamed from my heart, but I knew it would only be a waste of time.

I cooked breakfast for the entire group of Comancheros, but I made sure Ortega ate first. I did not wait to hear his opinion of my culinary abilities, but he did not complain.

Soon, everyone had awoken and were eating what I had prepared. Even Moreno, who looked like he had imbibed too much the previous night, ate hardily. Molina sat in his customary place, but instead of writing or reading, he bent his efforts toward consuming some eggs and bacon.

At the end of the meal, I received word that we were moving on, and Ortega warned me to leave the garbage where it was.

I tried to appeal to his paranoid side: "What if people are trying to track us? They will be able to find you by your leavings."

He grunted a laugh. "I like it when people track me. They are never any good, so it usually ends with me cutting their eyelids off."

Despite his carefree attitude toward garbage, he told me to clean up the dishes. When I finished, and they were all packed away where they belonged, I went to this wagon, where I write this entry now. The road is bumpy, so I hope you will forgive the scratchy handwriting. In school, the teachers complimented me often on my penmanship, and I hate to see it ruined by the hills and rocks of the West.

Gracie sits beside me, but she continues to stare out at nothing. Her ubiquitous grin is still plastered to her face. I wonder if there is anything inside of her. Is she just a human being who has forgotten to let her physical body die? Because I doubt that she has a mind anymore, and whatever soul she has left is a tattered ruin.

-

DAY FIVE OF CAPTIVITY

I have not been writing in this journal for a few days, and I am sad to say that the reason is simple: nothing of note has happened. As hard as it is to say, I think I have become accustomed to being abused. Perhaps I thought too much of it as a trip to the doctor's office, like I said before. But at the same time, Ortega has not been using me as often as he did those first two days. Why? Maybe he is just getting used to me, as I have gotten used to his ways. Maybe my flesh is less interesting. Maybe my novelty has worn off. He still keeps his fellow Comancheros away from me, and except for that one time with Moreno, they have obeyed him.

I find that I spend most of my day obeying Ortega's orders and finding something to do in between these commands. Occasionally, the idea to write about anything, or to perhaps make something up, flits about my mind. But it seems like too much trouble. Instead, I find a book to read in the wagon.

Unfortunately, half of them are written in Spanish. I have been picking up some of the language from those around me, but not enough to attempt to read one of their books. There are three Bibles back here, as well, but I have read that particular tome several times Back-East.

Another is *Typee* by Herman Melville. It was a good read, and I got through it in one day. I am currently reading a strange little comedy called *Frankenstein*. At least, I think it is a comedy. It is written by a woman, so it must not have been intended to be very dark.

Sadly, there are only three other books in English here, and when I am finished, I will have to start reading them again. One is a copy of William Shakespeare's *Titus Andronicus*, another is a collection of poems by Edgar Allan Poe, and the third is Cooper's *The Last of the Mohicans*.

Perhaps in the future, I will write about these books in this journal, if only to have something to write about.

-

DAY SEVEN OF CAPTIVITY

When I returned to the wagon after breakfast with some food for Gracie, I felt a wrongness in the air. I tried to place my finger on it when I realized that a few things had been moved, most notably the rags under which the books were kept.

I placed the tin dish down next to Gracie and pulled the rags away, revealing the books . . . and one of them was gone.

The one in which I had hidden this journal.

My throat dried up, and I cursed myself for being so stupid. Had I really thought my actions to be clever? Was Ortega this minute reading my innermost thoughts and laughing, perhaps reading them to his fellow Comancheros, translating the passages they wouldn't understand?

I wanted to cry, and my heart yearned to squirm out of my chest, but what could I do? Drive myself crazy? Or just try to keep it together?

I did what I always do: I survived. Calmly, I sat next to Gracie and began to fork food into her mouth. As always, she responded slowly, but surely. She did not gurgle as much when I held a cup of water to her lips, and the mess was not quite so bad as usual, almost as if she were trying to console me.

My blood did not stop racing. With each passing moment, I expected Ortega to burst into the wagon and rub my words in my face. Surely he would not be able to let some of the hateful things I have written about him pass.

Then, after the meal, as Gracie drank the last of the water, washing down the food, the flaps of the wagon practically ripped away, and I jerked. The cup fell from my hand and clattered on the floor. Water splashed Gracie as I braced myself for whatever punishment Ortega had in mind.

When I looked up, I saw not Ortega but Molina. He climbed into the wagon, and in one hand, he held the book which usually concealed this journal.

He glanced behind him. "You need to find a better place for this." He slid the pages out of the book and handed them to me. "There are others who are capable of reading around here, and I don't think it would be good if they found this."

I took the journal but remained silent. Perhaps he heard my unspoken thought, for he continued, "I didn't mean to read it, but curiosity got the better of me."

"I'm not angry," I said.

"Are you scared?"

At first, I didn't want to answer this question, but I gave in and nodded, unable to look him in the eyes.

"Good. If Ortega found this—and he *can* read—he would make things a lot worse for you. And I have something else to tell you."

This time, he was the one who hesitated. "I'm not a hero. Just because I'm nicer than the rest of these guys doesn't mean I'm going to rescue you. I am with them for a reason. Good guys aren't cut out to be Comancheros."

I bit my lip and nodded again. "What's your reason?"

"Huh?"

"Your reason. For being with them." I cocked my head toward the flap of the wagon.

He cleared his throat. "It's pretty lucrative work. I don't agree with everything they do. I certainly don't like trading in human flesh. But it's a living."

"Oh." I let my response hang in the air. "I see."

I could see him chewing the inside of his mouth, and his justification came almost scripted: "I'm not here to make friends with you. I want you to be comfortable until Ortega sells you. And if I can keep you safe from idiots like Moreno, I will."

"Thank you," I said.

His mouth worked, as if he wanted to say more, but he did not. Then, he turned to leave. As he pushed the canvas flap aside, he found himself face to face with Ortega.

"Good morning, Eddie," Ortega said. He wore a smile on his face so wide I could see his back teeth. "What are you doing in the wagon with my beloved?"

"I . . ." Molina trailed off.

My captor distracted, I took the opportunity to hide this journal under some rags.

Ortega started to sniff the air like a dog. "I don't smell . . . *anything* . . . on you, but that doesn't mean you weren't—"

"He came for a book," I said.

Molina caught on quickly and held the book up.

Ortega nodded, his smile now faded to a ghost of a grin. "That's good. You have to keep the ol' gray matter exercised, right? I recommend that you refrain from going into this wagon unsupervised, though."

Molina nodded. "I wasn't thinking."

"Good. I don't like it when my men start thinking. Thinking leads to ideas. Now get the fuck out of here."

Molina did not argue; he hopped down from the wagon and made his way toward the fire.

Ortega turned his attention to me, and the sun-bright smile returned. "I just wanted to let you know that I sent my men out to raid a nearby farm."

I tried to look unconcerned and focused my attention on wiping Gracie's water-splattered face. "What does this have to do with me?"

"Everything. You might have some new roommates by the end of today, so make some space in here, would you?"

Then, without waiting for an answer, he let the flap fall into place as he walked away.

I continued wiping at Gracie's face and hands. There were a few spots on her shirt, but those would dry in no time. Only when I finished did I pick up this journal to write today's entry. Soon, I will have to find a better hiding place for you. Until then, I will put you in a different book and hope that no one finds you again.

-

DAY EIGHT OF CAPTIVITY

Ortega's men did not come back last night, but in the morning hours, as I prepared breakfast, I heard a loud rumble of horses as the Comancheros charged into camp. A wagon rode with them but not one of theirs. I assumed they had gotten it from the farm they had raided, and it doubtless contained other spoils of war, perhaps even human beings.

Moreno rode at the front, and he wore a victorious grin. His teeth were straight, but there were wide spaces between them. Even from a distance, I could see bits of meat stuck in them.

He dismounted and strode over to Ortega, who waited patiently. The Comanchero spoke in Spanish to his leader, and he gestured with his hands a lot. Shortly after his speech, the two of them went to the wagon and peered inside. Moreno seemed to be pointing out their prizes.

Hernandez reached into the wagon and yanked out a young blonde girl, no more than ten years old. Tears cut streaks through her dust-caked face, but her eyes were wide and staring. I could only assume that she had witnessed the death of everyone in her family.

Hernandez groped her in a very unseemly fashion, and Ortega slapped the offending hand away. He said something harsh and then pointed to me. Hernandez scowled and led the girl over to where I stood.

The beastly Comanchero knew no English, but the language barrier between us did not stifle his intention. He grabbed my hand and then

169

placed the little girl's hand within mine. He tightened his grip, nodded and moved away.

I got a whiff of smoke on her. Not the noxious weed these Comancheros tended to smoke, but it smelled as if she had been in a fire. Some soot soiled the bottom of her white sleeping gown, and I figured she must have hidden in a fireplace to escape the flames that had undoubtedly taken her home (and possibly her family).

"What is your name?" I asked her.

She heard me, but all she could do was flick her eyes in my direction. It seemed like she wanted to cry but had no more tears.

"Never mind," I said. "Come with me."

I led her away from the crowd to our wagon. I helped her inside. "Wait for me. I'll be back."

She swallowed hard enough for me to see her throat work. I looked at Gracie and decided the two would be all right for now.

I took our bucket and went in search of the chuck wagon, where they kept the water barrel. Here, I dipped the bucket in. A lot of it slopped back into the barrel, but three-quarters remained. I then brought it back to the wagon and removed the girl's clothes.

After I had bathed her, I wrapped a blanket around her body, and I put her gown in the bucket. When I finished washing it, I went outside and untied one of the strings that hung from the canvas of the wagon. I tied the other end to a nearby tree and hung the wet gown on my makeshift clothesline.

When I went back into the wagon, I saw that the girl had curled up in Gracie's lap. Gracie's arm had been wrapped around her, and when I saw the woman's face, I wondered if maybe she had done it without the girl's help. Gracie looked down at the girl, not with a blank stare, but with the gaze of a mother. The seemingly endless smile vanished, and it looked like she was kissing the girl's crown.

For the first time, I thought Gracie might be returning to the real world. I decided they might need some time alone, so I closed the tent flap and looked for food for the both of them.

As soon as I had gotten them something to eat, I started writing in this journal. They are still holding each other right now, and I think I saw Gracie move to pet the girl's hair.

A lot seems hopeless right now, but it is a thing like this that makes me think there is some chance of us making it out of this mess.

Later—

I was reading a book when the little girl spoke to me. At first, I thought it to be just the whisper of the wind through the covered wagon, but I then discerned clear words: "Thank you, ma'am."

I looked up from Mary Shelley's tome to see the little girl looking at me. At the time, the only thing I could think of to say was, "You're welcome."

"Amy," she said.

"Pardon me?"

"You asked me earlier. My name is Amy. Amy Summers."

"Pleased to meet you," I said, and I told her my name.

"Meetcha', Miz Reeves."

I had to restrain myself from laughing. No one ever called me that. "Please, under the circumstances, I would appreciate it if you would call me Tessa."

"Okay, Miz Tessa."

I wanted to correct her, but I thought perhaps this admonishment might be too much.

"Where are we?" she asked.

I explained our situation, and she seemed to take it well. Maybe she did not understand what I told her, considering her youth, but she managed to keep her wits about her.

When I finished describing everything, she told me her story. The Comancheros had raided their farm, and while her parents and the farmhands prepared for battle, her mother put both her and her baby brother in the fireplace because the Comancheros had set their house on fire. It was the only place they would be safe, just so long as they kept their faces down.

Amy had done her best, but her baby brother choked on the fumes and died by the time the Comancheros had found her in the ruins. From her description, Hernandez had wrestled the baby out of her grip and, upon discovering it to be dead, tossed it aside like an empty grain sack.

The Comancheros had then loaded up everything of value, including her, and here they were.

I told her my own story (leaving out some of the more inappropriate parts, of course), and when she asked about Gracie, I said I did not know where she had come from, that she had been here before I was. I looked at Gracie, who no longer stared out into nothingness. She stared at Amy, yet she still remained in her coma-like state.

I thought about the girl who had been sold the day I arrived here, and she looked more than a little like Amy. Was it possible that the girl had been Gracie's daughter, and that Amy reminded her of her own flesh and blood?

I did not have much time to ponder this. The wagon stopped, and Ortega demanded that I join him for luncheon.

When I returned, Gracie and Amy had struck their former pose, and neither one of them were talking to me. Rather than return to Shelley's novel, I quickly wrote down everything that has just transpired, just in case I do not get the chance to do so again.

Later—

It is late, and everyone is asleep or drunk. I write this by the light of the moon.

I have just returned from Ortega's pleasure, and I arrived at the wagon just as Hernandez had snuck in. I rushed to the back flap and flung it open to see him crouching over Amy, trying to yank her from Gracie's grasp. It was like tug o' war, and Gracie's face was scrunched up from the effort. A terrible moaning sound came from her throat as she tried to wrestle the girl away from the Comanchero.

Amy had reverted to the shocked state in which I had met her, and she resisted neither party as they pulled at her. Hernandez muttered Spanish curses under his breath as he pulled. I could smell the whisky on his breath even from as far away as I stood.

I wanted to shout for help, but who would come? I do not think even Molina would have assisted me, as I had last seen him passed out by the fire, a bottle of mescal in his hand.

I could do only one thing: I jumped up into the wagon, grabbed Hernandez by the bandana around his neck, and yanked backwards with all my might and weight. The latter was not much, but the former was significant. Both of us tumbled back and out of the wagon.

We were both dazed for a moment, and our heads cleared up at the same time. He snarled something at me. I think he called me a whore in Spanish, but I am not sure. Regardless, he looked like he wanted to lunge at me.

I found a stray whisky bottle nearby. Feeling lucky that these men were such slobs, I grabbed it by the neck as he shot towards me. With the most speed as I could muster, I brought the bottle upside his head, where it shattered and carved several red lines down his face.

I expected him to scream, but I had knocked him out before the pain had a chance to register. He merely thumped to the ground and bled.

No one seemed to notice this scuffle, so I decided to leave him in the dust. Either he would die, or he would feel like trash the next day. One way or the other, I did not care.

Once again, Amy had found Gracie's lap, and they were hugging each other. I chose not to intrude, but went directly for these pages.

Midway through this entry, Amy turned to me and asked, "Whatcher writin'?"

My instinct was to hide this journal, but why hide such a thing from this little girl? "It's just an account," I said.

"Of what?"

"Things that have happened to me since I was kidnapped by Ortega and his men," I said.

"Would you read it to me?" she asked.

I thought about the inappropriate parts I had left out when I told her my story, and I thought reading my account to her would be a bad idea. "It would be best if I didn't. It's . . . personal."

"Oh. Sure." And she turned her face back into Gracie's bosom.

I regretted my choice of words, but what else would I say to her?

-

DAY NINE OF CAPTIVITY

As usual, I woke up first in the morning. When I looked over to Amy and Gracie, I saw that they had passed out in each other's arms, and both were sleeping soundly.

I stepped down from the wagon to see Hernandez where I had left him. Sadly, he still breathed. His wounds had scabbed over, and he snored into the dirt. The thought occurred to me that I could strangle him to death, and no one would be the wiser. He would not be the first man I had killed out in this wasteland.

Instead, I stepped over him and started preparing breakfast. While I did this, I wondered if Hernandez would remember the events of last night. I hoped he did, and I hoped that he wanted to take it up with me. Ortega, of course, would not allow this, and if things escalated far enough, he would be forced to kill Hernandez.

But what if the Comanchero had been too drunk last night to have much of a recollection? It would save a lot of trouble if this were true.

As always, I ate the first batch of food. If anyone were to ask why I did this, my answer would be simple: if I went hungry, how would I serve the others? As a doctor must watch after his own health first (for the good of his community), so must a cook watch after her own stomach.

Next, I prepared food for Amy and Gracie. When I brought it to them, I saw the little girl had awoken.

"Good morning," I said. "I brought you some breakfast."

She looked at the tin plate I held out to her and wrinkled her nose. "I don't like eggs. Momma always let me have flapjacks instead."

I gritted my teeth and tried to remind myself of her youth. She did not know any better. "Your mother isn't here," I said, "and you're in a bad situation. If you're going to keep your strength up, you have to eat what you can get, and right now, that's eggs."

Her lower lip pooched out, and I knew she wanted to cry.

I sighed. "We don't have flapjacks out here. All we have is eggs and bacon and toast. Maybe some sausages."

She sniffled. "What about milk?"

"I'm sorry, Amy. All we have is water."

She took the plate from me and turned around so she could eat and cry and not be seen by me.

At least she ate. I turned my attention to Gracie, who stared at Amy's back.

The feeding did not go well. I had to move Gracie's chin so she could chew. She was too preoccupied with the little girl who no doubt reminded her of her daughter.

About halfway through, Amy said, "Let me feed her."

She had finished her own meal and faced me with red, puffy eyes. Both hands went out, one for the plate and the other for the fork.

"Are you sure you can do this?" I asked her.

"Mm-hm. I used to do it for my little brother all the time."

I nodded and handed everything over to her. "Thank you, Amy."

She said nothing as she scootched over to Gracie and began to feed her. Gracie did not need help chewing this time.

Later—

We had not even reached our first rest stop for the day when Desmond and Norbert (both of whom I had determined were the scouts of this bunch) returned from the rear. They rode up to Ortega. Desmond said, "We got trouble."

Ortega laughed. "We sure do. Your breath stinks like shit. Have you been eating cowflops again?"

The Comanchero did not so much as flinch. "We're being followed. Norbert says it's a posse, probably trying to catch us for that barn-burner we pulled back there."

"So what?" Ortega said.

"There must be fifty of 'em," Desmond said.

Ortega shook his head. "Did your momma have any children who lived? That shit-splat of a town could not have raised fifty men, even if they had the help of an army."

"Well, maybe not fifty," Desmond said, "but there's plenty of men, and they're coming after us."

"So, they're coming. So what?"

"Shouldn't we leave a trap for them?" Norbert asked. "Enough men to kill 'em all?"

"Why bother? Let them come. We'll be ready for them."

The brothers exchanged a glance. The former said, "I think Norbert has an excellent idea, sir. If we leave a few gunmen behind, maybe stick 'em up in trees or somethin, they'll have a good chance of getten rid of them."

"I'm a good thot," Norbert said.

"Forget it," Ortega said. "Just keep riding drag, and if they get close enough, ride up and let me know."

The brothers looked at each other again and shrugged in unison. "You're the boss," Desmond said. The two rode back the way they had come.

This would have been the end of this entry, but just as I was finishing up, I heard a knock at the back of the wagon. We were riding, so I could not imagine what had caused it. When it came again, I got the distinct impression that someone wanted to come in.

I pushed open the flap and saw Hernandez, riding just close enough to the wagon so he could knock on the gate.

"What do you want?" I asked. He spoke no English, so I was fairly certain he could not understand me.

He said a few things in Spanish, and none of them could be repeated in polite company, or so I believe. At the conclusion of his tirade, he produced his blade and mimed drawing it across his throat.

I did not need to know Spanish to understand him. His message imparted, he rode away, and I pondered the wisdom of not having killed him when I'd had the chance.

-

DAY ELEVEN OF CAPTIVITY

It has been a couple of days since Desmond and Norbert noticed the posse following us, but the lawmen still did not reveal themselves. Occasionally, the brothers caught up to us to give Ortega a report, and I've been able to gather this much:

First, that the posse consists of anywhere between fifteen and eighteen men. Secondly, that three of them are law officers. The leader is a sheriff, and he is accompanied by two of his deputies. Most are armed with rifles and handguns, but there are a few who only have knives and pitchforks.

"Motht importantly," Norbert said, "they got thome whithky. Lotth, acthually."

"They'll run out of steam," Ortega said. "All posses do. They're all about justice until they start missing their families, a roof over their heads and a mattress under them at night. Besides, we're almost to

178

Mexico. If we keep outdistancing them, we'll be there by the end of the week."

Speaking of which, I have to note that the climate has been getting drier, hotter, and dustier. We are no longer heading east, as I had been with Iron Trail. South is our new route. I remember Ortega telling me that he would sell me to some bartender in Mexico, and I actually looked forward to it. How could it be any worse than living this lifestyle under the direction of the Comancheros?

-

DAY TWELVE OF CAPTIVITY

Today, only Desmond rode into camp for the update on the posse. Secretly, I hoped that his filthy brother had been gunned down by the law, but no such luck. Norbert had stayed behind to keep an eye on things while his articulate brother came back to give a report.

And Desmond had something interesting to say: "The sheriff is none other than Bixby Grant," he told his leader.

Ortega massaged the hair on his chin. "You don't say."

"Oh, I say, all right," Desmond said.

Stories of Sheriff Grant's exploits had made it all the way to New York, and I remember reading about him in the paper. Now that I think on it, I recall Sam Pepper reading a dime novel about the man and chuckling over the contents. To hear him tell it, Grant had killed just about every outlaw in the West.

I'd never heard of anything sillier. The person who followed us now was only a man, and anything said of him had to be more legend than truth. But still, I felt my heart flutter to have someone so famous "on our trail," as they say in the dime novels.

"And?" Ortega asked.

"And what?" Desmond asked.

"Bixby Grant is nothing but a man," Ortega said. "He'll die like any other of his kind."

"You ain't listenin', boss. Bixby Grant always gets his man."

Ortega laughed. "No one's perfect."

Desmond looked like he wanted to say more, but he closed his mouth.

"Forget these stupid tall tales," Ortega said. "The only reason that bastard's still alive is because people like you build him up and let it effect you when you're aiming for his heart. Return to your brother and come back when you have something interesting to tell me."

The bemused smile never left his face as he watched Desmond turn his horse around and ride out into the wilderness, leaving nothing in his wake but a plume of dust and a few horse-apples.

I never liked it when Ortega displayed some show of intelligence. I find it harder to plot against him this way. I hoped Sheriff Grant would catch up to us so I would not have to outsmart the leader of the Comancheros.

-

DAY FIFTEEN OF CAPTIVITY

Bixby Grant came upon us today, and I am very exhausted from the events that resulted from his attack. I can barely hold this pencil in my hand, but I know I must write this as soon as I can, or I might forget what happened.

The day had been quite uneventful, and we had stopped to camp for the night. We just started setting everything up, and I had begun preparing the fire, when Desmond and Norbert thundered into our midst, their horses covered in sweat and breathing heavily.

The brothers jumped down from their mounts and rushed over to Ortega, who practiced throwing cards into a nearby hat. Most of the time, he missed.

"Sir," Desmond said, "they're coming up on us, and they're coming fast."

"How long do we have?" Ortega asked. He flipped a card out, and it landed on the brim. Close, but not inside.

"Maybe half an hour, at most," Desmond said.

"Plenty of time." The next card landed on the previous one and almost slid into the hat.

"They mutht've theen our camp from up there," Norbert said. He pointed up at a cliff. It was about two miles away.

Ortega's next card struck its target. Of the thirty or so he'd thrown, it was only the second to get inside the hat.

"So, what are we going to do about it, boss?" Desmond asked.

"Set up camp and wait for them," Ortega said. He threw the remainder of the deck at the hat, and one of them managed to get in. Then, he stood and brushed his pants off. "Lock and load, boys!" he called. "We're gonna' have company!"

I looked up from the wood I had stacked. "What should I do?"

"Well, I hate to see my dinner delayed, but so be it. Get in the wagon with the other bitches."

I nodded, not wanting to betray my dislike of the word he had used. Without cleaning up, I went to the wagon and joined the girls. I appraised them of our situation.

"Are we going to be saved?" Amy asked.

"I hope so, darling," I said. "If anyone can do it, I'm sure it's Sheriff Grant."

"Sheriff Grant?!" Amy practically screamed these words. I supposed she had probably heard about his larger than life adventures.

"That's right. Now, keep your head down, all right? There will be a lot of gunfire, and we don't want you catching any of it."

Amy obediently pressed herself down on the floor of the wagon. I situated Gracie the same way before I took up a similar position. I kept myself by the back opening of the wagon so I could see the action. All I had to do was poke my head up, and I would be able to view everything.

As it turned out, Grant and his posse had a bit more of a head-start than Desmond had calculated. Within fifteen minutes, they had ridden in and were driven back by the first volley of gunfire. The Comancheros were not stingy with their ammunition, and by the time the lawmen had found cover, half of their number was bleeding into the dust.

One of the corpses wore a tin star. I hoped it did not belong to the good sheriff.

Moments later, I was relieved to hear a voice call out, "Put down your weapons! This is Sheriff Bixby Grant, and I'm here to arrest you all!"

The Comancheros laughed.

"You're surrounded!" the sheriff shouted.

"Horseshit!" Ortega yelled. "There isn't enough of you to surround a thimble!"

The gunfire started again, and this time, the sheriff's men shot back. The bullets came nowhere near where we sat hidden in the wagon, so I could see clearly that none of the posse were hit. Some Comancheros were, however.

We seemed to be at a bit of a stand-off. Every once in a while, someone would fire off their weapons, but after that, very few people were wounded or killed for a while.

Soon, it became apparent that Sheriff Grant had ordered men to discharge their rifles at regular intervals to keep the Comancheros occupied. They were trying to outflank us, and it might have worked if the deputy in charge of this maneuver had not tripped over his own feet. He let out a yelp as he rolled down the hill into camp, drawing the attention of just about everyone.

The deputy came to a stop against the wheel of the wagon we were in. I felt my heart freeze as I realized that we were about to be caught in a crossfire and were in all likelihood in the angel of death's presence.

I ducked down, and the world beyond the canvas exploded. Some bullets thumped into the wooden frame of the wagon, but only one passed through. I found it later, lodged into one of the Spanish books.

When I eventually found the courage, I looked up to see that the canvas itself had been Swiss-cheesed, but for the time being, I found the grainy swirls in the wooden floor much more interesting.

In the background, I could hear Amy wailing, and when I hazarded a peek, I saw that Gracie had moved so that her body could shield the little girl.

Later, I heard that when the flanking team had been discovered and fired upon, Sheriff Grant's team decided to descend on the camp, guns blazing. A considerable amount of people died on both sides of the conflagration, but Grant's side suffered more.

That is when the battle became a chaotic jumble. With the wagon no longer caught in a crossfire, I heard several bullets whiz nearby, some through the canvas above our heads.

When the battle burned most furiously, I saw the flap of the wagon whisked aside. I looked up, hoping to see one of Grant's posse.

No, it was Hernandez with his sloppy grin and wild eyes. He aimed his gun at me and gibbered something in the half-Spanish, half-Comanche language the Comancheros used. Then, he prodded me with the barrel of his weapon until I backed away enough so he could get in.

A bullet passed through his hat and out the top of the covered wagon. I do not think he noticed. He was too busy unbuttoning his pants with his free hand.

I thought this to be the wrong time for carnal thoughts, but then I changed my mind. For him, it was the perfect time. When he finished, all he had to do was kill me and claim that I had caught a stray bullet.

By the time he had his penis out, I pondered the possibility of kicking him in his dangly bit. Would he be able to shoot me before I managed to lash out in such a fashion? What if I missed? What if I did not hit him hard enough?

No, it was best to acquiesce. I went down on my back and started removing my pants. As I did this, I thought that since I was on the bottom and he was on top, perhaps astray bullet would find his head. A bit much to hope for, but—

Someone almost immediately granted my wish. I felt a splash of blood, and he stiffened between my legs. His brains sprayed the canvas, and his bowels released themselves onto the wagon's floor.

Then, his corpse fell on me, and I pushed it away. His dead weight pinned me down, but I still managed to roll out from under him.

Eduardo Molina stood at the back of the wagon, a smoking revolver in his hand.

"Thank you," I said.

He shook his head and let the flap fall back into place. Through the holes in the canvas, I watched as he jumped back into the fray.

Another bullet passed through the wagon, and I ducked down. From behind me, I heard Amy say, "It stinks in here."

Hernandez's final present to me. I turned my face away from the final lump of fecal matter he would ever pass, but it did nothing to relieve me of the stench.

Soon, the gunfire reduced itself to a shot every half-minute or so, and then to nothing at all. From the sound of the voices (and the language they spoke), I assumed Sheriff Grant's team had not won.

I turned to Amy and Gracie and looked them both over for wounds. Satisfied that they were all right, I spoke with Amy about what had happened with Hernandez.

"He came in here for shelter, but a stray bullet got him, all right?" I asked.

Amy nodded. "Why are we lying?"

"Because I don't want Eduardo to get into trouble," I said. "If we told the truth, Hector Ortega would kill him."

"All right," Amy said. When we gave Ortega our account of the battle, she stuck to her guns.

As soon as I knew that Amy was going to be fine, I emerged from the wagon to see how things stood. There were bodies everywhere. Most were strangers I had never seen before, but there were quite a few who were Comancheros. By my count, we were down to perhaps eleven men.

One of these eleven had been wounded. Desmond sat with his back to a tree while his brother dug around inside his shoulder, looking for a bullet. The more vociferous of the two now screamed his eloquence to the sky, begging for the pain to stop. He guzzled the contents of a closely-clutched bottle of whisky, but it did not seem to be doing the trick.

Ortega had returned to his cards and hat. "There you are, Tessa. Be a good girl and make me some dinner."

That was all he said to me. Later, he would interrogate me because Moreno had found Hernandez's body by then, but for the moment, all he wanted me to do was fill his belly. Too bad I had to do it with food rather than lead.

So now, here I am at the end of the evening, writing in this journal. After dinner, I had scrubbed the blood and shit out of the wagon while the surviving Comancheros drank and whooped and celebrated another day of life.

Just before I went out to pleasure Ortega, I saw Moreno hacking away at something with a machete. I stopped long enough to see his target: a body. A body with a badge pinned to it.

"Is that Bixby Grant?" I asked.

"You bet," Moreno said. With one great, final swing, he managed to separate the head from the rest. Blood poured, but did not pump, from the neck wound.

I watched as Moreno took the head and placed it on a spike, as per Ortega's instructions.

He stepped back to admire his handiwork. "So much for the legend, eh?"

I turned away and approached Ortega. Tonight, he was too tired. He only wanted me to suck his dick. I considered biting down hard, but we were all a bit too exhausted. Perhaps another night, I thought.

Amy does not want to go to sleep tonight because she is afraid of Hernandez's ghost. She sits curled up in Gracie's lap, and Gracie slowly pets the little girl's hair. This is the liveliest I have ever seen her.

Goodnight.

-

DAY SIXTEEN OF CAPTIVITY

I was too tired to write about this last night, but now that I am fresh from sleep, before I even venture out to prepare breakfast, I am ready.

I had awoken in the middle of the night with a full bladder, and I had stepped outside to satisfy nature's call when I noticed that Sheriff Grant's party had not all been wiped out. Apparently, the legendary lawman had brought a photographer with him, probably to take pictures of Ortega's dead body.

The photographer, a short, skinny man with a terrible comb-over, was being put to a new use. While the Brothers Hertell held guns on him, he set up his equipment. The apparent target of this photography session was Bixby Grant's head on a spike.

I was wrong, in part. Certainly, Grant's head was to be in the picture, but it was not the focus. A Comanchero, Villarreal, I believe his name is, removed his pants and placed his penis in the sheriff's open mouth.

Everyone laughed except for the photographer. He grimaced and wiped sweat away from his gaunt forehead. The display sickened me, but Villarreal waved his hand in a "get on with it" fashion.

"What? You tired of sticken yer dick in a dead man's mouth?" Desmond asked.

His brother laughed. "That mutht be hard work, Veeth."

Villarreal spat a stream of tobacco juice. "It's just uncomfortable, that's all."

Desmond dug his revolver into the photographer's back. "Hurry it up, some. My friend's chafing."

Norbert guffawed, and the photographer poked his head under the curtain of his device. He adjusted the camera a little bit, and then held up what looked like a very thin tray on a stick.

I turned away, not wanting to see the rest of this display.

Later—

We moved on shortly after breakfast. We did not bury the dead, not even the fallen Comancheros. The vultures had already flown down and were having a breakfast of their own by the time we rode out of camp.

The last thing I saw of the place was a vulture that had perched on top of Grant's head. It pecked his eyes out. At the bottom of the spike rested the photographer's body. His usefulness had run out as soon as he had developed the picture of Villarreal abusing the decapitated head. According to the Comancheros, it was a wonderful picture. They thought about sending it to the papers Back-East, mostly because they wanted it to be used on the cover of a dime novel, but Villarreal wanted to keep it for his personal collection.

Regardless, with the photographer superfluous around here, the Hertells had a bit of fun seeing how much of the camera's tripod they could fit into his asshole. As it turned out, quite a bit of it went in before the photographer died from shock.

But that is not what I really want to talk about now. For the first time since I met her, I noticed that Gracie looked a bit fuller. I did not think she could possibly put weight on, considering how little she ate. But there is a slight bump in her belly, and I cannot help but wonder if perhaps she is pregnant.

She has not bled since I met her, but I have not known her for a full month yet. I asked Molina if he knew when the last time she had bled was, but he shrugged and said the only way to find out is to ask around, to ask some of the men who had raped her, one of whom might be the father. I did not want him to do this, as it would probably not be very good for Gracie if she were indeed pregnant, and I did not want to raise any alarm among the men.

It is something I must keep an eye on.

-

DAY EIGHTEEN OF CAPTIVITY

Moments ago, Ortega burst into this wagon as I read. He practically ripped the canvas away and launched himself up into the back with me. Fury glared in his eyes as he advanced upon me, lips drawn back in a grimace, saliva-slicked teeth shining in the sunbeams thrown from the bullet holes.

Before I had the chance to say anything, he grabbed me by the front of my shirt and pulled me to him. "What the fuck have you been feeding Gracie?"

189

My roommate had been taken away about a half an hour before by the Hertell brothers, presumably for their pleasure. I wondered what events had transpired between then and now, with Ortega snarling like a beast into my face. Of course, I knew what he meant, but I could not understand how he had found out.

"I don't know what you're talking about," I said with just enough whine in my voice for him to believe me.

He threw me down and shook his head. "Desmond told me that when he was fucking her, he noticed she was starting to get a belly. We don't allow you to give her enough food for that. You have to be feeding her something on the side. Tell me. Now."

I could not believe my fortune. I nearly laughed at his blindness. Instead, I stammered, hoping he would take me for a fool. "W-w-why? W-w-what's wrong with . . .a-a-a-a . . . belly?"

He backhanded me. My neck cracked a little as my head whipped to the side. I could still feel the shape of his hand on my cheek, but it had not hurt me too much.

"You stupid cunt-whore," he said. "I can't sell a fat woman. No one wants a fat woman. What have you been feeding her?"

"I took a little extra from the chuck wagon," I said. "I didn't think anyone would miss it, and she looked too thin."

"Bullshit," Ortega said. "I checked the chuck wagon. Everything is present and acc—"

He broke off, and his eyes widened. I knew my ruse was over. It had been short-lived, too; it had lasted only a few days.

Ortega grabbed me by the shirt again and yanked me up. "You fucking cunt-whore. You're lucky you're good looking. Right now, I want to pound your face to clay, but I can't bring myself to destroy such marketable beauty."

Once again, he threw me down, but this time he left me there. I knew that he would never be able to sell Gracie now, not with her pregnancy so clear. There were no abortionists out here, but they had plenty of alcohol. My mother once called gin the cheapest abortion money could buy, and I know we have a bottle of the stuff. Or would violence be the quicker route to miscarriage?

I did not want to think about what Ortega no doubt considered. Gracie had come so far in the time I had known her, and I did not want to see this progress reversed.

I returned to my book, but I was unable to read more than a sentence.

-

DAY NINETEEN OF CAPTIVITY

Ortega is irritable today. Apparently, we have not been making the progress he hoped for. Mexico is still too far away for his likes, and he is taking his anger out on his men. Whisky has been banned for tonight, which is not sitting well with the Comancheros. If Ortega heard some of the things they said behind his back, I do not think there would be a single man alive in this group by sun-up.

I am surprised to find how much I am looking forward to seeing Mexico. It is not just the knowledge that my acquaintance with Ortega is almost finished, as he intends to sell me there, but also it is because I have never seen it before. I have never been to another country; the closest I had come was hearing Sam Pepper tell me about Paris. Now, here I was, about to see a different land and culture.

191

From what I heard the men talking about, however, it sounds like it might be more of the same ol' same ol', as Felton used to say.

At least I am learning some of the Spanish language. I have managed to pick up a few phrases from just listening to the Mexican Comancheros, and whenever I had a question, Molina helped me out. I would never say I am fluent, but at least I know something, perhaps enough to survive south of the border.

-

DAY TWENTY OF CAPTIVITY

Today is the most sorrowful day I have known since I saw Ortega torture Iron Trail to death, perhaps even more so than the day I learned of Felton's true intentions for me. I do not know how the world possesses so much cruelty, and it is not stingy with the spoon.

We did not leave camp this afternoon. When I asked Ortega about it, he told me it was none of my "cunt-whore" business. I later learned from Molina that we were to meet a customer, and with great reluctance, he told me we were selling Amy today.

"We can't do that," I said. "She's all the world to Gracie. That little girl has been bringing Gracie back from the brink of insanity, and if she's gone, all that work will be for nothing."

Molina shook his head. "Do you think we're running a charity, here? Ortega deals in flesh, ma'am, in case you've forgotten."

Every fiber of my being wanted to shout back, to object, but what good would it do? Wisdom lived in Molina's words, wisdom that I had apparently forgotten, although I am not sure how this came to pass. I have nightly reminders from Ortega himself as he sows his endless seed within me.

"Is there nothing we can do?" I asked. But I knew the answer.

"Do you think Ortega gives two shits about Gracie? Aside from the money she could earn for him?"

I could not look him in the eye.

He did not need to say anything else. He walked away.

The thought of escape stole into my head. Not that it had never visited me before, especially in the night when I cleaned myself of Ortega. But this time, it seemed much more real to me. Would it be so hard to take both Gracie and Amy with me from this godforsaken place? I would have to get them past Ortega's guard, but I thought I had a good chance of helping them survive until we found a town. Iron Trail had taught me well.

But there were so many factors. Would I be able to get a horse? Would I be able to steal food from the chuck wagon? Would I be able to steal *enough* food? And what about water?

And then, Ortega would not take well to us leaving. He would never let us get away. Perhaps upon finding us, he would decide that we were not worth a thing to him, and maybe he would kill us.

Well, he would kill Gracie for sure. Me? He would probably beat me around, to teach me a lesson. Amy? There is always a market for little white girls, I suppose.

There was nothing I could do, so I thought I would try to get Gracie used to the idea of losing Amy. I went to the wagon to do exactly this, and along the way, I noticed Amy playing in the dust with a doll she had made from some kindling and straw. She had no idea that she would be sold like an object today.

I tried to shake this thought as I climbed up into the wagon. Gracie sat in her usual fashion, her legs straight out and her hands laced as one in her lap. Her eyes stared out at nothing at all.

"Gracie," I said. "Can you hear me?"

I received no response.

"I have to talk to you about Amy."

I paused to let this sink in. Nothing, not even a twitch.

"Ortega is going to sell her today. They'll be taking her away from us."

She did not move.

I cursed and threw myself down by the books. Had I really expected some kind of reaction? I thought maybe I should talk with Amy about this, but the image of her playing with her makeshift doll changed my mind. Let her live in ignorance for just awhile longer.

What kind of people were buying her? Were they Indians or Mexicans? Were they buying a slave or an object to show off? Were they, perhaps, going to do to her what Sam Pepper did to me? I had not been that much older than Amy when I met that bastard.

Why think on it? I turned my attention to the books, but I could not read more than a line without being distracted by these horrid thoughts.

Later, I heard a commotion as two riders came into our camp. They were not loud themselves, but the Comancheros let out a cry of celebration when they had arrived. I went out to get a look at our "customers," surprised to find that they were white, one man and one woman. Both were a little bit on the elderly side, perhaps a shade before the sixty-year-mark.

The woman stayed on her horse while the man got down and ambled over to Ortega. Actually, he staggered. When he got close enough, I could see that his left leg was made of wood.

His name, I learned later, was Charles Seguinn, and although I could not hear him talk with Ortega, I gathered that he wanted to buy Amy because their own daughter had died a couple of years ago.

"I think you'll find young Amy to your liking," Ortega said. "Follow me."

"She's got a name already?" Mr. Seguinn asked.

"Well, yes," Ortega said. "But a name ain't nothing permanent, right?"

"I was kind of hoping her name was Julia."

"She goes by whatever you decide to call her," Ortega said.

Back-East, I had heard the same thing said by pimps, and I felt something go sour at the back of my throat.

Mr. Seguinn spent about ten minutes looking Amy over, as if he were considering a horse. He all but looked at her teeth. "How much?"

"This is one of the finest girls I have ever seen," Ortega said. "I do not think I'd be out of line asking for five hundred dollars."

Mrs. Seguinn cleared her throat. When her husband looked at her, she shook her head.

"That's out of the question, Mr. Ortega," Seguinn said. "We're just simple farmers. I'm afraid I can't go any higher than two hundred, and that's stretching the bank."

I felt my stomach churn as I watched them haggle over the price of a little girl. Heat flowed through my entire body, and I thought I would throw up. Something gurgled inside of me, and I turned away as they settled on three-fifty.

Amy remained quiet the whole time. She looked at nothing but the dust at her feet. Not even as Seguinn embraced her did she make a sound; she merely submitted like a ragdoll.

I did not know that Gracie watched from the wagon, but in the next few minutes, this became very much clear to everyone in camp.

Just as Mr. Seguinn took Amy by the hand and started leading her to his wife's horse, and Mrs. Seguinn handed the money over to Moreno, Gracie leaped from the wagon like a woman possessed. I do not think a beast could have been more wild than she. Her cries echoed over the land as she launched herself at Mr. Seguinn, her fingernails aimed at his eyes.

"No!" the old man cried. He released the little girl to put his hands up over his face, and just in time, too. Gracie's hands raked across the veins, opening them up and sending blood down to his wrists.

"You're not taking my daughter!" Gracie screamed. She made this proclamation time and again, and with each syllable, she attacked Mr. Sequinn anew.

Amy stared at the spectacle with no emotion, as if she were a doll herself. Mrs. Seguinn differed not from her perch above us all. Yet even Ortega seemed shocked by this display.

But not for long. As Mr. Seguinn's blood spattered the dust at our feet, Ortega finally broke his paralysis and marched toward the fracas. With very little ceremony, he punched Gracie in the face, breaking her nose with a sickening snap. Blood shot from her distorted nostrils as she dropped to the ground.

I did not know it at the time, but I could feel the pain of a scream in my own throat, tearing at the tender meat behind my tongue. The Comancheros' leader seemed to grow larger in my sight, and it took me a moment to realize that it was because I ran toward him in just as much of a rage as Gracie had. I jumped and landed on Ortega's back, seeking his eyes with my fingers.

"Cunt-whore!" He drove the back of his head into my face, and I fell away.

Gracie stood up again, and this time she went after Ortega. "I won't let you sell her!"

Ortega grappled with the woman, holding both of her wrists as she tried to claw at him. "She's! Not! Your! Daughter!" He roared these words as he fended off her attacks.

I went for his legs, and the both of them toppled to the dust. In that moment, as Gracie scrambled over Ortega's form to straddle him and force her hands down toward him, I noticed he had knocked out her two front teeth. Blood dribbled down from her chin, and she lisped her words as she mumbled obscenities under her breath.

I went to deliver a blow to his groin when I found myself hurled backwards. When I looked up, I noticed Moreno had stopped me, and he closed in on Gracie. Just as I pushed forward to intercept him, I felt arms twist around me, holding me back.

Helpless, I watched as Moreno flung Gracie away. I could do nothing as Ortega, using every curse word he could muster, staggered to his feet and wiped blood from his mouth.

I could never have stopped Ortega as he drew his pistol and leveled it at Gracie's head. "You're the stupidest cunt-whore I have ever laid eyes on."

She snarled her defiance at him.

In answer, he pulled the trigger and sent the back of her skull flying at the infinite sands.

I screamed my throat raw, and Ortega turned his attention on me. "You're lucky you're beautiful," he said. "You're lucky you have a sucking pussy. Or you'd end up like this stupid, pregnant cunt-whore." He spat on Gracie's lifeless body.

Tears burned a trail down my dirty cheeks, and I tried to burn holes into Ortega with my eyes. This had no effect. He strode to me, holstering his gun. "Molina, I think you have your hands on my woman."

Molina, who had restrained me and had probably saved my life, removed his hands. "I apologize, sir. I just didn't want to make matters worse."

"This is the second time I've caught you thus," Ortega said. "Don't make it a third time."

And then, as Molina retreated, Ortega thrust his fist into my belly, and I fell to the ground. "Don't worry, cunt-whore. I will never bruise your face."

He left me there as he concluded his business with the Seguinns. I could do nothing but stare at the empty husk that had once been Gracie. Her eyes stared into open space, as per usual, but this time it was because there really was nothing inside of her.

The Sequinns paid up, and the old man helped Amy onto his wife's horse. She cast one glance back at me, and all I could do was meet her eyes. I could not wave, and I could not say anything. I could not even nod.

And she rode away, fading into the dust.

I am the last person in my wagon now as I write this account. My tears have stained these pages, as I am sure you can tell. The pencil scratch has smeared here and there, but I hope it is still legible. I do not know who would ever read this account except for myself, but if there is someone out there . . .

But there is not. Is there?

Later—

As I tried to go to bed tonight, I overheard a discussion between Ortega and Moreno just outside of the wagon. Ortega had been too drunk to use me tonight, so he left me alone. Instead, he argued with his lieutenant in the night.

I did not understand everything they said, but considering how much time I have spent with them, I have picked up enough of their language to understand half of what they talked about. The dialogue that follows is as close to my understanding as I can make it.

"Why did you have to kill her?" Moreno asked. "She was a fine piece. She wasn't that bright, but she had a hole, and it was fun."

"She pissed me off," Ortega said.

"It's not like you to kill valuable pussy."

"She was pregnant."

A brief silence. "By who?"

"Who knows?" Ortega said. "I can't sell a pregnant woman. By the time I found a buyer for her, she would have been too far gone. Besides, she was crazy. No one wants crazy pussy."

"No disrespect, but I don't think you should have killed her," Moreno said. "I'm horny, and now I have no one to take it out on."

I heard a sharp crack, and it took me a moment to realize that Ortega had struck his second-in-command. "If that was a subtle hint that I should let you fuck my Tessa, then—"

"No! I swear it!"

"Then go into the darkness and beat off. It is not my concern. We've almost reached our destination, and then we can begin again. We're coming up on Socorro soon. At the very least, you can buy some pussy there."

I could tell Moreno wanted to argue more, and although I could not see him, I imagined the tenseness in his shoulders. But he gave in, and the conversation was over.

What did Ortega mean by Soccorro? Is this where I am to be sold? Could it be that my time with these miserable Comancheros is almost over? I pray this is the case.

-

DAY TWENTY-FOUR OF CAPTIVITY

I am sorry for not writing in this journal for so long. I just have not had the heart for it. Misery seems to weigh me down, as if I wear an anvil around my waist. I miss Gracie and Amy so much. It is hard to be the only woman around here. There is no one for me to turn to, to take care of, to confide in.

Except Molina, but I do not think he would risk Ortega's wrath in helping me any more than is humane. This seems like the worst insult of all, since I know he can help me get out of here, and he is just too cowardly to do so.

No, I should not blame him. He is, after all, a Comanchero. Perhaps he is not as vile as his companions, but his loyalty still lies with them. It is a shame, though. On my own, I would have a better chance of surviving in the wilderness. I do not know if I would be able to evade any trackers, but I have enough confidence in my survival abilities.

But, why bother? Is this not my grim fate? Should I not just give in to it? These last few days, I have gone through the motions of life with the Comancheros. My mind stayed a blank slate as I performed my duties. All of my duties, including those involving Ortega's sexual needs. And when I come back to this wagon, I do not even bother reading my books. What is the point? Why are books so important? The only good they have ever done for me is to help me escape, in my mind, my predicament. But so what? It does not change where I am. I have to return to this wretched existence. There is no escape from destiny.

Why am I even bothering to write this down?

I thought about ending my life, but I do not think I can. The courage it takes to make such a commitment does not live in my heart, for it is a faint organ. And besides, what purpose does this have? I no longer believe in God, and therefore there is no Heaven to which I can attain. No relief from this world. Only nothingness.

Try as I might, I can find no comfort in this.

My hand grows weary. Perhaps I will write in this journal again someday. Perhaps not.

T essa had just finished cleaning up after breakfast, and she wanted to get back to Mary Shelley's novel about the unfortunate creature and his unthinking creator. There were only a few pages left, and she could barely wait to find out how it all ended.

She hopped up into the wagon, but before she could reach for the pile of ragged books, she saw that she had company. Sitting with his back against the front end of the wagon was Ortega, and he held a bunch of loose pages in his knobby hands.

Her journal.

"What are you doing in here?" she asked.

He didn't answer. First, he finished the final page, and then he looked up at her. "I should have known, cunt-whore."

"What do you mean?" Hoping she could still play dumb.

"If a woman proves she can write a diary once, she will do it again. And this has not been a very good read." He crushed the pages in his hand, molding them into a ball.

"I don't know what you mean," Tessa said.

Ortega leapt to his feet and grabbed her by the throat. He pushed her against the canvas, and she felt like she was just about to be pushed through it.

"I read what you wrote about me," he hissed into her face. Spittle wet her eyelids in droplets. "Even more so, I read about your precious hero, Molina. Would you care to know where he is right now?"

"I . . . I don't . . ."

He backhanded her hard enough to drive her head to the right. Her neck crackled with the force, and her face burned. For good measure he did it again, and she felt blood squirt into her mouth.

"Stop!" she cried. Crimson dribbled down her chin.

"You're beautiful," Ortega whispered. His hot breath rolled over her nostrils, and she could smell whiskey. "You're the finest piece I've ever had. But I'm through with you."

He pushed her down, and she rolled over the books in the corner. Some of the spines, aged beyond their years by the dust and dry climate, cracked and splintered beneath her.

"Did you fuck him?" Ortega asked. "How many times?"

She mumbled something, but he couldn't hear it. He kicked her in the belly, and she cried out. "None! I haven't done anything with him!"

"I doubt it, cunt-whore." He kicked her again, and blood splattered the wooden boards of the wagon. "You are no longer mine. I will throw you to the other men tonight. And then, when we reach the town of Oso Feo in three days, I will sell you to the scummiest saloon owner I know. He won't be very picky with how ruined your pussy's going to be."

Tears poured down Tessa's face. Snot and blood bubbled from her nostrils. She tried to breathe, but too much mucous clogged her throat.

"Oh yes. I almost forgot. I want you to see something."

Ortega jumped out the back of the wagon, and he reached in to grab a handful of Tessa's hair. She screamed as he pulled on it, yanking her over the tailgate of the wagon. She thumped to the ground and sent up a dust cloud. Then, like a caveman, Ortega dragged her by the hair toward the outskirts of camp.

He tossed her down when they'd reached their destination. There was Molina, his shirt ripped open, his arms and legs tied to a large rock. The sun cooked him alive. Already his skin had turned a deep scarlet. Ants crawled all over his scorched back, leaving their tiny bites wherever they roamed.

Tessa gasped. "God!"

Molina squinted up. "Tessa? What's going on?"

Ortega drew his gun, and before anyone could do anything, he put a bullet into Molina's temple. His head snapped back, and a mass of meat and blood came out the other side of his face. One of his eyes rolled away, and the ants were on it before it came to a complete stop.

Tessa screamed, and when she tried to go to Molina, Ortega slapped her aside.

"I never did like his poetry," he said. "He was kind of a fuck, you know? I'm glad you finally gave me an excuse to put him down."

Hernandez and Moreno exchanged a glance which painted doubt in their boss with a light as clear as day. They both thought Ortega had finally lost it if he had sunk so low as to kill one of his own men in such a fashion.

"He didn't have the heart of a real Comanchero," Ortega said. He turned to Tessa. "And now you have no benefactor. Men!"

The Comancheros gathered around their leader. "This cunt-whore is yours. Do with her as you see fit, but don't mark her face. It's the only thing she has going for her, and I still have to sell her in Oso Feo."

The Comancheros closed in around her, and she felt lost because she had no moon to escape into. The sun hovered above, but it pained her to look at it, much less stare. No, she had nothing to take her focus off of the violence at hand, no place to which she could escape.

She closed her eyes and hoped it wouldn't hurt too much.

-

That night, as she lay in the darkness, feeling her life ooze out of her body, her wounds throbbing, her blood flowing, she could see by the light of the campfire as they rolled cigarettes with her journal pages and smoked them.

The sliver moon leered down at her, and she prayed that tonight would be her last night on earth. She didn't think she could take much more of this. And there would be more, night after night, until they reached Oso Feo, where she could expect to live the life of a saloon whore.

She wanted to die, and she thought this up to the moon, but all it offered was its crooked grin.

-

Tessa woke up the next morning, disappointed that she still possessed life. The others were passed out in their various places, and vultures had done their best to pick away at Molina's body. The corpse had baked under the sun, so all that remained was desiccated flesh. It did not even smell all that bad.

She gave herself a quick once-over and determined that while she had been bruised slightly, she only had two cutting wounds, and they'd sealed themselves. She probed inside of her to find that she was sore, but there were no rips.

All in all, the worst injuries she'd sustained were to her soul.

What to do now? She didn't ponder the question for very long. She merely went toward the guttering fire and stoked it up again for breakfast.

Over the next few days she tried to be the most obedient servant one could hope to find. Meals were always on time, and when pleasure was demanded, she acquiesced without question. She offered no resistance as they crossed the Rio Grande into Mexico. Soon she became so servile that Ortega decided to keep her for his own again. A certain level of trust had been regained in Ortega's eyes, and he wanted things to go back to the way they'd been before the unfortunate incident with Molina.

By noon the next day they would be in Oso Feo, and Tessa would belong to another man. On this occasion Ortega built up a separate campfire for himself and demanded that the other Comancheros stay away from this area. If it was to be their last night together, he wanted some modicum of privacy. This would be as special as possible since he knew that he would never encounter such beautiful property ever again.

Ortega had saved a steak from a fancy restaurant he'd visited before buying Tessa. He told her to cook it medium-rare, and to be very careful. He also had some wine, which he thought to be very good. He didn't know much about the grape, so he took the trader's word for it. The label had a bunch of pretty words on it, so he figured the trust had not been misplaced.

The other Comancheros were left to their own devices, their own food and drink, their own celebrations. Oso Feo was a well-known hell hole in Mexico, and they were all eager to explore its darker alleys and inexpensive depravities.

When the steak finished cooking, Tessa put it on a tin plate next to some potatoes she had prepared earlier. The fork and knife were already in place, so she put the meal in front of Ortega with great flourish. She even tucked a napkin into the front of his shirt.

"Tessa, you are a hell of a girl." He patted her on the cheek. "I'm going to miss you, I really am. But don't worry, you'll have plenty of company with Mendoza. He's the man who's going to buy you, and he has been a good friend of mine for many, many years. He will treat you well, just so long as you treat him well."

Tessa remained submissively quiet.

"Did you make anything for yourself?" he asked.

She nodded, still silent.

"Then bring it here and join me. I will pour us some wine."

Tessa shuffled off to the campfire where her own meal awaited her. Not quite so grand as Ortega's, it was a bit better than what the Comancheros were having. She brought it with her and sat next to Ortega, who handed her a glass.

"To your future," he said.

"And to yours." Her tone remained perfect and innocuous.

They both drank, and they started to eat. Ortega had nothing he wanted to talk about, so he stared at Tessa between bites. She felt no need to discuss anything with Ortega, so she let him look.

When they were done Ortega handed her his dishes. "Clean these up."

She did. As she scrubbed away at everything, she saw Ortega out of the corner of her eye drinking the rest of the wine directly from the bottle. She remembered the Scotch she and Iron Trail had possessed when Ortega had come into their lives, and she remembered the way that the Comanchero had guzzled the contents as if it had been common whiskey. Nothing changed with this man, did it?

Tessa came back to him, and by now he drank mescal. He eyed her. "How did you ever wind up out here? Someone as beautiful as you, you could have been someone. What are you doing here?"

"I was a mail order bride," she said. "My husband betrayed me and sold me to Iron Trail. Then you took me." She hoped her words didn't sound too terse.

"What were you in the East?" he asked. "A school marm?"

"No," she said. "I was a prostitute."

He shook his head, grinning. "Then you won't hate me for all the indignities I've visited upon you. You should be used to it all by now."

It occurred to her to say that as bad as Sam Pepper had been, he'd never humiliated and ruined her as the Comancheros had. But she kept quiet.

"Come here," Ortega said. "I intend to make full use of you tonight."

They kissed, and Ortega unbuttoned her shirt, grasping at her all too familiar breasts. His thumbs rubbed across the nipples, turning them into hardened points.

And then she slithered down his body, placing tiny kisses as she went. He pulled his shirt open so she could leave a few on his chest.

She reached his belt buckle, which she flipped open. Next, she unbuttoned his pants, and his cock practically shot out from the open flaps. The stink of many days without bathing came with it, and she nearly gagged. As she stroked his member, she tried to ignore the nearly overpowering reek.

He lifted his ass up a bit so he could remove his gun-belt and toss it aside. Her hands then grasped his hips, and he watched as she took him into her mouth.

As bad as the smell had been, the taste was worse, like licking uncooked pork. This time she did gag at the musk, but she pretended it to be a sound of pleasure. Ortega, who never paid too much attention to her, did not notice the difference.

"That's it," he whispered. "Take it all, cunt-whore."

Ortega was not a very large man, so she easily took this order. Tessa went all the way down to the base of his dick, and closing her eyes, drawing all of her strength together, she clamped down with her teeth and ground on him until her jaws met through his flesh.

Ortega couldn't scream at first. The unexpected pain encompassed him so much that he couldn't register what had happened.

Tessa continued to grind until she had severed the Comanchero's cock entirely. Then she pulled back, blood dribbling down her chin. And though it was a rather unpleasant morsel, she forced herself to chew on it as she gazed into his panic stricken eyes.

Ortega saw the pulped, bloody mess between his legs, and finally he screamed, grabbing the hole where once his dick once resided. He tried to form words, but his pain ravaged his mind so he couldn't do more than babble incomprehensible gibberish.

Tessa spat out the penis, and it flopped like a dead fish into the dust. No longer recognizable as the male sex organ, Ortega saw what had become of his manhood.

"You bitch!" he screamed. "I'll fucking kill you! I'll kill you! Cunt-whore!"

He scrambled for his gun belt, but his injury—and his insistence upon holding it—slowed him down. Tessa got there first, and she cocked the hammer back, pointing the barrel steadily at Ortega's head.

By now the Comancheros ran to their leader's aid. She couldn't let them help him, so while she wanted Ortega's misery to last longer, to perhaps equal Iron Trail's, she knew time was not on her side. Unceremoniously she pulled the trigger and blew Ortega's face out the back of his head.

"Holy fucking thit!" Norbert. He drew his gun as quickly as he could.

Tessa whipped around and with pure blind luck put two bullets into the uglier of the Hertells, killing him before he could clear leather.

"Norbert!" It was Desmond, but she couldn't see him. Smarter than his brother, he hid from her.

Villarreal did not. He took a shot at her, but he was too drunk to be accurate. The bullet struck Ortega's corpse, which alerted Tessa to her predicament. She whirled and easily put a bullet into Villarreal's throat. It took him a while to die, and he did so unnoticed by his target or his companions.

Another Comanchero, this one named Lopez, tried approaching her, but it was no good. She did not hesitate to put a bullet directly through his heart.

"You fucking bitch!" Desmond roared. "You killed my brother!" He took a shot, but drunk like Villarreal, he missed.

"And I'll kill you, too!" she snarled. "Come out and fight me like a man, you limp-dick splotch of goat cum!"

He did just this, firing his rifle as he did so. The bullet came very close this time. She felt it go through one of the open flaps of her shirt. But it did not strike her.

Tessa pulled the trigger a fifth time, but she only winged Desmond. He gave a yelp as a blood flower blossomed at his shoulder. No matter. She still had one bullet left. She took more careful aim this time as Desmond went to one knee, taking aim at her.

Stars exploded across her vision, and an unbearable sharp pain jolted the right side of her face. Blood squirted into her mouth as she collapsed to her side, dropping the gun. She had enough time to see crimson spray from her lips before she lost consciousness.

From what she could gather later, Moreno had snuck up on her and had buffaloed her, but instead of hitting her temple, he misjudged and got her on the jaw. Still, it had been enough to put her down.

She drifted in and out of the world, the only constants being the pain in her face and the stream of an argument between Moreno and Desmond. Most of it was in the Comanchero language, and she didn't understand it. Some was English, and some was Spanish, which she had a slight handle on. There was another Comancerho, Wolfpaw, and he seemed to be shouting the most.

From what she understood Moreno had been second-in-command, so he naturally thought he should be leader. Wolfpaw disagreed, since he was the most skilled. Desmond didn't care. He just wanted to kill Tessa, who had killed his brother.

Moreno said that they would not be killing her because she was still worth money. Wolfpaw said that with her face damaged, she would not get as much money as before. So she should be used and killed and left for the buzzards.

211

Tessa started coming back to herself. She coughed up some clotting blood and a few teeth. When she saw the latter, her stomach sank. All her life she had taken excellent care of her pearly whites, so much so that it surprised a lot of her clients and even Sam Pepper. When she arrived at Felton Reeves' door, even he had marveled at their beauty.

And now her smile was ruined. She probed her mouth and found that at least they had been back teeth, what she'd heard referred to as molars. There were no gaps at all. In fact if she didn't smile too widely, no one would ever notice.

Desmond pointed to her. "See? Her teeth are coming out. There's no way she's valuable to you guys. Let me kill her."

Moreno let fly with a string of Spanish curses. When Wolfpaw tried to interject, Moreno drew down and shot him through the forehead without warning. What he said next was unclear to Tessa, but she thought it was something along the lines of, "Does anyone else doubt my ability to lead you?"

No one wanted to take him up on the challenge.

Moreno turned to Desmond. "How about you, white man? Do you think you can take me?"

Desmond scratched his head. "Shit, man. I didn't mean anything by it. But she killed my brother."

"I know, and you will be compensated for it when I sell her," Moreno said.

"Do you really think you can sell her?" Desmond asked. "Look at that bruise. Mendoza's gonna want to know about that. It's not like we can use face paint to cover it up or nothin. And he's gonna want to see her teeth."

"It'll be fine," Moreno said. "I'll highball him, and he'll lowball me. We'll come to a satisfactory agreement."

"He's not gonna want her," Desmond said. "Not after he hears about what she did to Ortega."

"That's why he's not going to find out about that," Moreno said. "Now tie her up and throw her in the wagon. Garcia, I want you to bathe her tomorrow morning. Don't fuck her, just bathe her, got it?"

A smaller Comanchero with a bald head and an impressive mustache nodded.

"Good. Let's get some sleep, everyone. Tomorrow's a big day, and I know you'll want to reserve some energy for Oso Feo."

Desmond yanked Tessa's hands behind her back and tied her wrists with rawhide. He made sure to dig it in as much as he could. Already she could feel her hands becoming numb, and fire seemed to scorch her arms.

"You fucking cunt," he whispered. "Now that I think on it, not killing you'll be better. Killing you would end your misery. You're going to work for Alfredo Mendoza, and he's a hard man. You'll be all used up within a month, I promise ya."

He then whipped more rawhide around her ankles and tied them tightly enough so that it looked like a wire cutting into her flesh. Before she could feel her feet go fuzzy on her, he lifted her body across his shoulder and took her back to her wagon, where he threw her in with little consideration.

"I can't wait till yer off our hands, bitch," he said.

Later, when everyone else fell asleep, Desmond came back in and cut the rawhide around her ankles. While the feeling came tingling back to her feet, he yanked her pants off and finally achieved what he'd wanted to all this time. There were so many holes in the covering of the wagon that she couldn't miss the moon, and as always it accepted her into its embrace.

-

When Tessa came to she was outside, naked, and Garcia hovered over her with a wet cloth and a bucket by his side. The water spattered across her body, and it felt good under the beating warmth of the sun.

Garcia scrubbed at her body gently, especially over the bruises. When the cloth crossed over her breasts it was without sexual intention. Thinking back she remembered that this one liked little boys, so this probably disgusted him.

He moved down to her legs, and he roughly spread them so he could clean inside of her. Again the motion of his hands conveyed no desire at all. He just wanted to clean out her orifices. When he finished he looked at the goo on the cloth and tossed it aside for a new one.

Tessa closed her eyes and let the Comanchero do his job. Before long he flipped her over onto a buffalo blanket so he could clean her back. The washing motion satisfied her, almost like a massage. She couldn't help but enjoy the lack of dust and sand on her body.

Garcia's hands left her, and Tessa sensed a shadow fall across her body. When she opened her eyes she saw Moreno looming over her.

"Get dressed," he said. A pile of fresh clothes fell onto the blanket beside her. These were not rough garments but were ladylike.

Tessa didn't argue. She ignored the leering faces of the Comancheros as she wrapped herself in the vestments of a woman about to be sold. Presentable, they loaded her into the back of the wagon for the final time, and they started the last leg of their journey to Oso Feo.

Throughout the course of the trip Tessa tried to read from the books under the rags, but the words kept swimming around on the page, and her eyes weren't fast enough to catch them. Finally she gave up and stared out the holes in the canvas at the desolate wasteland through which they traveled. It looked pretty at first, for an Easterner's eyes at least, but it quickly became boring.

At about three in the afternoon they crossed a plank bridge over a dry creek and rode into the town of Oso Feo. It didn't differ much from what she'd seen north of the Rio Grande, but the style stood out. Most of the buildings tended to be made of stone, what she later learned to be pueblo. Very few structures were wooden, and those that were looked ready to fall down. A lot of the buildings were built low, and most had stairways that led down to the first floor.

The Comancheros parked their gear in front of a wooden saloon called El Gato Bonito. She watched as Moreno and a few others entered through askew batwing doors. The others remained outside, shifting from foot to foot, eager to begin the evening's festivities.

They emerged, accompanied by a tall bald man with a large gut protruding from under his chef's apron. His mustache curved, waxed in a French fashion, but the rest of his face betrayed his Mexican heritage. Could this be Alfredo Mendoza?

Moreno showed the portly bartender another wagon first. It looked like they haggled over the goods stowed away in there. Mendoza appeared to be very pleased, and he purchased the entire wagon shortly.

Moreno gestured toward Tessa's wagon, grinning. He spoke in Spanish, but she didn't need a translator to figure out what he said.

"Tessa! Step down, please."

Tessa gingerly made her way out of the wagon and lowered herself to the muddy ground. She straightened her spine, remembering her posture lessons from Back-East.

"Señor Mendoza," Moreno said, "this is Tessa Reeves. Beautiful, is she not?"

Mendoza stepped around her, examining every facet of her as if she were a diamond, and he circled around her body with his appraising eyes. "She's just about the prettiest woman I've ever seen," he said with a thick Mexican accent. "Let's see the tits."

Moreno nodded to her. "Open your dress. But not too far. We don't want anyone else spying on the merchandise."

Tessa unfastened a few buttons and unstrung some of her bustle in order to shimmy some cloth down, revealing the assets Mendoza wanted to view.

He nodded appreciatively. "You are right, Señor Moreno. This is a fine product. Has she been used?"

"A few times," Moreno said, "but she's not sloppy down there."

Mendoza bent down so he could lift her skirts. After he worked through the amazing amount of cloth down there, he dipped a finger inside of her and wiggled it around. Tessa closed her eyes and tried not to betray her revulsion.

"That's pretty tight," Mendoza said. "Almost brand new."

"Think of how much you could make off of this one," Moreno said. "That considered, I don't think you would blink at buying her for five hundred."

Mendoza rubbed the fat cleft in his chin. "I don't know. That's a bit steep."

"But think about the quality," Moreno said.

"Four hundred," Mendoza said.

"I'm sure you don't mean to insult me," Moreno said. "I don't think I could go lower than four-seventy-five."

"What about this?" Mendoza pointed to the bruise on her jaw. "Damaged goods."

Moreno smiled. "Aren't they all?"

"Four-twenty-five," Mendoza said.

"A bruise disappears after a while," Moreno said. "Within the week you'll never be able to tell she had one. Four-fifty."

Mendoza smiled and shook Moreno's hand. "I think we have a deal."

Tessa inwardly sighed. She hoped that this would mean she would never have to see the Comancheros again, but she was wrong, of course. They did not have any plans to leave town until tomorrow.

Mendoza produced a pouch and let a few gold coins fall into his red patchy palm. He counted a few of them, then poured a couple more out. These he gave to Moreno, and he put the rest of the pouch back on his belt.

"A sheer pleasure, Mendoza."

"Would you care for a drink?" Mendoza asked.

"Not now. We'll be back later."

Mendoza shouted orders in Spanish to a young man, gesturing to the wagon. He then turned to Tessa and grabbed her arm. "Let's go."

He practically pushed her through the batwing doors into a saloon that could only be described as greasy. Everything seemed to be smudged, and there were stains on the floor that she did not want to even consider identifying.

Mendoza went to the stairs. "Yvonne! Get your ass down here!"

"Coming!" The voice that answered was feminine but gruff. It belonged to someone who was clearly used to being ordered around.

Soon a stout figure descended from the balcony above. Painted so thickly she could have been a clown, her clothes quickly verified her true occupation. Perhaps she had been good looking once, but hard living had bloated her body and added wrinkles to her face. Her blonde hair, piled up on top of her head, looked like its color was fading.

"Yvonne," Mendoza said, "this is Tessa Reeves. She's the new girl."

Yvonne's cold blue eyes evaluated Tessa. "Not bad, Alfredo. I think this one's going to be a top earner."

"Not better than you," Mendoza said. But he made no pretense of hiding his mere flattery.

"She looks a bit fragile, though," Yvonne said. "She might break too easily."

"No offense meant," Tessa said, "but if you had experienced the things I've gone through over the past few weeks, you would know that I am made of oak."

Yvonne laughed. "She's got bottle, I'll give her that."

"Take her under your wing," Mendoza said. "Teach her the ropes. Then get her ready for tonight."

"Sure thing, boss," Yvonne said. "Let's start her out with a drink, what do you say?"

Mendoza looked reluctant. "Fine. Just take the house whiskey."

"I know, I know," Yvonne said. "You drink hard liquor, honey?"

Tessa nodded. How long ago would she have said no?

"You'll need a slug before we get started. I can see things have been rough on you."

They approached the bar, and Mendoza slipped them a bottle from the lower shelf. It had no label on it. Yvonne poured them two glasses practically to the brim.

"Bottoms up." She downed her drink in one go.

Tessa took a sip and felt her mouth ignite. She coughed and then pinched her nose shut so she could finish off the glass.

"Feel better, honey?"

Tessa cleared her throat, eyes wide. She nodded.

"Good. Let's take you on the grand tour. Since we're down here we'll start at the bar."

Tessa watched as Yvonne pointed out the different kinds of drinks Mendoza served. Most of it was slop, but behind the bar, she saw a row of clean bottles. "This is the finest whiskey we have. For our best customers only. The usual gaggle of dickheads we get in here should never know about this."

Tessa nodded.

Yvonne pointed out the roulette wheel and the faro tables. The rest were designated for whatever else was going on. If a bunch of customers wanted to get a game of poker going on their own, that was fine. Just so long as Mendoza got his share.

"Remember that, honey," Yvonne said. "Mendoza always gets his share. Ten percent. And if he doesn't, well, you'll meet Aguirre later. He's the guard."

Just before they moved into the storage room, Yvonne stopped them by the door. "All the stuff you just saw? You're responsible for cleaning it up. We all are. We don't take turns or anything, but at closing time we put up the chairs and sweep the place out. You know, polish whatever needs it."

Tessa nodded just to indicate that she understood. She had taken Yvonne's instructions for granted as soon as she had known she would be sold to a saloon keeper.

Yvonne opened the door to the storage room and pointed out the important things, like the extra kegs and barrels, the cleaning supplies and bedroom linens. "Try to keep this area clean, too. It's not an active chore just, you know, if you dirty it up, fix it up."

"I understand," Tessa said.

"Ready to move upstairs?"

They went toward the steps, and as Tessa ascended she couldn't help but notice how creaky they were. In addition to this the railing looked like it had been patched up many times. How many bar brawls did this place see?

When they reached the balcony, she saw five doors. "This one is Mendoza's office." Yvonne pointed to the first. "It is locked at all times unless Mendoza is in there. Sometimes when he's with a girl he locks it, but that's it."

They moved on. "These two belong to the other whores. Trixie and Lavender are out right now, but you'll meet them tonight."

"Okay."

"The next door is mine," Yvonne said. "If you ever need anything, and I'm not working, this is the door to knock on." She rapped her knuckles on the wood by means of demonstration.

"I'll keep that in mind," Tessa said.

"This last door is your crib," Yvonne said. She twisted the knob and threw open the door with much flourish.

Tessa glanced around the inside. Nothing fancy, not much space. She could probably touch the opposite walls at the same time. She had a bed, a changing shade, a dresser—complete with a porcelain basin—and just a little wiggle room.

"Where do I hang my clothes?" Tessa asked.

Yvonne laughed so hard that Tessa could see all of her teeth. Dentures. They were nice, but at the same time they were obvious. "This isn't a classy New York City-type place, honey. Stuff 'em in a drawer. The customers around here don't care if your undies ain't ironed."

Tessa restrained from sighing. It seemed like she would never be in a civilized place again. Would it have been too hard to supply her with a closet? Even a meager one would have sufficed.

"I notice you didn't come in with any belongings. There are a couple of dresses in the drawer for you, okay?"

Tessa wearily nodded.

"Sit down on the bed," Yvonne said. "Test 'er out."

Tessa gently sat down, surprised to find it had springs in it. "It's very comfortable."

"It's a bit loud when the customers are using it," Yvonne said, "but most of 'em like it that way. All that sound makes 'em feel like they're accomplishing something."

Tessa broke down at this remark. She'd been trying to keep a straight face the whole time, but this comment slapped her funny bone. Her laughter honked and echoed in the practically empty room.

"It's good to see you smile, kiddo," Yvonne said. "Not many new girls can do that. I think you're made of pretty stern stuff."

The smile faded like the sun setting over the horizon. "I seem to manage."

"Good, 'cause you'll need a lot of heart to get through this." Yvonne plopped down next to her, sending the springs screaming. "Now on to your duties."

"Yes. My duties."

"The first thing you should know is, as soon as we're done here I'm taking you to see Mendoza. He's going to want to test you out before he lets you loose on our customers."

"I see."

"Do you *understand*?"

"Yes."

"Good. After that you'll have some time to rest, but come six o'clock you need to be dressed, coiffed and downstairs, ready to work. Got me?"

"Yes."

"Mendoza charges five for a poke," Yvonne continued. "He expects to see that five the moment the customer leaves your crib. Take the time to put on a robe, but you come to see Mendoza immediately after that. Now I'm not saying that the customers can't tip you. If they choose to do so, and it is the custom in these parts, then you can keep that money. However, make sure Mendoza doesn't know about it. Keep in mind that you are his property, and property doesn't get to own things, right?"

"Yes."

"When you're done with one john, you move to the next. No lag time. Wipe the goo out of your pussy and come back downstairs. Play with the fellas. Show 'em that you're all about having a good time. Sit with them at the tables, or if the player piano's working, hang out around it and flirt. I'm sure you know the score."

"I've done work like this before," Tessa said. "Just not in a place like this. In New York City, it was different."

"I've been there, so I know. Just remember where you are now, honey."

Tessa nodded.

"Playful ribbing is permissible in this joint," Yvonne said, "but never outright make fun of a man. That's just asking for trouble. And if two dickheads make a fuss over you, do not get involved. Things will work themselves out, and we don't need a dead whore getting in the way. Do you understand?"

"Yes."

"Doors close here at five in the morning. If you've got a john who wants to stay the night, that's fine. Just remember that if he wants more from you, you're still on duty. Aside from that you're free to sleep here. You can come and go as you please, just so long as you're ready to work at six o'clock every evening."

"I can roam the town if I wish it?" Tessa asked.

Yvonne smiled. "You're thinking of running away. Don't deny it. I did, too, at first. It's a seductive thought. But it's pointless."

"Why?"

"Oso Feo is surrounded by nothing but desert, snakes and coyotes. You'd never survive. Not even the most skilled Apache would be able to get to the next town, and God made those bastards tougher'n buffalo hide."

"But with a horse—"

"No one in town would give you one. The livery stables know who we are, and they would not risk Mendoza's wrath. He doesn't look like much, but he's one of the most powerful men in this town."

"I could steal a horse," Tessa said.

Yvonne offered a lopsided grin. "Shit fire, I'm sure you'd try, honey. But I wouldn't recommend it. People are a tetch possessive around here, and everyone is armed. There's no way out, kiddo. Besides, there's one thing that makes staying worthwhile."

"What's that?"

"This job ain't as bad as it sounds," Yvonne said. "In fact it's kind of cozy. So you do a bit of cleaning up. So you get fucked by all manner of men and sometimes women. So what? Out there, in the world, most people have to work for a living. They have to worry about their next meal, or a roof over their heads. Guess what? We've got it made. Mendoza gives us food, and he gives us shelter. All we have to do is clean up a bit and take a few shots of *vaquero* cum every night. Sex is fun. I've been here for several years, and I've never complained about that aspect. Some of these guys even know what they're doing."

Tessa thought back over the last few weeks, thinking about all the times Ortega and his Comancheros raped her. The thought of sex made her skin want to turn inside out. If she never saw another penis again, she thought she would be happy.

"I know," Yvonne said. "I saw the disgust on your face just now. It's not that bad. You get used to it."

Tessa didn't think she'd ever get used to something like that. Granted, she'd sold her sex many times back when she was living with Sam Pepper, but this was different. Back then she kept a majority of whatever she earned as a whore, and trade came much less rough. Here she was a mere step above a slave.

"That's it, kiddo," Yvonne said. "Any questions?"

"No ma'am."

"Then come with me. It's time for Mendoza to have his taste."

Yvonne took Tessa's hand in hers, and she led the both of them out to the balcony and to the rail. "Hey boss! You still down there?"

Mendoza poked his head out from behind the bar. "Is she ready?"

"You bet."

He tossed a towel over his shoulder and rubbed his palms together. "Here I come."

Yvonne and Tessa waited patiently by Mendoza's door. "Don't you have a key?" Tessa whispered.

"Hell no," Yvonne said. "I'm just another whore. I'm the best in his stable, but I'm still just a whore. The only existing key is on a chain around his neck."

Mendoza thumped up the steps. He had no cadence to his movement. Because of his weight, these sounds came uneven, a little chaotic. When he finally reached the balcony his breath puffed a bit. "How's she doing?"

"I think we're going to have no problems with her," Yvonne said. "Quick learner, this one."

Mendoza removed the key from around his neck and unlocked the door. "Enter." He waved his hand over the threshold.

"This is where I leave you, honey," Yvonne said. "Good luck."

Tessa said nothing. With no argument she stepped into Mendoza's room, and he followed after. She did not turn when she heard the lock click.

Tessa found herself in a room that was part office, part bedroom. The two were separated by a portion of wall, and not by much. Anyone who did business in this office would have a clear view of where he slept in a fairly fancy bed. It even had a canopy.

A large desk stood guard near the entrance to the bedroom, and a gas lamp shone down on scattered papers. Nearby she saw a bar stocked with more of the shiny clean bottles like the top shelf stuff downstairs. There were three glasses, all upside down, surrounding the center bottle.

"Get on the bed," Mendoza said. He worked his way out of his shirt like a man trying to escape from a straight jacket.

Tessa obeyed.

Mendoza said, "Take off your clothes first. Jesus, woman. You'd think this was your first time."

Tessa stood and slowly started to remove her clothes.

Mendoza shrugged out of his suspenders and struggled with the button on his pants. The material stretched so tightly that it looked like the button was going to pop off from the strain.

By the time he stepped out of his pants she removed the last of her clothes. "Stand there. Let me look at you."

Tessa stared ahead like a soldier in the Army, and Mendoza circled around her, appraising her body. "Yep. You're a beauty, all right." His meaty hand grasped a buttock and roughly squeezed. She did not yelp, and she did not shiver.

"How many men have you been with?" he asked.

"I've lost count," Tessa said.

"Got any diseases?"

"Probably," Tessa said. "I've been with the Comancheros for weeks. I'm sure you know what they're like."

Mendoza caressed her cheek where Moreno had pistol-whipped her. "Oh yeah. I know. I don't see anything amiss, though, so you're probably good."

"Should I report to you if anything shows up?" she asked.

"Why?"

"For business," Tessa said.

"Why the fuck should I care? If some *vaquero* catches something off you, it's his business. Call it the Lord's penance or something."

"What about you?" Tessa asked. "Aren't you afraid of catching something off of me?"

"No. I'm only going to fuck you this once, and you can't catch anything from a woman on the first time."

Tessa wondered about Mendoza's seriousness, but after looking at his straight face for nearly a minute she knew his ignorance.

"Now get up on the bed. Hands and knees. I don't want to see your face, whore."

Quietly Tessa climbed into bed, and she offered herself to him. The bed trounced as he waddled up onto the mattress. Mendoza slapped his hand on her sex and held her open as he pressed into her. Although she couldn't see anything, she knew Mendoza wasn't packing much. Maybe he'd been considerable in his youth, but now the fat had taken over. If anything more than three inches had penetrated her, she would be surprised.

Less than two minutes later Mendoza rested on his back trying to catch his breath. Tessa rested next to him, feeling his muck oozing between her legs. She stared longingly at a towel by the wash basin, but she knew now wasn't the time.

"Hot damn," Mendoza said. "You will most definitely do. I think you're going to make me a rich man."

"Yes sir," Tessa said.

"Your pussy's like velvet to touch," he said. "I might have to charge ten for you."

"Yes sir."

"Now get the fuck out of here. I have business to attend to. And don't forget, be ready by six."

Tessa stood and bent to pick up her clothes.

"Leave 'em. They stink like shit. Use one of the dresses in your room. And don't forget to wash your pussy."

"Yes sir." Tessa dropped the rags and went for the door. The key still rested in the hole, so she let herself out and walked to her crib, stark naked for the world to see.

Only Yvonne watched her from downstairs. Even she felt surprised by how beautiful Tessa's body was, and she wondered how long it would be before the young woman started getting stout.

Stout like Yvonne. Life here was particularly hard on a woman's figure.

-

At five-fifty Tessa stood before the mirror in her boudoir, dressed and painted and ready to go. She marveled at how the dress really did accentuate her features. In fact she had never looked so good, not even in the Sam Pepper days.

All she had to do was gain the courage to go downstairs.

She considered the things that Ortega and his Comancheros had done to her, and she realized that nothing these men paid her to do could possibly be worse.

Tessa turned away from the mirror and made her way to the door. She'd been given the key to her crib, and she used it now, twisting it to unlock and unbar her way to a new lifestyle. As she strode down the stairs she dropped the key into her cleavage.

The saloon was not yet crowded. There were only a handful of *vaqueros* hanging around the bar, and two more by the faro table. A dark gentleman with well-manicured fingers dealt cards to the customers. His waxed mustache curled slightly at the ends, pointing at his eyes.

The girls milled about, and Tessa saw Yvonne working a man leaning against the bar. There were two others, but she couldn't tell who was Trixie, who Lavender. One was a hulking mass of flesh, jiggling as she laughed a little too hard at a customer's joke. The other was as skinny as a toothpick, but she knew how to use what she had. The man she worked on practically fell all over himself to praise her.

Near the batwing doors a very tall, very thick man stood guard. He leaned against the wall, arms crossed, and watched everyone around him, waiting for someone to start something. Anything. He had no hair on his head, but his ears were full of jewelry. This one could only be Aguirre.

As she stepped down from the staircase all eyes turned on her, and more than several jaws dropped. Even the ladies took a gander, and the skinny one nodded her approval . . . until she noticed how intently her prospect stared at this newcomer.

"Look what the angels brought to us," Yvonne said. "Come on down, Tessa. Let's show these guys what a real lady looks like."

The faro dealer didn't dare blink as Tessa made her way to the bar, to Yvonne's open arms. The two embraced, and the pants of every man suddenly became pleasantly tighter at the crotch. Even Aguirre abandoned his duties and let his eyes crawl all over Tessa's body.

"This is the new girl, everyone," Yvonne said. "Treat her well. Don't get too rough. And remember to have some fun, huh?" She winked at the crowd, and everyone began hooting.

Mendoza barked a few words in Spanish, and everyone hooted even louder. The faro dealer switched on the player piano, and music flooded the room.

The skinny one's client moved toward Tessa, but—Trixie, or was it Lavender?—pulled him back and nuzzled his head between her surprisingly considerable breasts.

Yvonne poured Tessa a drink and put it in her hands. "Good luck, honey. If any of these guys gives you a problem, let me know. If things get violent, go to Aguirre first. He's the guy by the door."

"I gathered," Tessa said.

"The skinny one is Lavender," Yvonne said. "The fat one's Trixie. And the faro dealer is Rodrigo. He might want a piece of you, but don't let him. He doesn't get anything until after hours, right?"

"Understood," Tessa said.

"Go get 'em, tiger," Yvonne said.

Tessa sipped her drink and looked around the room. Trixie and Yvonne seemed to be working the bar, and Lavender worked the faro tables. There weren't a lot of prospective clients around right now. But who knew? The night was early, and . . .

Three men entered, all dusty from the trail. They weren't *vaqueros*, but they certainly looked thirsty. One of them had gold in his mouth, a good sign. Tessa made sure she got to them first.

-

Tessa was surprised by the turn-around rate in Mendoza's saloon. Back-East, such business proceedings resulted in quality service with plenty of time to perform such quality service. It wasn't just Sam Pepper's policy, either; it was the custom in New York City. Here, though, the act could last anywhere between two minutes to a half an hour.

In her first evening she had gone through five men before midnight. No one managed to fuck for more than thirty minutes. Tessa watched the other girls, and they seemed to spend the same amount of time with their clients. Yvonne kept pretty quiet, but the sound of the bedposts slamming up against the wall betrayed her quickness. With Trixie, though, windows rattled within their frames whenever she cried out with pleasure. With Lavender, you could go either way. It depended upon the client.

As Tessa cleaned herself out for the fifth time this evening, she considered what she'd gone through with the Comancheros and realized this could be worse than she'd feared. With Felton it had been about deceit, and with the Comancheros, property. With these clients, they just wanted to get their pipes cleaned. There was a refreshing honesty about it, and Tessa wondered if maybe Yvonne had been right.

She gave herself a once-over, then went back downstairs for more business. Now the crowd went from wall to wall. Rodrigo had his hands full dealing faro, and a few private games of poker had broken out at the tables. The bar lacked elbow room as *vaqueros* drank their fill and regaled each other in loud Spanish. Tessa knew enough of the language to realize they were yelling stories about their sexual prowess to one another.

Yvonne was still upstairs getting her brains fucked out by the mayor, just as Trixie headed upstairs now with a *vaquero* who might have just turned eighteen three seconds ago. Only Lavender remained downstairs, working a poker player. The room spread wide open, and Tessa started moving toward the faro table.

The batwing doors flew open, and in stepped three men. Tessa recognized two of them as Comancheros from Ortega's bunch. They were nameless, and she remembered one had raped her when Ortega had ordered them to. The third, however, was none other than Desmond Hertell himself. Their eyes locked for a moment, and Desmond leered at her. He whispered something to the other Comancheros, and they all laughed. Desmond then went to the bar and ordered whiskey for them all.

Tessa went to the faro table with the intention of chatting up one of the players, but one of the Comancheros approached her, plucking at his pants around the crotch area, drinking from a glass of whiskey.

"*Hola, señorita,*" he said. It was the one who hadn't raped her. "*Tengo dinero. Vamos?*" He nodded to the stairs.

One of the faro players, an American, interjected. "I believe the lady was about to talk with me."

Desmond stepped over. "I don't see what's wrong with Cortez getting his dick wet. I think he's earned it. And he's got the money. So what the fuck?"

Tessa glanced at Mendoza, who kept an eye on the situation. She waited until he noticed her looking at him. He nodded. She said, "Nothing's wrong. Let's see the color of your money, Cortez."

Desmond said something to his comrade in Comanchero, and the young Mexican grinned, showing off his pouch. There were a few gold pieces in it. Not a lot, but definitely enough.

"You go on with Tessa," Desmond said in English. When he spoke he did not look at Cortez. "She'll show you a good time. One of the best, I'd say."

Cortez nodded, but it was clear that he didn't understand what Desmond had said.

Tessa held her hand out, and Cortez took it.

"Hey!" the American shouted. "Wait a goddam minute!"

Lavender swooped in. "It's all right, mister. Don't you like what you see over here?"

"She's got a purtier face, ma'am," the American said.

"You ain't seen my tits yet," Lavender said. "Care to take a gander?"

Tessa, already halfway up the stairs to her crib, didn't hear the answer.

Ten minutes later they were done, and Cortez was on his way. Tessa took a moment to cleanup a little bit, but as she retouched her make-up she heard a gunshot from downstairs. She ducked down, but when she recognized the sound she knew she could do nothing. She stood directly above the bar, and if a bullet went through the floor, then that was it. What else could she do? What god would protect her?

No more gunshots came, but she heard a lot of yelling, and it sounded like Desmond. She thought it might be interesting to see the action, especially if Desmond was hurt, so she exited her room and headed down the stairs.

Rodrigo lay on his back, blood spurting from his throat into a puddle surrounding his head. His fingers feebly tried to stem the flow, to no avail. It had been a killing blow, and Rodrigo was as good as dead. Standing over him was the other Comanchero, the one whose name she could not remember. He held a smoking gun, and Mendoza yelled at him. Desmond stood between them, trying to keep the peace and failing. Desmond shouted in the Comanchero mixed language, and the other two argued in Spanish. Neither paid much attention to Desmond.

Finally Desmond gave up. "Fuck both of you," he said in English. "I'm getting a drink."

The Comanchero went for his gun, but Mendoza beat him with a chop to the throat. The nameless guy dropped to the floor, gripping at the stricken spot, gasping for breath.

"You son of a bitch!" Desmond shouted. He drew down on Mendoza.

Aguirre had already drawn his weapon, and before Desmond could even cock the hammer of his six-shooter, the guard put three bullets into the prettier Hertell's chest, dropping him like a straw man.

The downed Comanchero gingerly went for his own weapon, but Cortez slapped a hand down on the gun. He whispered something in Spanish to his comrade, and then he helped his friend out of the saloon.

Tessa stood by the stairs as Desmond's life-blood ran out of the holes in his chest. One of the bullets had passed through, so more blood spread out behind him as he lay staring at the ceiling. His mouth worked like a suffocating fish's, but there was no doubt about his lingering death. He'd be gone in the next five minutes, and even that long would be a stretch.

Mendoza went behind the faro table and checked on his dealer, but it turned out to be an exercise in futility. He cursed in Spanish and told a *vaquero* to fetch the undertaker. By the time Mendoza stepped out from behind the faro table, Desmond had expired, too.

Tessa went to the bar and ordered a whiskey with the tip she'd gotten from Cortez. "Not the cheap stuff, either," she said. Yvonne, not as shocked as she'd been pretending, obliged her.

-

Two hours later, after the corpses had been cleaned up, and Tessa had been with three more men, Moreno pushed his way through the batwing doors. All four ladies were on the floor at the time, working various portions of the saloon, and all tried to ignore the Comanchero leader's entrance. Tessa looked up briefly, and when she saw the newcomer she'd turned her attention back on a poker player.

"Mendoza," Moreno said. "I would like to speak with you."

The bartender looked at the other Comancheros who had accompanied their leader. All were packing, and they did not look like they were drunk.

"Now," Moreno said.

Mendoza looked to the others. "Clear the bar. Everyone!"

The ladies went scattering, and the customers eased their way to the exit. Only Aguirre remained, and he stood behind his boss, arms crossed.

Tessa joined her co-workers in their rush for the stairs, but when the others hid away in their cribs, she remained outside peering through the bars of the balcony's railing, waiting to see how this all turned out.

Moreno and Mendoza both spoke exclusively in Spanish. While not good with the language, she vaguely determined what they said. It seemed like Moreno wanted to know what had lead up to the shooting of Desmond Hertell.

"Ravenous Tarantula accused my dealer of cheating," Mendoza said. "I run a clean saloon."

"I'm sure you do," Moreno said. "But at the same time, I trust my men."

Tessa thought that Mendoza said that Rodrigo came from unimpeachable references, and the two argued in staccato back and forth for the next few minutes. Finally Moreno sighed. "What about Desmond?"

"He was trying to mediate the issue," Mendoza said. "Then he gave up in favor of alcohol."

"And then?"

This next part was a bit confusing, but Tessa thought the bartender had said that the nameless Comanchero, whose name turned out to be Rivera, drew down on him, at which point he had to defend himself. "It wasn't like I had killed him or anything," Mendoza said. "I hit him in the throat. He would have lived."

"And then?" Moreno asked.

"Hertell drew down on me. If not for Aguirre's interference, I would not be having this discussion with you."

Moreno nodded. "Very well. Give us five bottles of whiskey and three hundred *pesos*, and we will not tear down this bar around your head."

"I am not to blame," Mendoza said.

"I have decided. Meet these terms, or you will regret it."

For a moment it looked like Mendoza wanted to fight back, but then his shoulders slumped. "Fine. I will accept these terms. But I don't want to see your Comancheros for at least a year."

Moreno smiled. "That shouldn't be a problem. As of tomorrow we're headed north for more spoils."

"Aguirre!" Mendoza called. He seemed surprised when his bodyguard cleared his throat behind him. Mendoza said, "Give them what they want. And be quick."

Aguirre nodded and went behind the bar. As he rooted around Mendoza looked up to the balcony, and his eyes locked with Tessa's. For a moment they watched each other, and then the whiskey and money came to the table.

Moreno quickly counted the cash and nodded. "Pleasure doing business, Mendoza."

Mendoza remained silent as the Comancheros filed out of the bar. When Aguirre looked to him, his eyebrows raised, the bartender shook his head. "No. Close down for the night."

Aguirre went to the front door and locked up. Tessa started to retreat when Mendoza pointed to her. "In my office. Right now."

Later, when Tessa laid her head down to go to sleep, she wondered if violence turned her boss on. This second bout of sex had definitely been more intense than the first, though still not very satisfying. She went to bed after cleaning up between her legs, and she dreamed of killing Ortega again. She smiled in her sleep.

-

At three o'clock Tessa's eyes opened. She didn't think she had been dreaming, and she had no idea as to what had awoken her. She waited in the darkness, hearing only the tick of the clock and the steady beat of her heart.

Sure that nothing was amiss, she closed her eyes again, but she couldn't find sleep. She tossed and turned, and after a half an hour of effort she finally gave up.

Her pitcher was empty, so she decided to go downstairs for a drink. As she quietly slipped down to the bar she thought she might take a slug of whiskey. Perhaps a nightcap would do her well. Not the fancy stuff, though. She knew from tonight's experience that Mendoza watched the stuff like a hawk and even drew lines to mark the levels. The cheap shit, however, was open market.

Water first. She bent down behind the bar and dipped her pitcher in a barrel. She then put the container on top of the bar and took a few extra handfuls of water to her mouth. It was warm but refreshing, especially after a night of tasting nothing but bar slop and unwashed men.

Tessa straightened out and grabbed the pitcher. Someone said, "You should wipe that up. Mendoza hates sweat circles."

Tessa whipped her head around, but she couldn't see in the darkness. Only the moon lit her way, and it was not generous tonight. "Who's there?"

A match flared up, and one of the lanterns blazed to life, revealing Yvonne's smirking face. "It's just me, honey. Thirsty?"

Tessa looked down at the pitcher and nodded.

"Yeah, the desert is hell on your tongue," Yvonne said. "Sometimes I make three or four trips down here in the summer. But don't go thinking about taking any of the hooch."

"No ma'am," Tessa said. As if she'd never thought of it.

"It's for your own health. Mendoza would get upset, but that doesn't matter. You'd only make yourself thirstier, and that doesn't do anyone any good."

Tessa nodded again.

Yvonne took a rag from one of the tables and dried the bottom of Tessa's pitcher. She then moved to the bar and wiped up the wet mark. "You did good tonight, honey. Better than almost everyone I've ever seen. Trixie and Lavender are kinda pissed at you."

"I thought they might be."

"When folks get used to you, things'll level out," Yvonne said. She tossed the rag aside. "What do you think so far?"

Tessa shrugged, and some water spilled, wetting her fingers. "It's all right."

"I think you're short-changing it," Yvonne said. "I saw the look on your face tonight. No one can act that good. You had some fun, right?"

Tessa smiled. "Maybe a little."

"That's the spirit. I can't tell you how many whores I've seen broken because they had no sense of fun."

"Is that what we are?" Tessa asked. "Whores?"

"We fuck for money. That makes us whores. But being a whore ain't so bad, eh?"

"I didn't come out West to be a whore," Tessa said.

"None of us did," Yvonne said.

"I just wanted to be a normal woman. I knew I'd never be cut out for high society, but I didn't want to be a whore. I had enough of that Back-East."

"What can I say?" Yvonne said. "Shit happens, and when it doesn't, it's going to."

"Why did *you* come out West?" Tessa asked.

Yvonne opened her mouth, but before she could say anything, someone shuffled upstairs. It sounded like the noise had come from Mendoza's room.

"That's a story for another time, honey. I think maybe we should go back to bed."

Tessa agreed. Just before they headed back to their cribs, she stood on tiptoes to blow out the lantern. In Luna's illumination, they made their way to their beds, and both slept the night through.

-

The next day Tessa noticed that she'd collected quite a bit of money in tips, so she thought she'd treat herself to something special. After she got dressed she went downstairs and saw Mendoza slumped at a table, reading the newspaper. From the way he rubbed at his temples she guessed that he had a hangover.

"Sir," Tessa said. "I'm going to go out for a while, if that's all right with you."

Mendoza scowled. "Out? For what?"

"Just to see the town," Tessa said. "I'll be back in time for tonight."

"You'd better be." Mendoza waved a dismissive hand, and Tessa took that to mean that she was free to go.

As soon as she stepped outside into the blinding sun and the baking air, she considered making a break for it. It would be easy. She had enough money for a horse. Nothing fancy, but a horse nonetheless.

But where would she go? Besides, she had no idea as to where in Mexico she was. Sure, she knew which direction was north, but would such information be enough?

She wasn't being beaten like she'd been with the Comancheros. All she had to do was offer some sex, and she didn't think that to be so bad.

Her thoughts jumbled together, and she decided it best not to consider these things. Not yet. Perhaps later, when she had a better lay of the land.

Wasn't this what got you into trouble with Iron Trail? a voice in her head asked.

This intrusion surprised her, but she found herself thinking back to a time before she'd fallen in love with her original captor. She'd given him sex in return for information on how to survive. She remembered how she thought she would break away from Iron Trail, perhaps even kill him, and all she had to do was wait until tomorrow. Except with each procrastination she fell more and more in love with him.

Did this indicate a healthy mind? Or had she gone temporarily insane under his supervision? Should she just make a break for it now?

Why go around in circles? She moved on, her mind a barren wasteland of thought. She took in her surroundings and nothing more. Some people tried to sell her things, others offered wolf whistles. Very few spoke English.

She found herself in a general store, glancing about the goods. The shopkeeper was a polite young man. He spoke very broken English, but enough with which to do business. He understood she was just browsing.

When she came upon a pile of notebooks with a cup of pencils next to it, she picked up a pad and flipped through the pages. All were blank, begging to have graphite scraped against them.

She grabbed a handful of pencils and prepared to bring them with a pad of paper to the clerk, but then she stopped. She thought back over all the time she had ever kept a journal, and she remembered what had happened to each one.

Tessa sighed, and she dropped the notebook back on the pile, the pencils back in the cup. There would be no more journals for her. The world seemed incessant upon making sure there would be nothing left of her when she died, so why bother kicking against the pricks?

She started to exit with no purchases when she saw that the store sold jerky. She stopped to buy a piece, and as she bit into the tough leathery stick, she tasted the wilderness. She tasted freedom from Comancheros and saloon keepers.

She tasted her memories of Iron Trail, and she wept for him. Not in front of the shopkeeper or anyone else, of course. No, she saved her grief for when she was alone with the past jutting juicily out of her greasy fist.

-

Tessa just finished cleaning up after one of her customers when she heard the banging from two doors down. Shouts were followed by a few screams. The former sounded masculine, and the latter sounded like Lavender.

Tessa opened her door just in time to see Aguirre clomping up the steps hard enough to rattle the walls. He came around the railing and charged up to Lavender's door. He did not wait long enough to knock. He threw his shoulder into the wood, splintering it from its hinges.

Tessa stepped out into the hallway so she could peek into the room. Mendoza arrived next to her within moments, followed by Yvonne. They all watched as Aguirre grabbed the offending customer by the throat and dragged him back. The customer managed to break free by scraping his boot along Aguirre's shin, but it was a small victory. Aguirre retaliated by buffaloing the guy. They heard a sharp crack, and the customer went down, eyes wide with death, blood oozing from his mouth and nostrils and the corners of his eyes.

Lavender sat on the corner of her bed, weeping, snot dripping from her nose and caking her upper lip. She had bruises on her face and arms, and one of her eyes had swollen shut. The brow above was split, and blood dribbled down her face from it.

"Ah, hell," Mendoza said. "This is fucking great."

As Mendoza went to her side, Aguirre knelt next to the corpse and checked it over, just to be sure he was dead.

"Show me your teeth," Mendoza said to Lavender. When she didn't he reached over and pushed her hands aside, opening her mouth to take a look. "Good. They're still there. What's this about?"

Lavender tried to speak, but her throat clogged up with tears.

"Does this happen often?" Tessa asked Yvonne.

"Not really," Yvonne said. "But it does happen. Sometimes. It's a hazard of the job."

Tessa nodded as she looked on.

"Forget it," Mendoza said to his property. "We'll talk about it later. Get down to the doctor's. While you're there, get your cunt checked out. Save some time." He turned to Aguirre and spoke in Spanish.

243

Tessa didn't know what he said, but from the way he gestured at the corpse, she figured that he had told his guard to get rid of the body.

"Better grab a mop from downstairs, honey," Yvonne said. "The boss is going to want that mess cleaned up. Ever scrub blood before?"

Tessa shook her head.

"Might as well learn now. Better grab one of those hard-bristle brushes, too."

An hour later, when Lavender had been escorted to the doctor's office and the customer's body had been dragged to the undertaker's, Yvonne and Tessa stood over the circle of wetness, sweating and shaking their heads.

"Not bad," Yvonne said. "There'll always be a mark there, but all in all not bad."

"Maybe Lavender can put a throw rug over it," Tessa said.

Yvonne laughed. "Hot damn, girl! You're a regular homemaker, ain't you?" She slapped Tessa on the back.

Tessa stared down at the faint blood stain, and she tried not to imagine it being in her room. She was tough. Her tribulations had made her that way. But what would she be able to do if something like this happened to her?

The next day when she went out for a walk, she went back to the general store and purchased a Derringer. It wasn't anything fancy; it looked just like the one she'd owned when she came to live as Felton's wife, the one Sam Pepper had given her for the trip out West.

The shopkeeper wanted to sell her something that would go better with her outfit, but she turned him away. "Just give me the bullets for this one."

"Yes, ma'am," the shopkeeper said.

When she left the store she did not look back. She just wanted to find a place where she could have a decent breakfast and forget about what she'd seen last night. Since she didn't give the store a second thought, she did not notice the shopkeeper emerge. She did not see him when he put the CLOSED sign over the door. And she was not aware of him crossing the street and running down toward Mendoza's saloon.

-

Tessa looked at the clock and noticed that she had an hour before work. She had whiled her day away at a restaurant, and after that she visited Lavender at the doctor's office. She had bruises, but no broken bones. She'd be off for the next few days while her black and blue marks went away, but she would be as good as new in no time.

The doctor took payment in trade.

Now Tessa thought that maybe she should get ready early and see how the pickings were downstairs. She stood up and headed to her dresser when there came a quiet knocking at her door.

"Who is it?" she asked.

"It's Alfredo Mendoza, darling. I was wondering if I could see you a moment."

"Come in."

The door cracked open, and Mendoza poked his fat head over the threshold. "I hope I'm not intruding."

"I was about to get dressed for tonight," Tessa said. She took an outfit from her dresser and laid it out on the bed. "What can I do for you?"

Mendoza entered and closed the door behind him. His fingers hesitated over the key, as if he wondered whether he should lock up or not, but he seemed to abandon this idea. Instead he ambled over to the dresser and leaned against the wall, watching her.

"What?" she asked.

"I wanted to ask your opinion of what happened to Lavender," he said.

She didn't think he was simply here to make conversation. But she couldn't come up with any other reason for him to be here. Did he want another taste of her? If so, he had no need to beat around the proverbial bush.

"Well?" he asked.

"It's a shame," Tessa said. She fiddled with some of the ruffles on the dress.

"And?"

"And what? It was an ugly thing to happen, and I hope to never see the likes again."

Mendoza oozed up behind her and rested his hands on her shoulders, massaging slowly. "I can understand a whore's fear. You're not tough like us men, and you find yourself in a horrible position if a customer gets rough. You feel the need to tip the scales in your favor."

Tessa remained silent.

"Give me the Derringer," Mendoza said. "Whores should not be armed. I have customers to think of."

Tessa thought to deny her ownership, but what would be the point? Mendoza clearly knew. It fell upon her to now prove that she needed the hardware. "I have no intention of letting someone do to me what that man did to Lavender. Besides, you have to think of your merchandise, too. Lavender isn't going to be able to earn for you until

246

the swelling goes down and the bruises go away. Not even the town drunk would want a piece of her right now."

Mendoza moved his hands to her upper arms and turned her around so he could look her in the eyes. "Look, Tessa." And with a sudden savagery she would never have believed his weight to have allowed, he shoved a fist into her belly, doubling her over.

She fell to her knees, gasping for air that nature denied to her. She tried speaking, but nothing came out.

"I'm the owner here." Mendoza's voice was now gruff, all sense of honey gone. "You don't question me, understand? I'm the law, and you're my property. You're lucky you're so beautiful, and I'm already down a whore, or I would have put your nose on the other side of your face. Now give me the fucking gun."

With a trembling finger, she pointed to her dresser. The garters were still in there, and she'd intended to tie the tiny pistol to one of them.

Mendoza shuffled through the drawer until he found his prize. He hefted it for a moment and barked a laugh. "You could barely put a dog's eye out with this piece of shit." He slipped it into his pocket. "Don't let this happen again. In case you were wondering, the shopkeeper told me. It's his job to tell me. So put firearms out of your pretty little head."

Tessa gritted her teeth as she pushed herself up to her feet. The pain still had her bent over a little, but she knew she'd live. There might be bruising, but it would be nowhere a customer would see it while on the floor. Maybe after they'd gone to her crib, but if she kept the lights low, then there would be no problem.

Mendoza looked at his watch before putting it back in his vest. "See you in an hour. Don't be late."

247

The door closed, and Tessa sat on the bed, breathing heavily. The pain already subsided, but that didn't bother her. No, the humiliation got to her more, and the sudden absence of a gun in her room.

She resolved to not let this defeat her. There were other ways of surviving. She stood and started getting herself ready for the evening.

-

On a Sunday afternoon Tessa worked at cleaning the saloon up with her fellow ladies. The people of Oso Feo were devout Catholics, and town law stated that all vice halls should be closed on the Lord's Day. Mendoza took advantage of this by having his employees clean the place up. Saturday nights were usually the nastiest, and cleaning up was no simple chore.

Maybe not for Mendoza. All he did was sit behind his bar and wipe down all the glasses. Aguirre had the day off, so it fell upon the ladies to do all the hard work. They whirled about the place, scrubbing and rubbing and wiping and sweeping.

Tessa worked with Yvonne in the back room, tidying up and organizing everything. Making sure that the empty barrels were dragged out to the alley and the full ones were on hand to be tapped. Making sure that all the fluid-encrusted bed-sheets were scrubbed clean in the wash basin.

They talked about the places they'd been to, people they'd seen, things like that. It turned out they were both from New York, and both had come West to be mail order brides.

"Small world, honey," Yvonne said. "I can only assume your hubby was a piece of shit, considering where you turned up. Tell me about him."

Tessa smiled, thinking back to her time with Felton Reeves. Had she really been happy there for a while? Just a short period of time? She almost wished she still lived in Felton's illusion.

"Well?" Yvonne asked.

"He was kind of silly looking," Tessa said. "He was skinny with an Adam's apple which really was about the size of an apple. And his hair. My God, the man couldn't tame it!"

Yvonne laughed. "My fella was the same way. Nothing on earth could have given him a decent pattern. I tried lard on him once, and that seemed to do the trick, but Lord, did he attract flies!"

The both of them laughed a little too loud. "Quit yer giggling and get back to work, whores!" Mendoza shouted from the bar.

Yvonne and Tessa exchanged devilish glances and tried not to giggle when they each put a single finger to their lips. "Go on," Yvonne said. "Tell me more."

"Well, he wore clothes that made him look like a scarecrow," Tessa said. "He was a nice guy, or so I thought. When I first met him, I thought he was just a fool, but a well-meaning fool. He never cursed, and he always went to church. His neighbors liked him and thought him to be harmless."

"But he wasn't," Yvonne said.

"No, he wasn't. He sold me to a Comanche gentleman by the name of Iron Trail—"

Yvonne's face went pale, and she almost dropped the bed sheets she carried to the wash basin. "Iron Trail, you say?"

"Yes. Is the name familiar?"

"Is the name of your husband Felton Reeves?" Yvonne asked.

Tessa blinked. "Yes. How did you know?"

"Because I was his second mail order bride," Yvonne said. "My name isn't Yvonne, really. It's Elizabeth Rivers. I just started calling myself Yvonne because some cowboy said he thought I looked like an Yvonne. Do you recognize my name?"

Hadn't she seen it on one of the graves behind Felton's house?

"And now your name is on a grave, too, huh?" Yvonne asked. "Some fuckin racket he's got going."

"Did he do the same thing to you?" Tessa asked.

"Damn right he did," Yvonne said. She told Tessa a story remarkably similar to her own. The only notable difference was that Iron Trail had come down to Oso Feo himself without bargaining with the Comancheros. There was no love between Yvonne and Iron Trail, however. The Comanche had respected her, and had taught her a few things about survival, but no other emotion passed between them.

Tessa then told her story in its entirety, starting with Sam Pepper, continuing with Felton and Iron Trail, skimming through Ortega, and ending with their meeting in Mendoza's saloon.

"I knew of that Sam Pepper fella'," Yvonne said. "Never met him, but I heard an awful lot of terrible things about him. Like, he was a murderer and maybe liked his girls a little too young."

"That's him, all right," Tessa said. "But there was a tender side to him, too. If he loved you, he could be very nice."

"I think that's all men, honey," Yvonne said. "They're nice enough when they need to be, but when they don't get their way they revert to the beasts they are."

Tessa nodded. There seemed to be a lot of wisdom in this.

-

Two months later she met the infamous outlaw, William King. She had never heard of him personally but later, when the other whores warned her about him, they told her about all the men he'd killed, not just as a bank robber but also as a soldier in Bill Quantrill's army.

When Tessa went downstairs on that fateful day, all she saw was a man hunched over a glass of whiskey, a bottle nearby at hand. No one else populated the saloon yet, and the other ladies were milling about. It struck her as odd that no one had approached the stranger, but she figured it was just her good luck.

"Hello, mister." She put an arm around the man's shoulders. "What are you drinking?"

The man looked up through the shaggy dark hair at his brow. His eyes were blue, but they were the darkest blue she had ever seen. He had a thick growth at his cheeks, and it looked like something weighed him down by an anvil tied around his neck. He seemed confused, as if he'd wandered into the middle of a lecture about a topic with which he was unfamiliar.

Perhaps she shouldn't have approached this man, and she tried to think of polite ways to show she had made a mistake. "Sorry, sir," she said. "I'll leave you—"

"Wait," the man said. He took her gently by the wrist. He offered no force to it, but it was clear that he had the strength to make her stay. If he wanted to.

She sat down next to him and let him hold her hand. "Mind if I have a drink?" she asked.

The man called for another glass, which Mendoza provided. Neither of them noticed when Mendoza tried to get Tessa's attention. He tried to shake his head by using only his eyes, but the motion went unrecognized.

The man poured her drink almost to the top of the glass and pushed it across the scarred wooden table to her. He watched as she picked it up and took one big gulp of it. Half the glass went down her throat, and he nodded approvingly.

"You don't look like much," he said, "but it seems you've got talents."

"I'm Tessa," she said.

"Call me William."

"Sure, William. You seem to be a man with troubles. I think I can help lighten the burden, don't you?"

William uttered a laugh. "I'll bet you can."

"Tell me about yourself," she said.

The brightness he just started to display suddenly died out, and he poured himself another drink. To the brim. With a short cough he downed the entire glass and licked his lips. "That's a long story. I don't think I know where I can begin."

Tessa patted his arm, trying to be the best servant she could. "You don't have to tell me anything, darling."

"How much?" he asked.

"How much what?"

"For your services."

She finished off her drink, and led him upstairs by the hand. Once in her crib money exchanged hands, unusual before the act but not unheard of, and they lowered themselves to her bed.

A half an hour later they fell apart and side by side panted up at the ceiling, trying to catch their breath. After a long moment of silence Tessa got out of bed, and washed up for the next customer.

"Wait," William said. He grabbed her wrist in much the same way as he had before.

"Yes, darling?" Tessa asked.

"How much for you to just lie down next to me for a few hours?" William asked. "No sex or anything, just resting."

"I don't do that."

"Fine," he said. "You charge five for a poke, right? Here's fifty. Tell your boss I poked you ten times."

She laughed. "That's just too . . . too . . ."

"Too what?"

She took the money and put it on the dresser. "Forty for the eight pokes," she said. "The rest is a tip. That should keep us going for a few hours."

"That's all I need," William said. "Thank you."

She went back to bed and grabbed his dick, but he showed no response. "No. I just want to rest next to you."

"Fine." She put her head on the pillow, and William curled up next to her. Within minutes he snored softly against her neck.

About an hour later a soft knock came to her door. Quietly she slipped out from his embrace. She opened the door a crack and poked her face out to see Aguirre looking back at her with his dead fish gaze.

"What?" she whispered.

"Mendoza says to check on you," he said. His English was bad, and he stuttered a lot, but he got his intent across.

"Take it easy," she said. "He paid for more than one poke."

"Money?" he asked.

Tessa swore. "Wait here." She closed the door, and when she opened it again, she poured a couple of double eagles into Aguirre's hand.

"How many pokes he have left?"

"Five," she said.

He nodded. "I be back later."

When she crept back into bed, back to William's arms, she watched the clock. She figured she could get away with another hour, maybe ninety minutes, but if Aguirre had to come upstairs again, things would not go very smoothly.

She did not sleep, but she listened to William's breathing and felt the rise and fall of his chest. She wanted to close her eyes, to pretend it was Iron Trail next to her, but she knew if she did she would fall asleep.

Instead she stared at the second hand as it swept across the face of the clock, counting out the minutes before she would have to wake her customer and send him on his way.

When the ninety minutes were up and no one bothered them, Tessa decided to see how far she could push it. It had been quite some time since she'd lain next to a man in such a fashion, and she enjoyed it. She knew William wouldn't mind the extra sleep.

But when they reached the two hour mark, she knew it was just a matter of time before Mendoza sent Aguirre back upstairs. Violence would ensue.

Tessa tapped William's shoulder. "Wake up. It's time to go."

William's eyes slowly peeled back, and he regarded her with a look that didn't seem sleepy. It was as if consciousness had never fully left him, and he had been counting the minutes just as she had been.

"If you don't get going, my boss will think something's wrong," Tessa said. "He'll send Aguirre up, and we don't want that."

"What are you doing here?" William asked.

"Pardon?"

"In this whorehouse."

Tessa laughed. "I'm not a prostitute with a heart of gold. I'm just a prostitute, and you're not my white knight."

William's eyes drifted from her face down her body to her feet, then back up. "Sure. Laugh it off. But when I look into your eyes, I see my own."

Tessa's smile faded. His eyes were dark hollows, and they made it look like he barely had a grip on his soul.

"You're here because you have no choice," William said. "Am I right?"

Tessa bit her lip and looked away.

"Me, too," William continued. "I guess we're both doomed by the great god circumstance."

"You'd better leave, William," she said.

He sat up and put his pants back on. As he buttoned his shirt, he turned to her. "A long time ago I was going to be a teacher. I had all the book learning you could imagine, but all it ever did was make me ask more questions. Free will was one of my favorite subjects, and back then I always believed in it."

"You don't anymore?" she asked.

"Nope. When you've been through the things I've experienced, you start to realize that someone, maybe God, set you down a certain path, and there was no way you could turn around and find another."

"I think I know the feeling," Tessa said.

William buckled his gun belt on and knotted the rawhide string around his thigh. "You ever kill someone?"

Tessa considered lying, but why bother? Would this stranger judge her? "Yes, I have."

"More than one?"

"Yes," she said.

"They have it coming?"

"Indubitably."

He drew his gun and held it up, barrel aimed at the ceiling, for her to see. "This thing has sent many souls to their makers. More than I care to count, both in wartime and when I robbed banks. Almost all of those sons of bitches had it coming, and those who didn't, well, they just got in my way. They had fair warning."

Tessa remained silent, waiting.

"There was one, though . . ." He trailed off, and his face distorted in the dimness. For a moment Tessa thought he would cry.

"William, you—"

"Never mind," he said. He holstered the weapon and went for the door. "I'll probably be back tomorrow."

"I'll be glad to see you," she said.

As soon as he left, Tessa cleaned up. Soon she went back downstairs. The place was a lot more crowded than it had been earlier, and she cast her gaze around for William.

He was gone.

But there were plenty of men who were willing to pay her to take his place.

-

The next day, as Tessa cleaned up the barroom, Mendoza waddled over to her and hovered for a moment, watching as she scrubbed at a puke stain.

She noted his presence, and ordinarily would have waited for him to say his piece, but she could feel her own irritation itching under the skin of her scalp. "What do you want, sir?" she asked.

"What did that gunman want last night?" he asked.

"What gunman?" Though she knew.

"Bloody Bill King," Mendoza said. "You were with him a long time."

"Oh. William. I guess he liked me a lot. He was a hell of a randy man, sir, and he paid in advance."

"I'm not arguing with that," Mendoza said. "Aguirre told me there were no fucking sounds coming from your crib. Why is that?"

She stopped scrubbing and sat up, balancing her ass on her heels. A strand of her hair had tumbled free from its restraints and hung in her face. She swept it back and sighed. "He got the animal out of him the first time. The rest were a lot sweeter."

"Sweeter? What the fuck is that supposed to mean?"

"I don't know. It wasn't rough. It was slow and tender."

"Tender? I don't like the words you're choosing."

"I don't have any others," she said.

"No personal relationships," Mendoza said. "You're here to fuck for money, and to give me my cut."

"I'm not in love with him," Tessa said.

257

"Good. Keep it that way." And he went upstairs to his office.

Lavender stopped polishing glasses behind the bar and approached Tessa. "Did you really give Bloody Bill King a poke?"

Tessa resumed scrubbing. "More than one."

"Why?"

Tessa started grinding her teeth. "He had the money."

"But he's a killer."

"So are most of our customers," Tessa said. "What makes him different?"

"Well, he's a famous outlaw," she said. "Like the James brothers. I heard he rode with them during the war. He's mercilessly killed hundreds."

"I'm sure that's a true story," Tessa said. She did not wonder if her sarcasm went noticed or not.

Lavender watched Tessa scrub for a while, showing no intention of returning to her own job. "What was it like?"

"Fucking William King?" Tessa asked.

"Yeah. Did he . . . hurt you?"

Tessa's mouth curled up into a tight grin. "He threatened me at gun point and then showed me his collection of scalps. One of 'em still had the face attached."

Lavender grimaced. "Really?"

"No. He was a customer, just like any other. Now can I please scrub up this sick stain in peace?"

Lavender remained, biting one of her fingernails, as if debating whether or not to mention something.

"Do you have anymore curiosity to vent?" Tessa asked.

"He killed kids, you know."

It was a disturbing thought, but Tessa knew enough to realize what things were like out here. It was probably just a rumor.

When she didn't answer, Lavender finally went away, leaving her to her task.

-

True to his word William King returned that evening and the next evening and the next. During the following night they both sat at a table, talking and drinking and laughing. Mendoza approached them with a bottle of the good stuff and joined them without an invitation.

"Who are you?" William asked.

Mendoza poured his good whiskey into three glasses and distributed them to everyone. "I'm the owner of this fine establishment. My name is Alfredo Mendoza. And you are William King."

William nodded. "My notoriety precedes me?"

"That's a fact," Mendoza said. "Drink up."

William took a sip at his glass and nodded. "That's some mighty fine liquor, Señor Mendoza. To what do I owe this gift?"

Mendoza downed his glass in one go and licked his lips. "You've been seeing a lot of my number one earner, Mr. King."

"I pay my way," William said.

"No doubt. Unfortunately, while she is busy taking care of your business, she is neglecting my other customers."

"I'll pay double the price. How's that?"

Mendoza's eyes lit up, and Tessa thought that whatever speech he had prepared would be canceled. However, he cleared his throat instead. "It's not a matter of money, although your offer is most generous, and I would be willing to take it. However, Tessa draws a lot of customers, and if she's too busy with you, she can't be with them."

"So it's a matter of servicing your customers," William said.

"Yes. I don't want to disappoint anyone. A lot of people come in here wanting real quality, and they don't like having to settle for Trixie. She's the fat whore."

William sipped at the whiskey again. "What do you propose?"

"Make your visits less frequent," Mendoza said. "Make them every other night. And in return I will throw in a bottle of this whiskey for each rendezvous, gratis."

William grunted a laugh. "You must really want Tessa on the floor."

"What can I say? She livens this place up. She's the most beautiful asset I have to offer this shit-splat of a town."

William nodded. "You're the first whoremaster I've ever known to turn perfectly good business away."

"But I'm sure you see my point," Mendoza said.

"You bet. I have a stipulation, though."

Mendoza poured himself another glass. "Name it."

"I promise to make my nocturnal visits later in the evening, but in return I expect to spend the rest of the evening with Tessa. I will leave your establishment in the morning."

Mendoza paused, his whiskey glass suspended in the air mere inches from his mouth. He seemed to be weighing the matter from the way his head tilted back and forth. "Might I inquire as to why?"

"Don't worry, Señor Mendoza. I have no intention of falling in love with her and stealing her away from your business. It's just that it has been quite some time since I've had the company of a woman as lovely as Tessa. I miss sleeping next to a woman, and I'm willing to pay for the privilege."

The glass finished its voyage to Mendoza's lips, and it surrendered the entirety of its contents to his mouth. It then clunked down on the table, empty. "You drive a hard bargain, sir, but I think the terms are acceptable."

"Good." William drank down the remainder of his own glass.

"There's just one thing," Mendoza said. "If you show any signs of falling in love with her, I will send Aguirre to cut your nuts off."

William smiled, already buzzed. "That's agreeable, Señor Mendoza."

They shook hands, and Mendoza stood. "Take the bottle. Remember, tomorrow you should stay away from here."

"I understand," William said. "I'll see you in the morning on my way out."

Mendoza held his hand out.

"Money up front?" William asked.

Mendoza nodded.

William returned the gesture and dropped a few coins into Mendoza's palm. "Good night, señor."

"Good night, Mr. King."

As soon as Mendoza left, William turned to Tessa. "I hope you don't find this arrangement objectionable. Perhaps I should have asked you before I struck this deal with your boss."

Tessa laughed. "You're so well spoken for a rogue."

William's face reddened slightly. Not much, but enough to betray his embarrassment. "I was going to be a teacher, remember?"

"You did mention that."

"Well? Was I putting the buggy in front of the horse?"

"No," Tessa said. "I don't mind at all. You remind me of someone else, and I'm glad for your company."

"That's funny," William said. "I was about to say the same thing."

Tessa stood and held out her hand. "Shall we?"

William grabbed her offering and the bottle. "Sure."

-

Hours later they came apart, both exhausted from exploring every niche and cranny of the other's body. Skin sticky with sweat and other fluids, they rested side by side, arms and hips touching but nothing more.

Panting, William rolled a cigarette and lit it. Lazy blue smoke rose up to the ceiling and wreathed the hanging lantern. One hand behind his head and the other perched on his chest, he said, "How did you come to be here?"

Tessa sighed. "That's a long story."

William looked at the clock to see it was only one-thirty. "I have the time."

"Why do you want to know?"

"I'm curious." He took the cigarette from his mouth and let it dangle from between his fingers for a while.

She almost laughed. Here was a new diary for her, only this time, instead of writing it all down, all she had to do was dictate. Even though she'd sworn she would never keep another journal she didn't think there to be any harm in telling William anything. Besides, he was pretty drunk, and he might not remember it the following day.

So she told him everything from Sam Pepper selling her to Felton Reeves via mail all the way until now. At first the going was awkward, and she found herself making adjustments to the story not for the purposes of lying, but to make the story easier to tell. But then, much to her surprise, it all came pouring out of her. Around the point where Felton sold her to Iron Trail, when the flood truly began, she refrained from any deviation of truth by then.

She did not cry, though. There were many times she wanted to, but by the end of her tale the only wetness on her cheeks was the sweat from their last bout of fucking, and it was almost dry.

William stubbed out his second cigarette and reached for the bottle Mendoza had left for them. He poured two drinks, and both were very tall. He handed one to Tessa.

She gulped it down at once. "Thank you."

"That was a hard story to tell, I'm sure," William said. He sipped at his own glass. "Why don't you just leave?"

"I told you why," she said. "There isn't another town for miles. If I tried to escape, Mendoza would—"

William held up a hand. "It doesn't matter. You're not shackled down. Anything is possible. All you have to do is walk out of here in the middle of the night, steal a horse and get going. I'm sure if you left now, you'd make the next town by dawn. That's about when they'd be noticing you were gone."

"It's just . . . too dangerous." Tessa held out her glass, and William filled it.

"I'm a pretty experienced man," William said. "I've been all over, done all sorts of things and lived to tell about it, if I was of a mind. Wisdom comes with survival."

Tessa grunted a laugh. "That's definitely the truth."

"The world's like a dog, Tessa. It's easy to impose your will on it. You just need to be careful, or the dog will eventually turn on you and bite."

Tessa stared into her glass. "I'm just tired of the world biting me."

"Then be careful," William said. And he finished his drink.

-

It happened on one of the nights William had agreed not to show up. Tessa worked the floor, having a quick drink between customers, when she saw a familiar face pushing his way through the batwing doors. He stank like cow shit, but his grimy appearance triggered some kind of memory within her mind.

She put her empty glass down and approached the newcomer, trying to place him. He certainly wasn't from Back-East. The only thing that struck any resonance with her was that he was from Felton's town. Yes, that had to be it. She didn't think she'd seen him in Tramonto.

And then it hit her. Jake Ellis. When she lived with Felton and ran all of his errands she often saw Jake Ellis in town, usually at the general store, where he spent most of his idle time talking with the shop's owner, Brett Hartford. Always friendly, Jake tipped his hat to her whenever they encountered one another.

Jake stepped up to the bar and ordered a whiskey. He removed his hat and showed off a mop of sweat-slicked hair. He slapped the dust from the brim and put it on the bar as Mendoza poured a drink.

"Make it a double, friend," Jake said. He ran his hand through his greasy hair, and motes floated around his head. Actually, as she got closer, she noticed they were flies. He had cowhand written all over him, or *vaquero*, as they were known south of the Rio Grande. Had he always been a drover? No, she thought he worked odd jobs around the town.

Jake took down half the drink and sighed. "I love the first belt after a long day's work."

Mendoza nodded. "Welcome to Oso Feo. I hope you enjoy your stay."

"If the whiskey's this good, I think I'll be able to fulfill them hopes, mister."

Tessa grimaced. Jake drank the bar slop. How did most men not recognize this?

"How much?" Jake asked.

"On the house," Mendoza said. "First one's always for free."

"I like that policy," Jake said. He let out a whoop and finished the rest of his drink. Mendoza stood by, ready to refill the glass.

Out of the corner of her eye Tessa saw Trixie making her approach. Quickly Tessa stepped in and took up the space next to Jake.

"Holy fucking shit," Jake said. "You got some high quality talent in here, friend." His gaze went up and down Tessa's body.

"Don't you recognize me?" she asked. Hazarding a glimpse she noticed that Trixie, frowning, had moved on to other prey.

Jake squinted. "You do look kind of familiar. Did I see you in San Antone?"

"I've never been," she said.

"How about Abilene?"

"Nope."

"Shit, I give up. Wait, I didn't get you up the stick, did I?"

"No."

He sighed. "That's a relief. But I do give up."

"Do you remember Felton Reeves?" Tessa asked.

Jake broke up laughing. "That loopy bastard? You bet I do. That fella looked weirder than a shaved cat. Hard to forget . . ." And he trailed off.

She smiled. "You remember."

Jake cleared his throat. "Ain't you dead?"

"That's the rumor," she said.

"So what? You left him, then?"

"He sold me to a Comanche gentleman by the name of Iron Trail."

Jake laughed again. "You're putting me on. I saw your grave. Tessa Reeves, right?"

"That's right."

"But Fell couldn't hurt a fly, not even if it made fun of his mother."

"I'm not the only one," she said. "All of his brides were sold to Iron Trail."

Jake paid for his next drink, but this time all he took was a sip. "That's just not true. Felton Reeves ain't that bright. If he had any brains in his head, he'd get a new farm. He just can't make a living off the shit he harvests."

"Yet he has enough money to send away for mail order brides?" she asked.

Jake paused, and she thought she'd finally broken through his mental barrier. He opened his mouth, as if he were about to say something, but nothing came out, not even a whistle of air.

And then Yvonne stopped by. "Fill me up, boss," she said to Mendoza. "Night's been hard for me."

Jake watched her, eyes wide with recognition. In fact it was more than just that. Tessa thought the cowhand might actually be afraid.

266

"Beth fuckin Reeves," he whispered.

Yvonne perked up and turned. "You know me?" And her mouth paused as the last word squeaked out of her mouth. "Jacob Ellis?"

"You're both supposed to be dead," Jake said.

"Death came to punch our tickets, but we kicked his ass and sent him packing." Yvonne smiled. "How you been?"

Jake's hand trembled as he brought the glass to his lips and finished off his drink. He placed the tumbler back down a little too hard on the bar. "I . . . I just, well, this is just . . ." He jammed his hat back on his head and made for the exit.

"Wait!" Tessa shouted.

Jake whirled around. "I don't want to know shit about this. I'm getting the fuck out of here. My world is finally coming together for me, and I don't need specters from beyond to ruin it all."

"Does he have a new one yet?" Yvonne asked.

"What do you mean?" Jake asked.

"A new mail order bride."

Jake nibbled at his lower lip, and his eyes seemed to dance in his skull. Finally: "Not yet. One's on her way."

He then jerked himself around and pushed through the batwing doors, out of their lives. Tessa turned to look at Yvonne, but the older whore had already finished her drink and returned to work.

Later when they were closing down for the night, Tessa had to talk to Yvonne. "So he has another."

"You mean Felton?"

"Yes. Another victim."

Yvonne shrugged. "From what you told me, Iron Trail's dead. I don't see how the scrawny twat can do business without such a good connection."

"His farm doesn't produce very well," Tessa said. "He's probably desperate. Desperate men usually find a way to get what they want." Her own words seemed to resonate in her head, and she remembered William's analogy about the world and a dog. Was she not desperate enough?

"He's not all that bright," Yvonne said.

"That's just a show for his friends, so they would never suspect what a monster he is. For all I know he's dealing directly with Moreno now."

"So what?" Yvonne said. "It's none of our concern."

Tessa didn't respond to this. She wanted to retort, but what if Yvonne was right?

Yvonne sighed. "Look, remember how I told you I was his second bride?"

"Yes."

"His first wife really did die," Yvonne said. "That's no scheme or anything. He sent for me because he was genuinely lonely. He got the idea for his little business venture when he was with me. I was there for his conversation with Iron Trail. It was the Comanche who convinced him, you know. There's a great deal of sadness in that man, honey."

"It doesn't matter," Tessa said. "He's a monster."

"Good for him," Yvonne said. "Now will you lock up for the night? I'm tired."

Tessa wanted to continue, but out of deference to Yvonne she complied, keeping her mouth shut the whole time. When they went to bed Tessa lay awake for hours listening to Yvonne snore away. Gears turned. Plans formed. Perhaps they were long-reaching. They depended on a lot, but really, nothing was impossible. She'd learned so much from Iron Trail, so why couldn't she learn from William King, too?

-

The next night, after they'd fucked a couple of times, Tessa asked William if he would buy her a gun. "It doesn't have to be anything special. A Derringer would make me happy."

William nodded. "All right. But why not get it yourself?"

"The last time I tried to buy a weapon, the shopkeeper told Mendoza on me," Tessa said. "It has to be you."

"Tired of letting the world bite you?"

"Something like that." She drew him close and they fucked again before going to sleep for the night.

Two days later William returned, and when they were in the privacy of her crib he presented her with a .32-caliber pistol. "I was going to honor your request for a Derringer, but you have strong arms. I think a .32 would be fine for you, especially if you're planning on what I think you are."

Tessa accepted the gun. She expected it to be heavier, but there were no bullets in it. "What do you think I'm going to do?"

"I think you're tired of living here," William said. "I know I am. Something tells me you're not leaving town alone. A few fellas are going to their makers before you're gone, am I right?"

"Maybe." She admired the shape of the .32. It stank of oil, but she thought it to be a good sign. An instrument of death should not smell like roses.

"I paid a 'bo to buy it for me," William said. "I remember you saying that there was a lot of suspicion around this town, and I thought it would look weird if I was buying a .32 for myself, especially when I have this on my hip." He patted the Peacemaker in its holster.

"That was very smart of you. Did you get bullets for it, too?"

"Yep," William said. "I just thought it would be a bad idea to give them to you now."

Her teeth clamped together, and she could hear them grinding in her head. Why did he keep the bullets from her? What use was a gun without ammunition? She supposed she could beat Mendoza to death with it, but she didn't want to be within punching distance of him. "Why?" she asked.

"Because you don't know how to use it," William said. "Without knowing what to do, that thing will be about as useful as a rock to you."

"But—"

"Yeah, I know. You want to get out of here now. I'm here to tell you, you need some patience. If you don't know how to use that thing, it won't do you any good."

"Then what do you propose?" Tessa asked. "You wouldn't give it to me unless you intended to give me bullets."

"I will, eventually," he said. "You have free time tomorrow afternoon, right?"

"Yes."

"You have no obligations to Mendoza at that time, right?"

"Well, he always owns me. But no, I'm not expected to be ready for work until six."

"Good. That will give us plenty of time for target practice. I'll leave at six in the morning, like I always do, and then you can meet me at La Tortilla at about noon. I'll have a buggy and horse ready, and I'll take you out into the desert for some shooting."

"You'd do that for me?" Tessa asked.

"Why wouldn't I?"

"I'm just a whore. Why should you care?"

"Well, you're a pretty whore," William said. When she did not laugh, he pursed his lips. "That's a joke. I mean, you are pretty, but that's not my only reason."

Tessa remained silent, waiting.

"I'm tired of people wanting more and not being able to achieve it," he said. "You're not weak, Tessa. I've never met a stronger woman. The things you've been through would have killed most people I know, and that includes some of the toughest men I've ever met. But you've been scared into submission, and I just can't stand it."

She muttered a soft chuckle. There was no mirth to it. "An experienced gunfighter like you would want to rescue me."

"Fuck that chivalry shit," William said. "You know the phrase about teaching a man how to fish?"

"I'm familiar with it."

"Same thing. If I save you from this, so what? There might come a day when I can't save you. What then? No, I agree with that Darwin fella. Only the strong survive. You're strong, you just don't know it yet. I'm going to help you realize this."

"By teaching me how to shoot this?" She held up the .32.

271

"Yep. It wasn't God who made all folks equal. It was Samuel Colt."

"Another familiar phrase," she said. She drew him closer and kissed him on the lips, something she had never done before, not for any man in the Gato.

When they disengaged William smiled. "What was that for?" His eyes seemed to be far away.

"For caring," she said. "And for being the smartest man I have ever known."

"I'm not that smart," he said. "If I was, I'd be in New York City, living off of Wall Street."

"You know what I mean," she said.

He sighed. "Don't let my charm fool you. I'm just as stupid as the rest of my kind. I just have some book-learning, that's all."

"Shut up and fuck me," she said.

He did.

Later, as they lay side by side, smoking and drinking and staring at the ceiling, Tessa realized she had to know. "I heard that you've killed a lot of people."

He nodded. "I have."

"Someone told me you've killed children. Is that true?"

He didn't answer. He only grimaced.

"You don't have to tell me," she said. "I just wanted to know."

"One kid," William said. "I'm down here in Mexico because of that . . . incident."

Tessa turned on her side, bracing her head up with one hand. Her breath stirred the hair on his chest. "What do you mean?"

William reached over to his gun-belt, which hung on one of the bedposts. "This thing," he said. "Remember how I said that this gun has killed a lot of people? Some who didn't have it coming?"

"Yes."

"One of those who didn't deserve to die was this little kid. I was robbing a bank, and my stupid Italian partner decided to kill everyone. He got shot up, which he definitely deserved, but the marshal's men were shooting at me, too. If it came down to it I'd rather get out of a scrape without killing anyone, but they were making it very hard for me. One of the deputies jumped behind a water trough, and I killed him. I saw another head pop up, and I shot before I realized it was just a child. If he was more than ten years old I'll eat every bullet in this gun."

"But it was an accident," Tessa said.

"I try to tell myself that," William said. "But a split-second before I pulled the trigger I knew those small brown eyes belonged to a kid. My hand was just a little bit faster than my brain."

"I'm sorry," she said.

"So am I."

They were quiet for a while, and William lit another cigarette. Though he did a good job of keeping his cool she could hear his heart beating harder through his chest, and his breath hitched. He was close to tears, but any bystander would not be able to tell.

"I'm wanted in the States," he said. His thick voice did not betray his true feelings, not in the way the rest of his body did. "I came down here to escape from that. But mostly I came down here to hang up my gun. After I realized what I'd done I swore to myself I would never use my .45 on anyone ever again. I think the only place I'd be able to do that is where no one knows me. If you heard about me, then I'm sure I'm not far enough south. Some day, though, I will find a quiet place to retire, where no one will know me, where no one will even suspect my capacity with a revolver."

Finally the wetness in his eyes overflowed the lids, and a tear rolled down his face. No remorse shone in the trail. Tessa knew doom when she saw it. This man had big dreams and knew he would never be able to achieve them.

She knew because she often saw such tears on her own face. She wrapped her arms around him, and they drifted off to sleep like that.

When he woke up at six, as he always did, no matter where he was in the world, William saw Tessa's closed eyes. Softly he pulled himself out from under her arms, trying not to wake her. First he pulled on his underdrawers, and then he sat on the side of the bed, holding his tobacco pouch in one hand and a rolling paper in the other. Finally he put them both back and poured himself a drink to keep the hangover at bay.

He didn't notice one of Tessa's eyes open. He had no idea that she watched him as he pulled his clothes on, buckled his gun-belt and finished off the glass of whiskey. He left the remainder of the bottle for her.

She closed her eye just in time as he turned around and regarded her. He stood over her sleeping form and contemplated kissing her forehead. But no, that would be too much like a lovesick fool. Instead he turned around and left.

-

At noon Tessa met with William at La Tortilla, just as they had agreed. He came out of the restaurant with a picnic basket full of what smelled like burritos, but when he lifted the red checkered cloth, it turned out to be the .32 revolver and a box of ammunition. The food rested on top, merely for show.

"But it's good stuff," he assured her. "It'll keep our bellies full."

William led Tessa to a horse-drawn buggy and helped her up before lashing the horse into a walk. They headed for the town outskirts, and it seemed that every person on the way looked at them. The children waved and the women scowled, but the men seemed to pay extra attention to them as if recording this moment in their memories, perhaps for later reference.

They left town, and they rode for quite some time before they came to a place that almost resembled the land from up north. A stretch of the desert had been replaced by a stream and some tall grass. A lively tree offered shade. William called this an oasis, but Tessa disagreed. The only word she could think of for it was "dreamy."

"Set up our picnic," William said. "I'll be right back."

Tessa took the picnic basket and knelt in the grass, clearing a space for their blanket. She laid it out and weighed the corners down with rocks before emptying the basket of food. The tortillas were fresh, the meat juicy. The cheese had just melted, and the greens were leafy, almost as if they'd sprouted from the earth this morning. She also found wine in the basket and two glasses, which she laid out.

She left the gun in the basket. For now.

Meanwhile William took a box of empty whiskey bottles from the back of the buggy and started setting them up on a fallen log. He spaced them out evenly and stepped back to admire his work. "That should be easy," he said.

"What should?" Tessa asked.

"You'll see. Forget the food for now. Bring the gun and the box of bullets."

She took them from the picnic basket and brought them over to William. "Do you know how to load the gun?" he asked.

"Of course." She demonstrated.

"Good. Let's see what you can do."

Tessa stood in front of the bottles and took aim at each one. Iron Trail had not taught her a lot about guns, but she knew enough from what she'd overheard and from what she'd read. She sighted down on the first bottle and twisted her head so she could see everything evenly. Then she squeezed her hand gently until the hammer came down, sending a bullet directly through the stout part of the bottle.

"Good," William said. "Better than I expected. Get the next one."

She fired five more times, and with each shot she sent shattered glass across the ground.

"That was incredible," William said. "Why do you need me?"

Tessa stared at the shattered glass, all that remained of her targets.

"It's easy to do that," William said. "Most people don't see it that way, but it is. The hard thing is to draw down on human flesh. But you don't have any problem with that, do you?"

Tessa shook her head.

"Are you fast enough?" he asked.

"I don't know."

"Maybe it doesn't even matter," William said. "You're a woman, and no one expects you to draw down on them. No, chances are, when you finally shoot your way out of this town, you'll have the gun in your hand already. Let me see how fast you are."

William handed over the box of bullets, and he set up new targets, only this time on all sides of her. She reloaded the gun while watching him. He was still getting ready by the time she'd finished reloading, so she slipped a few bullets into her pocket. Just in case he didn't give her the rest of the box.

"All right," he said. "This one over here is Bottle One." He pointed. He then rattled off the other bottles' numbers and made sure she understood when he finished. "Now, I'm going to call out which bottle you need to break next. Let's see how quickly you can take 'em all out."

She nodded.

"Two!" he shouted.

She twisted and fired at the bottle in question, busting it to pieces. She barely had enough time to admire her handiwork when William called out again. "Four!"

She whirled and sent another bottle across the grass, broken into shards.

The game continued until she'd knocked the guts out of each bottle William had set up. He approached her from behind, even though the gun was empty. "I don't know if I have anything to teach you, darling."

"I learn quickly," Tessa said.

"I'll bet. Reload." He handed her the box of bullets again, but this time he didn't set up any bottles. Instead he grabbed a couple from the ground and held them loosely by his sides until she was ready.

"What's this?" she asked.

"Moving targets," William said. "Let's see how well you do with something in motion. Go for it!" He threw the first bottle.

She blew it out of the sky with little to no effort.

He picked up another bottle, so now he held two, one in each hand. "Multiple targets," he said. "Go!"

The two bottles went up into the air like birds, and Tessa shot them both to pieces just as they reached their apexes.

William made as if he were about to reach for more bottles, but then he straightened up, running the back of his hand across his wet forehead. "Shit, woman. I've never seen anything like you. Do you know how long it took for me to learn how to fire a gun?"

"How long?"

"Years. I'm surprised you haven't made your own way out of this town by now. Tessa, there is nothing holding you back. You know your way out of every situation. I wish I knew how to handle myself as well as you do now when I was your age. Maybe . . . well, maybe things would have been different."

"Iron Trail taught me a lot, I suppose," Tessa said. Even though he'd refused to teach her about guns, she thought he might have taught her the common sense of killing.

"The Comanche?"

"Yes."

"I guess he did. I don't know what else I can teach you, darling."

"Maybe you should just give me the bullets, then," Tessa said.

William smiled. "You already took a few. What, you thought I wasn't counting what you were using?"

"I still have three in here." Tessa waved the pistol.

"And the six you stored away in your pocket," William said.

She looked away from him. "Maybe."

"I was going to chastise you for it," William said, "but honestly, I don't think you'll have a problem. You know how to take care of yourself."

"Thank you," Tessa said.

"Well, we still have some bottles left, so we might as well shoot at them, right?"

"Sure," she said.

"More moving targets." William threw a bottle into the sky, and just as Tessa drew down on it, he pulled his own gun and shot at her. Not close enough to accidentally hit her, but close enough to unnerve her.

She fired, and the bottle came crashing down. It split open on the ground, but not before.

"What are you doing?" Tessa yelled.

"That's the final test," he said. "How well you can shoot at something that's shooting back."

"You bastard!"

"Maybe. But if this were a real situation, you would have been knocked out of your pretty little shoes."

She gritted her teeth. "Let's do it again."

"You're ready now," William said.

"Make it two bottles, then," Tessa said.

William shrugged. "You got it."

She waited as he grabbed two more bottles. He hesitated before he threw them, but one sidelong glare from her made him realize the futility of arguing. Instead he threw both bottles into the air, and before she had the time to track their course he drew down on her and fired, kicking up the dirt at her feet.

She fired the last two bullets into the air, and both bottles exploded, raining shattered glass onto the weeds. She did not so much as flinch.

William holstered his weapon and approached her, the dry grass crunching beneath his boots. "That's impressive, Tessa. I've never seen anything like it. So long as you know an attack is coming, I'm certain that you'll come out on top."

"I'm the instigator," she said. "There will be no surprises."

"Good," William said. They were now face to face with nothing between them but her smoking gun. He took it from her and reloaded it. "You don't need my help. You don't need anyone's help."

She leaned across the gap between them and gently planted a kiss on his lips. It bloomed into a smile, and he handed over the box of bullets. "Good luck, Tessa."

She took the gun from him. "It sounds like you're leaving."

"I am. I didn't think it would be this soon, but then again I didn't think you were this good."

"You're leaving me?"

He took her hands. "This isn't far enough south for me. Sometimes I wonder if I'll reach Bolivia before I think it's south enough. I have a lot of ghosts on my trail."

"You're leaving me now?" she asked.

"Yes," William said. "I was going to wait a few days until I was certain you could handle yourself, but you surprised me. They say Jesse James is good with a gun. Well, I rode with the man. He's good, but not nearly as good as you are. I think you were born for this."

"Then, this is it?" she asked.

"Not yet," he said. He took the gun and box from her hands and threw them aside. They landed in the grass, the barrel poking into the sliding door of the box. He then led her to the red checkered blanket and lowered her down.

There they made love, and afterward they ate. As the sun began its steady decline to the west they loaded everything up and rode back to town. Neither of them said a word.

William dropped her off at Mendoza's, and they took a moment to share a final kiss.

"I hope I see you again," he said. "For now I'm heading back to my hotel to get my things."

"I'm sure we'll meet again," she said.

"Probably. We're both bad pennies, so we'll always turn up." He laughed.

She smiled. "Goodbye, Mr. King."

"Good luck, Mrs. Reeves." He tipped his hat and then rode away into the rising full moon.

Once she walked into the bar, before she could even turn toward the stairs leading up to her crib, pain erupted in her right cheek, and she practically fell against the wall behind her.

"You fucking whore!" Mendoza reared back to slap her again.

"No!" she cried.

"Where were you?" Mendoza yelled.

"I . . . I . . ."

"You were fucking that degenerate cowboy, King," he said. "Did the cocksucker pay you?"

"I . . ."

"Shut the fuck up! Answer me! Did he pay you?"

She wanted to tell him the truth, but such would no doubt be folly. The truth could only make matters worse. Too scared to tell a lie, she tried to avoid the question. "I was on my own time!"

"You cunt!" Mendoza snarled. He grabbed her by the hair and yanked her up. He did this so quickly that she didn't notice him draw his knife, not until the blade came firmly against her throat. "You don't have your own time, or have you forgotten that I own you?"

Her heart beat so hard that she could barely hear his voice over its thumps. Sweat tickled the small of her back, and she clutched her purse closer to her breasts. The gun and bullets were heavy inside, but it never occurred to her to try to use them.

"You thought you'd earn a little on the side, huh?" he whispered. His breath stank of whiskey, and it crawled across her face like a giant slug. "How much?"

"I . . . uh . . ."

"Don't you fucking lie to me! If you tell me something, and it doesn't ring right, I will slit your bitch throat and bathe in your blood. I don't care how great your tits look."

She blurted the first number that came to mind: "Twenty!"

"Bullshit," Mendoza said.

"I swear it!"

"How much do you have in your purse?" Mendoza asked. He released her hair and held his hand out.

"Twenty and some change," she said. She wanted to swallow, but she feared that even such a slight movement might be enough for the blade to cut into her.

Mendoza stared into her eyes. It was hard to look back, but she had enough hard living in her soul to make the task a possible one.

When he saw she wasn't going to give, Mendoza backed down. "Give me the purse."

There was no way she could let that happen. If he found the gun, everything would be over. Maybe this time Tessa wouldn't survive. Instead she reached in and felt the butt of the .32. She felt tempted to use it now, but it was not loaded. She grabbed a handful of change and pulled it out, offering it to Mendoza.

As it turned out, she indeed held a double eagle in her palm. Twenty American dollars, enough to satiate Mendoza's greed.

He took the money. "You're not to leave this building for a week," he said. "If I find that you have violated this edict, I will cut your throat ear to ear, and Aguirre will chop you up into little pieces. We'll dispose of your body a piece at a time. By the end of the week you'll be coyote shit, scattered about the desert. Do you understand?"

She didn't trust herself to speak. She merely nodded.

"Get out of my fucking sight. And if you earn less than forty dollars this weekend, I will carve your pussy out like an apple core and sell it to the highest bidder."

"Yes sir."

Tessa managed to hold it together until she reached her crib. As soon as she closed the door, she slid down to her butt and threw her face into both palms. Tears came so fast and hard that they seeped between her fingers and left tiny circles on the floor.

Her tears did not wet her hands for very long. Soon she pushed herself up, and she walked to the bed. Here she sat down and removed the gun from her purse. There were still about twenty-five bullets left in the box. It wasn't enough for a grand display, but it might just be enough to get her out of Oso Feo forever.

Her eyes became twin deserts as she loaded the gun and placed it into her drawer, along with the remaining bullets from the box. Tonight was not the night. It might not even be tomorrow, but some time in the near future, she knew she would get out of here.

Just as she closed the drawer, there was a knock at her door. "Who is it?"

"It's me, Alfredo. I'm coming in." Not, "May I come in?" Never that.

The key plate shook, and the door knob turned. Mendoza stepped in, one hand in his pocket, the other twirling a key on a tiny chain.

"What do you want?" Tessa asked.

"William King. Where did he go?"

This was a bit more direct than Tessa had expected, but she had an answer. This time, the truth would be sufficient. "He left town."

"I'm fucking aware of that," Mendoza said. "I just sent Aguirre over to his hotel to cut his balls off, but he wasn't there."

"We had a picnic today," Tessa said. "It was a special occasion, because he was leaving."

"Is that so?" Mendoza asked.

"That's so."

Mendoza nodded, licking his lips. There was a moment of silence. He broke it before long. "What did the two of you eat?"

"What does it matter to you?" Tessa asked.

"Just answer the fucking question."

"Burritos from that restaurant on Guillermo Street," she said.

"That checks out, then," Mendoza said.

"Are you trying to figure out if I'm lying?" Tessa asked.

"It's just business," Mendoza said. "I've got to keep an eye on my investment."

Tessa remained silent.

"He's really gone?"

"William King?"

"No, the goddam Pope. Yes, I mean Bloody Bill King."

"Yes."

"That's probably for the best. He was a good paying customer, but things have just gotten too unorthodox for my likes. It would have been nice to have his scalp, though. I hear he's worth a couple thousand dollars north of the Rio Grande."

Tessa ignored him.

"It's five-thirty. Start getting ready." Mendoza then turned and went away.

Tessa sighed, closing her eyes. Her lids burned, but she knew there would be no more tears. She hadn't strength enough left in her.

-

For the rest of the week she played by Mendoza's rules. She never left, and she made more than sixty dollars that weekend. It seemed to be business as usual in El Gato Bonito except every night, after she sent her final customer off for the evening, she went to the drawer and pulled out the revolver William King had bought for her. She hefted it in her hand and wondered what it would be like to fire .32-calibers of lead into Mendoza's fat frame.

It wasn't time. No, not yet. Her coffers were too insubstantial. Soon though. She almost had enough to survive, if it came down to that.

Two weeks after William King left, Tessa finally gained the courage to leave Mendoza's saloon. She went to the general store and bought some jerky beef, for old time's sake. She hovered around the paper and pencils, and it took her a long time, but finally she decided to buy a journal and three pencils. She didn't think she'd be using them any time soon, but it comforted her to know that she owned them.

The following day she sat at the edge of her bed with a pencil in hand, the empty pad of paper before her. She wanted to write something, but the blank page seemed too daunting.

So she gave up. Perhaps, she mused, she would give it a shot another day.

Tessa put the paper aside and got ready for another evening of whoring.

-

A month after Tessa had bought the journal, it was still blank, and she still worked at Mendoza's saloon. By this point she had secreted away enough money to last her the next couple of years, but for some reason she still couldn't find the courage to do what she'd wanted to do ever since William King had gotten her the gun. Every night before she went to bed she argued the points in her mind, and it always came out that she should hold her peace, at least for now. The opportunity would eventually present itself, and she would finally be free on that day.

But she kept putting it off.

It took Lavender to convince her that she should leave Oso Feo, and Lavender did not feel happy about it.

It was a slow night for a Saturday. Only five *vaqueros* were in the saloon, drinking and playing cards. No one had gone upstairs yet, despite the best efforts of all Mendoza's women. Though Tessa had finally perfected her Spanish, none of their customers wanted to go to her crib. Not yet. They said perhaps later, after they had won everything they could.

After a few tries Tessa retired to the bar next to Yvonne, and they both had a couple of shots. Neither said anything. They didn't have to. Both knew that any words would be fruitless at this point. They could only bide their time until the customers were finally drunk enough for a poke. Even Trixie had given up and was lounging by the bar, nursing a beer. Only Lavender still worked the floor, trying to rake in some business.

"It's hard out there," Trixie said.

Yvonne and Tessa both nodded, but neither said a word. What could they say?

The three ladies waited by the bar, drinking as sparsely as they could as they watched their prey. Lavender still had not gotten the idea, and she whirled about the customers, trying to get someone interested in a poke. No bites.

Finally, after about an hour or so of not having any interested parties, Lavender broke down. "What the fuck is wrong with y'alls? You queer or something? You a pack'a cocksuckers? You like to pull each others dicks? You've got a grade-A woman over here, and all y'alls wants to do is play cards?"

"Lavender," Mendoza said from behind the bar. "Shut the fuck up."

"It's Saturday goddam night," Lavender said. "Nine o'clock. I haven't had my pussy pounded yet, and there's at least seven able-bodied men. Why haven't I been fucked yet?"

"'Cause you're stupid as a pile of shit-hammers," Mendoza said. "More trade'll come in later."

Lavender lifted up her skirt, showing the world what God had given her. "You boys not man enough to purchase a fine pussy like this?"

"Lavender," Yvonne said.

"Fuck you, bitch!" Lavender howled. "I haven't had a customer in a week, and now it's our busiest day! None of these Mexi-queers want me! What am I supposed to do?!"

"Shut the fuck up and wait for new customers!" Mendoza roared. "It's still early, you cunt-face!"

"You know what?" Lavender said. "Fuck this. I'll be in my crib. Let me know when a real man comes through those doors." She started for the stairs.

The *vaqueros* glanced at each other. None of them knew English, and they had no idea what had just happened. Mendoza knew, though, and he would never let something like this go. He strode out from behind the bar, tossing his apron aside.

"Wait, boss," Yvonne said. "She don't—"

Mendoza slapped her hand away. "Keep back, whore."

Yvonne kept silent.

Tessa watched as Aguirre came out from his shadowy corner and approached the stairs with his boss. They reached Lavender before she could so much as touch the handrail. They flung her back so hard there was a crunch as she landed on her ass.

"I've had just about enough out of you, twat-mouth," Mendoza said. "Remember what I said the last time you got into trouble?"

Lavender's lower lip quivered. "You can't do anything. You need me."

"Like shit."

"I'm the best looking whore you have, except for maybe Tessa," Lavender said.

"You're a skinny cunt," Mendoza said. "You're better than Trixie, but that's about it. Are you done whining?"

"What'd I do?" Lavender asked. Her voice was on the edge of a snivel.

"You've been nothing but trouble since Ortega brought you down here last year," Mendoza said. "I can't count how many customers you shot, and now you're calling them queers? What's wrong with you?"

"I . . . I . . ."

Mendoza shook his head. "Aguirre?"

The guard did not hesitate. He drew his blade and flicked it across Lavender's throat, sending a spray of crimson up against the wall and ceiling.

"No!" Tessa screamed.

Yvonne was the only one who noticed. Mendoza grabbed the knife from Aguirre's sticky hand and planted the blade into Lavender's face several times. "Teach you to fuck with me, whore." He cut pieces from her head.

Tessa stepped forward, but Yvonne held her back. "It's too late, honey. She's gone."

Mendoza stabbed away at a piece of meat that had once resembled Lavender. When he finished he relinquished the knife to Aguirre. "Get her out of here. Send the maid in to wipe up this mess."

Aguirre nodded and took a tablecloth from a nearby table. He wrapped the dripping corpse up with it and put it in the corner. For later. He ignored the part about the maid. He knew his boss meant the whores.

Mendoza stopped by the player piano. "What the fuck? Why so grim, everyone? Get back to your celebration." He plugged a nickel into the piano and wound it up. Before his hand left the crank, an old-timey tune filled the saloon.

Tessa walked like a zombie to the stairs, and when she reached the top she ambled toward her crib. When finished loading up the .32 William King had bought for her, she came back downstairs. Before anyone could do anything she shot Aguirre in the back of the head, sending his brains out in a spray all over the floor. His body fell, and it turned over, showing how the exit wound had left very little of his identity intact.

Everyone stopped what they were doing. Mendoza, who was in mid-polish on a pint glass, paused and looked up. The poker players dropped their hands, all forgotten even though one of them was a solid flush. The faro dealer and his one player paused in mid-bet. The ladies, who watched all the action on the floor, averted their eyes to their colleague. And the player piano continued its tin tune.

"Honey?" Yvonne asked.

Tessa regarded her with blank eyes. "Get out of here," she whispered. "You and Trixie, both."

The ladies did not argue. They cleared out as soon as they were given the order. Before they reached the batwing doors Mendoza ducked his hands behind the bar and came up with a shotgun. Tessa was quicker, though, and she put a bullet in her owner's chest, sending him down to the floor.

The *vaquero* by the faro table drew his gun, but Tessa's instinct took over and she blew him out of his boots. The bullet had struck dead center between his eyes, and he died before his body hit the hardwood floor.

The other *vaqueros* glanced at her, afraid to meet her eyes. She had counted three bullets gone, and she had three left. If the *vaqueros* wanted to push it, they might win, but they had seen her skills. She was willing to bet they wanted nothing to do with her.

The one who seemed to be the trail boss lifted his hands and spoke to her in Spanish. Tessa shushed him. She nodded toward the door. "Get out."

They didn't need to be told twice. The player piano finished up its paid song as the last of the *vaqueros* slipped out the front door.

The sudden silence was so loud that Tessa could hear it ringing in her head. "The music of the spheres," her father used to tell her. It had been a joke, but never before in her life had it seemed so real to her.

A hand slapped at the bar, and Mendoza grunted as he forced himself up into a standing position. "You . . . fucking . . . whore."

"Sit down, Mendoza," Tessa said. "Or I will put another one of these in you." She waved the pistol.

Mendoza struggled to lift the shotgun, and Tessa fired again, this time in his upper chest, blowing out the bottles behind him. He stumbled backwards, and the firearm dropped from his hands. He tried to use all of his strength to keep himself propped up against the shelf behind him.

"You can still get out of this," Tessa said. "That's more than I promised anyone else. That's more than Ortega ever got."

291

Mendoza touched his wound and marveled at the red fingertips that came away. Very slowly, like a toddler learning how to walk, he bent over and picked up the shotgun with tremulous hands. He struggled to figure out which end to aim from before he put the stock up to his shoulder. Blood coursed out of the hole in his chest and saturated the weapon as he lifted it up.

Before he got any further Tessa put her fifth bullet into her boss's head. More bottles shattered. More blood sprayed the walls. And Alfredo Mendoza dropped down behind the bar, spitting his last breath out in a red mist.

Tessa approached the bar, the .32 in front of her like a feeler, and she reached over the counter, ready to fire if Mendoza showed any sign of life at all. He didn't. His empty eyes stared up at the ceiling, as if offering a final prayer to God.

One bullet left. She reached into her purse and pulled out the box of ammunition. She plugged five fresh cartridges into the .32, but she knew she wouldn't need them. Anyone who had to die had already lost their lives by her hand. There was no law in Oso Feo. Perhaps she had already shot everyone she needed to.

She looked back down at Mendoza's corpse, and she could not believe she had really done this. William King had been right. She could have escaped at any time. To think of all the days she had wasted in this wretched bar, letting countless men spend their seed between her legs. Why had she not come to her senses sooner? Had she really been this afraid?

She heard a loud clacking sound behind her, and she whirled, pointing her gun at the batwing doors. A wayward stranger had just wandered in, but as soon as he saw the long dark tunnel of her .32, he turned around and fled from the saloon.

"Shit," she muttered. She had to get going before more customers came in. It was, however, prudent to close the place down, first. She locked the outer doors and blew out the candles, hoping that would give any potential drunkards and gamblers the idea that they should seek out their vice elsewhere.

That done she went into the back room and scrounged together some supplies. Three skins filled with water. A pound of jerky beef. Some eggs and bread. Even a wrapped parcel of bacon. She threw them all together into a sack, and on her way back up to her crib she stopped to grab three bottles of Mendoza's good stuff. The desert wasn't a good place for such spirits, but she knew that if she didn't take some with her, she would regret it, especially late at night with nobody to warm her in the chilly darkness.

She did not want to go back up to her crib. Really, she had nothing up there except for a few things, but she knew she would need them when she made her way out of town. She had a set of clothes up there that made riding a horse easy, and then she had her journal. Though she had not written in it yet, she thought it would be important to take with her. Not to mention the money she'd managed to collect.

Tessa dropped the sack of her spoils on the table nearest the door, and she went up the stairs to her crib to gather together the things she would need. It did not take long. She thrust her working clothes aside and dressed in her riding duds. She stuffed her tight pockets with money, and clutched her journal—and a few pencils—to her chest.

She closed the door behind her, and just as she started to head for the stairs, she noticed Yvonne standing by the balcony, tears in her eyes, a Derringer in her hands. The gun was pointed at Tessa's breast.

"What are you doing?" Tessa asked.

Yvonne's face contorted. It looked like it wanted to melt from her skull. "You have no idea what you've done to me, do you?"

"I don't give a fuck," Tessa said.

Yvonne nodded her head. Her mouth worked, as if she had something to say, but nothing would come out.

"You finally have whatever life you want," Tessa said. "You're free."

Yvonne convulsed, and it looked like she chewed on her lower lip. "Don't you remember? This *was* the life I wanted!"

Tessa grunted. It may have been a chuckle, it may have been a sneer. "Are you going to shoot me, then?"

Yvonne sniffled so hard it sounded like she had slurped at ice through a straw.

"If you are, just do it. It's too late in the game for me to give much of a shit. Do it, Yvonne. Do it, Elizabeth."

At the mention of this second name, Yvonne's shoulders slumped. The gun weighed her hands down, and it broadcast her intention to do nothing.

As Tessa passed, she paused. "You're free. You can do whatever you want."

Yvonne didn't even look up from the floor.

Tessa moved down the stairs, and she grabbed the sack she'd left down there. Just before she stepped out through the doors, she looked back up to the balcony. Trixie and Yvonne both stood up there, and it didn't seem like they would be looking for new employment.

What had Yvonne said? Didn't she say she liked this lifestyle? Well, maybe some people were built for it. Tessa Reeves certainly wasn't.

She stepped outside of El Gato Bonito, and thankfully, she never saw it again in the remainder of her life.

-

"You know how things are around here," the livery man said. "I can't let you buy anything without Mendoza's approval."

"Alfredo Mendoza is dead," Tessa said. She reached into her pocket and tossed a few coins up into the air. She didn't know how many she'd unleashed upon the stable, but the hay at her feet glittered with double eagles as if they were stars.

The stable man dove to the floor and grabbed up as much money as he could. "You can have whatever horse you want! With whatever saddle."

Tessa said, "I know. Get me your best. And don't fuck around with me, or you'll be shaking hands with Mendoza. In hell."

The livery man didn't know politics, but he was uncanny with money. He scooped up Tessa's coins and supplied her with a horse. Even at such a late hour, the roan was shoed and ready to go.

Tessa didn't think about the implications. She loaded up the saddle bags and mounted her horse. Before long they were pointed north, to a new destination, to a place where she thought she could win something back.

-

That night, three miles from the town of Oso Feo, Tessa Reeves sat near the edge of a campfire, staring into the wild flames, eating from the jerky beef she'd taken from her most recent boss. Periodically she gulped from a bottle of Mendoza's finest whiskey. But nothing happened.

Tessa drew a pencil from her bag and tried to start a new journal, all for naught. Instead of marking down anything about her history she put the diary and pencil back into her saddle bag and wrapped herself in a blanket by the fire.

As she fell asleep she looked up to the stars and remembered Iron Trail's lessons. The constellations were known to her. She could not mistake her direction.

There would be a lot of land through which to travel, and she knew that she had to make it back. She had but one thing to do, and only then would she allow the world to destroy her.

And destruction seemed very, very likely.

-

Brett Hartford swept at the ubiquitous dust on the boardwalk in front of his store. Motes swirled through the air, illuminated by the afternoon sun. Sweat trickled down the small of his back in a cool stream and from the bottoms of his eyes he could see it glisten in his mustache. He hailed from Back-East, and he thought he would never get used to the heat out here, even though it was only March.

He heard boots clopping against the hardwood, so he turned to see Joe Ridgway ambling down the walk. "Afternoon, Joe," he said.

"Brett." Joe stopped, backhanding sweat from his forehead. "Sure is a scorcher."

"Yep," Brett said. "How's the wife?"

"A shrew, just like usual. I'm headed over to the bar. What say you close up shop for an hour and join me?"

Brett smiled at the idea. "Can't do it, Joe. You know how it is."

"Sure as shit. Just thought I'd try."

Then, just before Joe turned back on his way to the bar, someone came riding into town from the south end. Both men looked up to see it was only a stranger, and a woman, no less. She looked like she'd been on hard times, covered in dust and filth, but the worst were her eyes: cold green, as if they belonged on a snowman.

But something else seemed familiar about her, and Brett said so.

"I don't know," Joe said. "Now that you mention it, she *does* reminds me of someone. You remember that one wife that Felton Reeves used to have?"

Brett chuckled. "Which one?"

"Good point. Naw, she looks like the real gorgeous one. Tessa, I think her name was."

"She's dead," Brett said.

"Shit, I know that. I'm just saying, is all."

Both men watched as she rode past, and Brett felt a chill when he got a better look at her. Joe had been right, she looked an awful lot like Tessa Reeves. She had to be an older sister, come to see where Tessa was buried. But something on her face implied that this was no social visit. Rage seethed in her squinted eyes and in the deep set of her mouth.

"She doesn't look too happy," Joe said.

Brett nodded.

"Fact, I think she's got killing on her mind."

Brett nodded again.

"If she keeps heading down that way, she'll be going out to Felton's place."

Brett let the implication set in. "What do you want me to do about it?"

"Maybe we should let the sheriff know," Joe said. "Just in case."

"You don't think . . ." Brett trailed off. He thought about how many wives Felton Reeves had had, but then he also knew how harmless the farmer was. Dull? Yes. Lonely? You bet. A killer? No.

Still, maybe Tessa's sister had ideas. Maybe she rode out there to face off against the man who had done her sister wrong. And there was just no way that Felton could have done anyone wrong, but a backyard full of his ex-wives' graves probably would not ease her heart.

"Let's get the sheriff," Brett said.

Joe nodded. "Just in case."

-

Tessa felt her heart hammer away at her insides as she approached the farm of Felton Reeves. How long had it been since she'd seen this place? The last time in her life she had ever been happy was here, and she intended to be happy again as soon as she finished with this errand.

And then what? She had a few ideas.

Tessa rode up to the hitching post and tied her horse down. She then took the time to tie the rawhide strip from her gun belt around her thigh, just in case she had to draw down quickly. Only then did she ascend the steps to the porch.

Her boots clopped heavily on the old wood, which creaked beneath each footstep. Her stomach boiled inside of her, and she forced her hands to stop shaking. How long had she waited for this? How many times had she fallen asleep out in the desert, dreaming of this moment?

She knocked on the door. She didn't hear the dainty sound of a cowed woman but the rich bass sound of a church bell striking at the top of the hour. Her hand then fell to the butt of her gun. This was a .45, much different from the .32 William King had bought her. She'd spent hours in the wilderness practicing with her new gun, and with very little effort she had become proficient with it.

Felton Reeves, she thought, required a higher caliber than most men.

The door opened, and a young woman stood there wearing a fine dress with a kitchen apron tied around her. Blonde hair trickled down her shoulders in waves, and her ruby red lips spread out in a smile. "Ma'am?" she asked.

"Is Felton Reeves home?" Tessa asked.

"He's out working the fields," the woman said. "He should be in within a half an hour. Come on in. Do you want something to drink?"

"Water, please," Tessa said. She stepped in and removed her hat, letting her own hair flow down her body. Dust caked her all over, but she did not slap it away.

"Have a seat, Miss . . . ?"

"Call me Tessa."

"I'm Gloria Reeves. Nice to meet you." She held out a hand.

Tessa did not take it. She pretended not to have even seen it. She looked around and noticed that the house hadn't changed. Felton's new wife had not bothered to redecorate, which did not surprise her. Although Tessa, back in the old days, had seen a few flaws, she'd had no desire to fix them. Felton seemed like a man who wanted everything to stay the same.

Gloria stepped away for a moment and then returned with two cups of water. She handed one to Tessa and then sat down near the fireplace. "What brings you out here, Tessa?"

Tessa sipped from the cup and contemplated telling Gloria a bunch of lies. Why put her on alert? It would be all the more surprising for Felton if Gloria didn't know the truth.

But she couldn't do that. "I have a few things to tell you, Gloria, and you're not going to like any of them."

Tessa then told her the story. Not everything. The parts with Iron Trail, the Comancheros and Alfredo Mendoza she skimmed over. The important part involved Felton Reeves. At first Gloria listened and nodded, because she knew of her husband's bad luck with wives. But when Iron Trail entered the story she listened a bit more attentively, and when Tessa reached the point where she'd been sold by the seemingly innocuous Felton Reeves, Gloria had to stop herself from interjecting.

At the conclusion Gloria felt free to talk at last. "I just can't believe anything you've just said. You don't know Fell like I do. He couldn't harm a fly."

Tessa set her cup down on the table. "There's a way to prove my story. That is, if you care to give me a chance."

"And what is that?" Gloria asked.

"Get a shovel."

Moments later they stood out in the bone yard, and Tessa dug into her own grave. TESSA REEVES, it said. Nothing more, not even the date of her supposed death.

Gloria wrung her hands, and her mouth twisted with anxiety. She clearly wanted to say something, to object to this, but she didn't have the courage to stand up to someone, at least not someone as frightening as Tessa.

"Did you ever know a man named Samuel Pepper?" Tessa asked Gloria. Sweat trickled down from her hairline, and she swiped it away.

"Yeah," Gloria said. "Back-East. He was my . . . well, you know."

"I know," Tessa said. "How is he?"

"My answer isn't very appropriate for polite conversation."

Tessa laughed. "He finally get the clap or something?"

"Syphilis," Gloria said. "An evening with Venus—"

"A lifetime with Mercury," Tessa said. "Old joke."

"Yeah."

This time when Tessa threw a clump of dirt, something went with it. She paused and bent down only to find her very first journal. She marveled at it, surprised that very little had decomposed. Almost all of it remained legible.

"What is it?" Gloria asked.

"My journal. There's another one in my saddlebags, if you'd care to get it and compare the handwriting."

"I . . . I trust you. What else is down there?"

Tessa pushed aside more dirt only to find her old belongings. A suitcase. Some clothes. A few knick-knacks. No corpse.

"And the others are the same?" Gloria asked. Her face had gone pale, and her fingers twitched.

"Yes," Tessa said. "Except the grave of his first wife. As I heard, that one actually has a body in it."

"God!" Gloria cried. Her face dove into her hands. "What was I thinking? Just when I thought my life was finally going someplace!"

301

"That's all right," Tessa said. She climbed out of the hole and put a hand on Gloria's shoulder. "You're not the first person to fall for it. Besides, when you think about it, what kind of man sends away for a mail order bride?"

Gloria pulled away from her hand and took up the shovel. Frantically, she dug into the grave next to Tessa's. Dirt flew everywhere, and she resembled a dervish as she plowed into the ground, seeking anything she might find.

And she did not seem surprised when she found another woman's belongings, and not a corpse.

"Gloria? Honey? What are you doing?"

Gloria dropped the shovel and turned in the direction of her husband, her blistered hands aching against the gentle breeze. Felton Reeves came ambling over the rise, a scythe balanced over one shoulder.

"Don't," Tessa whispered to her. "Just go. I'll take care of him."

"But . . ."

"Just go."

"I didn't know we had company," Felton said. He stood about twenty yards away. "Have we met, sir?"

The fool, Tessa thought. He wasn't even close enough to recognize her yet.

"Don't hurt him," Gloria whispered.

"Why?"

"Because . . . I don't know what I'd do without him."

Tessa would have been disgusted, but she recognized so much of herself in that comment. "You'll manage. You'll be surprised at what you can do. Now get back in the house."

Gloria sniffled, biting her lip. She looked like she wanted to say more, but in the end, as Felton drew closer, she gave up. She left without so much as looking at her husband.

"Hey, Gloria! Where are you going?"

Tessa turned to him, giving him the best look at her face that she could. Finally he stopped short and dropped the scythe. His eyes widened, and it looked like he had a hard time breathing.

"Hello, Fell," Tessa said. She brushed a sweaty strand of hair out of her face.

"Do I . . . do I know you?" Even though recognition blossomed clearly on his face.

"I think you know who I am, Fell. I told your new wife everything. She saw what was really in my grave."

"But . . . it can't be. You're gone. You're in Mexico, selling . . . well, doing whatever they want you to do down there."

Tessa laughed a dry, crackly sound. "You can't even bring yourself to say it."

"I . . ."

"Iron Trail's dead," Tessa said. "I don't know if you knew that. If you didn't, well, there you go. He won't be by to get Gloria."

Felton's considerable Adam's apple worked up and down. "Tessa, please . . ."

"Don't bother," she said. "I will admit, out of all the scoundrels I've met over the course of time since last we'd seen each other, you probably are the most innocuous. But you're still the piece of shit who sent me to hell. And now I'm back. And I'm not leaving until I've had my pound of flesh."

"We can work something out," Felton said. "Honey, please!"

Tessa drew her gun. "You don't get to call me honey anymore."

"Gloria!" Felton yelled. "Help me! I can explain everything! Just get the shotgun from my bedroom and help me!"

"She's not going to help you," Tessa said. "Not now that she knows the truth."

Felton almost whimpered. "Come on, Tessa. What did I ever do to you, really? You were a mail order bride. Back-East, you were just a whore. Did I really put you through something that you couldn't handle?"

Tessa's palm itched, and she wanted to put a bullet through Felton now. But no, she wanted to draw this out for him. She wanted him to *suffer.* "Go fuck yourself, Felton Reeves. I'm here to kill you, and there's no getting out of it."

"But, you're a whore," Felton said.

"I'm a human being," Tessa said. "Even whores deserve consideration. Are you ready to die?"

At this point Felton laughed. He almost simpered, "You're not going to do it. You're just a whore. You're scared, that's all. Just a scared woman. It's all right. You don't have to put on the act."

Tessa drew back the hammer and took aim. Felton ducked down and grabbed up the scythe. With a roar he charged forward, closing the distance between them. They had been about five yards apart, and now they were two.

"No!" a voice from the house cried.

Too late. Tessa pulled the trigger several times, and Felton's body jigged like that of St. Vitus before he fell to the ground, dead.

Tessa turned, counting in her head how many times she'd fired. Four, she thought. No more than five. At the very least, she had one bullet left.

When she turned she saw herself face to face with a lawman of some kind, perhaps middle-aged with a gray mustache on his face and a dim tin star on his chest. He was puffy around the edges, and she thought that he probably wasn't much of a sheriff.

Tessa started to walk around the house.

"Wait!" the sheriff called out. "Stop! Don't you move!"

He still had not drawn his gun, so Tessa ignored him as she continued around the house.

The sheriff cursed and started running through the building until he made it to the front door. As he got there, Tessa swung up into the saddle and started pulling away from the Reeves farm.

The sheriff rushed down the porch steps, and his hand dropped to the butt of his gun. "Stop! This instant!"

Tessa listened. As she turned the horse around she put her own hand on her gun. Eyes squinted and teeth clenched, she tensed. "Are you the man to stop me?"

The sheriff farted, and he nearly let his bladder loose. This woman had to be the devil herself, and considering what she'd done to Felton Reeves, he had no doubt that she was faster and meaner than he was. His hand dropped away to hang loose by his side.

Then Tessa turned around and gigged the horse forward. She headed north, and she didn't think anyone from town would be following her, not least of all the lily-livered sheriff.

As soon as she was gone the sheriff let loose all of his tensions in a sigh. Gloria stood behind him, tears in her eyes. They looked at each other for a long time. Finally he spoke. "Who the hell was that woman?"

"A dead woman," Gloria said. "Come inside, and I'll tell you all about it. Would you care for a drink?"

"Whiskey, if you've got it," the sheriff said.

"Well, Felton told me he wasn't a drinking man, but one day while I was cleaning up I did find some amber spirits. Probably for medicinal purposes, but you're free to have it, Sheriff."

"Thank you, kindly." They both went into the house, into the shade and out from under the unforgiving sun.

-

That night, as Tessa sat under the stars warmed by the campfire, she cleaned her weapon. The powdery grime from the bullets that had killed her husband flaked away, which she thought to be depressing. She hoped she could take it with her for the rest of her life, to comfort her as she sat around various campfires, in search of a life of her own.

When she finished she reassembled everything and put the revolver into her holster, which she placed close to her bedroll. Just in case.

She'd already eaten dinner and now sat back against her saddle, which she used as a pillow, to enjoy a few sips from the final bottle of Mendoza's good whiskey. It was almost gone. In fact she thought this would be her last night with it, which seemed almost poetic.

With a sigh she took up a pencil and her journal. She'd managed to write a few things in it since that first night out in the desert when she had left Oso Feo, but there wasn't much of true meaning in here, just an account of her days.

She glanced over the last few pages, surprised by the lack of emotion in them. She thought this close to the actualization of her fondest desires, she would have written something with more meat to it.

She turned to a fresh page, and the pencil hovered over it, ready to transform it from blankness into something else.

F ROM THE JOURNAL OF TESSA REEVES:

March 15, 18—

Today I killed Felton Reeves. It felt just as satisfying as I had hoped it would, but there still seems to be something eating away at my soul. Something that feels unfinished.

As if I did not know what that was. As if I had not been planning further vengeance ever since I left Oso Feo.

I have not been entirely honest with you, Journal. I learned something a couple of weeks ago that I should have mentioned.

I have heard that Juan Moreno is hiding out in the Nations. It is not far away from here, but I think I can find him in a month, no less . . .

THE END

BONUS STORY
"GTT"

1

S am Pepper packed his pecker in his pants and closed the door gently behind him. It wasn't often that a virgin fell into his hands. The urge to take that from the young fourteen year old girl had been strong, but he restrained himself. He knew she would be worth a lot, and he didn't want to spoil that. He could always fuck her later. For now he was satisfied with sowing his seed in her mouth. She had a lot to learn, and he looked forward to teaching her.

He hopped down the stairs with a jaunt in his step and turned the corner into the saloon. Smoke filled the air, its acrid odor almost strong enough to overcome the bitter scent of whiskey. He bellied up to the bar and waved Grimes over.

Grimes lived up to his name. As far as Sam could tell the man had never bathed, not once in his entire life. His cheesy stink reminded him of the smell of gangrene, and Sam thought he could probably grab Grimes by the wrist and slough his ratty skin off his bones. He had no teeth even though he was only twenty years old. A cheap cigar stuck out of his mouth like a toothpick. "She any good?"

"Not yet," Sam said. "I'll work on her, though. Gimme a whiskey."

Grimes took a bottle down from the top shelf—it was still rotgut hooch—and poured it into a glass to the tippy-top. He pushed it over to Sam, who downed half of it in one go. It burned like he'd swallowed a match, but at least it took the god awful stink of the room out of his nostrils.

"Dick was looking for you," Grimes said.

"Christ. What did that bastard want?"

"What he always wants."

Sam sighed and plugged more whiskey into his mouth. "I have no idea where he gets so much cum. You'd think he'd run out considering how many times he's around here."

Grimes shrugged and helped himself to some booze. He knew enough to pour it into a glass first. When he started working for Sam he'd swigged from the bottle everyone would use. Sam had kicked seven shades of shit or more out of him. He'd still had a couple of teeth at that point. He found them later wedged into one of Sam's boots.

"How much does he owe?" Sam asked.

"Ten bucks," Grimes said.

Dick Lyman swore he was good for it. He usually was, too. But it had been a while since he'd offered payment for Sam's services, and that made Sam a bit leery. He didn't think Lyman deserved any more credit than that. Sam would have to mention it when he saw him.

"He said he wanted Tessa," Grimes said.

That was a hard no. Tessa was class. Sam was saving her for the mail order business. A lot of men Out West needed marriage material, and Tessa would make one of them a fine wife. For a hefty fee, naturally.

Sam felt something tickle at the back of his throat, and he coughed into a handkerchief. Blood came up with a hunk of meat. He thought maybe he should move Out West, himself. He'd heard the dry climate worked wonders for lungers.

"He's not good for that," Sam said. His voice had a bit of liquid to it, so he coughed out more blood until his loogies turned greener. He threw more whiskey down his throat for good measure.

"I know the rule, boss," Grimes said. "Send him to you when he comes back?"

"Posthaste." Sam poured more of what was undoubtedly actual poison into his glass and went into the back room, his office. As filthy as the rest of this place was, his office was fairly clean. He made sure of that. His desk had a minimum of clutter on it because he liked to kick his feet up on the surface. He did that now, sipping at his drink, looking for a cigar of his own. He found a fresh one and lit it. The first pull always made him sweat a little, but after that the rest went smoothly. As he blew smoke up to the dirty gilded ceiling he pondered who he should offer the girl's virginity to. Who could *afford* it.

A knock came at the door. "Enter," Sam said.

Dick Lyman sauntered in, spinning a knife in one hand. He was only a little taller than Sam, but he had the swagger of a much bigger, much more confident man. He grinned, showing off a perfect set of teeth. The skimpy mustache above his mouth looked like a third eyebrow, and it always sickened Sam. Why did this guy bother with a mustache if he couldn't grow one? Sam smoothed over his own impressive handlebar mustache with one hand, unaware that he was doing it.

Lyman sat down across the desk from him without asking. He gave his knife one final expert twirl before jabbing it into the scabbard at his belt. "Sam. How's everything?"

"Everything is good," Sam said. He let his feet drop from the desk and felt his drying dick scritch loose from the inside of his pants. He adjusted himself and leaned forward. "I heard you were in earlier."

"Lemme have a go at Tessa. I gotta have her."

"Not a chance," Sam said. "You know she's not in regular rotation. I'm saving her—"

"For being a mail order bride, I know." Lyman sighed, running his fingers over his face. "I'll be gentle. I promise."

"You put that one girl through a window," Sam said.

"I paid for it, didn't I?"

"I couldn't sell her after that. She lost an eye."

Lyman grinned. "I had a few ideas about that empty eye socket."

Jesus. Sam had a certain unsavory reputation, but that was a bit too much even for him. He thought changing the topic was the better part of valor for now. "Speaking of money . . ."

"Ten bucks, I know. Here." Lyman reached into his pocket and plunked down a double eagle. Freshly minted, from the looks of it. "Consider the other ten a down payment on Tessa. As a gesture of good faith."

Sam looked at the coin for a moment before picking it up and hefting it in his palm. It felt heavy enough to be real. He put it between his teeth and took a gentle bite before looking at it again. Yep, it was real, all right.

Lyman laughed. "Don't trust me?"

"Well."

"Come on, Sammy. Tessa's worth a lot, but is she worth ten bucks?"

Sam hated being called "Sammy." Still, that was a lot of money for a poke. "Maybe."

"Bullshit. That's almost half a month's wages. No woman is worth that much. I don't care how tight her pussy is."

It was more like a third of a month's wages, but Sam decided not to argue the point. He put the double eagle in his pocket and stood. "Okay, Dick. You got it." He led the way to the door.

313

Lyman almost giggled as he stood and followed. They went upstairs, past the room where the virgin was still washing out her mouth, to the end of the hall. Sam knocked a couple of times before he opened the door. Lyman moved to go in the room, too, but Sam closed the door before he could.

Tessa Elder sat at her dresser, applying makeup while looking into a large round mirror. She glanced behind her long enough to see it was Sam, then went back to work. "I'm almost ready."

"I know," Sam said. "Take your time, but make it look good. You've got a high roller paying for you right now."

"Oh?" She smiled, and Sam could practically see the dollar signs in her eyes. "How high are we talking?"

"He's paying ten bucks. But there's a catch."

"Oh?" She didn't seem too concerned.

"It's Dick Lyman."

She jerked, and the eyeliner she was touching up dipped too far, leaving a line going down her cheek. "No. Absolutely not."

"Not your call," Sam said.

Tessa pursed her lips and turned around. "Please, Sam. Please?"

"Aw." He caressed her cheek and ran his hand under her chin, pushing his thumb across the slight cleft there. "It won't be so bad."

She took her face back and rubbed at the extra eyeliner with a rag. "Can I get a bigger piece of the action, then? I mean, he did pay you ten."

Sam mulled it over for a moment. Lyman didn't usually have much money. He'd gone a while without paying his bill, after all. The decision came swiftly. "I'll make him tip you. Is that fair?"

"You think he's got the money for that?" she asked.

"Sure." Probably not, but what the hell? That wasn't Sam's problem.

Tessa looked askance upon Sam for a moment before deciding she believed him. "Fine. Send him in."

Sam opened the door to see Lyman licking his lips and fluffing himself through his pants. "Go on, then, Dick. But you have to tip her, got it?"

Lyman didn't look like he heard him. "Yeah, yeah."

Sam stepped aside and let Lyman pass, then closed the door and went downstairs.

Grimes stood at the front of the establishment, shaking his head while he looked out the window. He hunched down so he could look under the backwards words that would spell out "Pepper's Pleasure Palace" if you stood outside. "Goddammit," he muttered.

"What?" Sam asked. He went to the bar to pour himself another drink. Medicine. He felt today would be a rough day on his lungs.

"Another dead morphinomaniac," Grimes said. "He's blocking the front door."

"Anyone I know?"

"He looks kind of familiar," Grimes said. "Maybe he was in here before?"

"Well, he's not a customer anymore. Sweep him into the alley with the rest of he trash and dogshit."

"We already have a corpse back there. Some dickhead last night tried to stab another dickhead and got shot in the throat for his troubles."

"Grimes, this is the Five Points. No one cares about corpses in alleyways. Just get it sorted out."

Grimes sighed and went out while Sam took his fresh drink back to his office and sat back down, relaxing, hoping he wasn't wrong to let Lyman have Tessa.

Grimes came back in and set a couple of dollars on the desk. "From the dead guy's pocket. Thought you should have it."

Sam took the money and put it with the double eagle to keep it company. He knew to a moral certainty that Grimes was holding out, but he figured it wasn't worth thrashing him over a few bucks. He let Grimes go back to the bar.

Just then a scream came down from above, followed by a roar of anger and possibly pain. Lyman, of course. Sam cursed under his breath and grabbed a pistol from under his desk. Grimes already stood at the foot of the stairs, looking up, and Sam breezed past him. He kicked Tessa's door down and moved in, ready to shoot anything and everything in sight.

Tessa pushed herself against a wall, using her blankets to cover her naked chest. Lyman rolled on the floor, cursing and spitting blood. When he looked up at Sam, he snarled, showing off a space where his front teeth had been.

"Fucking bitsh kicked my teef out!" he yelled.

Sam glared at Tessa. He wanted to slap her around a bit, remind her of the fucker-fuckee relationship in this business, but she looked too pissed for a life lesson.

"Fuck him, Sam! He tried to cut my titty off!"

"Fuck you, bitsh!" he yelled. "I justht wanted the nipple!"

Fuck's sake. Sam sighed and packed the gun away. "What did I tell you, Dick? No hurting the merchandise."

"What the fuck I pay you for?" Lyman said.

"To get your dick wet, *Dick*," Sam said.

"You're taking her bitsh cunt word over mine?!"

That was a good point. Sam would be a lousy whore master if he regularly took his girl's word over a customer's. As much as it pained him, he would have to do something for Lyman. Not a refund, of course. That would be crazy.

"Tell you what," Sam said. "I'll take care of your dentistry bill. And I'll get you someone else to poke at. Let's get you out of here."

"Sam!" Tessa said. She looked hurt.

"Later," he said. He helped Lyman to his feet and out the door. Miserably, Lyman packed himself away and buttoned up his trousers. Then, at the front door to the Pleasure Palace, Lyman turned to Sam. "You gotta get rid of that bitsh cunt."

"Let me worry about my problems," Sam said. "Send me the bill, and I'll take care of it."

"You better."

"Hey Grimes," Sam said. "When Lyman comes back, he gets a free poke for his troubles. Anyone except Tessa. Got it?"

Grimes nodded.

"That'th more like it," Lyman said. Mercifully he left, walking through the blood stain left by the dead man.

Sam sighed, rubbing his eyes. "I need a fucking break from this shit. This job is getting too political. Just a few years ago I would have cut Dick Lyman's throat and told God he'd died."

Grimes offered a lopsided smile. "Simpler times, boss."

"Simpler times, indeed."

2

— • —

The barber/dentist paused, holding up a set of pliers. "You sure you don't want me to pull 'em all? Dentures would be a lot easier for me."

"I don't give a thit what'th easy for you," Lyman said.

"It's less expensive that way."

"I'm not paying. Tham's footing the bill, and fuck him."

"Have it your way." The dentist took a slug of whiskey before passing the bottle to his patient. "Have a drink. I have to take measurements, and your gums are looking tender still."

Lyman took three slugs for good measure, swishing the third around in his mouth. Just in case. The dentist took the bottle back, took another drink for himself and went to work.

After a bit the dentist straightened out and went to his desk. "I think I have a couple of corpse teeth that would fit your mouth perfect."

He turned back to Lyman after a moment and clipped something into his mouth, then stepped back to admire his work. "Not bad."

"Lemme see," Lyman said.

The dentist picked up a piece of mirror and handed it over. Lyman peered at his dingy reflection for a moment, his upper lip pulled back. "They're too big."

The dentist shrugged. "They're the closest I got."

Lyman tested the clipping mechanism, and when it didn't pop off he nodded. "I guess it'll do."

"That'll be fifteen bucks."

"Goddam. Good thing I'm not paying for this shit." Lyman stood up to leave.

The dentist stepped in front of him. "I can't let you leave without paying."

"I look like I got that much money? Get it from Sam fucking Pepper."

"That's not how this works."

"Hell, charge him twenty. He'll pay it."

The dentist brightened up. That was a good point. Hell, while he was at it, why not charge thirty? Take the rest of the day off. Maybe Pepper would throw a poke on top of it all. The possibilities were endless.

Lyman—slightly drunk—struggled out of the chair and shrugged into his coat. He didn't bother with pleasantries like saying goodbye. He left the dingy office, stepping into the alley that served as the storefront. Two drunks fucked in a pile of garbage. Lyman stopped to watch them until he realized they were men. His burgeoning hard-on deflated, and he spat on the indiscreet fuckers. Neither of them noticed.

Just before he left the alley he paused, wondering if he should go back and rob them. He didn't want to see that again, and he figured they were transients, or they could afford a room. He shook his head, forgetting the whole thing.

He stepped over a dead dog and crossed the street, eyes on the bar in front of him. He didn't owe too much here. Drinking on credit had become a habit for him. He'd have to find someone to strong-arm soon. Why did he have to give Sam Pepper that double eagle?

Well. Lyman had wanted to fuck Tessa Elder for a long time. He felt he still hadn't. He'd gotten his dick inside her, but it didn't count unless he shot his muck up her.

Which reminded him, he hadn't blown his load yet. He'd been too worried about fixing his teeth that he'd forgotten about it. Grizelda worked here. She didn't speak a lick of English, and she looked like she'd taken buckshot to her face, but pussy was pussy. Pink and slick did the trick.

Some red-headed Irish prick puked rotgut up on the bar while two Germans arm wrestled in the corner. Someone bragged loudly about murdering voters, hired by a certain local politician to ensure his reelection. A Negro cleaned up the Irish prick's mess just in time for the Irish prick to puke his guts up on the bar again.

In other words, just another day in the Five Points.

Lyman got a whiskey and showed the bottom of the glass what the ceiling looked like. Someone won the arm wrestling match, much to the displeasure of the loser, who promptly shot his companion in the face.

The Negro sighed and went to clean up the blood with a mop. Lyman grimaced. It was bad enough that they let Irish scum in this place. He thought about the letter he'd written to President Lincoln. Lyman disliked anyone who wasn't as white as the purest snow, but he thought slavery was crazy. Why put dangerous tools in *their* hands and teach *them* how to use them? He felt that if the abolitionists had their way and freed the slaves, the slaves would then rise up and use those tools to kill all white people. Lyman had implored the president to instead send the slaves to death camps at his earliest convenience.

He'd not heard back from Lincoln. His beseeching letter had probably been tossed in the circular file.

He got another whiskey and asked after Grizelda.

"She's got the syph," the bartender said. "You okay with that?"

Lyman pursed his lips. "An evening with Venus, a lifetime with mercury," as the saying went. And Grizelda was no Venus. "Nah, it's not worth it. I don't suppose you have other pussy on tap?"

"Not yet. Later toni—"

Someone burst through the door, whooping in celebration, laughing as he sauntered up to the bar. He had a pencil stub behind one ear, which he just remembered about, so he plucked it out and flicked it away. "Bartender! Gimme a triple of the finest hooch you got! It's a good goddam day!"

The bartender moved away from Lyman and took down a dingy bottle from the top shelf, pouring a drink into an even dingier glass before pushing it to the newcomer. "What's so goddam good about it?"

The new guy slapped a coin on the bar and slugged down his drink without so much as a shiver. "President Nigger-lover is dead!" He whooped again.

"Bullshit," Lyman said.

"It ain't hit the papers yet, but just you wait! Tomorrow, news'll be all over town. The world, even!"

"Oh yeah?" the bartender said. "How do *you* know so soon?" Winking to Lyman.

The newcomer, it turned out, was Norris Headley, and he worked at a telegraph office. A half an hour earlier the lines went crazy with news that Lincoln had been assassinated at Ford's Theatre during a play. "Shot in the head like a cunt," Norris said.

"Who did it?" the bartender asked.

"John Wilkes Booth." Norris, satisfied with himself, took another drink.

"No," Lyman said. "Now I know you're full of shit. The actor? Edwin Booth's brother?"

"The one and only," Norris said.

"Fuck you. Liar. A famous actor? And who killed Johnson, Charles fucking Dickens?"

That earned a laugh from everyone in the saloon except for Norris. He slapped two coins on the bar. Double eagles.

"I'll bet you this that I'm right. If it ain't all over New York tomorrow morning, I'll owe you forty dollars."

That made Lyman pause. He couldn't afford to lose that kind of bet. The guy had to be bluffing, right? Right?

Even Dick Lyman knew he was pretty stupid. He didn't dare take the bet. Probably not. He thought about his empty pockets and wondered what the odds might be. Maybe he'd be stupid to *not* take the bet.

"Define tomorrow morning," Lyman said.

"If it's not in the first edition when it hits newsstands," Norris said, "then I'll owe you forty."

That sounded oddly specific, and Lyman felt a tinge of fear cool his guts.

Ah, fuck it.

"You're on," Lyman said.

Norris cackled. "Easiest money I'll have ever made!"

Bullshit, Lyman thought. They drank on it and made plans to return to this shithole tomorrow morning. Six sharp.

3

"Howdy, Sam! How's Tricks?"

Sam Pepper reached across the desk and shook hands with the congressman. The congressman smiled when he felt the coin in his hand and made it disappear like a fart in the wind. He gestured to a chair.

Sam sat. "Tricks is well, sir. I'll tell her you asked after her."

"Lascivious" didn't quite cover the smile on the congressman's face. "Please do. I'll be by to see her when my wife takes my children on vacation. All things considered, I think they're leaving today."

Sam felt like he'd missed something. "When you're ready, let Mr. Grimes know," he said. "We'll give you the gold star treatment, as usual."

The congressman laughed and slapped his desk. "You, sir, are a peach!" He presented two cigars, offering one to Sam. After he lit them he leaned back. "To what do I owe the pleasure?"

"I think you know, sir."

"The bill banning whorehouses on the island? Even in the Five Points? Surely you don't think that will pass."

Sam blew smoke up to the ceiling. "Never turn your back on a Puritan. Look what happened to Rome."

"A good point, to be sure." The congressman tapped out some ash and reached into a drawer for his whisky. He poured two glasses and passed one to Sam.

Sam, not used to actual good whisky, drank his so quickly he felt unexpected euphoria as an immediate buzz took hold.

"Mr. Pepper, it is goddam un-American to ban whorehouses anywhere. I predict a hundred years from now—no, two hundred!—there will be whorehouses stretched from sea to shining sea. Not that I won't take your money, of course, but I wouldn't worry about it."

"I'm not so sure," Sam said. "How many people still worship Mithras in Rome?"

"Catholics are scum. No one will ever elect them to public office much less let them decide policy."

"Then how did the bill get introduced in the first place?"

"Ah." The congressman waved a dismissive hand. "They're hypocrites just as much as the rest of us good Christians. They see a hole, they want to fuck it, just like us. And they'll pay for the pleasure, too. I'll bet we hand this country back to the English before we ban whorehouses."

"This pope fella seems to think he has God's ear," Sam said.

"All the more reason that the bill's not going to pass. Popes are fucking crazy. I'm shocked anyone believes in that shit. It's like witches casting spells as far as I'm concerned."

The congressman poured Sam another drink, and Sam sipped at it this time. He cleared his throat and leaned forward. "All the same, I'd like to hedge my bets."

"You're a fool, Sam Pepper, but a well-regarded fool. Rest assured, I'll vote against it. A lot of my colleagues feel the same way. I'm sure there is maybe one asshole who will buck the system. There's always one, at least. But this vote will get shot down almost unanimously. Just you wait."

Sam accepted this. It was all he could do at this point. On to other business. "Anything else you can give me a head start on?"

"Have you read the newspaper this morning?" the congressman asked.

"No. They weren't out yet by the time I got on the train. I planned to read it on the way back home."

"I'll save you the trouble of buying one." The congressman reached to a table behind him and picked up the folded newspaper, spreading the front page open on his desk upside down so Sam could read it. It showed a picture of Abraham Lincoln with a hangdog look on his face. Beneath it said: EXTRA. 8:10 A.M. NEW YORK, SATURDAY, APRIL 15, 1865. DEATH OF THE PRESIDENT.

"What the fuck?" Sam said.

The congressman only nodded.

Sam thought Lincoln had been a do-gooder with misbegotten ideals who had plunged the country into a civil war, but he had the best of intentions. He could imagine a lot of people who wanted to kill the president but couldn't think of anyone specific. Did Jefferson Davis even want to do the deed? "How?"

"Shot in the head while watching a play," the congressman said.

"Who did it? Some Confederate?"

"They're saying it was John Wilkes Booth."

Sam paused. "What? The actor? That's crazy."

The congressman took a careless puff on his cigar and let the smoke dribble out of his mouth onto the paper. "That's what they're saying."

Sam picked up the *Herald* and glanced over the words, still not believing this could happen. He tried thinking of a president who had been assassinated before and came up with nothing. Mentally he ran the list of presidents through his head, something he hadn't done since his school days. He got all of them except James Madison, and none of them had been killed. Died in office? Sure. Killed? No.

"Gonna close down the palace today in his honor?" the congressman asked. He had a glint in his eye meant to be a sure sign he was fucking with Sam.

Sam didn't notice. "Hell no. Could be more people will want to drink and fuck because of the news."

"I could be one of them," the congressman said. "You should get back home to prepare for the grieving and their money. I'll probably be by tonight at some time."

Numb, Sam picked up the paper and folded it under his arm. He drank down the rest of his whisky and stood. "I'll see you then."

The congressman watched him leave the office, amused. He'd never seen Sam Pepper like that before, and he almost liked him for it. Still, today would be a busy day. He had a few letters to write, so he called for his secretary, getting ready to go to work.

Outside, Sam passed by a couple of people holding up signs protesting the bill to ban whorehouses. Or maybe they were for it? Sam didn't notice. He didn't care. He ghost-walked back to the train station, thinking about how Lincoln's death would affect his plans. And possibly the bill. Would the papists spring on this as a distraction to get the bill passed?

Fuck. He hoped not.

4

"**M**otherfucker!"

Norris threw his head back and laughed like a madman. The rest of the saloon laughed with him except for Dick Lyman, who stared with fury at the front page of the newspaper. Never before had he felt such rage looking at a picture of the president. *Any* president, not just Lincoln.

"Pay up, *Dick*," Norris said.

Lyman hated it when people said his name like that. Earlier in life he'd tried to go by Rich. For some reason unknown to him no one ever called him that.

"A bet's a bet," he mumbled. He didn't reach to his pocket, which was empty. Instead he grabbed the drink in front of him and drained it in one go. He knew he'd have to leave in a hurry—probably never to return—and he didn't want to leave a man behind. Now he pretended to go for his pocket, hoping no one in here would have a gun.

The odds of anyone being unarmed were, of course, low.

Swift and blinding violence would get him out of this. He slowly drew his knife while reaching into his pocket, making a show of getting the supposed money.

Norris saw the knife. "Hey, what the fuck?" He reached under his coat, and Lyman could practically smell the gun under there.

Swift and blinding.

Lyman didn't have enough time to lead with the knife. He lashed out with his foot, getting Norris's shin. Norris yelped, and his gun fell to the floor, its clatter lost in the noise of raucous morning boozers. Lyman, with his free hand, palmed the empty glass, slapping it toward Norris, hoping to break it on his face. It thunked him squarely on the nose, and he fell back to the floor, one eye looking in a different direction than the other.

"Hey," the bartender said.

Lyman didn't hear him. He beat it to the door and rushed out into the hazy sun. He ran wildly down the street, not daring to look back. He imagined the saloon emptying out behind him, bloodthirsty denizens chasing after.

By the time he made it two blocks he stopped, gasping, holding his knees. No one gained on him. He wondered if running had even been necessary and decided, yes, it had been. Too bad. He liked that place.

Only now did it occur to him that Lincoln really had been killed. He wondered how that would change the country. He hoped it wouldn't roll back to slavery. No, genocide would be a lot better. But who would want to destroy—he never thought "kill"—their own property?

A white America was a right America.

Lyman chuckled at his own joke. Perhaps he should write a letter to the newspaper with that phrase in it. It would at least make his old man laugh.

He walked now at a leisurely pace, wondering what the hell he could possibly do now. He tried to think of other saloons where he still had credit. He doubted the story of what just happened would get around. There were at least a dozen worse stories about him—all true—and if they'd made the rounds he'd be *persona non grata* in the Five Points.

Would Sam Pepper turn him away? Maybe not. Didn't he say he owed Lyman a free poke?

It was worth a shot. Why not take it?

Well. He might still be pissed about Tessa.

Ah, the hell with it.

Lyman realized he was still holding his knife. On the one hand he felt angry that he didn't get to cut on anyone. On the other the story might get around if he had. All the same he thought he should pack the blade away. A fancier part of the island might still not have cared, but it never paid to be reckless.

He sheathed the knife and started heading north, seeking out Pepper's Pleasure Palace.

5

S am Pepper wiped blood from his lips and put his handkerchief away. Thoughts of moving Out West really appealed to him in moments like these. He didn't want to be away from the action of a major city like New York, but at the same time he went through three handkerchiefs a day. He wondered if maybe he should see his doctor again.

Grimes stood perched on top of a ladder while he nailed up some red, white and blue bunting, all in honor of Lincoln's assassination. No one would probably give much of a shit, but it gave people an excuse to celebrate, and it seemed like more and more people needed an excuse these days.

Sam glanced over to Eudora, one of his girls, who he had painting promotional signs. Half off whisky and beer in honor of the president's passing. Sheila, another of his girls, painted another sign declaring a dollar off pokes. Both would go up in the window at the front. Sam sold alcohol and sex at a high markup, so he didn't anticipate losing much money. It helped that he'd marked them both up for tonight and put a slash through those new prices, giving the impression that his customers would be getting quite a deal. The regulars might pitch a fit, but he figured he could cut them a break. The new customers, on the other hand, could go fuck themselves if they didn't like it.

Two boys he'd hired off the street carried a rolled up corpse down the stairs. An old man had a heart attack while fucking Bonnie, one of Sam's youngest girls. He'd been too busy to deal with it himself, so he found a couple of ten-year-olds smoking cigarets in the alley and offered them two bits to take care of it. They giggled when the corpse farted as they jounced it down the steps.

Sam, ever the entrepreneur, frisked Bonnie, who had indeed emptied the old man's pockets. He let her keep twenty percent, which he felt was generous. On any other day it would have been ten, but a dead president softened him up at the edges. The boys had also checked the corpse's pockets, annoyed when they only came up with lint.

"We'll take them two bits now, mister," one of the boys said.

"After," Sam said. "Dump him out in the alley first."

They looked annoyed, like maybe they were planning on dropping the body and dashing out the door once paid. Both boys grumbled as they maneuvered out the door and carted the body to the nearest alley.

Bonnie emerged from her crib and stood at the top of the stairs. "Sam! Those rats are fighting in the blood stain!"

Sam sighed. The old man had fallen off the bed backwards and hit his head on the floor. Rats were pretty quick in the Palace. He thought he'd discouraged them by shooting a third member of their confederacy. "Jefferson! Get up there and kill those fuckers!"

The janitor, a former slave from South Carolina, grabbed a club and started humping it upstairs. He'd been mopping the floor, getting rid of all the tobacco stains and boogers and peanut shells. He left the mop leaning against the bar, and Sam—annoyed—picked it up and put it in the bucket.

The door behind him opened, and he prepared himself to greet another customer. Then he saw it was Dick Lyman and restrained himself from grimacing. "Dick. I got the dentist's bill."

Lyman grinned, showing off his new false teeth. "They look pretty good. And they stay in more often than not."

They looked a little big, but Sam thought it would be better to not mention it. "Back so soon? I don't know if I can take another of your visits after last time."

"Come on," Lyman said. "I had to get dental work. And you said I could have a free poke."

Sam couldn't stop his lips from pursing in distaste. Still, Lyman had a point. Not only that, but he'd paid with a double eagle the other night. He might even have more of those. Why turn away a good customer?

"No cutting on my women," Sam said.

Lyman held up a hand like he was about to testify in court. "Your lips to God's ears."

Sam sighed. "All right. We're closed right now because we're throwing a shindig tonight. Did you hear about President Lincoln?"

Now Lyman's lips pursed in distaste. "Yeah, I heard."

"We're giving him a proper sendoff, as good as the Five Points can give him. Why don't you come back tonight? We'll have plenty of booze and cooze. I'm even bringing a few girls in from out of town, so you'll have plenty of new quim to sink your dick into."

Lyman laughed, thinking about that unexplored cuntry. "I'll be here."

"And bring more of those double eagles," Sam said.

Lyman kept smiling. "You got it."

As Lyman headed out the door, the two boys came rushing back in. "It's done, boss," one said.

332

Sam dug into his pocket for the two bits, but one of the boys held up a hand. "You can pay us with whisky instead."

"You're not getting a fifth," Sam said.

"Did we ask for a fifth?" the other boy said. "We'll take a pint."

Sam considered. "A half pint for a couple of half-pints."

"There's no call for that kinda talk, mister."

"Or I could just give you the two bits?"

The boys looked at each other. "We'll take the half pint."

Sam got one from behind the bar and handed it to the boys. They each took a quick slug and then ran out into the streets to do whatever boys their age did while drunk. Sam guessed they were either peeping toms or animal torturers, just like any other good boy in the Five Points.

Outside, Lyman stopped to think about where he could get some money. He knew a woman off Mulberry Street near Bandit's Roost. It was probably the roughest area in town, but she had money. It might even be worth the risk of getting the mortal shit beaten out of him by the guards or possibly getting his throat cut. If he could only figure out a way to convince her to let him into her crib. Then he could just beat the shit out of her and take her money. But he didn't think she would be receptive to letting him get that close to her. He had, after all, knocked out three of her teeth. Too bad she'd only had a couple of dollars at the time. But he knew now she had more. Word got around fast.

No, he couldn't see a way where he could make that happen. Unless he murdered her and got away without being seen. Lyman didn't believe in God, but he thought it a mortal sin to kill a whore.

Perhaps he had to do this the old fashioned way. There was an Irish bar not too far from here. He hated the thought of going inside with that trash, but he knew those micks were probably already three sheets. All he had to do was wait in the alley until one of them went outside for a piss or a puke. Then he could let his knife do all the talking.

Hell, maybe he'd luck out and one of them would have a bottle on him. Weren't the Irish born into this world with their dicks in one hand and a bottle of whisky in the other?

6

━ ● ━

A knock at the door. "Sam? The congressman's here."

Sam put his pencil down and closed his book. The Palace made a lot of money, but it would never make enough. He had designs on being he premier whoremaster of New York City, but he needed a better class of clientele. Perhaps the congressman would pass word among his colleagues.

He hacked up blood into his handkerchief and threw the sodden thing in the trash before selecting a fresh one and putting it in his jacket pocket, making sure a corner stood up at a jaunty angle. He took another belt of whisky and walked out into the saloon where he saw Grimes pouring a drink for the congressman.

Sam plastered on a grin and stepped up to the bar. "Good to see you, sir."

The congressman quaffed his drink quickly and motioned for another. "The Palace looks good, Sam. Real good. Oh, I brought a friend." He gestured to another man standing next to him. He wore a Union uniform—impeccably—with one shortened sleeve pinned up at the shoulder. "Sam, this is Bettis, formerly of the Union Army, now one of my bodyguards."

Bettis nodded, and Sam noticed that one of his eyes didn't move. A glass eye? What kind of fucking bodyguard could this guy be? He thought mentioning it would be rude, though.

"Good to meet you, Bettis," Sam said. He turned his attention back to the congressman so quickly that he knew Bettis couldn't take the pleasantry as anything more than a token gesture. "I have a surprise for you tonight. A new girl."

"Oh?" the congressman asked.

"A fresh one. A virgin."

"Do tell."

"Her parents sold her to me a few days ago," Sam said. "They claimed she was sixteen, but something tells me that her fourteenth birthday was maybe last week."

The congressman grinned so wide Sam could see the metal clasps that held his bridgework in place. "Pure and unspoiled! You're a good man, Sam Pepper."

"She's freshening up for you now, good sir. In the meantime, I hope you enjoy everything the Palace has to offer. Drinks are discounted tonight, but you drink for free, sir."

The congressman plugged a cigar into his mouth and searched his vest for a lucifer. Sam produced one and fired it up. Soon the congressman sent puffs of acrid smoke to the ceiling. "Anything good to eat?"

"We have the best beef in the Five Points," Sam said. That wasn't strictly true. There were a few other places that had access to fresh meat, but Sam didn't make enough for that. At the least, though, his meat wasn't maggoty like most of the beef in the Five Points. No one would actually die from eating it. Probably. It could be even worse than that. He'd heard that some of the mick establishments in the area served human flesh taken from bodies found in local alleys. But Irish depravity never surprised Sam. Not anymore.

"I'll have a steak this thick." The congressman held his index finger and thumb apart about two inches.

336

Sam turned to Grimes. "You heard the congressman." He then, painfully, turned his attention back to Bettis. "For you, sir?"

Bettis lipped some chaw and spat a stream at the nearest spittoon, hitting it with a sharpshooter's accuracy. Not bad for a one-eyed man. "Not while I'm working."

Sam felt relief. Paying the congressman's way was an investment, but he was glad he didn't have to pay for the bodyguard, too, which would be a waste of good money.

"He'll have a whisky," the congressman said.

"Sir," Bettis said, "I—"

"He loves a good tipple," the congressman said.

Ah fuck. Sam kept his pleasant grin up as best he could.

"But sir—"

"No buts," the congressman said. "What's going to happen to me here? None of my enemies even know of this place."

Bettis started to sigh, then pursed his lips. He nodded to Grimes, who poured him a tall glass.

Sam would have to have a word with him later about that. For now he held out a hand, gesturing to a table. "Follow me, sir."

He led them to the table and pulled out the chair for the congressman. Bettis didn't sit. He sipped at his whisky and glanced around the room. He moved close to his boss but not so close that he might miss a threat.

More patrons entered and bellied up to the bar, ordering drinks. Sheila came downstairs and approached them with a winsome smile, and so commenced the dance.

Sam went upstairs to check on the new girl—what was her name again?—to make sure everything would go swimmingly.

As he hopped up the stairs, Dick Lyman entered the Palace with an eager grin on his face and a jangling pocket. He looked down Sheila's cleavage, winking to her with approval, and went straight to the bar. Grimes finished up serving the new customers and moved down towards him.

"Whisky," Dick said. "Make it a double. No, a *triple*."

"Let's see your money first," Grimes said.

"What, I ain't good for it?"

Grimes didn't say a word. He merely waited, his eyebrows raised.

Dick cursed while pulling out his change. The mick bar had paid off big time. He probably had a double eagle's worth in small change. Small change was all that could be expected from those Catholic bums, but they were dependable in that way. He didn't even have to kill any of them. He just had to make sure he didn't go around for a while on the off-chance that one of them was sober enough to remember his face.

"There's blood on 'em," Grimes said.

"It spends, don't it?"

Grimes sighed. "Fair enough." He took one of the coins and poured a triple, sliding it to Dick.

Dick drank. It wasn't his first of the day. That had been from the flask he'd taken off a drunk mick in that alley. But it was the best of the day. It warmed him in all the right ways. He rolled a cigaret with his slim fingers and poked it in the corner of his mouth. "Tessa here?"

"She's with another customer," Grimes said.

"Sam Pepper tell you to tell me that?" Dick asked.

"No." But Grimes was a terrible liar.

"Ah, fuck it then. Who's on tap tonight?"

Grimes grunted. "I'll let the girls know you're looking for a poke."

Dick blew smoke in his face. "You do that."

Grimes didn't cough. He didn't even blink. He turned away to greet new customers, and he made sure Dick saw that his wishes weren't a priority.

7

— ◆ —

Within the hour the Palace was packed with people drinking, smoking, gambling, fucking and generally enjoying themselves.

Bettis blew out a 180-proof breath and wiped sweat from his forehead. He had a nice buzz going, but he felt confident enough to order another drink. Hey, the congressman had given Bettis permission to drink. If he passed this up now, he felt, he'd never get permission to do it again.

Bella would give him grief later, but fuck her. If she didn't like it she could stay with her mother for a few days. All the better to bring Cynthia home. His manservant wouldn't say a word to Bella about it. He knew his place and knew the consequences of moving out of it. He would take care of the sullied bedsheets and—

Whoa. Bettis stared at one of the whores. Her bust practically spilled out of her top. He tried to imagine his hand around each of her breasts, but it just wasn't big enough for even one of them. He didn't even think his cock would poke through the other side of her cleavage if he was fucking her boobs from underneath.

"Get your dick wet," the congressman said.

"Huh?" Bettis snapped back to himself, only slightly aware of the spot of drool in the corner of his mouth. He absently wiped it away and took a sip of his fresh drink.

"Your eyes are popping from your head," the congressman said. "Get the poison out."

He thought about Bella and how she didn't even bother to fuck back during their rare bouts of passion. He didn't know what having sex with a corpse was like, but he had a pretty good idea thanks to her. Hence his need for Cynthia. And for this whore in front of him. But could he afford it?

In the back of his head he thought perhaps he should do his job, but he didn't pay any heed to that little voice.

"I'll buy," the congressman said. He flipped a coin to Bettis.

Bettis missed it and had to duck down to the floor to pick it up. It took him a couple of tries, but he got it and held it aloft like a prize. Maybe he was drunker than he'd thought.

Grimes arrived at their table. "Sir, she's ready."

The congressman grinned and turned back to Bettis. "Don't worry about me. I'll be in good hands."

Bettis didn't need any further convincing. He approached the whore while Grimes led the congressman upstairs.

As they approached the door the congressman stopped. "I think there's been a mistake. This is Tessa Elder's room, is it not? I was hoping for someone . . . younger."

"That's what Mr. Pepper said," Grimes told him. "The one you want is new and doesn't have a crib of her own yet. She's borrowing Tessa's for now."

Relief flooded the congressman's heart. "Good. Very good. You may continue."

Grimes opened the door and waved the congressman in. The young girl sat on the edge of her bed in a low-cut top designed for a woman with larger assets. She looked like she was a child wearing her mom's clothes. She *was* a child. Her pale face looked too fresh, and her eyes looked more like a puppy's than a doe's.

"This is Mildred," Grimes said. "Compliments of the boss."

"Thank you, Mr. Grimes," the congressman said. "That will be all."

Grimes went out the door before he could see the girl's face quiver, desperate to please and yet scared to enter womanhood in such a disrespectable way. The congressman approached, holding a hand out to her face just as Grimes closed the door and went back downstairs.

At the bar Dick downed yet another drink and looked around. Grimes hadn't returned yet, so Dick looked to both sides trying to gauge if anyone would notice him reaching behind the bar. The customers were so plastered that they danced to a crazy bastard hammering away at a player piano while it was trying to play a song. Dick, fairly drunk himself, almost thought it was music. The whores plied their trade with all the attention they could muster. The only customers not out of hand at this time were the gamblers at a back table, and they were too busy to notice anything.

Fuck it. Dick reached behind the bar and grabbed a bottle of hooch so vile that it didn't even have a label. He poured a tall drink and put it back, taking another look around to make sure no one noticed. Only when he took his first sip did he see Grimes coming back. Dick held the glass in one hand to shield the level of booze inside of it just in case Grimes remembered how much had been left before he went to the congressman's table.

Someone laughed and started shouting something with an Irish lilt to it. Fuck, when did the micks show up? He gave them a dirty look as they threw darts, completely missing the target and hitting the wall. One of them cursed, and another playfully tossed a dart at him, getting him in the shoulder. Drunken prick didn't even notice.

"Scum of the earth," Dick muttered.

"What's that?" Grimes said.

"Fuckin' Irish. You shouldn't let them in here. Next thing, it'll be niggers."

Jefferson, cleaning up a puke puddle, stiffened when he heard it, but they didn't notice. He gritted what few teeth he had and continued mopping.

Grimes shrugged. "They got money, same's you."

Dick grunted and finished off his purloined drink before putting the empty glass down in front of him, pointing to it.

Grimes poured. "Careful. You keep on like this, you're gonna get whisky dick, *Dick*." He chortled, amused with himself.

Dick briefly considered downing the drink and breaking THIS FUCKING GLASS on Grimes's fucking face, but he knew better. The bartender was a lot tougher than he looked, and Dick had had enough dental work recently. He thought keeping the guy who poured the alcohol conscious and healthy would be a good idea.

"Say, where's Tessa, anyway? She can't still be with another customer."

"She's got along wait list," Grimes said. "One of the other girls should be freed up shortly."

Dick pinched his hog through his pants. "I hope so. I got a lot of tension to work off."

Grimes didn't know what to say to that, so he moved on to another paying customer.

About then the alcohol truly hit Dick. One of his eyes hung at half-mast, and his head tilted to the side to straighten out his vision. He giggled to himself, wondering if he could walk straight. Everything seemed slightly distorted, almost like looking into a trick mirror at a sideshow. The whores around him looked all the more delectable, and he grinned stupidly at them, hoping to get their attention.

Then he remembered he was saving himself for Tessa. Where was she? She fucking owed him. All right, perhaps trying to cut her nipple off was a little forward of him, but she had to be over it by now. He still had plenty of change rattling around in his pocket.

Fuck it. Time to go up to her. He downed his drink and shifted his feet while waiting for Grimes to come back with the bottle. The filthy bastard spent too much time talking with other customers. Fuckin' fuck. Dick gritted his teeth and felt his falsies shift a little. He pushed them back into place with a finger.

Grimes finally arrived, pouring a fresh drink.

"About fucking time, you fucking fuck," Dick said. Or at least he thought he'd said it.

"I didn't get that," Grimes said. "What the fuck are you saying?"

Dick said it again, but this time he actually heard the garbled mumble that came from him. Whoops. Definitely too drunk. He had to get to Tessa fast so he could blow his load before the blackout took over. He clutched his drink and walked toward the stairs. He thought he was doing a good job, although he fought pretty hard to remain on his feet. No one seemed to notice him, so that had to be a good sign.

The stairs gave him more trouble. He had to grip the railing and lean his hip against it to keep standing. When he felt certain of himself he pushed forward and felt like he was on a rocking chair. He laughed to himself and licked the spilled booze off of his hand.

Finally he reached the top of the stairs, and for an unsettling moment he tipped backwards. Thank fuck he still held the railing, or he knew he would have fallen down every step. Probably would have broken his neck. With his luck he'd wind up in a wheelchair for the rest of his life in some kind of asylum. No way to live, that.

He stopped thinking about it as he moved towards Tessa's crib. He stood swaying in front of her door, a fist raised to knock. But why would he do that? She knew she had to service him. She had to be waiting for him. And if she really was with another customer?

Well. Dick knew how to handle himself.

He grabbed the doorknob and pushed with all his might. He hooted with joy, holding his drink aloft like a champion. "Hey Tessa! Your troubles are over! Dick is here!"

Someone screamed, and Dick looked at the bed, confused. He didn't see Tessa there but a set of skirts hiked up and two small legs pointing up in the air. A hairy fat ass stood positioned between them, and an equally fat face turned to look back at him.

"How dare you, sir!" the congressman shouted. "Shut that door immediately!"

Dick's face flushed, but not out of embarrassment. Rage flowed through him, boiling the drunken haze away. He saw the congressman clearly and knew that his beloved Tessa had been violated by someone else.

"Me?" Dick said. "Fuck you! That's my girl!"

The congressman struggled to pull his pants up, showing off a wilting shiny dick before managing to push it to the right of his trousers. "Sam Pepper!" he shouted. "I need Sam Pepper up here immediately!"

"No need for Sam," Dick said. "Let's take this outside."

"How dare you!" the congressman said again. "Don't you know who I am?"

That did it. If there was one thing Dick couldn't stand, it was when people put on airs. Especially if they were in the same whorehouse as he was. Dick whipped out his knife and plugged it into the congressman's belly.

The congressman made a huff sound as the air escaped him entirely. His eyes went wide, and he clutched at the hilt of the blade, but Dick's hand was still around it. He yanked it up until the blade caught against bone, and the congressman's insides flopped out of the rift in his flesh.

Dick felt the slimy organs on his feet, but he ignored them as he yanked the knife out and stuck it in again.

The congressman hacked blood up on Dick's face, and still Dick ignored it. He had to stop this fat prick from fucking his girl, and this was the best way to handle it. Now he shoved the knife between the congressman's ribs, nailing him in the heart. The congressman stiffened and collapsed. His weight—and the fact that the knife was stuck in his chest—brought Dick down with him.

Dick, still drunker than he'd thought, felt confused for a moment as he untangled his legs and tried to stand. He realized that someone was still screaming. Tessa?

He looked to the bed to try to explain himself when he realized that it wasn't Tessa after all. It was a different girl. A younger girl. And something twisted in his guts. He looked down at the congressman, who no longer breathed, and realized what he'd done. Now completely sober he reached down and yanked the knife out of the corpse, wiping it off on the congressman's underpants before putting it back in its sheath.

He had to get out of there. Right fucking now.

Dick turned, but before he could get far he saw Sam Pepper's face, aghast at the scene before him.

8

— • —

Bettis panicked as he tried to breathe, but he couldn't sneak a breath between convulsions. Puke kept pouring out of his mouth all over the body of a dead alley cat between sacks of garbage. The pressure built up in his head so much that his glass eye popped out, and his real eye felt like it could go at any second.

He tried to stop himself, but he couldn't. The next bout of puke soaked his glass eye.

His body seized up one more time, and finally nothing else came out of him. The booze came up the same as it had looked going in, and it smelled the same, too. If he hadn't had something to eat earlier in the day it would have still been serviceable alcohol. Not that he wanted to redrink it.

He finally caught a breath and sagged against the brick wall, trying to let the revulsion die down. Goddam, he didn't even get laid. He was about to take a whore up to her crib when the sickness came over him. He knew that if he hadn't dashed out to the alley right away he would have thrown up all over her. He'd never live that one down. Even the congressman would look askance upon him in the future.

Bettis felt normal-ish again. To take the gross taste out of his mouth he lit a cigar and waited. Only then did he pick up his eye—wiping it off on his shirt—and head back to the door of the Palace.

Just before he reached it a flood of people came pouring out, almost all of them drunk and angry. Someone shouted something from inside, and it sounded like Sam Pepper. Bettis knew something had gone wrong, and if his stomach had been up to it, he would have felt a bit of fear prickle in his guts.

He waited until the others were gone before he went back in to an empty saloon. The bar stood unattended, and even the gamblers were gone, all the winnings taken with them. Bettis looked upstairs to see the whores gathered at the top around one of the doors.

Where was the congressman?

"Oh God," Bettis whispered. He still felt shaky from vomiting, but he took the stairs as quickly as he could.

"You've got to get out of here," Sam Pepper said. "I don't care where you go. Get the fuck out of here. Out of town. Out of the state."

Someone rushed out of the room. Bettis didn't know who Dick Lyman was, but that was who rushed down the stairs past him. Dick went behind the bar and grabbed two bottles before running out of the Palace.

Bettis didn't have time to deal with petty larceny. He dreaded learning what had happened, but he knew he had to find out. He kept going upstairs and pushed past the whores until he could see the inside of the crib.

He saw what remained of the congressman and felt his gorge rise again.

"Goddammit!" Sam shouted. "Get him out of here!"

Grimes pushed at Bettis. "Go on. You don't want to see this."

"But . . . but . . ." All other words failed him. He knew his career was over in that moment. No one would hire him to guard someone ever again. He'd heard that, due to the president's assassination, the government was forming a secret service to guard future presidents, and he'd dreamed of getting that job.

349

But they would never give it to him now.

He'd be lucky getting a job swabbing out saloon floors.

"Oh God," he said. It came out in a croak. No one could ever find out about this. Then again, who could hide it?

"Jesus Christ," Sam said. "Jesus fucking Christ. This is a disaster. Oh fuck."

"Oh fuck" was right. Sam would lose the Palace, but Bettis would lose everything. There wasn't a goddam thing he could do about it.

Except for one thing. He backed away from Grimes just far enough so he could draw the pistol from his holster. It was always loaded and ready to fire its minie ball, so he didn't have to do anything except cock it.

And pull the trigger, which he did as soon as he put the barrel to his own temple.

9

━ ● ━

Sam Pepper rubbed his eyes. "This day can't get any fucking worse, can it?"

He heard a gun go off just outside the door. He jerked, eyes wide, then went to see what had happened.

Grimes stared down at the crumpled bodyguard watching blood pouring from the corpse's open head. He turned back to see Sam standing there. "Boss, I didn't do it. He did it to himself."

Sam looked down at yet another dead body in his fucking saloon, incredulous. "Motherfucker. Goddam motherfucker."

"What do we do?" Grimes said.

Sam knew he couldn't handle this like the usual corpses that wound up in his Palace. This was a fucking congressman. He couldn't just be chucked out into the alley or fed to the Irish. This would come with real consequences. He'd have to shut down the Palace. He'd be run out of town. He might even get tarred and feathered and carried out on a rail.

The whores chattered like crazy birds behind him, and he whirled on them. "Shut up!" Once they had, he blew out a breath. "We need to keep this quiet. If I find out any of you have talked about this, I will cut your goddam throats and tell God you went Out West."

He turned to Grimes. "Pay them each double what they usually get a night. Then remind them that if they want to continue working this gravy train, they need to keep their mouths shut about this."

Grimes nodded and started downstairs.

"And get Jefferson! We need to make the congressman disappear."

There was no way the congressman could ever be found. No one would give a shit about Bettis, so he planned to have Jefferson throw him in the gutter somewhere. But the congressman had to be chopped up and dispensed with across the Five Points. Or maybe in the river.

If someone found even one piece of him, would that cause more questions to be asked? Maybe it would just be better for the congressman to be found somewhere else. Anywhere else.

Didn't he have some Irish blood in him? Sam had heard that rumor. Maybe they could get rid of him in the alley outside an Irish bar across town from here.

Goddam that Dick Lyman. If he never saw that bastard again, it would be too soon.

10

Dick went back to the shithole he slept in and grabbed everything he wanted to keep, throwing it into a suitcase held together with two belts. The bottles he'd grabbed from the Palace went in, but not before he took a few healthy swigs from one of them. He had the jitters and needed to smooth them out somehow.

He couldn't have possibly known that man was a congressman. But he should have known those skinny legs didn't belong to Tessa. Tessa was powerfully built, and he should have seen that and known it wasn't her. Goddammit.

He still owed back rent, but fuck that. He took every coin he had with him and went out the rear window, rushing toward the train station.

Despite Sam's best efforts, word of the congressman's murder passed quickly on the streets, and the denizens of the Five Points already joked about it pretty freely. Dick tried to ignore them all as he made his way to the clerk's office. He glanced at the chalkboard, wondering where he would live out the rest of his life. He could already feel the authorities looking for him.

Sam Pepper wouldn't rat on him. Not out of kindness, of course, but he would want to hide the fact that a congressman had died in his establishment in such a gruesome way. But that didn't mean other witnesses wouldn't talk. He knew there would be wanted posters of him out there in no time. He just had to stay ahead of them, at least until he hit the state border.

The farthest terminal the train went to was the Republic of Texas. Dick glanced back at the Five Points, knowing that it was the last time he would ever see home-sweet-home. He would miss it, but he really didn't want to see it from inside of a jail.

Fuck it. What did the Southerners say? Gone to Texas? GTT?

Dick went to the window and bought a ticket for Texas to save his life.

THE END

ABOUT THE AUTHOR

John Bruni is the author of, most recently, *Eye Cutter* and *Something to Consider*, among others. His novel, *Trail of Blood*, details the adventures of William King after his sojourn to Mexico, where he met Tessa Reeves in this book. An Elmhurst resident originally, he now lives in Joliet, IL, where he finally finished a 20-year project of watching *Gunsmoke*. Not that anyone cares . . .